D0447235
FOR
MEN

Look for these exciting Western series from bestselling authors William W. Johnstone and J.A. Johnstone

The Mountain Man

Luke Jensen: Bounty Hunter

Brannigan's Land

The Jensen Brand

Preacher and MacCallister

The Red Ryan Westerns

Parley Gates

Have Brides, Will Travel

Guns of the Vigilantes

Shotgun Johnny

The Chuckwagon Trail

The Jackals

The Slash and Pecos Westerns

The Texas Moonshiners

Stoneface Finnegan Westerns

Ben Savage: Saloon Ranger

The Buck Trammel Westerns

The Death and Texas Westerns

The Hunter Buchanan Westerns

Tinhorn

Will Tanner, U.S. Deputy Marshal

BAD DAYS FOR BAD MEN

SMOKE JENSEN'S AMERICAN JUSTICE

WILLIAM W. JOHNSTONE

AND J.A. JOHNSTONE

PINNACLE BOOKS
KENSINGTON PUBLISHING CORP
www.kensingtonbooks.com

PINNACLE BOOKS are published by
Kensington Publishing Corp.
119 West 40th Street
New York, NY 10018

PUBLISHER'S NOTE: Following the death of William W. Johnstone, the Johnstone family is working with a carefully selected writer to organize and complete Mr. Johnstone's outlines and many unfinished manuscripts to create additional novels in all of his series like the Last Gunfighter, Mountain Man, and Eagles, among others. The two novels in this omnibus edition were inspired by Mr. Johnstone's superb storytelling.

First Printing: December 2022
ISBN-13: 978-0-7860-4999-8
ISBN-13: 978-0-7860-5000-0 (eBook)

10 9 8 7 6 5 4 3 2 1

Printed in the United States of America

CONTENTS

Betrayal of the Mountain Man
1

Rampage of the Mountain Man
243

Betrayal of the Mountain Man

Chapter One

Smoke Jensen saw the calf struggling through a snowdrift. The little creature had separated from its mother and the rest of the herd, and was bawling now in fear and confusion. He also saw the wolves, two of them, about twenty-five yards behind the calf. They were inching up slowly, quietly, hunkered down on their bellies to reduce their presence.

Smoke snaked his Winchester from the saddle sheath, then jacked a round into the chamber. He hooked his leg across the saddle horn, rested his elbow on his knee, then raised the rifle to his shoulder and sighted on the lead wolf. He was about 150 yards away from the two wolves, and he was looking down on them so it would be a difficult shot. But he figured that even if he didn't kill them, he might at least be able to drive them away from the calf.

Smoke squeezed the trigger. The rifle kicked back against his shoulder as smoke bellowed from the end of the barrel. When the smoke rolled away, he saw the lead wolf lying on its side, a spreading pool of red staining the snow.

The other wolf turned and ran quickly toward the trees, kicking up little puffs of snow as it did so. Smoke jacked another round into the chamber and aimed at the second wolf. His finger tightened on the trigger; then he eased the pressure, and lowered his rifle.

"Don't reckon I should shoot you for doing what your instinct tells you to do," Smoke said quietly. "I just don't want you doin' it to my cows. Specially not this year."

Smoke rode down to the wolf he had killed, then dismounted. His bullet had hit the animal just behind his left foreleg, penetrated the heart, and killed it instantly. The wolf's eyes were still open, his tongue still hanging out of his mouth. Strangely, Smoke felt a sense of sadness.

"I'm sorry I had to do this, fella, but you didn't leave me any choice," Smoke said. "At least it was quick for you."

Smoke remounted, then rode on toward the calf. He looped his rope around the calf, then half-led and half-dragged it back to the herd. There, he removed the rope and watched as the calf hurried to join his mother.

What had once been a large herd was now pitifully small, having come through what they were calling the "Great Winter Kill." Hundreds of thousands of cattle had died out throughout the West this winter, and Smoke's Sugarloaf Ranch was no exception. He had started the winter with fifteen thousand head; he was now down to less than two thousand.

Smoke's only hope to save what remained of his herd was to push them into a box canyon and hope that it would shield them from any further winter blasts. He, Cal, and Pearlie were doing that very thing when he came across the wolves.

Looking up, Smoke saw Cal approaching him from the north end of the canyon opening, while at the same time Pearlie was approaching from the south. Even if he had not been able to see them, he would know they were coming toward him, because each of them was leaving a long, black trail in the snow.

Cal reached him first.

"What was the shootin'?"

"Wolves," Smoke answered.

"Yeah," Cal said. "Well, you can't much blame 'em, I guess. They're probably havin' as hard a winter as we are. Same with all the other creatures, which is why they're goin' after cattle, rather than deer."

"Wolves?" Pearlie asked, arriving then.

"Yes, they were after a calf," Smoke said.

"Too bad you didn't see them a little earlier."

"What do you mean?"

Pearlie twisted in his saddle and pointed back down the black smear that marked his path through the snow. "Three calves back there, or what's left of 'em. Killed by wolves."

"Maybe we ought to put out some poisoned meat," Cal suggested.

Smoke shook his head. "I don't care to do that. Besides, there are enough animals around, frozen to death, that they probably wouldn't take the bait."

"You'd think they'd go after the dead ones, and leave the live ones alone," Pearlie said.

"The dead ones are frozen hard as a rock. They want something alive because it's warmer, and easier to eat," Smoke said.

"Speaking of something warm and easy to eat, you think maybe Miss Sally fixed us up any bear claws?" Pearlie asked.

"Does the sun come up in the east?" Cal asked.

Smoke chuckled. "I expect she did," he said. He stood in his stirrups and looked down toward the small herd.

"We've got them in the canyon now; that's about all we can do for them. Let's head for the house."

The three started back toward the house, which was some five miles distant. A ride that, in good weather, would take no more than thirty minutes stretched into an hour because of the heavy fall of snow. The horses labored to cut through the drifts, which were sometimes chest high, and their heavy breathing formed clouds of vapor that drifted away into the fading light.

The three riders said nothing, lost in their own thoughts as they rode back toward the main house.

The oldest of the three, and the ranch owner, was Kirby "Smoke" Jensen. Smoke stood just over six feet tall, and had shoulders as wide as an ax handle and biceps as thick as most men's thighs. He had never really known his mother, and when he was barely in his teens, he went with his father into the mountains to follow the fur trade. The father and son teamed up with a legendary mountain man called Preacher. For some reason, unknown even to Preacher, the mountain man took to the boy and began to teach him the ways of the mountains: how to live when others would die, how to be a man of your word, and how to fear no other living creature. On the first day they met, Preacher, whose real name was Art, gave Kirby a new name. That name, Smoke, would one day become a legend in the West, and after a while, even Kirby thought of himself as Smoke Jensen.

Smoke was in his thirties, a happily married landowner whose ranch, Sugarloaf, had the potential to be one of the finest ranches in the state. For the last three or four years, Sugarloaf had lived up to its potential, so much so that Smoke had borrowed money to expand the ranch. He bought more land, built a new barn and bunkhouse, added onto the big house, and bought more cattle.

Then the winter hit. Blizzard followed blizzard as the temperature plummeted to record lows. All across the West cattle died in record numbers. Tens of thousands of cattle froze to death, thousands more died of starvation because they couldn't get to the food, while nearly as many died of thirst because the streams and creeks were frozen solid under several feet of snow.

Ironically, the smaller ranchers were better able to ride it out than the bigger ranchers, who had more land, more cattle, and much more to lose. In one terrible winter, Smoke Jensen had gone from being one of the wealthiest ranchers in Colorado to a man who was struggling to hang onto his ranch.

"Smoke, if you want, I'll take the lead . . . let my horse break trail for a while," Pearlie called up to him. The three men were riding in single file, the two behind the leader taking advantage of the lead horse breaking a trail through the snow.

"Sure, come on up," Smoke invited, moving to one side of the trail to let Pearlie pass.

A few years earlier, Pearlie had been a gunman, hired by a man who wanted to run Smoke off the land so he could ride roughshod over those who were left. But Pearlie didn't take to killing and looting from innocent people, so he quit his job. He had stopped by to tell Smoke that he was leaving when Smoke offered to hire him.

Since that time Pearlie had worked for Smoke and Sally. He stood just a shade less than six feet tall, was lean as a willow branch, had a face tanned the color of an old saddle, and a head of wild, unruly black hair. His eyes were mischievous and he was quick to smile and joke, but underneath his friendly demeanor was a man that was as hard as iron and as loyal to his friends as they come.

"I'll ride second," Cal said, passing with Pearlie. "That way I can take the lead in a few minutes."

Not too long after Pearlie had joined the ranch, a starving and destitute Cal, who was barely in his teens at the time, made the mistake of trying to rob Sally. Instead of turning him over to the sheriff, Sally brought him home and made him one of the family, along with Pearlie. Now Calvin Woods was Pearlie's young friend and protégé in the cowboy life.

The three men rode on in silence for the next fifteen minutes, frequently changing the lead so that one horse wouldn't be tired out. Finally they crested a hill, then started down a long slope. There, half a mile in front of them, the ranch compound spread out over three acres, consisting of the main house, bunkhouse, barn, corral, and toolshed.

In the setting sun the snow took on a golden glow, and the scene could have been a Currier and Ives painting come to life.

The main house, or "big" house as the cowboys called it, was a rather large, two-story Victorian edifice, white, with red shutters and a gray-painted porch that ran across the front and wrapped around to one side. The bunkhouse, which was also white with red shutters, sat halfway between the big house and the barn. The barn was red.

A wisp of smoke curled up from the kitchen chimney, and as the three approached, they could smell the aroma of baking.

"Yep! She made some," Pearlie said happily. "I tell you the truth, if Miss Sally don't make the best bear claws in Colorado, then I'll eat my hat."

"Hell, that ain't no big promise, Pearlie," Cal said. "The kind of appetite you got, you eat anything that gets in your way. I wouldn't be that surprised if you hadn't already et your hat a time or two."

Smoke laughed.

"That ain't no ways funny," Pearlie complained. "I ain't never et none of my hats."

"But there ain't no danger of you eatin' your hat anyhow 'cause you're right," Cal said. "Miss Sally does make the best bear claws in Colorado."

Sally was a schoolteacher when Smoke met her, but she was far from the demure schoolmarm one most often thought of when picturing a schoolteacher. Sally could ride, rope, and shoot better than just about any man, and yet none of that detracted from her feminine charms. She was exceptionally pretty and her kitchen skills matched any woman and surpassed most.

The bear claws that Pearlie was referring to were sweet, sugar-coated doughnuts. They were famous throughout the county, and some men had been known to ride ten miles out of their way to drop by the Sugarloaf just on the off chance she'd have a platter of them made up and cooling on the windowsill.

The three men rode straight to the barn, where they unsaddled their horses, then turned them into warm stalls with hay and water. They took off their coats, hats, and boots on the enclosed back porch, dumping the snow and cleaning their boots before they went inside.

The house was warm and cozy, and it smelled of coffee, roast beef, fresh-baked bread, bear claws, and wood burning in the fireplace. Sally greeted Smoke with a kiss and the other two with affectionate hugs.

Around the dinner table the four talked, joked, and laughed over the meal. And yet, as Sally studied her husband's face, she knew that, just beneath his laughing demeanor, he was a worried man. It wasn't so much what he said, as what was left unsaid. Smoke had always been a man filled with optimism and plans for the future. It had been a long time since she had heard him mention any of his plans for improving and expanding the ranch.

Sally had no idea what time it was when she rolled over in bed, still in that warm and comfortable state of half-sleep. She reached out to touch Smoke, but when she didn't feel him in bed with her, the remaining vestige of sleep abandoned her and she woke up, wondering where he was.

Outside, the snow glistened under the bright full moon so that, even though it was the middle of the night, the bedroom was well lit in varying degrees of silver and black. A nearby aspen tree waved in a gentle night breeze and as it did so, it projected its restless shadow onto the softly glowing wall. Smoke's shadow was there as well, for he was standing at that very window, looking out into the yard.

"Smoke?" Sally called out in a soft, concerned voice.

"I'm sorry, darlin'," Smoke replied. "Did I wake you?"

Sally sat up, then brushed a fall of blond hair back from her face. "Are you all right?" she asked.

"I'm fine."

"You're worried, aren't you?"

Smoke paused for a long moment before he answered. Then, with a sigh, he nodded.

"I won't lie to you, Sally," he said. "We may lose everything."

Sally got out of bed and padded across the room. Then, wrapping her arms around him, she leaned into him.

"No," she said. "As long as we have each other, we won't lose everything."

Chapter Two

The banker leaned back in his chair and put his hands together, making a steeple of his fingers. He listened intently as Smoke made his case.

"I'm sure I'm not the only one coming to you with problems," Smoke said. "I reckon this winter has affected just about everyone."

Joel Matthews nodded. "It has indeed," he said. "Right now our bank has over one hundred fifty thousand dollars in bad debt. I'll tell you the truth, Smoke. We are in danger of going under ourselves."

Smoke sighed. "Then it could be that I'm just wasting my time talking to you."

Matthews drummed his fingers on the desk for a moment, then looked down at Smoke's account.

"You have a two-thousand-dollar note due in thirty days," he said.

"Yes."

"What, exactly, are you asking?"

"I'm asking for a sixty-day extension of that note."

The banker turned at his desk and looked at the calendar on the wall behind him. The picture was an idealized night scene in the mountains. Below a full moon a train was crossing a trestle, its headlight beam stretching forward and every car window glowing unrealistically.

"Your note is due on April 30th," he said. "A sixty-day extension would take you to June 30th. Do you really think you can come up with the two thousand dollars by then?"

"I know that I cannot by April 30th, and I'll be honest with you, Joel. I don't know if I will have the money by June 30th either. But if any of my cattle survive the rest of this winter, I will at least have a chance."

"Smoke, can you make a two-hundred-dollar payment on your note? That would be ten percent."

Smoke shook his head. "Maybe a hundred," he said.

"A hundred?"

"That's about the best I can do right now."

Matthews sighed. "I'll never be able to convince the board to go along with it, unless you can at least pay ten percent on the loan."

Smoke nodded. "I understand," he said. He started to stand, but Matthews held out his hand.

"Wait a minute," he said.

Smoke hesitated.

"I know how you can come up with a hundred fifty dollars, if you are willing to do a job for me."

"A job for you?"

"Well, for the bank, actually," Matthews said. "It will take you about three days."

"Three days work for a hundred fifty dollars? I'll do it," Smoke said.

"Don't you even want to know what it is?"

"Is it honest work?"

"Oh, yes, it's honest all right. It might also be dangerous."

"I'll do it," Smoke said.

"Yes, I didn't think you would be a person who would

be deterred by the possibility of danger. But just so that you know what you are letting yourself in for, we have a rather substantial money shipment coming by stagecoach from Sulphur Springs. If you would ride as a special guard during the time of the shipment, I will pay you one hundred fifty dollars."

Smoke gasped. "One hundred fifty dollars just to ride shotgun? It's not that I'm looking a gift horse in the mouth, Joel, but shotgun guards make about twenty dollars a month, don't they?"

"Yes."

"So why would you be willing to pay me so much?"

"We are bringing in over twenty thousand dollars," Matthews said. He sighed, then opened the drawer of his desk and pulled out a newspaper. "And the damn fool editor over at Sulphur Springs has seen fit to run a front page story about it."

Matthews turned the paper around so Smoke could see the headlines of the lead story.

HUGE MONEY SHIPMENT!

$20,000 In Greenbacks

TO BE TRANSPORTED

by Sulphur Springs Express Company

to BIG ROCK.

"Why in the world would he publish something like this?" Smoke asked.

"Well, if you asked the editor, I'm sure he would tell us that he is merely exercising his freedom of the press," Matthews said. "But I would call it idiocy. Anyway, the cat is out of the bag, and no doubt every outlaw in three states knows about the shipment now. Do you know Frank Simmons?"

"No, I don't think I do."

"Frank Simmons is the normal shotgun guard on this run. He's sixty-six years old and blind as a bat. Ordinarily it's not a problem. About the only thing the stage ever carries is a mailbag with letters from grandparents, a few seed catalogues, and the like. But this? Well, Frank just isn't up for the job."

"I see what you mean," Smoke said. "When do I go?"

"You can take the stage over Monday morning," Matthews said. "The money will arrive by train Tuesday night. Marshal Goodwin and a couple of his deputies will meet the train with the banker just to make sure it gets in the bank all right. Then, Wednesday, you'll take personal charge of it until you get it back here."

"Sounds easy enough," Smoke said.

Matthews laughed out loud. "For someone like you, I imagine it is," he said. "But I'll be honest with you, Smoke. If I had to guard that shipment, knowing that every saddle bum and ne'er-do-well from Missouri to California is after it, why, I'd be peeing in my pants."

Smoke laughed as well. "I'll have the money here Wednesday evening," he said. "And I'll be wearing dry pants."

"You want me to go with you?" Pearlie asked over the supper table that night.

"No, why should you?"

"Well, if it's like Mr. Matthews says, you're liable to run into some trouble between here and Sulphur Springs."

"No. I thank you for the offer, Pearlie. But I want you and Cal to stay here and look after what few cattle we have left. You'll have to take hay out to them, since they won't be able to forage. And you'll have to watch out for the wolves, and any other creatures that might have a yen for beef. The only chance we have of saving Sugarloaf is to keep enough cows alive that I can sell to raise the two thousand."

"All right, if you say so," Pearlie said as he reached for the last of the bear claws.

"That's four," Cal said.

"What's four?"

"That's four of them things you'n has had."

"Cal," Sally said sharply.

"What? You think I'm lyin', Miss Sally? I been a'countin' them."

"I'm not concerned about that. I'm talking about your grammar."

"That's four of *those* things *you have* had," Pearlie said, correcting Cal's grammar. "Not them things you'n has had."

"Have you had four of them, Pearlie?" Sally asked.

"Well, yes, ma'am, but I believe these are somewhat smaller than the ones you usually make," Pearlie replied.

Sally laughed, then got up from the table and, walking over to the pie saver, opened the door and pulled out an apple pie.

"Then you won't be wanting any of this, will you?" she asked, bringing the pie to the table.

"*I* sure do!" Cal said, licking his lips in anticipation as Sally cut a large slice for him.

"Maybe just a little piece," Pearlie said, eyeing the pie she was cutting. "With, maybe, a slice of cheese on top."

* * *

That night, Sally cuddled against Smoke as they lay in bed.

"You take care of yourself, Smoke," she said.

Smoke squeezed her. "I've spent a lifetime taking care of myself," he said. "I'm not likely to fall down on the job now."

"It was nice of Mr. Matthews to offer you the job," Sally said. "He did say we would get the extension?"

"Yes." Smoke sighed. "For all the good it will do."

"What do you mean?"

"We've got thirty days until the loan is due, with the extension ninety days. Then what? We are still going to have to come up with the money."

"You don't think we'll have enough cattle to sell?"

"What if we do?" Smoke said. "Then what? At best, we'll just be buying time. A cattle ranch without cattle isn't much of a ranch."

They lay in the quiet darkness for a long moment before Sally spoke again.

"I know a way we might be able to come up with it," she said.

"Oh, no," Smoke said.

"Oh, no, what?"

"I'm not going to let you go on the line for me. I mean, I appreciate the offer, but I just wouldn't feel right, you becoming a soiled dove."

"What?" Sally shouted, sitting up in bed quickly and staring down at him.

Smoke laughed out loud. "I mean, I have given that very idea some thought too, but I wasn't sure you would do it. Then I figured, well, maybe you would, but I just wouldn't feel right about it."

"Kirby Jensen!" Sally said, laughing at him as she

realized he was teasing. She grabbed the pillow, then began hitting him with it.

"I give up, I give up!" Smoke said, folding his arms across his face as she continued to pound him with the pillow. Finally, winded, she put the pillow down.

"Truce?" Smoke asked.

"Truce," Sally replied. Then, she smiled wickedly at him. "How much do you think I would make?"

"Sally!" Smoke gasped.

This time it was Sally's turn to laugh. "Well, you are the one who brought it up," she said between giggles.

Sally lay back down beside him and, again, they were quiet for a moment.

"How?" Smoke asked.

"How what?"

"You said you may have a way to raise the money. How would we do it?"

"Light the lamp," Sally said as she got out of bed, "and I'll show you."

Sally walked over to the dresser and opened the top drawer. Removing a newspaper, she returned to the bed just as a bubble of golden light filled the room.

"Read this advertisement," she said, pointing to a boxed item in the paper.

Smoke read aloud. "New York Company desires ranch land to lease. Will pay one dollar per acre for one-year lease."

"If we leased our entire ranch to them, we could make twelve thousand dollars," Sally said.

Smoke shook his head. "No," he said.

"Why not?"

"Sally, you know why not. If we lease this ranch to some outfit like this"—he flicked his fingers across the page—"they'll send their own man in to run things. We'll be tenants on our own land. Only the land won't even be ours, at least not for a year."

"Smoke, you said yourself we are in danger of losing everything," Sally said. "At least, this way, we could hang onto the ranch. All right, we won't make any money this year because everything we get will have to go toward the notes. But next year, we could start fresh."

"Start fresh with no money," Smoke said.

"And no debt," Sally added.

Smoke stared at the advertisement for a long moment. Then he lay back on the bed and folded his arm across his eyes.

"Smoke?"

Smoke didn't answer.

"Smoke, you know I'm right," Sally said.

After another long period of silence, Smoke let out a loud sigh.

"Yeah," he said. "I know you're right."

"Then you'll do it?"

"Is this what you want to do, Sally?"

"No, it isn't what I want to do," Sally admitted. "But I don't see any other way out of this. At least think about it."

"All right," Smoke agreed. "I'll think about it."

The man standing at the end of the bar had a long, pockmarked face and a drooping eyelid. He picked up his beer, and blew the foam off before taking a drink. His name was Ebenezer Dooley, and he had escaped prison six months ago. He was here to meet some people, and though he had never seen them, he knew who the three men were as soon as they came in. He could tell by the way they stood just inside the door, pausing for a moment to look around the main room of the Mad Dog Saloon, that they were here to meet someone.

The room was dimly lit by a makeshift chandelier that consisted of a wagon wheel and several flickering candles. It was also filled with smoke from dozens of cigars and pipes so that it took some effort for the three men to look everyone over. Dooley had told them that he would be wearing a high-crowned black hat, with a red feather sticking out of a silver hatband. He stepped away from the bar so they could see him; then one of them made eye contact and nodded. Once contact was made, Dooley walked toward an empty table at the back of the saloon. The three men picked their way through the crowd, then joined him.

One of the bar girls came over to smile prettily at the men as they sat down. She winced somewhat as she got a closer look at them, because they were some of the ugliest men she had ever seen.

Dooley had been in town for a few days, so she had already met him. He was tall and gangly, with a thin face and a hawklike nose. He was not handsome by any standard, but compared to the other three, he was Prince Charming.

"Girlie, bring us a bottle and four glasses," Dooley said.

The bar girl left to get the order, returned, picked up the money, then walked away. None of the men seemed particularly interested in having her stay around, and she was not at all interested in trying to change their minds.

"You would be Cletus, I take it?" Dooley said to the oldest of the three men. Cletus had white hair and a beard and, as far as Dooley could tell, only one tooth.

"I'm Cletus."

"A friend of mine named McNabb told me you would

be a good man to work with," Dooley said. "And that you could get a couple more."

"These here are my nephews," Cletus said. "This is Morgan." Morgan had a terrible scar that started just above his left eye, then passed down through it. He had only half an eyelid, and the eye itself was opaque. Morgan stared hard at Dooley with his one good eye.

"And this here'n is Toomey," Cletus continued. "Neither one of 'em's too quick in the mind, but they're good boys who'll do whatever I tell them to do. Ain't that right, boys?"

"Whatever you tell us, Uncle Cletus," Toomey said. "Mama said to do whatever you tell us to do."

"His mama is my sister," Cletus said. "She ain't none too bright neither, which is why I figure she birthed a couple of idiots."

Neither Morgan nor Toomey reacted to his unflattering comment about them.

"Can I count on them to do the job I got planned?" Dooley asked.

"I told you," Cletus said. "They'll do whatever I ask them to do."

"Good."

"You said this would be a big job?"

"Yes."

"How big?"

"Twenty thousand dollars big," Dooley said.

Cletus let out a low whistle. "That is big," he said.

"The split is fifty-fifty," Dooley said.

"Wait a minute, what do you mean, the split is fifty-fifty? They's four of us."

"I set up the deal, I'm in charge," Dooley replied. "I take half, you take half. How you divide your half with your nephews is up to you."

Cletus looked at his two nephews for a moment; then he nodded.

"All right," he said. "That sounds good enough to me. Where is this job, and when do we do it?"

"Huh-uh," Dooley replied.

Cletus looked surprised. "What do you men, huh-uh? How are we goin' to do the job iffen we don't know what it is we're a'supposed to be doin'?"

Dooley shook his head. "I'll tell you what you need to know when the time comes. I wouldn't like to think of you gettin' greedy on me."

"Whatever you say," Cletus replied.

Chapter Three

Even though Smoke had nothing to do with the money yet, he was in the Sulphur Springs Railroad Depot when the eleven o'clock train arrived.

The depot was crowded with people who were waiting for the train. Some were travelers who were holding tickets, and some were here to meet arriving passengers, but many were here for no other purpose than the excitement of watching the arrival of the train.

They heard the train before anyone saw it, the sound of the whistle. Then, as the train swept around a distant curve, the few people on the platform saw the headlamp, a gas flame that projected a long beam before it.

The train whistled again, and this time everyone could hear the puffing of the steam engine as it labored hard to pull the train though the night. Inside the depot, Smoke stepped over to one of the windows, but because it was very cold outside, and warm inside, the window was fogged over. He wiped away the condensation, then looked through the circle he had made to watch the train approach, listening to the puffs of steam as it escaped from the pistons. He could see bright sparks embedded in the heavy, black smoke that poured from the flared smokestack. Then, as the train swept into the station, he saw sparks falling from the firebox and leaving a carpet of orange-glowing embers lying between the rails and trailing out behind the train. They glimmered for a moment or two in the darkness before finally going dark themselves.

The train began squeaking and clanging as the engineer applied the brakes. It got slower, and slower still, until finally the engineer brought his train to a stop in exactly the right place.

Much of the crowd inside went outside then, to stand on the platform alongside the train as the arriving passengers disembarked and the departing passengers climbed aboard. But Smoke and three men remained inside the depot. Smoke had met with the others earlier in the day when he had presented them with the letter from Joel Matthews, authorizing him to take possession of the money.

"Well, Mr. Jensen," the banker said, noticing Smoke for the first time that night. "On the job already, I see."

"I just came down to see if I would actually have a job tomorrow."

"That's probably not a bad idea," the young deputy said. "Coming down here now to watch us can give you a few pointers."

"Ha," the marshal said, laughing. "I can see Smoke Jensen picking up some pointers from the likes of us."

"Everybody can learn something," Smoke said.

The station manager stuck his head inside the door then.

"Mr. Wallace, you want to come sign for this now? The railroad is anxious to get rid of it."

"I'll be right there," the banker said.

The marshal and his deputy both drew their pistols,

then followed Wallace out to the mail car. Smoke went outside with them, and he turned up the collar of his sheepskin coat as he watched Wallace take the money pouch from the express messenger. Then he followed the banker and his two guards down to the bank, where the money was put into the safe.

"There you go, Mr. Jensen," Wallace said when the money was put away. "All safe and sound for you tomorrow."

"Yes, well, I'll feel a lot better when it is safe and sound in the bank back in Big Rock," Smoke said.

Smoke was just finishing his breakfast the next morning, sopping up the last of the yellow of his egg with his last biscuit, when someone walked over to his table.

"You're Mr. Jensen?"

"Yes."

"I'm from the bank, Mr. Jensen. Mr. Wallace said to tell you to come over and get that . . . uh . . . package now," he said cryptically.

"All right," Smoke said, washing down the last bite with the end of his coffee. He put on his coat, turned up his collar, and pulled his hat down, then followed the messenger back to the bank.

"I didn't think the bank would be opened yet," Smoke said, his words forming clouds of vapor in the cold morning air.

"It isn't open yet," the young man said. "Mr. Wallace thought it would be better to give it to you before we had any customers."

"Sounds sensible," Smoke said.

Smoke thought they would go in through the front, but the young man walked alongside the bank until they reached the back. Then, taking a key from his pocket, he opened the back door and motioned for Smoke to go inside.

Wallace was sitting at a desk in his office when the young man brought Smoke in. The pouch that the money had come in was open, and there were several bound stacks of bills alongside.

"You want to count this money?" Wallace asked.

"It might be a good idea," Smoke replied.

"Jeremiah, pull that chair over here for Mr. Jensen."

"Yes, sir," the young messenger said.

Thanking him, Smoke sat in the chair and began counting. When he finished, half an hour later, he looked up at Wallace. "I thought it was supposed to be twenty thousand dollars."

"How much did you come up with?" Wallace asked.

"Twenty thousand four hundred and twelve dollars," Smoke replied.

Wallace smiled, and slid a piece of paper across his desk. "That exact amount is recorded here," he said. "It's good to see that you are an accurate counter. Sign here, please."

With all money accounted for, Smoke took the pouch and walked down to the end of the street to the stage depot. The coach was already sitting out front and the hostlers were rigging up the team.

Although it had not snowed in nearly a week, there were still places where snow was on the ground in many places, some of which could not be avoided. As a result, Smoke had snow on his boots, but he stomped his feet on the porch, getting rid of as much as he could.

The stage depot was warm inside, and he saw five people standing around the potbellied stove, a man, two women, and a young boy. There were three more men over by the ticket counter and one of them, seeing Smoke, came toward him. He was an older man, with white hair and weathered skin. He stuck his hand out.

"Good morning, Mr. Jensen. I'm Frank Simmons."

"Call me Smoke," Smoke said. "You would be the shotgun guard?"

"Yes, sir, normally that would be me," Simmons said.

"Normally?"

"Well, the truth is, if you have that much money to look after, ever'one figures it'd be better if you'd just go ahead and ride shotgun yourself." Simmons held out his hands and both were shaking. "I got me this here palsy so bad, why, I couldn't no ways hold a gun to shoot. Only reason I go along now is to keep Puddin' company. We don't never carry nothin' worth stealin'. That is, until now."

"Puddin'?"

"That would be me," another man said, coming over to shake Smoke's hand. "Puddin' Taylor is the name. I'm the driver. You'll be sittin' up on the high board with me, if you don't mind."

"No, I figure that's probably the best place for me," Smoke said. "Not looking forward to getting that cold," he said.

"Ah don't worry none 'bout gettin' too cold," Puddin' said. "We keep us a really warm buffalo robe up there. Why, you'll be as warm as the folks down in the box with their wool blankets."

"Puddin'," someone called from the front door. "Your team is hitched up, you're all ready to go."

"Thanks, Charlie," Puddin' replied. "All right, folks, let's get on the stage. I'm 'bout ready to pull out."

Smoke went outside with the others and watched as the

passengers boarded the coach, then wrapped themselves in blankets to ward off the cold. Smoke climbed up onto the high seat alongside Puddin', who then released the brake and snapped the ribbons over the team. The coach jerked forward, then moved at a clip faster than a brisk walk through the town and onto the road.

Dooley stood on a rock and looked down the road.

"What we stayin' here for?" Cletus asked. "It's cold up here."

"We're here because by the time the coach reaches this point, the driver will have to stop his team to give 'em a breather. That's when we'll hit them," Dooley said.

Cletus, Morgan, and Toomey were sitting on a fallen log about forty yards away from the road. Morgan got up and walked over to a bush to relieve himself. He began to giggle.

"What are you laughin' at?" Toomey asked.

"Lookie here when I pee," Morgan said. "There's smoke comin' from it."

"That ain't smoke, you idiot," Dooley said. "It's vapor, same thing as your breath when it's cold."

"That don't make no sense," Morgan said. "There ain't no breath a'comin' offin' my pee."

"Wait," Tommey said. "I'm goin' to see if I can piss smoke too."

"Quiet!" Dooley said sharply. "I think I hear somethin'."

In the distance, Dooley could hear the whistle and shouts of the driver as he urged his team up the long grade.

"They're comin'. Ever'one get ready," Dooley said, climbing down from the rock.

* * *

"Git up thar, git on with ya'!" Puddin' shouted, urging the straining team up the grade. He leaned over to spit a chew, and a wad of the expectorated tobacco hit the right front wheel, then rotated down.

"Will you be stopping at the top of the grade?" Smoke asked.

"Yeah," Puddin' answered as he wiped his mouth with the back of his hand. "We got to, else the team'll give out before we reach the next way station."

Smoke pulled his pistol and checked the loads.

"What you doin' that for?" Puddin' asked.

"If I were planning to hold up this stage, this is where I would do it," Smoke said.

"Yeah," Puddin' said, nodding. "Yeah, you're prob'ly right."

It took another ten minutes before the team reached the crest of the grade.

"Whoa!" Puddin' called, pulling back on the reins.

The team stopped and they sat there for a moment, with the only sound being the heavy breathing of the horses. Vapor came, not only from their breath, but from their skin, as the horses had generated a lot of heat during the long pull up the hill.

Suddenly three armed men jumped out in front of the stage. One of the men fired and his bullet hit Puddin' in the arm.

Even before the echo of that shot had died out, Smoke was returning fire, shooting three times in such rapid succession that all three of the would-be robbers went down.

"Puddin', are you all right?" Smoke asked.

"Yeah," Puddin' replied, his voice strained with pain. "It just hit me in the arm, didn't do nothin' to any of my vitals."

"What's happening? What's going on up there?" someone from inside the coach called. The door to the coach opened.

"No!" Smoke shouted. "Stay inside!"

With his pistol at the ready, Smoke climbed down from the driver's seat, then moved slowly, cautiously toward the three men he had just shot. That was when he heard hoofbeats and looking toward the sound, he saw a rider bending low over the neck of his horse as he kept the horse at a gallop.

Smoke raised his pistol and started to shoot, but decided that whoever it was offered no immediate danger, so he eased the hammer back down and examined the three men.

All three were dead, their faces contorted in grimaces of pain and surprise.

"Did you kill the sons of bitches?" Puddin' called.

"Yeah," Smoke said.

"Good."

"Keep everyone on the stage until I have a look around," Smoke said.

Smoke followed the tracks of the three would-be robbers back into the edge of the woods. There, he saw a fallen log. There was also enough disturbed snow around the log that he knew this was where the men had been waiting. He also saw three horses tied to a branch. He walked over to the animals and patted one of them on the neck.

"Don't worry," he said. "I'm not going to leave you out here. You didn't try to hold up the stage."

Further examination showed that there had been a fourth horse, and Smoke was satisfied that that was the horse of the man he had seen running away. Nobody else was here, or had been here.

Smoke came back out of the tree line leading the three horses. He stopped at the bodies of the three outlaws.

"See anyone else back there?" Puddin' asked.

"No, it's all clear," Smoke said. He began putting the bodies on the horses, belly down. "Don't know which one of you belongs to which," he said to the horses. "But I don't reckon it matters much now."

Puddin' tied off the team, then climbed down. "You folks can come out now," he called to his passengers. "If you need to, uh, rest yourselves, well, there's a pretty good place for the ladies over there," he said.

"Let me take a look at your arm," Smoke said. He tore some of Puddin's shirt away, then looked at the wound.

"How's it look?"

"It went all the way through. If it doesn't get festered, you should be all right." Smoke tore off another piece of the driver's shirt. "Give me a chaw of tobacco," he said. "I'll use it as a poltice."

The driver chewed up a wad of tobacco, then spit it into the cloth.

"Here too. I'll need it on the entry and exit wound."

Puddin' complied, then Smoke wrapped the bandage around his arm, putting the tobacco over each wound.

"There was another'n, wasn't there?" the driver asked as Smoke worked.

"Yes. But I don't expect we'll have any trouble with him."

The passengers came back from their rest stop then, and the boy, who was about eleven, walked back to look at the bodies draped over the horses.

"Timmy, come back here," the boy's mother said.

"Wow," Timmy said to Puddin'. "There were three of them and just two of you, but you beat 'em."

Puddin' shook his head. "Not two of us, son," he said. "Just one." He nodded toward Smoke, who had already climbed back up into the seat. "He did it all by himself."

"What kind of man could take down three armed outlaws all by himself?" one of the male passengers asked.

"Well, a man like Smoke Jensen, I reckon," Puddin' replied.

Dooley rode his horse at a gallop until he feared that the animal would drop dead on him. Then he got off and walked him until the horse's breathing returned to normal.

He had told Cletus and his nephews to stay out of sight until he gave the word to confront the stage. He'd had it all planned out, which included staying separated so as to deny the stage guard any opportunity to react.

But before he knew it, all three jumped up in front of the stage. At first, Dooley couldn't understand why they would do such a damn fool thing. But as he was riding away from the scene, he began thinking about it, and he was fairly certain that he had figured it out.

Dooley was convinced that Cletus and his two nephews had planned to rob the stage, then turn on him, keeping all the money for themselves. But it didn't work out that way for them because the shotgun guard killed all three.

What sort of man could take on three gunmen and kill all three? Dooley wondered.

From the moment he had learned of the money shipment, he had begun planning this robbery. He'd even taken a trip on the stage, just to make certain that he knew the route it would travel. That's how he'd learned about the long grade and the necessity of stopping to rest the horses.

But the shotgun guard on the trip he took was an old man with the shakes. He wouldn't have presented any trouble at all. In fact, Dooley even watched the coach depart two more times, and it had been the same guard for each trip. This guard today was new and, as it turned out, deadly.

Dooley resented the fact that he didn't get the money, but he was just as glad that Cletus and his nephews got themselves killed. As it turned out, they were nothing but a bunch of double-crossing bastards anyway.

Chapter Four

"Folks, can I have your attention please?" Sheriff Carson called.

At the sheriff's call, everyone in Longmont's Saloon grew quiet and turned to see what he had to say.

Sheriff Carson smiled, then nodded toward a table where Smoke was sitting with Sally, Pearlie, Cal, and Louie Longmont, owner of Longmont's Saloon.

"As you all know, our own Smoke Jensen here foiled a robbery last week, and that's why we're here celebratin' with him and Sally." Sheriff Carson turned toward Smoke, and held up his mug of beer. "Smoke, if those no-'counts had managed to steal the money you were guarding, the folks around here would be in a lot more trouble than we are. I thank you, and the town thanks you."

"Hear, hear," Longmont said, and the others in the saloon applauded.

"Mr. Longmont, another round of drinks if you please," Joel Matthews said. "The bank is buying."

"All right!" someone shouted, and there was a rush to the bar.

"I'll get ours," Pearlie said, getting up from the table.

"I'll have a beer," Cal said.

"He'll have a sarsaparilla," Sally declared.

"Miss Sally I . . ." Cal began, but Smoke cut him off with a steely gaze. Cal was about to say that he drank beer all the time when he was out with just Smoke and Pearlie, but he knew that if he told her that now, Smoke would curtail those privileges.

"May I join you?" Matthews asked, coming over to the table.

"Yes, please do," Sally said with an inviting smile.

Matthews sat down, then pulled an envelope from his inside jacket pocket.

"Smoke, the board voted to give you a reward of three hundred dollars, in addition to the one hundred fifty you earned," Matthews said, handing the envelope to Smoke.

"Smoke!" Sally said happily. "That will pay our interest, plus allow us to keep the money we were going to use."

Smoke nodded. "Thanks, Joel."

"I just wish it could be more," he said. "I wish it could be enough to pay off your entire note."

"Well, with the extension this will buy for me, maybe we'll come up with a way of handling that note," Smoke said.

At that moment, Emil Blanton came into the saloon, carrying a large pile of papers. Blanton was publisher of the local newspaper, the *Big Rock Vindicator*. Smiling, he brought one of the newspapers over to Smoke.

"Since you are the star of my story, I thought I might give you a free copy," Blanton said, holding it up for Smoke and the others to see.

SMOKE JENSEN FOILS ROBBERY ATTEMPT.

On the 9th instant, the well-known local rancher Smoke Jensen volunteered his services as a shotgun guard for the Sulphur Springs Express Company. The reason for this was a special shipment of twenty thousand dollars, said money to be made available at the Bank of Big Rock in order to provide loans for those of the area who have been made desperate by the brutal winter conditions.

According to Mr. Puddin' Taylor, who was the driver of the coach, the would-be robbers accosted them just as they reached the top of McDill Pass. Before Taylor could question the intent of the three who had flagged down the coach, the highwaymen presented pistols, and opened fire with mixed effect. Mr. Taylor was wounded, but the other bullets missed. Smoke Jensen fired back, but not until after the robbers had fired first.

Smoke Jensen, as his reputation so nobly suggests, did not miss. Within scarcely more than the blink of an eye, all three outlaws were sent on their way to eternity, where they will be forced to plead their case before St. Peter and all the angels of heaven.

This newspaper joins other citizens of

> the fair city of Big Rock in congratulating Smoke Jensen for his quick thinking and courageous action.

Ebenezer Dooley was at the Cow Bell Saloon in the small town of Antinito, Colorado. A traveler had left a copy of the Big Rock newspaper in the saloon, and because Dooley had nothing else to do, he picked it up, took it over to an empty table, and began reading it.

The paper was over two weeks old, but that didn't matter because it had been several weeks since Dooley had read any news at all. He read about his botched robbery attempt.

"Smoke Jensen," Dooley said, scratching his beard as he read the weathered newspaper. "That's the name of the son of a bitch who stole my money."

Dooley folded the newspaper and put it in his pocket. "I'll be keepin' that in my memory."

"Beg your pardon?" the man at the next table over said.

"Nothin'," Dooley said. "I was just talkin' to myself, is all."

The man laughed. "I do that my ownself sometimes," he replied. "I guess when you're used to talkin' to your horse all the time, why, a man will sometimes just wind up talkin' to hisself."

"I guess so," Dooley said, not that interested in getting into a conversation with the man.

"You was readin' about Jensen, wasn't you? Smoke Jensen."

"Yeah," Dooley said. "Yeah, I was. How did you know?"

"You spoke his name."

"Oh, yeah, I guess I did."

"You know him?"

"No, I, uh, ran across him once," Dooley replied.

"So you wouldn't say he's a friend of yours?"

Dooley shook his head. "He ain't no friend. Do you know him?"

"Well, we ain't ever actual met, but I know who the son of a bitch is. He kilt my brother."

"He killed your brother? Why isn't he in prison for that?"

"Well, my brother was rustlin' some of Jensen's cattle at the time."

"Where were you when that happened?"

"I was in prison."

Suddenly Dooley smiled. "I'll be damned," he said. "I know who you are. You're Curt Logan, aren't you?"

Logan smiled, then picked up his glass and moved over to join Dooley. "I was wonderin' when you would recognize me. I mean, I recognized you right off. Course, we was in different cell blocks, so we didn't see each other all that many times. Then I done my time and got out." Logan looked puzzled. "What are you doin' out? I thought you was supposed to be doin' twenty years."

"Well, let's just say that the State of Colorado had its idea of when I should leave, and I had mine," Dooley said.

Logan chuckled. "I'll be damned. You escaped, didn't you?"

"Yes, I did. Fact is, you could get five hundred dollars just for turning me in to the law."

"Is that a fact?"

"It is," Dooley said. "But I'm not worried about you doin' that."

"Why not?"

"Because I know somethin' that would be worth a lot more than five hundred dollars to you. That is, if you are interested."

Logan nodded. "I'm interested," he said.

"What have you been doin' since you got out?" Dooley asked.

"Tryin' to make a livin'," Logan said. "I've punched some cows, worked at a freight yard, mucked out a few stalls."

"Haven't found anything to your likin', though, have you?"

Logan chuckled. "What's there to like about any of that?"

"I might have an idea," Dooley said, "if I can get enough men together."

"How many do you need?"

"Besides the two of us, I'd say about four more."

"Six men? Damn, what you plannin' to do? Rob a bank?"

Dooley smiled again. "Well, that's where the money is, ain't it?"

Smoke sat in his saddle and watched as his hands dragged the dead cattle into large piles, then burned them. It was the only way to clear away the carnage left from the brutal winter just passed. He and all the cowboys were wearing kerchiefs tied around their noses to help keep out the stench.

When the pile was large enough, Pearlie and Cal rode around the carcasses, soaking them with coal oil. Their horses, put off by the smell of death, were skittish, and would occasionally break into a quick gallop away. Cal's horse did that, reacting so quickly that Cal dropped the can of kerosene.

"Whoa! Hold it, hold it!" Cal shouted, fighting his mount. Cal was an exceptionally skilled rider who sometimes broke horses for fun. Because of that, he generally rode the most spirited horses, and not many of the other riders would have been able to stay seated. Cal rode easily, gracefully, until he got the horse under control again.

When the gallop was over, Cal brought his reluctant horse back to the task at hand, bending over from the saddle to retrieve the can he had dropped.

Finally, when the pile of dead cows had been sufficiently dosed with kerosene, Pearlie lit a match and dropped it onto one of the animals. The match caught, and within a few minutes, large flames were leaping up from the pile.

Pearlie and Cal rode back to where Smoke was, then reined up alongside him and turned to watch the fire.

"It's like a barbeque," Cal said.

"If it is, it's the most expensive barbeque you'll ever see," Pearlie said.

"Yeah," Smoke said, answering in one, clipped word.

"Sally," Smoke said that night as they lay in bed. There was agony in the sound of his voice.

"Yes?"

"I had to let all the men go today."

"I figured as much. I saw them all riding off."

"I even let Pearlie and Cal go."

"Oh," Sally said.

"Don't worry. They aren't going anywhere. I explained that I cannot pay them, but they said they would stay anyway."

"Yes," Sally said. "I figured they would."

"We can't do it," Smoke said. He sighed. "We lost too many head. Even if we sold every cow we have left, we wouldn't make enough money to pay off the note on the ranch."

"Oh, Smoke," Sally said, putting her head on his shoulder.

"I've let you down," Smoke said. "I've failed you."

"No, you haven't let me down, and you haven't failed. You had no control over the weather."

"That's true, I had no control over the weather," Smoke said. "But if I hadn't borrowed so much money against the ranch, we could have ridden out this winter. Now, we're going to lose Sugarloaf. And I know how much you love this place."

"Oh, you silly darling," Sally said. "I do love this place, but don't you know that I love you much more? In fact, I love this place because of you. And no matter where we go, or what we have to do, it will be fine as long as we are together."

"Yeah," Smoke said. He tightened his arm around her. "That's good to know, but it doesn't make me any less a failure."

They lay in silence for a moment longer before Sally spoke again.

"We don't have to lose this place," she said.

"You have an idea as to how to save it?"

"Yes. Don't you remember? I told you about it last winter."

"You're talking about leasing the ranch, aren't you?"

"Yes."

Smoke sighed. "I don't want to do that. I don't want to give up control of my own place."

"But it would only be temporary. You would give up control for one year. Surely that would be better than losing the ranch, and giving up control forever?" Sally insisted.

Smoke didn't answer for a moment, and Sally thought about pressing her case, but she held back. She had lived with Smoke long enough to know that he was thinking it through.

"All right," he finally said. "Suppose I decide to do this, what would be the first step?"

"There is a land broker's office in Denver," Sally said. "I saved the address. We can go there and talk to him."

"No, you stay here with the ranch," Smoke said. "It's ours for thirty more days. I wouldn't want to give anyone the wrong idea that we were abandoning it, and someone might think that is exactly what is happening if we both leave."

"All right, I'll stay."

"Besides, if we do lease the ranch, I expect the tenants will want to live in this house. So you, Pearlie, and Cal need to find someplace for us to go. The line shack over on Big Sandy might work. It's the biggest of all of them."

"We'll get it in shape while you're gone," Sally said.

"I hate having to ask you to live in such a place."

"It will be fine, Smoke, you'll see," Sally said. "I'll have it looking really nice by the time we move in. And it's only a year; then we'll be back in our own house."

"The Lord willing," Smoke said.

"Smoke, when you make the deal, don't forget that you must get the money in advance, in order to be able to pay the note."

"I know," Smoke said. "Don't worry, I will."

"It's going to be all right, Smoke," Sally said. "I know it will."

"Pearlie?"

Cal got no response.

"Pearlie?" he called again.

Although the bunkhouse had beds enough for twelve

cowboys, Cal and Pearlie were the only two occupants at the present time.

Cal sat up in the darkness. He couldn't see Pearlie, but he could hear him snoring.

"Pearlie!" he said again.

"What?" Pearlie answered, sitting up quickly. "What's happening?"

"Are you asleep?" Cal asked.

Pearlie let out an audible sigh, then fell back in his bed.

"Well, I was asleep," Pearlie said.

"Oh. Well, then, I won't bother you."

Pearlie got out of his bunk, then walked over to Cal's bunk. He jerked all the covers off Cal.

"Hey, what did you do that for?" Cal shouted, reaching for the covers that Pearlie was holding away from him. "Give me my covers."

Pearlie handed him his covers, then sat back down on his bunk. "I'm listening now," he said. "So tell me what was so important that you had to wake me up." Pearlie ran his hand over the puff of purple flesh that was on his chest, the result of a bullet wound.

"We was goin' to bury you under the aspen trees," Cal said.

"What?"

"Last year, when we was down to the Santa Gertrudis Ranch, helpin' out Captain King, you got shot, remember?"

Pearlie laughed. "Well, Cal, that ain't somethin' that you just forget all that easy."

"Anyway, we didn't figure you'd live until we got you home, so we was already plannin' your funeral. We decided to, that is, Miss Sally decided to bury you under the aspen trees. That would'a been a real pretty spot too."

"Sorry it didn't work out for you," Pearlie said, teasing.

"Cal, please tell me you didn't wake me up just to tell me where you had planned to bury me."

"Miss Sally planned."

"All right, Miss Sally planned. Is that why you woke me up?"

"No."

"Then why did you?"

"I'm worried," Cal said. "What if Smoke can't get the money? I mean, he's got to come up with all that money in less than a month. I can't see no way he's goin' to be able to do that."

"He's been in some tough spots before," Pearlie said. "I reckon it'll work out all right."

"What if he don't?"

"What do you mean?"

"What if he don't get the money? Then he'll lose the ranch. And if he does, then where will we go? What will become of us?"

"Cal, are you worried about Smoke? Or are you worried about us?" Pearlie asked.

Cal ran his hand through his hair. "I guess I'm worried about both," he said.

"Well, at least you are honest about it," Pearlie said. "Truth is, I don't know what will become of us."

"You know what I think? I think we ought to leave," Cal said.

"Leave? You mean run out on Smoke and Miss Sally?"

"No, not run out on them," Cal said. "Just leave, so they don't have us to have to feed and worry about."

"Yeah," Pearlie said. "Yeah, I see what you mean."

"I think we ought to go now," Cal said.

"You mean just leave, without so much as a fare-thee-well?"

"Yes," Cal said. "Think about it, Pearlie. If we stick

around long enough to tell them good-bye, you know what they are going to do. They are going to try and talk us into stayin' on."

"Maybe they need us to stay on."

Cal shook his head. "No, right now, we're a burden to 'em. I know how it is, Pearlie. I was on my own when I was twelve 'cause I didn't have no family to speak of, and I didn't want to be a burden to nobody."

"All right, we'll go," Pearlie said. "But I ain't goin' without leavin' 'em a letter. There ain't no way I'm goin' to just run out on 'em. Not after all the things they have done for us.'"

"I agree," Cal said. "The least we can do is leave 'em a letter tellin' 'em what happened to us."

Chapter Five

"Smoke!"

Smoke was in the bedroom, packing for his trip, but the anguish in Sally's call to him caused him to drop the saddlebags on the bed and hurry to the kitchen. He saw her standing just inside the kitchen door, leaning against the counter. She was holding a letter in one hand, while her other hand was covering her mouth. Her eyes had welled with tears.

"What is it?" Smoke asked. "What has happened?"

"They are gone," Sally said in a strained voice.

"Who is gone? What are you talking about?"

"It's Pearlie and Cal," she said. "When I went out to the bunkhouse to call them in for breakfast, they weren't there, and all their stuff was gone. I found this lying on Pearlie's bunk." Sally handed Smoke a sheet of paper.

Smoke read the letter.

Dear Smoke and Miss Sally,

By the time you get this letter, me and Cal will be gone. We figure, what with all the problems you're havin' with the ranch and all, that you don't really need two more mouths to feed. And since you ain't got no cows to speak of, why, there ain't enough work to justify you keepin' us on just so's you can feed us.

We are both grateful for all the good things you two has done for us, and for all the good times we've had together. I know you ain't either one of you old enough to be our parents, but it's almost like that's just what you are, the way you have took care of us and looked out for us for all this time.

I hope you can save the ranch somehow. We'll be looking in now and again to see how it is that you are faring, and if we see that you got the ranch all put back together again, why, we'll come back and work for you again. Fact is, if we can find work now, why, me and Cal has both said that we'll be sending some money along to help you out.

Your good friends,
Pearlie and Cal

"I can't believe they would do something like that to us," Smoke said.

"Oh, Smoke, I don't think they believe they are doing it to us. I think they believe they are doing it for us."

"Well, that's just it. They didn't think," Smoke said. He sighed. "That means you are going to be here all alone while I'm gone. Will you be all right?"

"Why, Kirby Jensen," Sally said. "How dare you ask me such a question?"

Smoke chuckled. "You're right," he said. "That was pretty stupid of me. I pity the poor fool who would try and break in here while I'm gone."

"Did you pack your white shirt and jacket? I think you should wear that when you talk to the broker."

"I packed it," Smoke said. He put his hands on her shoulders. "It's a long ride to Denver," he said. "I'll be gone for at least two weeks, maybe a little longer. I'll send you a telegram when I get there, just to let you know that I arrived all right. Then I'll send you another one when I get something worked out with the broker."

"I'll miss you terribly, but I'll be here when you get back," Sally said. "I'll spend the time while you are gone getting the line house ready for us. I intend to move some of my favorite pieces of furniture down there."

"How are you going to move them with Pearlie and Cal gone?"

"I'll go into town and ask Mr. Longmont to find someone to help me," Sally said. "Don't worry, I'll take care of it."

They kissed, and as the kiss deepened, Sally pulled away and looked up at him with a smile on her face.

"What would it hurt if you left an hour later?" she asked.

Smoke returned her smile. "Why, I don't think it would hurt at all," he said as he led her toward their bedroom.

It was just after dark when Pearlie and Cal rode into Floravista, New Mexico Territory. From the small adobe houses on the outskirts of town, dim lights flickered through shuttered windows. The kitchens of the houses emitted enticing smells of suppers being cooked, from the familiar aromas of fried chicken to the more exotic and spicy bouquets of Mexican fare.

A barking dog ended its yapping with a high-pitched yelp, as if it had been kicked, or hit by a thrown rock.

A baby cried, its loud keening cutting through the night.

A housewife raised her voice in one of the houses,

launching into some private tirade about something, sharing her anger with all who were within earshot.

The main part of Floravista was a contrast of dark and light. Commercial buildings such as stores and offices were closed and dark, but the saloons and cantinas were brightly lit and they splashed pools of light out onto the wood-plank sidewalks and on into the street. As Pearlie and Cal rode down the street, they passed in and out of those pools of light so that to anyone watching, they would be seen, then unseen, then seen again. The footfalls of their horses made a hollow clumping sound, echoing back from the false-fronted buildings as they passed them by.

By the time they reached the center of town, the night was alive with a cacophony of sound: music from a tinny piano, a strumming guitar, and an out-of-tune vocalist, augmented by the high-pitched laughter of women and the deep guffaw of men. From somewhere in the Mexican part of town, a trumpet was playing.

Pearlie and Cal dismounted in front of the Oasis Saloon, tied their horses to the hitching rail, then went inside. Dozens of lanterns scattered throughout the saloon emitted enough light to read by, though drifting clouds of tobacco smoke diffused the golden light.

As they stood for a moment just inside the door, Cal happened to see a pickpocket relieve someone of his wallet. The thief's victim was a middle-aged man who was leaning over the bar, drinking a beer and enjoying his conversation. While he was thus engaged, the nimble-fingered pickpocket deftly slipped the victim's billfold from his back pocket. Instead of putting the billfold in his pocket, though, the thief walked down to the end of the bar and, casually, dropped it into a potted plant. Then the thief ordered a beer and stood there, drinking it casually.

"Pearlie, did you see that?" Cal asked.

"Yeah, I saw it," Pearlie answered.

"Maybe we should. . . ."

"Wait," Pearlie said. "Let's see what happens."

The victim ordered a second beer, then reached for his pocket to get the money to pay. That's when he realized that his billfold was gone.

Puzzled by the absence of his billfold, the man looked on the floor to see if he had dropped it. Then he picked up his hat, which was lying on the bar, to see if it was there.

"Hey," the man called. "Has anybody seen my bill-fold?"

"I know where it is," Cal said.

Cal and Pearlie were still standing in the middle of the floor, having just come in.

"You know where my wallet is?" the man replied in disbelief.

"Yes, sir, I know where it is."

"Well, where is it?"

Cal pointed to the potted plant that sat on the floor at the end of the bar.

"It's down there under that plant" Cal said.

The victim looked toward the plant; then he turned back toward Cal. "Now how in the hell would it wind up down there?" he asked. "I haven't moved from this spot since I got here."

The pickpocket, suddenly sensing danger, put his beer down and started walking toward the door. As he did, Pearlie stepped in front of him to stop him.

"Here, get out of my way," the pickpocket growled. "What are you doing."

Cal pointed to the pickpocket Pearlie had stopped. "Your billfold is in that pot, because this fella put it there. Only, he didn't put it there until after he took all the money from it and stuck it down into his own pocket."

"What?" the pickpocket said. "Mister, are you crazy? I just come in here to have a beer."

"And steal some money," Pearlie added.

By now the confrontation had stopped all conversation as everyone looked toward Pearlie, Cal, and the pickpocket.

"I ain't goin' to stand around here and be accused of stealin'," the pickpocket said. He pointed toward the bartender. "What kind of place are you running here anyway? Do you just let anyone accuse an innocent person of picking someone's pocket?"

The barkeep brought a double-barrel shotgun up from under the bar, and though he didn't point it at anyone, its very presence lent some authority to his next comment.

"Mr. Thornton, you want to step down there and look in the potted plant and see if your wallet is there?" the bartender asked.

The men who were standing at the bar between Thornton and the potted plant stepped back to let him by. He walked to it, then looked down inside.

"I'll be damned!" he said. "He's right! My wallet is here!" Thornton reached down into the pot, then came up with the wallet, holding it high for everyone in the saloon to see.

There was an immediate reaction from all the other patrons.

"Any son of a bitch who would steal another man's wallet ought to be strung up," someone said.

"Or at least tarred and feathered," another added.

"I don't know what you are talkin' about," the pickpocket said, his voice and expression showing his anxiousness. "I didn't put that there."

"Is your money gone, Mr. Thornton?" Pearlie asked.

Thornton opened his wallet and looked inside.

"Yes!" he said. "Every dollar of it is gone."

Pearlie stuck his hand down into the pickpocket's vest pocket and took out some folded bills. He handed the bills to the bartender.

"Hey! That's my money!" the pickpocket said. "You all seen it. He just stole my money!"

"How much money did you have in your billfold?" Pearlie asked.

"I had nineteen dollars," Thornton answered. "Three fives and four ones."

The bartender counted the folded bills, then held them up. "Three fives and four ones," he announced to all.

The pickpocket tried to run, but two men grabbed him, then hustled him out of the saloon bound for the sheriff's office.

"Well, now, I would like to thank you two boys," the victim said, extending his hand. "The name is Thornton. Michael Thornton."

"I'm Pearlie, this here is Cal," Pearlie said, shaking Thornton's hand.

"Pearlie and Cal, eh? Well, I reckon that's good enough for me. Could I buy you boys a drink?"

"Later, perhaps, after we've had our supper," Pearlie replied. "That is, if a fella can get anything to eat in here," he added to the bartender. "Do you serve food?"

"Steak and potatoes, ham and eggs, your choice," the bartender replied.

"Yes."

"Yes, which?"

"Yes, we'll have steak and potatoes, ham and eggs," Pearlie said.

Thornton laughed. "These young men are hungry," he said. "Bring them whatever they want. I'll pay for it."

"You don't need to buy our supper," Pearlie said. "We were just doin' what we figured was right."

"I know I don't need to. It's just my way of thanking you."

"If you really want to thank us, you can tell us where we might find a job in this town," Cal said.

"You two boys are looking for a job?"

"Yes, sir," Cal answered.

"You aren't afraid of hard work, are you?" Thornton asked.

"Not if it's honest."

"Good enough. I own the livery," Thornton said. "I can always use a couple of good men if you are interested."

"We're interested," Pearlie said.

"Then the job is yours."

Chapter Six

Ebenezer Dooley turned in his saddle and looked at the five men who were with him. Buford Yancey, Fargo Masters, and Ford DeLorian were men he had worked with before. He had never worked with Logan, but he vaguely remembered him from their time together in prison. Curt Logan had brought along his brother, Trace, as the fifth man. Curt and Trace Logan were wearing identical red and black plaid shirts.

Dooley spit out a wad of tobacco as he stared at the two brothers.

"Logan, would you tell me why in the hell you and your brother are wearing those shirts? Don't you know they stand out like a sore thumb? Ever'one in town is goin' to see 'em, and remember 'em."

"There's likely to be some shootin', ain't there?" Curt Logan asked.

"I told you there might be. Robbin' a bank ain't like stealin' nickels off a dead man's eyes."

"Well, I already lost me one brother when he got hisself kilt by Smoke Jensen, and I don't plan to lose me another'n. That's why Trace 'n me is wearin' these here plaid shirts."

Dooley shook his head in confusion. "What's wearing a shirt like that got to do with it?"

"Things gets real confusin' when there's a lot of shootin' goin' on, and I don't plan for me'n my brother to shoot each other by mistake. As long as we're wearin' these here shirts, that ain't likely to happen."

"If you lead the posse to us 'cause of them shirts, I'll be doin' the shootin' my ownself," Dooley growled.

"Dooley," Fargo said. "The sun's gettin' on up. I figure it's nine o'clock for sure. The bank'll be open by now."

"Right," Dooley said. "All right, men, anybody got to take a piss, now's the time to do it."

Three of the men dismounted to relieve themselves, then all remounted and looked at Dooley.

"Fargo, you, Ford, and Yancey will ride into town from the south end. Me'n the Logans will come in from the north. That way, we won't be drawin' no attention on account of so many ridin' together."

"All right," Fargo said. "Come on, boys," he said to the others. "We'll need to get around to the other side."

Jason Turnball, the city marshal for the town of Etna, was a big man, standing almost six feet six and weighing well over two hundred pounds. He was sitting in a chair on the porch in front of Dunnigan's General Store. Dunnigan had reinforced the chair just for the marshal, because he liked having the marshal parked on his front porch. That tended to keep away anyone who might get the idea to rob the store, almost as if he had hired his own personal guard.

Marshal Turnball had his feet propped up on the porch railing, and his chair tipped onto the back two legs. He was peeling an apple, and one long peel hung from the apple all the way to the porch.

Billy Frakes, an eighteen-year-old who worked as a store clerk for Dunnigan, was sweeping the front porch.

"I tell you true, Marshal Turnball," Frakes said. "I believe that's about the longest peel you've ever pared."

"Nah," Turnball said as he cut it off at the end, then held it up for examination. "I've done longer." He tossed the peeling to the bluetick hound that lived under the porch. The dog grabbed the peel, then backed up against the front wall to eat it.

"Look at them folks," Frakes said, pointing to the three riders who passed by in front of the store. "Two of 'em's got shirts just alike."

Turnball laughed. "Wouldn't think two of 'em would be dumb enough to wear a shirt that ugly, would you?"

Frakes laughed with him.

Fargo, Ford, and Yancey reached the bank just before Dooley and the Logan brothers. They stopped across the street from the bank and dismounted in front of a leather goods store. Yancey and Fargo examined a pair of boots in the window, while Ford dismounted and held the reins of the three horses. Dooley and the Logans arrived then, and Dooley nodded at Fargo, just before he and the Logans went into the bank.

"That's funny," Frakes said.

"What's funny?" Turnball replied.

"Them fellas over there in front of Sikes Leather Goods. How come you reckon that one is holdin' the horses, 'stead of tyin' 'em off at the hitchin' rail?"

"Maybe them other two just wanted to look at the boots and they was goin' to ride on," Turnball suggested.

"Well, if they're just wantin' 'em some boots, maybe one 'em would be interested in buyin' a pair of boots I just made," Frakes said. "I think I'll go down there an' see."

"If you go down there and sell your boots in front of Al Sikes's store, takin' business away from him, you never will get him to sell your boots for you," Turnball said.

"No, sir. I think it's just the opposite. If Mr. Sikes seen that folks would be willin' to buy boots that I've made, why, that might just make him want to sell 'em in his store," Frakes insisted as he stood the broom up against the wall. He stepped inside Dunnigan's for just a moment, then came back out carrying the boots he had made. He held them out for the marshal's inspection.

"What do you think of 'em?" he asked.

"They're good-lookin' boots all right," Turnball agreed. "Can't nobody say you don't do good work."

Smiling under Turnball's praise, Frakes started down the street toward Sikes Leather Goods.

Trace Logan stayed out front holding the horses, while his brother Curt and Dooley went into the bank. There were only two people inside the bank, Rob Clark, the owner, and Tucker Patterson, the teller. Both were just behind the teller's cage, and Patterson looked up as the two men came inside.

"Yes, sir," Patterson said. "Can I help you gent . . ." he began. Then he paused and gasped as he saw that both men were wearing hoods over their faces. They were also holding guns.

"This here is a holdup," Dooley said in a gruff voice. He held up a cloth bag. "Fill this bag with money."

"Mr. Clark?" Patterson said. "What shall I do?"

Dooley pointed his pistol at Clark and pulled the hammer back. It made a deadly-sounding click.

"Yeah, tell him, Mr. Clark," Dooley said. "What should he do?"

"T-Tucker," Clark said in a frightened voice. "I think you had better do what the man says."

"Yes, sir," Patterson said.

"Now you're getting smart," Dooley said.

Patterson started taking money from the cash drawer and putting it into the sack.

"Take a look out in the street," Dooley said to Curt. "Anybody comin' in?"

"Don't see nobody," Curt answered.

"That's all the money we've got," Patterson said, handing the sack back.

Dooley looked down into the sack. "There's not more'n a couple hundred dollars here," he said. "I know you got more'n that. I want the money from the safe."

"I . . . I don't have the combination to the safe," Patterson said. "Only the bank president has the combination."

"Where is the bank president?"

Patterson glanced toward Clark, but he said nothing.

"I see," Dooley said. "All right, Mr. Bank President, I'll ask you to open the safe."

Clark didn't move.

Dooley pointed his gun at Patterson. "Open the safe or I'll kill him right now," Dooley growled.

"Mr. Clark, please!" Patterson begged.

Nodding reluctantly, Clark walked over to the safe. Within a few minutes he had the door open. Dooley could see several small, filled bank bags inside.

"Damn!" Curt Logan said with a low whistle. "Have you ever seen so much money?"

"Put them bank bags in the sack," Dooley ordered, handing the sack over to Clark.

"What's takin' 'em so long?" Yancey asked, looking back toward the bank.

"Maybe there's lots of money and it's takin' 'em a while to get it all," Fargo suggested. "You don't worry about them; you just do the job you're supposed to be doin'. Keep a lookout all around you."

"There ain't nobody payin' no attention to the bank," Yancey said.

"Fargo, Yancey, there's someone comin'," Ford called from his position holding the horses.

"Where? Who?" Fargo asked.

"Up there," Ford said, nodding. "He's comin' right for us."

"He's carryin' a pair of boots," Yancey said. "Maybe he bought some boots here and he's bringin' 'em back."

"This is a hell of a time for him to be doin' that," Fargo said.

At that moment, Dooley and Curt Logan ran from the bank, still wearing hoods over their faces. Clark appeared in the front door of the bank, right behind them. He was carrying a pistol, and he fired it at the three men as they were getting mounted.

"Holdup!" Clark shouted. "Bank robbery! These men just robbed the bank!"

Dooley and both of the Logan brothers shot back at the banker, and Clark dropped his gun, then fell back into the bank.

"Shoot up the town, boys!" Dooley shouted. "Keep ever'one's head down!"

Frakes, who was nearly to the leather goods store by

then, was surprised to see that the three men he was coming to see were also part of the robbery. He dropped his boots and ran as they began shooting up and down the street, aiming as well at the buildings. Window glass was shattered as the bullets crashed through.

One of the bullets hit the supporting post of the awning in front of the meat market, just as Frakes stepped up onto the porch. Frakes turned, and dived into the watering trough right in front of the meat market. Sinking to the bottom, he could hear the continuing sound of shots being fired, though now it was muffled by the water. Frakes held his breath as long as he could, then lifted his head up, gasping for air. By that time he could see the six men just crossing over the Denver and New Orleans railroad track. They galloped out of town, headed almost due west toward Thunder Butte, which rose some twenty miles away.

Frakes climbed out of the trough and stood in the street alongside, dripping water. The town was in a turmoil with men yelling at each other, dogs barking, and children crying. Several men were running toward the bank.

"Was anybody hit?" someone asked.

"Help me," Patterson was calling from the front of the bank. "Help me, somebody! Mr. Clark has been shot!"

By now there were several men gathered at the bank and as Frakes started toward it, he saw Dr. Urban going there as well. Urban was carrying his medical bag, and when he reached the bank he started shouting at the people to let him through.

"It's the doc," someone said. "Let him through."

Frakes went over as well, and because there were too many people crowded around for him to see, he climbed up on the railing. That gave him a good view, and he saw Dr. Urban kneeling beside Clark's prostrate form.

"How is he, Doc?" someone asked.

Dr. Urban put his fingers to Clark's neck, held them there for a moment, then shook his head.

"He's gone," Dr. Urban said.

"Somebody better go tell Mrs. Clark," Tucker Patterson said.

Dr. Urban looked up at Patterson. "Well, Mr. Patterson, I expect that should be you," he said. "You know her better than anyone else."

Gulping, Patterson nodded. "I expect that's so," he said.

"Did anyone get a good look at the ones who did this?" Turnball asked.

"Marshal, it was them same fellas we seen comin' into town," Frakes said. "The ones with them plaid shirts."

"Yeah, I seen them shirts too," one of the other townspeople said.

"That's right, Marshal," Patterson said. "Two of them were wearing red and black plaid shirts."

"Did you see their faces?" Turnball asked Patterson.

Patterson shook his head. "No, I didn't see their faces. They had their faces covered with hoods."

"The ones outside wasn't wearin' hoods," someone said.

"Yeah, well, wearin' hoods or not don't make no difference," one of the others said. "Near'bout all of us seen them shirts. You can't hide a shirt like that."

"You goin' after them, Marshal?"

"There are six of them," Turnball said.

"I don't care how many of 'em there is, they got our money. Hell, after this winter we just come through, that's near'bout all the money the town has left."

"I'll need a posse."

"I'll ride with you."

"Me too."

"You can count on me."

"I'll ride with you, Marshal," Frakes said.

"All right, men, get yourselves a gun, have your women put together two, maybe three days' food, get mounted, and meet me in front of my office."

"When?"

"I figure you should all be ready within an hour."

"An hour? Marshal, them outlaws can get a long ways in an hour," one of the men said. Like Turnball, he was wearing a badge, because this was Turnball's deputy.

"Pike, they've already got fifteen minutes on us," Turnball said. "If we go off half-cocked now, we ain't got a snowball's chance in hell of catchin' up to them. Best thing for us to do is be prepared. Now, are you plannin' on riding with the posse or not?"

"You know I'm goin'," Pike said. "I'm your deputy, ain't I?"

"Then get you some food, then get on back down to the office and wait until we are ready to go."

"All right, all right," Pike said. "I just don't want them sons of bitches to get away, that's all."

Turnball looked at the others, who seemed to be standing around awaiting further instructions. "What are you all a'waitin' on? Now!" he said gruffly, and with that, the posse scattered.

"Marshal, you want I should get some cuffs so we can cuff 'em when we find 'em?" Pike asked.

"Of course," Turnball said. "Unless you were plannin' on just askin' them not to try and get away."

"No, it's not that, it's just that I thought, well . . ." Pike hesitated.

"You thought what?"

"I wasn't all that sure we would be bringin' 'em back in, if you know what I mean."

"No, I don't know what you mean."

"I mean men like that, shootin' down Mr. Clark and stealin' all the town's money like they done. Well, some folks might think they don't have no right to be brought back in alive."

"Pike, I'm going to pretend I didn't hear that," Turnball said.

"It's not like I'm talkin' lynchin' or anything," Pike said. "I meant, uh, well, I meant, what if they put up a fight and we have to kill 'em? I mean, all legal like."

"Now, you get back down to the office and get ready, like I said."

"Sure, Marshal, sure," Pike said. "Like I said, I didn't really mean nothin' by it. I was just thinkin' on what might happen, is all."

"Do me a favor, will you, Pike? Don't think," Marshal Turnball said.

Smoke was riding north through a level forest. Just behind him a boulder-covered hillside rose almost ten thousand feet to the wooded and still-snow-covered peak of Thunder Butte. It was getting toward midday when Stormy started limping and Smoke had to stop. He had just lifted the left foreleg of his horse to look at the foot when he saw six men riding toward him.

Smoke didn't pay that much attention to them at first. He was on relatively level ground, which meant that anyone who was traveling through here would have to come in his general direction. Right now his biggest concern at the moment was the shoe. But the approaching horses made an obvious turn so that they began moving directly toward him.

Smoke had no idea what they wanted, so he kept an eye on them as he examined Stormy's hoof. He saw that the horse had picked up a rock between the shoe and the hoof, so he started working to get it out.

The riders came right up to him, then reined to an abrupt halt. Smoke looked up at them again.

"Howdy," he said.

"Howdy," one of the riders—a man with a long, pock-marked face and a drooping eyelid—said, swinging down from his horse. The other five riders dismounted as well.

There was something peculiar about the riders, the way they all dismounted and the way they stared at him. It was also curious how they let one man do all the talking. Two of the riders were wearing identical red and black plaid shirts, and as he looked at them more closely, he saw that they looked enough alike that they must be brothers. He didn't have a good feeling about the whole situation, and he decided that the quicker they left, the better it would be.

"Are you havin' any trouble?" the man with the pock-marked face and drooping eyelid asked.

"Nothing I can't handle," Smoke answered. He squinted at the men. "You folks headed anywhere in particular?"

"Yeah, we're lookin' for work," the man with the drooping eyelid said.

Smoke shrugged. "Don't know as you'll have too much luck there. The winter was pretty bad on most of the ranches. What few spring roundups there were are probably over now. Far as I know, none of the ranches are hiring. Maybe if you go farther south, down into New Mexico Territory where the winter wasn't so bad, you'll have some luck."

"What are you trying to do, mister? Put a shoe on a split hoof?" one of the men in a plaid shirt asked.

Smoke should have known better than to fall for an old trick like that, but out of concern for the horse, he looked at Stormy's foot. That was when one of the other riders stepped up and slammed the butt of his pistol down on Smoke's head. After that, everything went black.

Chapter Seven

Opening his eyes, Smoke discovered that he was lying facedown in the dirt. He had no idea where he was or why he was lying on the ground, though he sensed that there were several people standing around, looking down at him.

His head throbbed and his brain seemed unable to work. Who were these people and why were they here? For that matter, why was he here?

Smoke tried to get up, but everything started spinning so badly that he nearly passed out again. He was conscious of a terrible pain on the top of his head, and when he reached up and touched the spot gingerly, his fingers came away sticky with blood. Holding his fingers in front of his eyes, he stared at them in surprise. That was when he saw his shirt sleeve. He was not wearing the blue shirt he had started out with that morning. Instead, he was wearing a red and black plaid shirt . . . one of the shirts he had seen on the men who had accosted him.

"What happened?" Smoke asked. His tongue was thick, as though he had been drinking too much.

"I'll tell you what happened, mister. Looks to me like there was a fallin'-out among thieves," a gruff voice said.

"The other boys turned on you, didn't they? They knocked you out and took the money for themselves."

Smoke got up slowly, trying to make sense of things. He wasn't sure what the man was suggesting, so he just hesitated.

"That's right, ain't it?" the man asked. The man talking to him was a very big man, wearing a tan buckskin vest over a red shirt. Peeking out from just behind the vest was a lawman's star.

"I'm not sure I know what you are talking about, Sheriff," Smoke said.

"I'm not a sheriff, I'm marshal for the town of Etna. And lyin' ain't goin' to do you no good. Too many people seen you in that shirt you are wearing. And just because you wound up without any of the money, it don't make you no less guilty. You're going to hang, mister. I don't know which one of you killed Mr. Clark back there in Etna when you held up the bank, but it don't really matter none who pulled the trigger. Every one of you sons of bitches is just as guilty."

Smoke had been right in sensing that there were several people around him, because as he looked around now, he could see several more men glaring at him, all of whom were brandishing weapons, ranging from revolvers to rifles to shotguns.

Again, Smoke put his hand to the wound on his head. It was extremely painful to the touch, and he winced.

"Who are you?" Smoke asked.

"I'll be askin' the questions, mister," the big man replied. "But for your information, the name is Turnball." Turnball pointed to a thin-faced, hawk-nosed man who appeared to be in his mid-twenties. He was also wearing a star.

"This here is Pike, my deputy, and the rest of these men

are temporarily deputized for posse duty. What is your name?"

"Jensen. Kirby Jensen, though most folks call me Smoke."

Turnball smiled broadly. "Smoke Jensen, eh?"

"You've heard of me?" Smoke said, relieved. Sometimes having a reputation could be an intrusive aggravation. But in a case like this, it would be helpful in preventing a case of mistaken identity.

"Oh, yes, I've heard of you all right," Turnball said. "Fact is, I've got paper on you tacked up on my wall."

"Paper?"

"You're a wanted man, Mr. Jensen."

"No," Smoke said. "If you've got wanted posters on me, they are old. Very old. All the dodgers on me have been withdrawn. I'm not wanted."

"Well, if you wasn't wanted before, you're sure wanted now, seein' as how you robbed our bank. I reckon you and your friends figured you could get away with it 'cause Etna is so small. But you got yourselves another think coming."

"I didn't rob any bank."

Turnball pointed to Smoke's shirt. "Anyone who would wear a plaid shirt while robbing a bank is just too damn dumb to be an outlaw," he said. "Hell, half the town of Etna described you."

"They may have described this shirt, Marshal, but they didn't describe me," Smoke said.

"Same thing."

"No, it isn't the same thing. This isn't my shirt."

Turnball laughed. "Oh, you mean you stole the shirt before you stole the money from the bank?"

"No. I mean whoever attacked me took my shirt and put this one on me."

Turnball and the others laughed.

"Now if that ain't about the dumbest damn thing I've ever heard. Why would anyone do that?"

"It's obvious, isn't it? They did it to throw the suspicion on me," Smoke explained. "I guess they figured the law around here would be dumb as dirt and buy into it. Looks like they were right."

Turnball laughed again. "You say I'm dumb, but you are the one who got caught. Quit lyin' and save your breath. I know what happened. You boys got into a little fight, and they lit out on you. I'm arresting you for the murder and bank robbin' you and the others done in my town," Turnball said.

Deputy Pike and one of the other riders grabbed Smoke roughly, and tried to twist his arms behind his back. Smoke broke loose.

"Oh, do it!" Pike said, cocking his pistol and pointing it at Smoke's head. "I'm just lookin' for an excuse to shoot you, you murderin' bastard!"

"Pike!" Turnball said gruffly. "I told you, we're takin' him back alive. You kill him here, we never will find the others."

Smoke glared at Pike. "If you want to shackle me, just ask," he said. "No need for you to pull my arms out of their sockets."

"Put your hands behind your back," Pike ordered.

"Shackle his hands in front of him," Turnball said. "He's got to ride his horse back into town."

Smoke held his hands out in front, and Pike shackled them together.

"Help him on his horse," the marshal ordered. "And

pick up them empty bank wrappers. Like as not, we'll be needing them as evidence."

"Marshal Turnball, my horse picked up a stone," Smoke said. "I was working on his foot when the bank robbers jumped me. He'll go lame if it isn't taken care of."

"Check it out, Frakes," Turnball said.

Frakes, who was the youngest of the bunch, had been staring unblinkingly at Smoke from the very beginning. He made no effort to move.

"Frakes?" the marshal said again.

Frakes blinked, as if just aware he was being spoken to. "What?"

"He said his horse picked up a stone. Check it out."

"Left foreleg," Smoke said.

Frakes lifted the horse's left foreleg. "Yeah, there's a stone here, all right," he said. He took a knife from his pocket and, after a moment, got the stone out.

"Thanks," Smoke said.

"You're welcome," Frakes said.

Pike held the reins as Smoke got mounted.

"You're making a big mistake," Smoke said. "I did not hold up any bank. I was on my way up to Denver to meet with a land broker. I own Sugarloaf Ranch down in Rio Grande County. I haven't even been in Etna before today."

"You want to explain these empty bank wrappers here?" Turnball asked, holding one of them out for Smoke to examine. Printed on the side of the wrapper was $1,000.00 BANK OF ETNA.

"They must've been left here by the men who jumped me. They're the ones you are looking for."

"Jumped you, you say?"

"Yes, I told you, I was seeing to my horse when they rode up. They started talking to me, and the next thing I knew, they knocked me out. That must have been when they took my shirt and left this one. That's also when they left these bank wrappers lying around. They set me up."

"You got any witnesses to that?"

"Well, no," Smoke answered. "The only witnesses are the ones who did it, and they certainly wouldn't testify against themselves."

"Too bad you got no witnesses, mister. 'Cause I do have witnesses. At least half a dozen of 'em. And they'll ever'one of 'em swear they seen you and the other robbers ridin' out of town."

"Your witnesses are wrong, Marshal. They are either mistaken, or they are lying."

"Mister, I am one of them witnesses," Turnball said. "And I don't cotton to being called a liar. So, don't you go tellin' me what I did and what I did not see." He pointed at Smoke's chest, adding, "I remember them plaid shirts you and one of the other robbers was wearin' like as if there was a picture of 'em drawn on my eyeballs."

"I told you, this isn't my shirt," Smoke said again. "You are making a huge mistake."

"No, friend," the lawman responded. "The only mistakes made around here was made by you. And you made three of 'em." Ticking them off on his fingers, he enumerated: "Your first mistake was in pickin' a bank in my town to rob. Your second was in havin' a fall-out with the other thieves, and your third was in getting yourself caught. Now, let's go."

The ride back to town took about two hours, and as Turnball and his posse rode into town, several of the town's citizens turned out along either side of the street to watch.

"They caught one of 'em!" someone yelled.

"Good job, Marshal!" another said.

"Hang 'im! Let's hang the son of a bitch now!" yet another shouted. "Ain't no need for a trial! Hell, the whole town seen him kill Mr. Clark!"

The last citizen had several others in the town who agreed with him, and the mood grew much uglier by the time Turnball got Smoke back to the jail.

"What you goin' to do with him now, Marshal?" someone asked as the riders all dismounted.

"I'm going to put him in jail and hold him there until Judge Craig can get down here and hold a trial," Turnball said.

"Hell, there ain't no need in wastin' the judge's time or our time," one of the citizens said. "If you ask me, I say we hang the son of a bitch now, and get it over with."

"Fremont, I hope you are just mouthin' off to hear yourself talk," Turnball said. "I hope you aren't really talkin' about lynchin'."

"Come on, Jason, you seen what he did to poor old Mr. Clark. His wife has been grievin' something pitiful ever since it happened," Fremont said. "It ain't right that poor Mr. Clark is dead and the son of a bitch that killed him is still alive."

"Pike," Turnball said gruffly. "Get the prisoner in the cell."

"These folks are pretty worked up," Pike said. "Maybe Fremont's got a point. I mean, why should the town pay to feed the prisoner when he's just goin' to hang anyway?"

"Get the prisoner in the cell like I told you to," Turnball said. Turnball pulled a shotgun from the saddle boot of his horse. "The rest of you," he said to the crowd. "Get on about your business and let me get about mine."

"Marshal, you know damn well if we try him, the judge

is goin' to find him guilty. Then we'll hang him anyway," Fremont said.

"Then you can afford to be a little paitent."

"To hell with patience. I say let's do it now and get it over with," Fremont insisted, still undeterred by Marshal Turnball's chastising.

Turnball pointed the shotgun at Fremont. "You aren't listenin' to me, are you?" Turnball asked menacingly.

"Whoa, hold on there!" Fremont said, his voice showing his fright. Fremont held his hands out in front of him and took a couple of steps back. "What are you doin', Turnball? You'd shoot an innocent man to save a murderer?"

"There's nothin' innocent about a lynchin', or about anyone who would suggest one," Turnball said. He pulled the hammer back on one of the barrels of the double-barrel shotgun he was holding. "Now if these here people don't leave in the next ten seconds, I'm goin' to blow your head off."

"Wait a minute! What do you mean you're going to blow my head off? I'm not the only one here," Fremont said, obviously frightened at having the gun pointed at him.

"No, you aren't. But you are the one doin' all the big talk, and you are the one I'm going to kill if the others don't leave."

"Why would you shoot me if *they* don't leave?" Fremont asked.

"'Cause I won't be able to kill all of them," Turnball said impatiently. "One, two, three . . ."

"Let's go!" Fremont said to the others. "Let's get out of here!"

Turnball watched as the townspeople left. Then he looked at the men who had ridden with him in the posse.

"You folks can go too," he said. "I thank you for ridin' with me."

The posse members left as well, some of them remounting and riding away, others leading their horses. Frakes remained behind.

"You may as well go on too, Frakes."

"You think the town would really lynch Jensen?" Frakes asked.

"It sounded for a few minutes there like they were giving the idea some thought," Turnball said. "But I don't intend to let it happen. I can't say as I blame them, though. Mr. Clark was a good man, and he carried a lot of people through the winter, givin' 'em time on their loans and all."

"What if we don't have the right man?" Frakes asked.

Turnball laughed. "What do you mean, what if we don't have the right man? Hell, you was right over there on Dunnigan's porch with me when they rode in. We commented on the shirts two of 'em was wearin', remember?"

"Oh, yes, sir, I remember all right," Frakes said.

"Then what makes you think we ain't got the right man?"

"I remember the shirt," Frakes said. "But I don't know as I remember the face. I know for a fact he wasn't the one standin' out front. And when the other two come out of the bank, why, they was both wearin' hoods."

"Well, don't worry about it. We got the right man, all right. And soon as he gets his day in court, why, we'll prove he is the right one. Then we'll build a gallows right here on Front Street, and all these people that's got a bloodlust out will have their hangin'. Only by then, it'll be legal."

"Yeah," Frakes said. "Yeah, I guess you're right." Frakes climbed onto his horse, then started riding it toward the livery.

Turnball watched him for a moment, then went inside.

He saw Pike standing over at the utility table by the wall. Pike was leafing through all the wanted posters.

"You got him into the cell with no problem, I take it?" Turnball asked.

"No problem," Pike said as he continued to page through the wanted posters. "I reckon his kind knows better than to mess with me."

"No doubt," Turnball replied sarcastically.

"Aha! You was right!" Pike said, suddenly holding up one of the posters. "We do have some paper on a fella named Smoke Jensen. Hey, Marshal, did you know there's a five-thousand-dollar reward on him!"

"No. I just remember having seen the name on a dodger, that's all."

Pike whistled. "Five thousand dollars," he said. "Damn that's a lot of money. Just think what we can do with that money."

"It don't do us any good to think about it," Turnball said.

"What do you mean it don't do us any good to think about it? We're the ones that caught him. I'd like to know who has a better claim on it."

"It ain't a point of havin' a better claim on it. We're the law," Turnball explained. "If you're the law, you can't collect on a reward. That's just the way of it."

"Well, that ain't right," Pike said, crestfallen. "That ain't no way right."

"Marshal," Smoke called from the cell at the back of the room. "Check the date on that poster."

Turnball looked at the poster, front and back. "There ain't no date," he said.

"Well, take a good look at the poster then," Smoke said. "Can't you see how the paper has already turned color? That alone should tell you how old it is."

Turnball shook his head. "It don't matter how old it is. I've never received anything cancelin' it."

"All right, it tells what county issued it, doesn't it?" Smoke asked. "Doesn't it say it came from Hinsdale County?"

"Hinsdale County, yes."

"Then it is easy enough for you to check," Smoke said.

"Check, how?"

"All you have to do is send a telegram to the sheriff of Hinsdale County and ask if the poster is still good."

Turnball stroked his chin for a moment. "I could do that, I suppose, but what difference would it make?"

"What do you mean, what difference would it make? It would prove that I'm not a wanted man."

"Oh, it might prove that you aren't wanted for this crime anymore," Turnball said, pointing to the poster. "Whatever the crime was. But that don't have anything to do with why you are in jail now. You are in jail now because you robbed a bank and killed a good man, and near half the town seen you do it. That's somethin' you can't get out of."

"I didn't do it," Smoke said.

"Yes, well, I guess we'll just have to let a judge and jury decide that, won't we?"

Dooley, the Logan brothers, Fargo, Ford, and Buford Yancey had watched from an elevated position near the place where they had encountered Smoke. They saw the posse arrive, confront Smoke, then ride away with him as their captive.

"Ha!" Yancey said. "That was smart leavin' them empty bank wrappers like that. They think he done it."

"Yeah, but this is what gets me. They got to know that

there was more'n one person," Fargo said. "How come they're all goin' back with him? Why ain't they still searchin' for the rest of us?"

"Come on, Fargo, you know how posses is," Curt Logan explained. "When they first get started, why, they're all full of piss and vinegar, ready to chase a body to hell and back. But they run out of steam just real quick. Especially if they find just enough success to make 'em feel good about themselves. And what we done was give 'em somethin' to make 'em think they done good."

"Let's go," Dooley said, turning away.

Dooley led them up into the high country and through a pass that was still packed with snow.

"Damn, Dooley," Curt Logan said. "Couldn't you find a place that's easier to get through? The snow here is ass-deep to a tall Indian."

"Nobody who's looking for us will expect us to come this way," Dooley said. "And if they do come this way, it'll be just as hard for them as it is for us."

"Well, you seen 'em. They ain't even comin' after us at all," Curt Logan said. "I sure don't see no need to be workin' so hard just to get away from a posse that ain't even chasin' us."

"If you don't like followin' me, just go your own way," Dooley offered.

"Well, hell, we ain't got no choice now but to keep on a-goin' this way," Curt Logan said. "Now it'd be as hard to go back as it is to keep goin'."

"Besides which, we ain't divided up the money yet," Yancey said.

"We'll divide it up soon as we get through the pass," Dooley said. "Then we can all go our separate ways."

Chapter Eight

"Come on, Pearlie, why won't you go with me?" Cal asked.

"I just don't care that much about travelin' shows, that's all," Pearlie said.

"But they say that Eddie Foy is really funny."

"You go, Cal," Pearlie said. "Have a good time."

"You're sure you don't want to come? I mean, I won't go if you . . ."

"Go," Pearlie said. "We aren't joined at the hip. You can do something by yourself if you want to."

Cal smiled. "All right, if you're sure." He started down the street toward the music hall. A large banner that was spread across the front of the music hall read: EDDIE FOY—DANCER—HUMORIST.

"Cal?" Pearlie called.

Cal turned toward him.

"If you hear any good jokes, tell me tonight, will you?"

Cal nodded. "I will!" he said.

Pearlie watched his young friend walk away; then he headed for the saloon. It wasn't that he didn't want Cal's company, or even that he didn't enjoy his company. It was just that he intended to play a little poker tonight and he knew how Sally felt about such things. He didn't want to be blamed for getting Cal mixed up in a card game.

There was another reason Pearlie wanted to play cards tonight. On the few nights he had come in for a beer, which was all he could afford before his first payday working in the livery stable, he had noticed that the Oasis Saloon employed a woman as dealer for the card games.

The woman's name was Annie, and through the week, Pearlie and Annie had flirted with each other. She had invited him into the game several times, and Pearlie sometimes got the idea that the invitation might be for more than just a game of cards.

He had turned her down every time, not because he didn't want to, but because he couldn't afford to. Tonight, he felt like he could, so he nursed a beer at the bar, then went straight to the table the moment a seat opened up.

"My, my," Annie said, smiling up at him. "Look who has finally come around."

"I thought I might give it a try," Pearlie said, sitting in the open chair.

"New player, new deck," Annie said. She picked up a box, broke the seal, then dumped the cards onto the table. They were clean, stiff, and shining. She pulled out the joker, then began shuffling the deck. The stiff, new pasteboards clicked sharply. Her hands moved swiftly, folding the cards in and out until the law of random numbers became king. She shoved the deck across the table.

"Cut?" she invited Pearlie. She leaned over the table, showing a generous amount of cleavage.

Pearlie cut the deck, then pushed the cards back. He tried to focus on her hands, though it was difficult to do so because she kept finding ways to position herself to draw his eyes toward her more interesting parts.

"You aren't having trouble concentrating, are you?" Annie teased.

"Depends on what I'm concentrating on," Pearlie said.

Annie smiled. "You naughty boy," she said.

"Here, what's goin' on here?" one of the other players asked. "You two know each other?"

"Not yet," Annie answered. She licked her lips. "But I have a feeling we are going to. Five-card?" She paused before she said the next word. "Stud?"

"Fine," Pearlie said.

The cards started falling for Pearlie from the moment he sat down. He won fifteen dollars on the first hand, and a couple of hands later he was ahead by a little over thirty dollars. In less than an hour, he had already tripled the money he'd started with.

Eddie Foy, wearing a broad, outlandish black and white plaid suit, along with a bright red shirt and a huge bow tie, pranced and danced across the stage. He was a very athletic dancer who often twisted his body into extreme positions, but did so gracefully.

Sometimes he would stop right in the middle of his dance and look at one of his legs in a seemingly impossible position. When he did so, he would assume a look of shock, as if even he were surprised to see his leg there. Then, with that same shocked expression on his face, he would stare at the audience, as if asking them how this had happened.

The audience would react in explosive laughter; then the music would start again and his dance would resume.

Sometimes in the middle of his dance, the music would stop and Eddie would walk to the front of the stage, turn sideways, then stare out at the audience, almost as if surprised to see them there. He was carrying a cane, and he had a method of holding the cane behind him in such a way as to cause his hat to seem to tip on its own.

As he spoke, he affected a very pronounced lisp.

"Yethterday wath thuch a nith day that I went for a thmall thtroll," he began.

The audience grew quiet, and Cal leaned forward in anticipation of the upcoming joke.

"I took mythelf into the bank and gave the teller a twenty-dollar bill. My good man, I thaid, I would like to trade thith bill for two ten-dollar billth.

"The teller complied with my requeth.

"I then thaid, my good man, tho well did you perform that tathk, that now I would like to trade my forty-year-old wife for two ladieth of twenty."

Eddy Foy tipped his hat as the audience exploded with laughter.

Cal decided that would be one of the jokes he would have to remember to tell Pearlie.

Back in the Oasis Saloon, most of the other players were taking Pearlie's good luck in stride, but the one who had asked if Annie and Pearlie knew each other, a man named Creedlove, began complaining.

"Somethin' kind'a fishy is goin' on here," Creedlove said.

"Fishy, Mr. Creedlove?" Annie asked sweetly.

Creedlove looked at Annie, then nodded toward Pearlie. "I think you'n him's workin' together," he said.

"And just how would we be working together?" Annie asked. Almost instantly, the smile had left her face and her words were cold and measured.

"You think I believe that him winnin' all the time is just dumb luck?" Creedlove asked.

"It's not luck, it's skill," Pearlie said. "And the only dumb person in this card game is you. You need to calculate the odds so as to know when to bet and when to fold. That's somethin' you haven't figured out."

"You think you have me pegged, do you?" Creedlove asked. He stared across the table through narrowed eyes. "Suppose me'n you have a go at it? Just the two of us."

"Don't ask me," Pearlie said. "Ask the others if they'd be willing to sit it out."

"I come to play cards," one of the others said. "I don't plan to sit nothin' out."

"Twenty-five dollars to sit in," Creedlove said.

"That's too rich for my blood."

"Anyone else?"

"Play your game, Creedlove. I'll just drink my beer and watch," one of the others said.

"How about you?" Creedlove asked Pearlie.

"All right, I'll play. Name your game," Pearlie said.

"Five-card stud."

"I'm in," Pearlie said, sliding twenty-five dollars to the middle of the table.

Creedlove reached for the cards, but Pearlie stuck his hand out to stop him. "You don't think I'm going to let you deal, do you? We'll let the lady deal."

"Huh-uh," Creedlove said, shaking his head. He nodded toward one of the other players. "We'll let Pete deal."

"How do I know that you and Pete aren't in cahoots? Suppose we get someone who isn't at this table right now," Pearlie suggested.

"Who?"

Pearlie looked around the saloon and saw that there

were at least four bar girls working the tables. "How about one of the ladies?" Pearlie asked. "You can choose."

"All right," Creedlove said. He looked over toward the nearest one. "You, honey, come here," he called.

The girl looked up in surprise at being summoned in such a way.

"It's all right, Sue," Annie said. "It'll just take a minute."

"We want you to deal a hand of cards," Creedlove said to Sue when she came over.

"She gets ten dollars from the pot," Annie said.

"What? Why should she get ten dollars?"

"If she gets ten dollars from the pot, it won't make any difference to her who wins," Annie said. "It will guarantee you that it's a fair game."

"That's fine by me," Pearlie said. "How about you?"

"All right," Creedlove agreed.

Sue dealt a down card to each, then an up card. Creedlove showed a king, Pearlie a five of hearts.

Creedlove laughed. "Not lookin' that good for you, is it? Bet five dollars."

Pearlie matched the bet.

The next card gave Creedlove a pair of kings showing. Pearlie drew a six.

"Bet ten dollars," Creedlove said.

Pearlie called the bet, and Creedlove's next card was a jack. Pearlie drew another six, giving him a pair of sixes.

Creedlove bet another ten dollars and Pearlie called.

Creedlove's final card was another jack. Pearlie drew another six.

"Well, now," Creedlove said. "I have two pair, kings and jacks, and you have three of a kind." Creedlove lifted his down card. "So the big question is, do I have a jack or a king as my hole card? Or do your three little sixes have my two pair beat?" He chuckled, and put twenty dollars in the pot. "It's going to cost you twenty to find out."

Pearlie called and raised him twenty.

The smile left Creedlove's face. "You're puttin' quite a store in them three sixes, aren't you? How do you know I don't have a full house?"

"I'm betting you have two pair, and I have you beat," Pearlie said.

Creedlove hesitated for a second, then, with a big smile, he pushed twenty dollars into the center of the table. "All right, I've got you right where I want you. I call." He smiled and flipped over his down card to disclose a king. "Well, lookie here, a full house, kings over jacks. It looks like you lost this one, friend. A full house beats three sixes."

Creedlove reached for the pot as Pearlie turned up his down card showing another six.

"Yes, but it won't beat four sixes," he said, reaching for the pot and pulling it toward him.

"What?" Creedlove gasped. He pointed at the table. "That's not possible!" he said.

"Of course it's possible," Pearlie said. "There are four of everything in a deck. Or hadn't you ever noticed that?" he added innocently.

By now, everyone in the saloon was aware of the high-stakes game and they had all gathered around to watch. They laughed at Pearlie's barb.

Creedlove slid the rest of his money to the center of the table. "I've got thirty-six dollars here," he said. "What do you say we cut for high card?"

Pearlie covered his bet; then Sue fanned the cards out.

"I'll draw first," Creedlove said.

Creedlove drew a queen.

"Ha!" he said triumphantly.

Pearlie drew a king.

"What the . . ." Creedlove shouted in anger. "You cheated me, you son of a bitch! Nobody is this lucky!"

"How did I cheat?" Pearlie asked. "You had the same chance I did."

"I don't know how you cheated," Creedlove said. "I just know that, somehow, you cheated."

Pearlie stood up then, and stepped back from the table. "Now, mister, you might want think about that for a moment," he said in a quiet but ominous voice. "You can always get more money, but you can't get another life."

"No," Creedlove said, shaking his head and holding his hand out in front of him as he backed away. "No. I ain't goin' to draw against you. But I ain't takin' back my words either. You are a card cheat."

"Both you gents just hold it right there," someone said loudly and, looking toward the sound of the voice, Pearlie saw the bartender pointing his shotgun toward them.

"Callin' someone a cheat is the kind of thing that can get a man killed if he can't back it up," the bartender said. "Annie, Sue, you been watchin' this. Was there any cheatin' goin' on?"

"Not a bit of it, Karl," Annie replied. "The game was aboveboard in every respect."

"All right, then that leaves you at fault, Creedlove. So I reckon you'd better get on out of here."

"You got no right to run me out of here," Creedlove said.

The bartender pulled back the hammers of the shotgun.

"This here scattergun gives me the right," the bartender said. "Now, you can either walk out, or your bloody carcass will be pulled out. Which is it going to be?"

Creedlove glared at the bartender for a moment. Then he glared at Pearlie.

"This ain't the end of it," Creedlove said to Pearlie. "Me'n you will run in to each other again sometime."

"I can hardly wait," Pearlie replied.

"Don't let the door hit you in the ass on your way out," Annie called to him.

A thunderous laughter from the saloon patrons chased Creedlove out of the saloon.

"Marshal?" Smoke called from the cell.

"What do you want, Jensen?"

"I appreciate you standing up to the mob like that."

"That wasn't a mob," Turnball said. "That was a group of concerned citizens. Maybe you don't realize this, Jensen, but folks around here had a hard winter."

"We all had a hard winter," Smoke said.

"Yes, well, a lot of the folks hereabout wouldn't have their homes or businesses if not for Mr. Clark. You picked the wrong man to kill."

"I didn't kill him."

"And you expect me to believe that?"

"Marshal, send a telegram to Sheriff Carson, back in Big Rock. He can tell you who I am."

"I might just do that," Marshal Turnball said. Turnball walked away from the cell and saw Deputy Pike standing at the front window.

"What are you lookin' at?" Turnball asked.

"Them fellas you run away is all standin' down there in front of the Bull's Head."

"I don't have any problem with them as long as they're standin' down there talkin' and not up here makin' trouble," Turnball said.

"That wasn't right, you runnin' 'em off like that," Pike

said. "Ever'one of 'em is our friend. I can't believe you would'a shot Mr. Fremont over somethin' like this."

"I didn't shoot him, did I?"

"Would you have shot him?"

"I didn't shoot him, did I?" Turnball repeated.

Chapter Nine

"And then he said, 'I walked into thith church,'" Cal was saying.

"Thith?"

"This," Cal explained. "But that's how he talked. He would say words like Mithithippi instead of Mississippi. It was real funny the way he talked."

"All right, go on with the joke," Pearlie said. It was the morning after, and Cal and Pearlie were mucking out stalls in the stable.

"All right. So Eddie Foy says, 'Thith cowboy went into thith church and took a theat on a long bench, neckth to a pretty woman.' And then Eddie Foy asked everyone in the audience, 'What do you call that long bench that people thit on in a church?'

"And everyone in the audience yells back at him, 'Pew!'"

Cal laughed. "So then Eddie Foy says . . . he says, 'No, thath what the pretty woman thaid when the cowboy that down bethide her. Pew.'"

"So the pretty woman told him what the bench was called?" Pearlie asked.

"No!" Cal said in exasperation. "Don't you get the

joke? She said 'Pew' 'cause the cowboy was stinkin' up the place."

"Oh," Pearlie said. He laughed. "Yes, that is funny."

"He was real funny," Cal said. "He told a lot of funny stories and I can remember most of 'em, but they aren't as funny when I tell them."

"Well, that's 'cause Eddie Foy does that for a livin', and he's good at it," Pearlie said. "You're a cowboy who . . ." Pearlie paused and looked at the rakes he and Cal were holding. "No, we are cowboys," he corrected, "who muck out horse manure for a living."

Cal laughed. "I reckon that's so."

"Cal, how would you like to go back?"

"Go back? Go back where?"

"To Sugarloaf."

"I thought we wasn't going to go back there as long as we were a burden on Smoke and Miss Sally," Cal said.

"Miss Sally would correct you and say weren't," Pearlie said.

"Well, but didn't you say we *weren't* going back to be a burden on Smoke and Miss Sally?"

"That's what I said all right," Pearlie said. "But if we go back now, we won't be a burden."

"How do you figure that?"

Pearlie stopped mucking and looked around the stable to make sure no one was close enough to overhear him.

"I played some cards last night," Pearlie said. "And I won some money."

"How much did you win?"

"Two hundred seventeen dollars," Pearlie replied with a broad smile.

"Two hundred dollars?" Cal asked in amazement.

"Two hundred seventeen," Pearlie corrected.

"That's a lot of money!"

"It sure is," Pearlie said. "It's enough to go back and help out."

"When do we leave?"

"Today," Pearlie said.

"Have you said anything to Mr. Thornton?"

"Yes, I told him we would be leaving today. In fact, we could leave right now if we wanted to, but I promised him we would finish with the stalls before we left."

"Yeah," Cal said. "That's only right."

The two men began raking with renewed vigor. Then, after a few minutes, Cal looked up.

"That's why you didn't want to go see Eddie Foy last night, isn't it?"

"Yeah," Pearlie said. "I just had a feelin' I was going to be lucky. And it turns out that the feelin' was true."

Creedlove sat nursing his drink in the back of the saloon in the little town of Solidad. He had left Floravista shortly after his run-in with Pearlie at the card game in the Oasis Saloon. He had lost so much money in the card game that he barely had enough money to get by, and wouldn't have any if he hadn't stolen twelve dollars from a stage way station.

That was three days and fifty miles ago, and he didn't figure he would ever see Pearlie again. But when he looked up as two men came in, there he was—Pearlie, and another cowboy who was even younger.

Because Creedlove was sitting alone, at a table in the back of the saloon, he was blocked from Pearlie's direct view by the cast-iron stove, which, though cold now, still smelled of its heavy winter use.

Creedlove watched as Pearlie said a few words to the

bartender; then Pearlie and his friend took their beers to a nearby table.

Creedlove got up from the table, pulled his gun from his holster, then, holding it down by his side so it wouldn't be obvious that he had already drawn his weapon, stepped around the stove and started across the floor.

Pearlie was just pulling the chair out from the table when out of the corner of his eye, he saw Creedlove moving toward him. Pearlie wondered, briefly, what Creedlove was doing this far north of Floravista.

"Draw your gun, you son of a bitch! I aim to shoot you dead!" Creedlove shouted, raising his own pistol at the same time he was challenging Pearlie.

"Pearlie, he already has his gun out!" Cal shouted.

Pearlie didn't need Cal's warning because even as Creedlove was bringing his pistol to bear, Pearlie drew his own pistol and suddenly the room was shattered with the roar of two pistols exploding.

The other patrons in the saloon yelled and dived or scrambled for cover. White gun smoke billowed out from both guns, coalescing in a cloud that filled the center of the room. For a moment, the cloud obscured everything.

As the cloud began to roll away, Creedlove stared through the drifting white smoke, glaring at Pearlie.

Creedlove smiled and opened his mouth, but before he could say anything, there was an incoherent gagging rattle way back in his throat. His eyes glazed over, and he pitched forward, his gun clattering to the floor.

That threat over, Pearlie looked around the saloon, checking to see if there was anyone else laying for him. Pearlie's pistol was cocked and he was ready to fire a second time, if a second shot was needed. He saw that Cal had drawn his own pistol and was also looking around the room for any potential danger.

Satisfied that there was no further danger, Pearlie holstered his pistol. Cal holstered his as well, and seeing them put their pistols back in the holsters, the other patrons began, slowly, to reappear from under tables, behind the bar and stove, and even from under the staircase.

A lawman came running in then, but seeing that it was all over, he put his gun away. He looked toward the body on the floor.

"Anybody know this man?" the lawman asked.

"His name is Creedlove," Pearlie said.

"Did you shoot him?"

"I did."

"It was a fair fight, Sheriff," the bartender said. "The fella on the floor drew first."

"That's right, Sheriff," one of the others said. "Fact is, this Creedlove fella not only drew first, he already had his gun out before he even challenged this man."

After that, several men at once began telling the story, each adding embellishments from his own perspective. When they were finished, the lawman came over to Pearlie and Cal.

"You got 'ny idea why he would come after you like that?"

"I won some money off him playing cards the other night," Pearlie said.

"Were you cheatin'?"

"No, sir, I wasn't."

"What's your name, mister?"

"Smith," Pearlie said. "John Smith."

Cal looked at Pearlie in surprise, but said nothing.

"Are you staying in town for the night, Mr. Smith?"

"I hadn't planned on it," Pearlie said. "My friend, Bill Jones, and I are heading toward California."

The sheriff realized then that Pearlie hadn't given his right name, and he sighed and shook his head.

"All right," he said. "No need for you to give me your right names, if what everyone here says is true. And there's no need for you to stay in town any longer. Fact is, it might be better all around if you just kept passing through."

"Soon as we finish our beer, we'll be on our way," Pearlie said.

The sheriff looked over at the bartender. "I'll get someone to come down here and get the body out of here," he said.

"Thanks, Sheriff," the bartender said. Looking around the saloon, he saw that several new customers had come in, drawn by the excitement. The bartender smiled.

"No big hurry, though," he said. "It seems to be good for business."

Carrying the wanted poster on Smoke Jensen, Marshal Turnball walked down toward the telegraph office.

"Good job catchin' that murderer and bank robber, Marshal," one of the townspeople said.

"Thank you," Turnball replied.

"Too bad he didn't have any of the money with him."

"Yes, it is. But at least we have him," Turnball said.

When Turnball stepped into the telegraph office, a bell on the door announced his entrance. Rodney Wheat, wearing a green visor and red suspenders, was sitting behind the counter reading a penny-dreadful novel. Wheat looked up as the marshal entered.

"I hear you caught one of the bank robbers," Wheat said.

"Yes," Turnball answered. He showed Wheat the poster. "It was this fella."

Wheat looked at the poster.

PROCLAMATION

$5,000.00
REWARD

For the Apprehension

DEAD OR ALIVE

Of the Murderer
KIRBY "SMOKE" JENSEN.

This Notice Takes the Place
Of All Previous
REWARD NOTICES.

Contact: *Sheriff,* Hinsdale County, Colorado
IMMEDIATELY.

"I want you to send a telegram to the sheriff out in Hinsdale County, telling him that we have this fella in custody," Turnball said.

Wheat shook his head. "I can't do that," he said.

"What do you mean you can't do that? Why can't you do it?"

"The telegraph line is down. It's been down for a couple of days now."

"Well, when do you think you'll get it back?"

Wheat shook his head. There's no way of telling. Last time it took two weeks."

"Two weeks?"

Wheat nodded. "Two weeks," he said. "And it might even take longer this time. If the line is out up in the higher elevations, there will still be so much snow that the line crew might not be able to get to it."

Turnball stroked his jaw as he contemplated the situation. Then he nodded. "All right. I'll send a letter. What's the county seat of Hinsdale County?"

"Lake City," Wheat answered. "But I don't know if you are going to have any more luck with the letter than you are with sending a telegram. That's on the other side of the mountains, and I'm sure none of the high passes are open yet."

"Maybe not," Turnball replied. "But I'm going to try."

Smoke was lying on the bunk in his cell with his hands laced behind his head, staring at the ceiling. He had to admit that the cell was solidly built. The bars didn't go all the way to the ceiling, but came up only about six feet. Between the top of the bars and the ceiling itself was a two-foot wall of solid brick. At the back of the wall there were three small windows, enough to let in light and air, but not one of the three large enough for a man to pass through, even if there were no bars.

When he heard the marshal come back into the office, he sat up.

"Marshal?" he called.

"What do you want, Jensen?" Turnball answered.

"Did you send a telegram to Sheriff Carson, back in Big Rock?"

"No."

"What about the Sheriff of Hinsdale County? Did you contact him about whether or not the poster was current?"

"I told you, it doesn't matter whether or not the poster

is current," Turnball said. "I'm only interested in the man you killed here, and the bank that you robbed here."

"I didn't do it," Smoke said. "I told you, contact Sheriff Carson. He'll vouch for me."

"I'll send him a letter," Turnball said.

"A letter?"

"The telegraph wire is down," Turnball explained. "Fact is, if Judge Craig wasn't scheduled to come into town tomorrow, we wouldn't even be able to send for him. At least, we can have us a fair trial."

"Hold on there, Marshal," Smoke said. "You aren't planning on holding a trial before you can check up on my story, are you?"

"We're holding your trial tomorrow," Turnball said. "We don't get that many visits from a judge, and I don't intend to waste this one."

"What about a lawyer?" Smoke asked. "Do I get a lawyer?"

"We got two lawyers in town," Turnball said. "If it's the way they normally do it, they'll flip a coin to see who prosecutes and who defends. It seems to work out all right."

Chapter Ten

There was no courthouse in the town of Etna, so the trial was held in the school. At the top of the blackboard in the front of the room, the alphabet was displayed in both cursive and block letters, in capital and lowercase. On the side panel of the blackboard were the work assignments for each of the six grades that attended the single-room schoolhouse. A stove sat in a sandbox in the corner of the room, and artwork of the children was pinned on the wall.

Two tables had been placed in the front of the classroom. One table had two chairs, and that was for Smoke and his lawyer. The other table was the prosecutor's table, and it had only one chair. The jury occupied the two first rows of desks in the classroom, while the citizens of the town squeezed into the remaining desks. Others were standing along the two side walls and the back wall. The judge's bench was the schoolteacher's desk, while Miss Garvey, the schoolteacher, was pressed into service as the court reporter.

Smoke felt a sense of melancholy as he looked around the schoolroom. His Sally had been teaching at a school exactly like this one when he met her. It was a cruel irony that his fate was about to be decided in a place like this.

"All rise!" Marshal Turnball shouted. In his capacity as city marshal, Turnball was also acting as the bailiff.

At Turnball's call, everyone seated in the classroom cum courtroom stood to await the arrival of the judge.

Judge Arlie Craig was a short, fat man who filled out his black robes. He was bald, except for a tuft of white over each ear. He took his seat at the bench, then looked out over the courtroom.

"The court may be seated," he said.

As the people sat, Judge Craig removed his glasses and cleaned them thoroughly. Then he put them back on, hooking them very carefully over one ear at a time. During this process the courtroom was very quiet, almost as if mesmerized by it. The only sound came from outside the courtroom, and that from a barking dog.

"Bailiff, would you call the case, please?" Judge Craig said.

"Your Honor, there comes before this honorable court one Kirby Jensen," Turnball said. "Mr. Jensen is charged with the murder of Robert J. Clark, said murder committed during the act of robbery of the Bank of Etna."

"Was this charge issued by a grand jury?"

"It was, Your Honor. The grand jury met this morning."

"Thank you," Judge Craig said. "And is the accused now represented by counsel?"

"He is, Your Honor," the lawyer sitting beside Smoke said. "I am Asa Jackson, duly accredited by the bar of the State of Colorado to practice law."

The judge looked over at Smoke.

"Is the defendant satisfied with counsel?"

"I am not, Your Honor," Smoke said.

His response surprised the judge and startled many

who were in the court. Several reacted audibly, and one man shouted, "At least you have a lawyer! That's more than you gave Rob Clark!"

Others shouted out as well, and Judge Craig had to bang his gavel several times to restore order.

"Mr. Jensen, what complaint do you have against Mr. Jackson?"

"Your Honor, I have no complaint against Mr. Jackson personally. But I would prefer to select my own lawyer."

"There are only two lawyers in town," Judge Craig replied. "Would you rather have the prosecutor act as your defense counsel?"

"No, Your Honor. I ask for a delay so that I may get a lawyer from my own hometown of Big Rock."

"Mr. Hagen, you are the prosecutor," Judge Craig said. "How say you to this request?"

"Your Honor, the crime is still fresh upon the minds of all the witnesses. I fear that any delay may cloud their memories, perhaps even to the detriment of the defendant. All that is required by the law is that he be provided with counsel, and we have done so. I move that his request for a delay be denied."

Judge Craig nodded, then looked back at Smoke. "Due to my own busy schedule, it would be several weeks before I could return to Etna. And, as Mr. Hagen has pointed out, the closer the trial is held to the event, the sharper the memories of the witnesses who are called. Therefore, your request for a delay in the trial is denied. Has there been voir dire of the jury?"

"There has, Your Honor, and both defense and prosecution have accepted the jury as it is now constituted," Hagen said.

"Very good," Judge Craig replied. "Now, Mr. Jensen, how do you plead to the charge against you?"

"Not guilty," Smoke said.

"Very well," Judge Craig said. He cleared his throat. "The defendant represented and the jury accepted, I declare this case in session. Mr. Hagen, make your case."

Lester Hagen was a tall, gangly-looking man with a wild shock of hair and prominent ears. Standing, he turned to face the jury, which was seated just behind him.

"It won't take me long to do this," he said, speaking so quietly that those in the back had to strain to hear. "Practically everyone in this town was a witness to the robbery of the Bank of Etna on the sixth day of this very month. I could call any of them, and all would give compelling and damning testimony. Ten thousand dollars was taken, money that belonged to the fair people of this town."

Turning back to the table, he picked up the red and black plaid shirt Smoke had been wearing when he was arrested.

"Look at this shirt," he said. "It is not a shirt one can easily forget. And if you see this shirt on a man who is in the act of killing another, then the shirt becomes even more vividly burned into your memory. This shirt alone is enough to convict the defendant. No matter what he or his lawyer may say to obfuscate the issue, the facts are indisputable. A man wearing this very shirt killed Rob Clark. This man," he said, with a dramatic pointing of his finger toward Smoke, "was captured wearing this very shirt. I think that when this trial is finished, you will have no difficulty in finding Mr. Kirby Jensen guilty as charged."

As Hagen took his seat, there was a spontaneous outbreak of applause from the gallery.

"Hear, hear, there will be no such demonstration in this courtroom!" Judge Craig said with an angry bang of his gavel.

The court grew quiet; then all turned their attention to

Asa Jackson. Like Hagen before him, Jackson stood to address the jury. Considerably shorter than Hagen, and with eyes made almost buglike by his thick glasses, Jackson made less of an impression by his appearance.

"The law states that before you can find someone guilty, you must be convinced beyond the shadow of a doubt that he is guilty. You will hear the witnesses say that there were three men shooting into the bank. Since three men were shooting, it impossible to say that Kirby Jensen was the one who actually murdered Mr. Clark."

Jackson sat back down and Smoke leaned over toward him.

"The way you presented that, it made it sound as if I was there," Smoke complained.

"It's going to be hard to say you weren't there, with the evidence that the prosecutor has," Jackson said. "Our best hope is to sew doubt as to who actually did the shooting."

"Prosecution, you may call your first witness," Judge Craig said.

"Prosecution calls Mr. Tucker Patterson," Hagen said.

Tucker Patterson walked to the front of the room and put his hand on the Bible.

"Do you swear to tell the truth, the whole truth, and nothing but the truth, so help you God?" Turnball asked.

"I do."

"The witness may be seated," Judge Craig said.

Hagen approached the witness chair. "For the record, Mr. Patterson, what is your employment?"

"I am the head teller of the Bank of Etna," Patterson replied.

"Hell, Tucker, you're the only teller," someone shouted from the gallery, and everyone laughed.

Judge Craig slammed his gavel down, then, with an angry scowl, addressed the gallery. "If there is one more outbreak, I will hold the person responsible in contempt of court. You will be fined, and you will spend time in jail."

Patterson looked at Hagen. "Mr. Barnes is right," he said, identifying the person who spoke up. "There is only one teller, but Mr. Clark had assured me that, if we were ever to hire a second teller, I would be the chief teller. Therefore my position, technically, was that of head teller."

"Mr. Patterson, were you in the bank on the sixth instant?"

"I was."

"Tell the court what happened that day."

"Mr. Clark and I were both behind the teller's cage, counting the money to make certain that the books were balanced, when two men came in."

"Can you describe the two men?"

"One of the men was wearing a shirt like that one," Patterson said, pointing to the shirt that was still lying on the prosecutor's table.

"Let the record show that the witness identified the prosecution exhibit as the shirt worn by one of the robbers."

"Object, Your Honor," Jackson said. "The witness said it was a shirt like that one. He didn't say he was wearing that one."

"I stand corrected, Your Honor," Hagen said. "Mr. Patterson, you said there were two men?"

"Yes. The other man was wearing a white shirt."

"I object!" Smoke called out. "He is describing the clothes, not the men."

"Mr. Smoke, if your attorney cares to make that objection, he may do so," Judge Craig said. "But as the defendant, you are not allowed to object."

Smoke turned to Jackson. "Are you going to object?" he asked.

Jackson nodded. "I object," he said. "Mr. Jensen is correct. The witness is describing clothing, and not the men themselves."

"Sustained," the judge said.

"Mr. Patterson, could you see the men's faces?" Hagen asked.

"No, they were covered by hoods," Patterson replied.

"So, by looking at the defendant, you cannot say, as a matter of actual fact, that he was not one of the robbers, can you?"

"I object," Jackson said. "He just said that the men's faces were covered."

"Listen to the question, Counselor," Judge Craig said. "He asked if he could positively say that Jensen was *not* one of the robbers."

"Oh," Jackson said.

"Objection is overruled."

"So, since you cannot positively say that he was not one of the robbers, it is possible that he was one of them?"

"Yes."

Hagen continued with Patterson, eliciting from him the details as to how Clark got a gun, then ran to the front door to challenge the bank robbers as they were leaving.

"I told him not to go, that there were too many of them," Patterson said. "But Mr. Clark was a brave man, and he wouldn't hear of it. He ran to the front door and started to shoot, but got shot instead."

"Thank you, Mr. Patterson. Your witness," Hagen said as he sat down.

Jackson stood, but didn't approach the witness. "Did you see who actually did the shooting?"

"No, I was inside the bank. I saw Mr. Clark get shot, but from where I was, I couldn't see who shot him."

"So even though you saw Mr. Jensen wearing this shirt in your bank, once the robbers got outside, you have no idea who did the actual shooting?"

"I object!" Smoke said loudly.

"You are objecting your own lawyer?" Judge Craig asked.

"Your Honor, I ask the court's permission to act as my own lawyer."

"Are you saying you wish to dismiss counsel?"

"Yes, Your Honor, that is exactly what I am saying."

"Court is going to stand in recess for half an hour," Judge Craig said. "Marshal Turnball, clear the courtroom of everyone except you and the defendant."

"Yes, sir," Turnball said. "All right, people, you heard the judge. Everyone out."

"Your Honor, if there is going to be a sidebar, I request permission to remain," Hagen said.

"Permission denied," Craig said. "You will leave with everyone else."

"What about me?" Jackson asked. "Since the defendant is my client, shouldn't I be present?"

"You heard the defendant, Mr. Jackson," Craig said. "You have just been dismissed."

It took less than a minute for everyone to leave. Then Turnball, who had been standing at the door watching them leave, came back to the front of the room.

"They are all gone, Judge," he said.

Craig removed his glasses and cleaned them again. Watching him, Smoke realized that it was more of a nervous action than because the glasses actually needed cleaning.

"Mr. Jensen, there is a saying in the legal profession

that a person who defends himself has a fool for a client." He put the glasses back on, again looping them very carefully over each ear, one at a time. "Do you know what I am saying to you?"

"Yes, sir, I believe I do," Smoke replied.

Judge Craig pointed at Smoke, and began shaking his finger. "Disabuse yourself of any idea that I will go easier on you because of your inexperience or lack of knowledge of the law. Regardless of your competence or incompetence, this case will be tried under the rules of law. Do you understand that?"

"Yes, sir, I do."

"Very well. Mr. Jackson is dismissed, and I hereby declare you sui juris."

"I beg your pardon?"

"Sui juris," the judge repeated. "It is a Latin term meaning that you have the capacity to act for yourself in legal proceedings. You are hereby acting as your own counsel."

"Thank you, Your Honor," Smoke said.

"Marshal Turnball, you may reassemble the court."

"All right, our take come to ten thousand dollars," Dooley said after he counted out the money. "That's a thousand dollars apiece for each of you."

"Wait a minute," Yancey said. "You think they can't none of us cipher? I make that over sixteen hundred dollars for each of us."

Dooley shook his head. "I set it up, I take half," he said.

"That ain't right," Yancey protested. "We all of us took our chances when we robbed that bank. We should all of us get the same amount of money."

"Tell him, Curt," Dooley said.

"Maybe you ain't never done nothin' like this before," Curt said to Yancey. "But the one that gets the job set up is always the one that gets the most money."

"There didn't nobody say nothin' like that when I got asked to join up," Yancey said. "And I don't intend to just stand by and get cheated like this."

"Look at it this way," Curt said. "You got a thousand dollars now, which you didn't have before. You know how long you'd have to cowboy to make a thousand dollars?"

Yancey shook his head. "I don't care, that ain't the point. I don't intend to be cheated like that."

While Yancey was talking, Dooley pulled his pistol. Yancey didn't notice it until he heard the click of the hammer being pulled back.

"Then I reckon you can't be reasoned with, can you?"

"What? What are you doin' with that gun?"

"Go, Yancey," Dooley said.

"Go? Go where?"

"Anywhere," Dooley said. "I don't want you around anymore."

"All right," Yancey said. "It ain't right, but give me my money and I'll be on my way."

Dooley shook his head. "No money for you."

"What do you mean no money for me?"

"One thousand dollars wasn't enough for you, so you get none. Now, get out of here."

Yancey glared at Dooley; then he started toward his horse.

Dooley pulled the trigger, the gun roared, and Yancey's horse dropped in its tracks.

"What the hell did you just do?" Yancey shouted. "You son of a bitch! You just killed my horse!"

"You're lucky I didn't kill you," Dooley said. "Curt, get his gun."

Curt walked up to Yancey and pulled his pistol from his holster.

"All right, Yancey, start walkin'," Dooley said, making a motion with his pistol.

"This ain't right," Yancey said.

"I thought we already had that settled," Dooley said. "I decide what's right."

Dooley shot again and the bullet hit the ground right next to Yancey's feet, then ricocheted through the valley, whining as it did so. Even before the echo died, Yancey was running back down the trail, chased by Dooley's evil laughter.

"Dooley," Fargo said. "Leavin' him out here without a horse or a gun . . . he could die."

"Yeah, he could," Dooley said. "Now, each one of you boys is two hundred dollars richer. That is, unless you don't want the money."

"Hell, I want the money," Ford said.

"Me too," Curt said.

"I'll take my share," Trace said.

"Fargo, that just leaves you," Dooley said. Dooley had not yet put his pistol back in its holster and a little wisp of smoke curled upward from the end of the barrel. The implication was obvious to Fargo.

"Yancey was a troublemaker," Fargo said. "You was right to do what you done."

"I thought you might see things my way," Dooley said as he counted out the money.

Chapter Eleven

As the trial continued, the prosecution called witness after witness to the stand to testify as to what they saw on the morning of the robbery. In every case the testimony was the same. They had seen two men leaving the bank; then they'd heard Clark shout out the warning that the bank had been robbed. They talked about seeing and hearing the exchange of gunshots, and seeing Mr. Clark go down.

"Did all of the robbers shoot at Mr. Clark?" Hagen asked a witness.

"No, sir, just the two who come out of the bank, and the one that was holdin' the horses in front of the bank. There was three more men across the street, waitin' in front of Sikes Leather Goods, but they didn't shoot at Mr. Clark."

"How do you know that those three men were involved with the robbery?" Hagen asked.

"'Cause they all left town together, and all of 'em was shootin' and hollerin' as they rode away."

"I see," Hagen said. "But as far as who actually shot Mr. Clark, it was the two men, who were wearing red and black plaid shirts, and the one man who was wearing a white shirt. Is that what you are saying?"

"Yes, sir."

"From your point of observation, could you tell which one of the three actually killed Mr. Clark?"

"No, sir, I could not."

"In fact," Hagen continued, "if I told you that there were four bullets in Mr. Clark's body, would you be able to believe that all three may have had a hand in killing him?"

"Yes, I would say so."

"Mr. Jensen," Judge Craig said quickly. "Counsel is leading the witness. Are you not going to object?"

"I'm not going to object, Your Honor, because I don't care which of the three, or if all three, killed him. I wasn't one of the three."

"Very well, I will disallow it myself. Jury will disregard counsel's last comment. You may continue, Mr. Hagen."

"I'm through with this witness, Your Honor."

"Did you see me in the street in front of the bank that day?" Smoke asked.

"Yeah, I seen you. I seen you in that shirt," the witness replied.

"I've no doubt but that you saw the shirt," Smoke said. "But I want you to look at my face closely. Is this the face of the man you saw in front of the bank?"

"No, you ain't the one that was standin' in front of the bank," the witness said. "But I done told you, and everyone has done told you. The faces of the two that come out of the bank was covered by masks."

"Thank you, that's all," Smoke said.

"But I seen that shirt you was wearin'," the witness added.

"Thank you, that is all," Smoke repeated.

Billy Frakes was Hagen's next witness.

Frakes was pointed out as having had a unique perspective on the robbery, because he had gone down to try and sell a pair of boots to three men who were waiting across the street from the bank, and who subsequently turned out to be in collusion with the robbers.

As the prosecutor had done with all the other witnesses, Hagen held up the red and black plaid shirt.

"Have you ever seen this shirt before, Billy?"

"Yes, sir."

"Where did you see it?"

Frakes pointed to Smoke. "He was a'wearin' it when we found him," he said.

"Let the record show that the witness has pointed out that the defendant was wearing this very shirt when he was captured," Hagen said.

"Had you ever seen the shirt before?"

"Yes, sir."

"When and where did you see it before?"

"I seen it on the sixth of this month," Frakes said. "I seen it when the two men who was wearin' them come ridin' into town. Then, I seen it again when the two bank robbers come runnin' out of the bank."

"Wait a minute," Hagen said in sudden interest. "Are you saying that you saw him when he rode into town?"

"Yes, sir."

"And this was before the robbery?"

"Yes, sir."

"So, you saw him without the mask?"

"Maybe," Frakes said.

"Maybe? What do you mean, maybe?"

"I seen their faces, but I didn't look at them that long. I couldn't tell you if this was one of the men or not."

"But you do remember the shirt, right?"

"Yes, sir."

"You saw this shirt on one of the men who came into town?"

"Yes, sir."

"And you saw it again when you were with the posse as they arrested him?"

"Yes, sir."

"No further questions. Your witness, Mr. Jensen."

"Did you get a good look at the man who was standing in front of the bank, the man wearing a shirt just like that one?" Smoke asked.

"Yes, sir, I got a good look at him."

"Am I that man?"

"No, sir, you ain't that man."

Smoke turned away as if to sit down. Then, getting an idea, he stopped and turned back toward the witness.

"You said you were going to try and sell a pair of boots to one of the robbers?"

"Yeah, I was. See, I make boots and I figured if I could sell a few pair, well, maybe Mr. Sikes would carry 'em in his store," Frakes said. "And I thought maybe one of them might buy my boots since I seen 'em lookin' at boots in Sikes's window."

"You make boots, do you?"

"Yes, sir."

"So, you must know quite a bit about boots."

Frakes smiled. "I know more'n most folks do, I reckon."

"Do you take notice of the kind of boots people wear?"

"Oh, yes, sir, I'm always lookin' at folks' boots."

"Can you tell me what kind of boots I'm wearing?" Smoke asked. He started to stick his boot out so Frakes could see it, but Frakes waved it off.

"You don't have to show me," he said. "I've done looked

at 'em. Them boots you're wearin' is what's called black cherry brush-off boots. They're real nice boots, and kind of expensive."

"Were any of the bank robbers wearing boots like these?" Smoke asked.

"Ha!" Frakes said. "Are you kidding? None of 'em had boots like those."

"Not even the two men who were wearing the red and black plaid shirts?" Smoke asked.

Frakes shook his head. "No, sir." He chuckled. "They was wearing old, scruffed-up boots, the kind you can buy anywhere for no more'n two dollars."

Suddenly, the smile left Frakes's face, and he looked over at the judge. "That's right," he said. "They wasn't none of 'em wearin' boots like these here boots."

"Thank you. No more questions," Smoke said.

In redirect, Hagen tried to get Frakes to say that he couldn't be sure about the boots, that maybe one of them could have been wearing boots like the boots the defendant was wearing, but Frakes couldn't be budged.

"They was all six wearin' scruffed-up boots," he insisted.

When the prosecution finished its case, Judge Craig invited Smoke to call any witnesses he might have for his defense.

"Your Honor, in order to call any witnesses for defense, I would have to bring some people here from Big Rock."

"Could any of the people from Big Rock testify that you were somewhere else on the day of the robbery?" Judge Craig asked.

"No, sir. They would be more on the order of character witnesses," Smoke said.

"I see. Mr. Jensen, is there any witness, anywhere, who could testify that they were with you on the sixth of this month?"

Smoke shook his head. "No, Your Honor," he said. "I was on the trail for that entire day. I did not see a soul until I encountered the bank robbers."

Craig removed his glasses and polished them vigorously for a moment. Then he put them back on.

"If you cannot find a witness who can testify in direct contradiction to any of the witnesses the prosecution has brought to the stand, then I see no reason for granting a stay on this trial. I'll give you half an hour to compose your thoughts. Then I will expect you to make your closing arguments." Judge Craig slammed the gavel down on the desk. "This court stands in recess for one half hour."

As Smoke sat back down at his table, he saw the prosecutor summon Pike over to him. Hagen and the deputy spoke for a moment, then Pike left.

"Do you want me to help you with your closing argument?" Jackson asked.

Smoke shook his head. "No, thanks," he said. "I'm sure you mean the best, Mr. Jackson. But seeing as this is my life we're talking about here, I think I'd feel better if I did it myself."

"All right," Jackson said. He got up and started to leave. Then he turned and looked back at Smoke. "Mr. Jensen, don't try to make a speech. Just talk to the folks in the jury as if you were telling a friend what happened."

Smoke nodded. "Thanks," he said. "I appreciate the tip."

All too soon, it seemed, Marshal Turnball stepped up to the front of the room.

"All rise," he shouted.

Again, the gallery stood as Judge Craig came back into the court and took his seat.

"Mr. Jensen," Craig said after everyone was seated. "You may begin your closing argument."

"Thank you, Your Honor," Smoke said. He turned to face the jury.

"I must say that I am a little surprised that nobody in this town knows me," he began. "I guess this is a little far from Big Rock, so it's out of my home area. But I am well known back home. And, I'm proud to say, that I am known as a man of honesty and integrity. One of my closest friends in Big Rock is Sheriff Carson. I own a ranch there, a rather substantial ranch, and I am what you might regard as a pillar of the community.

"Now, normally, it isn't my style to blow my own horn, so to speak. But, since I don't have anyone over here to blow it for me, well, I reckon I don't have much choice." Smoke smiled broadly, and tried not to let it show when nobody returned the smile.

"I did not rob the bank here. I did not kill Mr. Clark. I did not know Mr. Clark, but from some of the testimony I've heard today, I'm sure he was a very good man. I can understand how having a good man killed so senselessly could get a town upset. But wouldn't it be better for you to find the person who actually did it?

"I wish I could tell you that I know who did it, but I don't. I was set upon by six men, two of whom were wearing shirts identical to the one prosecution is using as his evidence. While I was distracted, one of them knocked me out, and when I came to, I saw that my own shirt was gone, and I was wearing that shirt." He pointed toward the shirt.

"I was angry that someone had stolen my shirt, and puzzled as to why they would do it. But when Marshal Turnball and his posse came along a little later, I learned the reason. One of the bank robbers, perhaps even the killer, put this shirt on me to throw suspicion my way.

"Before you vote on your verdict, I want you to think about two things. Number one, nobody saw the face of the second man who was wearing the plaid shirt, and number two . . ." Smoke held out his foot. "We heard Mr. Frakes say that not one of the six was wearing boots like these."

Satisfied that he had done his best, Smoke sat down. Just as he did so, he saw Pike, smiling from ear to ear, come back into the school cum courthouse. He was carrying a bag, which he showed to Hagen. The two spoke about it for a moment, then looked over at Smoke.

Pike chuckled.

"Mr. Hagen?" the judge said.

"Please the court, I'd like one minute," Hagen said.

"Make it quick."

Hagen took the sack over to Frakes and showed it to him. Frakes looked into the bag, then nodded.

"Thank you," Hagen said. Hagen returned to the front of the room, facing the jury.

"Gentlemen of the jury," he began. "In Kirby Jensen's closing argument, you heard him say that he owned a large ranch near Big Rock. That is true, he does own a large ranch. However, according to papers found on him when he was arrested, that ranch is encumbered by a mortgage note of two thousand dollars, due in just over one month. If he fails to make that payment, he will lose his ranch.

"That, I submit, is incentive enough to make an otherwise honest rancher rob a bank.

"Where is that money, you may ask? Why was it not found on him? That is a good question, and the answer is as simple and as old as the sin of thievery itself. There is no honor among thieves, and he had none of the money when he was arrested because Jensen was beaten and robbed by his own fellow thieves.

"Did Kirby Jensen kill Mr. Clark? There were four bullets found in Mr. Clark's body, so it is likely that one of the bullets was his. But according to the law, it doesn't matter whether any of those bullets came from Jensen's gun or not. According to the law, everyone who was there is equally guilty of his murder.

"Now there comes only the question, was he there? You have heard witness after witness testify that they saw this shirt on the back of one of the killers. You also heard Billy Frakes testify that he saw the faces of the two men when they rode into town, and, having seen the faces, cannot rule out the possibility that Kirby Jensen was one of them. And not even Jensen can produce one witness who can testify that he wasn't there.

"So, what did Jensen do? He showed Billy Frakes a pair of fancy boots, and asked if any of the robbers were wearing such boots. Billy Frakes said no."

Hagen reached down into the sack and pulled out a pair of boots.

Smoke felt his heart sink. He had brought along those old and worn boots, intending to wear them to keep his better boots from getting scuffed. But they were uncomfortable as riding boots, so he kept them rolled up in his blankets.

"Mr. Pike took these very boots from Kirby Jensen's bedroll about half an hour ago," Hagen said, continuing with his closing argument. "You all saw me show these boots to Billy Frakes. Billy just told me that, if need be, he is prepared to testify that the two men in the red and black plaid shirt were wearing boots exactly like these.

"Gentlemen of the jury, your task is solemn, but it is simple. Your task is solemn, because you are charged, by your fellow citizens, with the responsibility of bringing justice to our fair town. But your task is simple, because there is overwhelming and irrefutable evidence to help you come to the right decision. And the right decision is to find Kirby Jensen guilty of murder in the first degree."

Hagen turned and started back toward his seat.

"Good job, Hagen, you got the son of a bitch!" a man shouted, and several others cheered and applauded.

It took Judge Craig several seconds of banging the gavel until he was able to restore order in the court. Finally, when the gallery was subdued, he charged the jury.

The jury filed out through the back door of the schoolhouse, then gathered under a shade tree to discuss the case. They returned in less than half an hour.

"Who is the foreman of the jury?" Judge Craig asked.

"I am, Your Honor. The name is Jeff Colfax."

"Mr. Colfax, has the jury reached a verdict?"

The jury foreman leaned over to spit a wad of tobacco into a spittoon before he answered. He wiped his mouth with the back of his hand.

"We've reached a verdict, Your Honor," he said.

"Would you publish the verdict, please?"

"We, the jury, find this here fella"—he pointed to Smoke—"guilty of murder and bank robbin'."

"So say you all?"

"So say we all."

"Thank you, Mr. Foreman," the judge said. "The jury is dismissed. "Mr. Turnball, you are hereby relieved of your duty as court bailiff, and may resume your duties as city marshal. Now, Marshal Turnball, bring your prisoner before the bench to hear his sentencing."

Marshal Turnball stepped over to the defense table and looked down at Smoke.

"Stand up and hold your hands out," he ordered.

Smoke did as he was directed, and Turnball clamped the manacles on his wrists before leading him up to stand before the judge.

"It is the sentence of this court that a gallows be constructed in the city street so that all may bear witness to the inevitable result that befalls a person bent on following the path of crime. Then, on Thursday next, at ten o'clock of the morning hour, you will be removed from your jail cell and taken to this public gallows where a noose will be placed around your neck, a lever will be thrown, a trapdoor will fall from under your feet, and you will be hurled into eternity.

"May God have mercy on your evil, vile, and worthless soul, sir, because I have none."

The judge ended his pronouncement with the banging of his gavel, and Marshal Turnball and one of his deputies led Smoke out of the court and down to the jail.

Chapter Twelve

"One hundred dollars!" the big man with the white, handlebar mustache shouted above the din in the saloon. "I'll bet one hundred dollars that no man can stay on Cannonball for one whole minute."

Pearlie and Cal were on their way back to Big Rock, but had stopped in the town of Jasper. They were having a quiet beer together in the Good Nature Saloon when they heard the offer.

"That ain't much of a bet, Stacey," one of the others in the saloon said. "Hell, there ain't nobody ever stayed on him for more'n ten seconds. Can't nobody stay on him for a full minute."

"I'll try it, if you give odds," another cowboy said.

"What kind of odds?" Stacey asked.

"Two to one," the cowboy answered. "I'll put up twenty. If I can stay on for a whole minute, you'll pay me forty."

"You got twenty dollars, cowboy?" Stacey asked.

"I got twenty," the cowboy answered.

"Take 'im up on it, Stacey. I'd like to see if anyone really could ride Cannonball."

"Yeah, give us a show," another shouted.

Stacey stroked his mustache for a second; then he nodded.

"All right," he said. "Put up the twenty dollars. Let's see what you can do."

"Yahoo!" one of the others shouted, and everyone poured out of the saloon to see the ride.

"Come on, Cal, let's go see this," Pearlie said, standing and tugging on Cal's arm.

There had been no more than twenty men in the saloon when the challenge was issued, but as they started down the street toward the corral, word spread through the rest of the town so that many more joined. By the time they reached the corral, which was at the far end of the street from the Good Nature Saloon, there were nearly one hundred spectators.

Pearlie and Cal found a seat on the top rail of the corral fence and watched as they saddled Cannonball.

Cannonball was a big horse with a well-defined musculature. He was also a very aggressive horse, fighting even against being saddled.

"Hey, Stacey, if Pete can't do it, can I give it a try?" one of the cowboys shouted.

"Have you got 'ny money?" Stacey replied.

"I've got money."

"All right, you're next."

When, at last, they got the saddle on Cannonball, Pete climbed up on the top rung of the fence and crouched there, ready. Pete nodded toward the two men who were handling Cannonball, and they led the horse over.

Pete pounced onto the horse's back, and the two handlers let go, then jumped out of the way. Cannonball exploded away from the fence, then went through a series of gyrations, bucking, twisting, coming down stiff-legged, and ducking his head. Pete was thrown in less than ten seconds.

"Whoowee, that's some horse!" someone shouted.

"My turn," the one who had put in the bid to be second said. But like Pete, he was thrown in a matter of seconds.

"I'll try it for twenty dollars," another said, and Pearlie and Cal watched as the third rider was thrown even faster than the first two.

"Look," Cal said to Pearlie as still a fourth man tried to ride the horse. "See how he ducks his head to the left there, then sort of leans into it? If a man would sort of jerk his head back to the right, he could stop that."

"You think you could ride him, Cal?" Pearlie asked.

Cal didn't answer right away. Instead, he watched another rider try and get thrown.

"Yeah," Cal said. "I think I could."

"Do you think you could a hundred dollars worth?"

"Ha! Are you kidding? I don't have a hundred dollars."

"*I* do. I'll give it to you to bet, if you think you can ride him."

Cal shook his head. "No, Pearlie, that's your money. That's money you said you were going to give to Smoke and Miss Sally."

"Yes, it is," Pearlie said. "But if you could win two hundred dollars more, don't you think that would be even better?"

"Well, yeah, sure, but . . ."

"Do you think you can ride him, or don't you?"

Cal looked at the horse just as it threw another rider.

"Yeah," Cal said. "I think I can ride him."

The two wranglers grabbed Cannonball and brought him back to the end of the corral.

"Anybody else?" Stacey called, holding up a fistful of

money, all of it won from would-be riders within the last few minutes.

Nobody responded.

"This is your last chance, boys. Anybody else want to try before we put Cannonball back in his stall?"

There was still no answer.

"All right, men, get the saddle off him," Stacey said to his wrangler.

"Here, Cal, here's the money," Pearlie said.

Cal hesitated but for one second; then he called out loudly.

"I'll have a go at it for one hundred dollars," he said.

Several had started to leave the corral, but when they heard Cal call out, they stopped and came back.

"What did you say?" Stacey asked.

Call held up the one hundred dollars that Pearlie had given him.

"I said I would ride him," Cal said. "And I'm betting one hundred dollars that I can stay on him for an entire minute."

"Who is that fella?" one of the men in the crowd asked.

"I don't know," another answered. "I think he must've just come into town. I ain't never seen him afore now."

"Where did you get a hundred dollars?" Stacey asked.

"What difference does it make where I got it?" Cal answered. "You didn't ask anybody else where they got the money."

"And you want to wager that one hundred dollars that you can stay on Cannonball for a minute?"

"Yes, sir."

"That's one whole minute, mind you," Stacey said. "Not fifty-nine seconds."

"An entire minute," Cal agreed.

"All right, I'll bet you a hundred," Stacey said.

"Huh-uh," Cal replied, shaking his head.

"What do you mean, huh-uh? That's what you're wantin', ain't it? To bet a hundred dollars?"

"I am betting one hundred dollars," Cal said. "You are betting two hundred dollars."

"Two hundred dollars is a lot of money," Stacey said.

"The boy's right, though, Stacey," Pete said. Pete was the cowboy who was the first to try to ride Cannonball. "That's what you said. You said you was givin' two to one. If the boy bets a hunnert and he stays on the horse for a whole minute, you give him two hunnert."

"Pete's right," one of the others called out.

"All right," Stacey said. "All right, it don't matter none. There ain't no way this boy, or anyone, can stay on Cannonball for a whole minute."

"Ride 'im, boy!" someone shouted.

"Yeah! Let's see you take Stacey's money!" another called.

"Who is this fella Stacey anyway?" Pearlie asked as several men gathered around Cal to offer him their best wishes.

"He owns the mercantile here in town," someone said. "He got rich during the winter by sellin' his goods at about three or four times what they was worth."

"They ain't nobody here but what wants to see him ride that horse and take some of his money away from him," Pete said to Pearlie.

"Well, come on, boy!" Stacey called. "Are you goin' to ride or not?"

"I'll ride," Cal said. He gave the one hundred dollars back to Pearlie. "Hold onto it."

"Well, get over here and do it," Stacey said.

"Ride 'im, cowboy," the others said by way of encouragement.

Cal walked down to the other end of the corral, climbed up on the fence, then dropped down onto Cannonball's back.

Cannonball leaped away from the fence, throwing Cal into the air as he did so. The others groaned as they saw the saddle slipping to one side. Then Cal did an amazing thing. Instead of coming back down on the saddle, he came back on the horse's hindquarters, just behind the saddle. He held on as the saddle slipped off; then he moved forward and riding bareback, stayed with the animal.

The horse tried every maneuver to throw Cal off. He porpoised and sunfished; he twisted and turned; he reared on his hind legs, then jumped up on his forelegs; he dipped his head and leaned, a maneuver that had been successful with all previous riders. Cal countered that move just as he told Pearlie he would, by jerking the horse's head back and kneeing him in the neck on the opposite side.

Unable to lose his rider any other way, Cannonball began galloping around the corral, running close to the fence trying to rake him off. Those who were on the fence had to jump back to get out of the way.

When the horse reached the end of the corral, he leaped over the fence, and continued his bucking out in the street. The spectators hurried out into the street to watch.

Cannonball leaped up onto the front porch of Stacey's Mercantile Store.

"No!" Stacey shouted, running out into the street in front of his store. "Get him down from there!"

Cannonball twisted and kicked, and when he did, he kicked out one of the front windows of the store. A second kick took out the door and a third kick took out the other window. Then, coming down off the porch, Cannonball hit the pillars, causing the porch roof to collapse.

Cannonball came out into the street and, seeing Stacey, started galloping toward him.

"No!" Stacey shouted again. He leaped to the left just in time to keep from being run down, and he landed face-first in a pile of horse apples. He screamed in anger and frustration as he stood up with gobs of manure sticking to him.

Cannonball ran at full speed to the far end of the street, then came to a sliding stop. Cal stayed on his back.

Everyone watched as horse and rider remained motionless at the far end of the street. Then Cal turned Cannonball around, and they walked back up to the corral at a leisurely pace. When they got back, Cal was sitting sideways on the horse's back.

"How long has it been?" Cal asked.

"One minute and thirty-seven seconds," the timer said.

"You owe me two hundred dollars," Cal said as he slid down. He reached up and patted the horse, which stood calmly beside him.

"I never thought you would be able to stay on," Stacey said.

"Yeah," Pete said. "Especially after you loosened the saddle.

"I did not loosen the saddle."

"Then I guess you did it on your own, huh, Jerry?" Pete asked one of the two wranglers.

"I . . . I . . ." Jerry began nervously. Then he looked over at Stacey and pointed. "I didn't do it on my own," he said. "Mr. Stacey, he told me to do it."

"You're fired, Jerry," Stacey said with an angry growl.

"No need for you to be firin' me," Jerry replied. "I quit." Jerry looked at Cal. "Sorry, fella, I ought'n to have done that. I reckon I was just tryin' to hang onto my job."

"No need to apologize," Cal said. "I won't be holdin' onto any hard feelings. I just want my money, that's all."

Stacey stared at Cal for a long moment; then, with a loud, audible sigh, he pulled a roll of money from his pocket and counted off two hundred dollars. "Here!" he said angrily. "Here's your damn money!"

"Hey, Mr. Stacey," one of the cowboys called out. "Does that bet still hold? I think I could ride ole Cannonball now."

"You go to hell!" Stacey said gruffly as all the cowboys laughed.

"Four hundred twenty-six dollars," Pearlie said as he and Cal counted their money that night.

"That ain't the two thousand Smoke needs to save the ranch," Cal said.

"Maybe it ain't," Pearlie agreed. "But it ain't no small potatoes either. And it might help him. If nothin' else, it'll give 'em a little money to start with, if they have to start all over again."

"Yeah," Cal said.

"You're all right with this, ain't you, Cal?" Pearlie asked. "I mean, givin' our money to 'em and all. When you think about it, this is a lot of money to be givin' away like this. In fact, I don't know as I've ever had that much money on my own before."

"I know I ain't," Cal said.

"Are you goin' to be able to give it up? 'Cause if you don't, I don't think anyone would fault you."

"I'm goin' to give it up," Cal said.

Pearlie smiled, then reached out his hand and took Cal's hand in his.

"Good man," he said. "Good man."

Chapter Thirteen

Smoke was lying on the bunk in the small, hot, and airless cell, listening to the sound of the carpenters at work as they were busily constructing a gallows.

The hammers banged and the saws ripped through the lumber.

"Joe? Hey, Joe, hand me up that two-by-four, will you?"

"You are going to need more than one two-by-four there. Jensen is a big man. Hell, he could fall through the floor and break his neck," Joe called back.

Smoke heard the exchange, as well as the laughter that followed it.

Turnball stepped up to the cell.

"Sorry 'bout all the noise out there," Turnball said.

"Yeah, well, it's not like it's keeping me awake," Smoke replied.

Turnball chuckled. "I'll say this for you. For a man who's about to be hung, you've got a sense of humor. Anyway, your lunch will be here in a few minutes. The jail has a deal with Emma's Café to furnish meals for the prisoners."

"Thanks," Smoke said.

"Oh, and I also have some paper and a pencil here,"

Turnball said. "If there's anyone you'd like to write a letter to, I'll see to it that it gets mailed."

"Any chance of sending a telegram?" Smoke asked.

Turnball shook his head. "The line is still down. If you want to send word out to anyone, a letter is the only way you can do it."

"All right, let me have the paper and pencil," Smoke said.

Turnball nodded, walked over to his desk and got the paper and pencil, then brought them back and passed them between the bars. Smoke took them, then returned to his bunk and sat down. He lifted the pencil to write, but didn't begin right away.

He didn't want to hurry into the letter. He realized that by the time Sally got this letter, he would be dead. Because of that, he needed to think, very carefully, about what he would say.

His lunch came before he started writing, so Smoke ate the ham, fried potatoes, and biscuits while he contemplated what he would say to Sally. Then, with his lunch eaten and the sound of construction still ringing in his ears, he began to write.

My Dearest Sally,

If you are reading this letter, it means I am dead.

That's a very harsh thing to be telling you, so maybe you should pause for a minute so you can catch your breath.

I know this isn't the kind of opening sentence you would expect to read in a letter from me, and believe me, it's not one I wanted to write. But there is no other way to say it, other than to come right out and say it.

I also realize that some explanation is in order

so, as well as I can, I will bring you up on just what has happened to me since I left home a week ago.

The trip up from Sugarloaf was a lot more difficult than I expected, as there is still a lot of snow in some of the higher elevations. Coming through Veta Pass, which normally should take only a matter of hours, took two days. Stormy had to break through snow that was up to his chest, and by the time we did get through, I had to give both him and me a pretty long breather.

We did not see another living soul for those two days. And that is bad, because if we had seen anyone else, anyone at all, I probably wouldn't be in this fix.

It's time now for me to explain just what kind of fix I am in. I am, as of this writing, sitting in a jail in Etna, Colorado. It seems that the Bank of Etna was robbed on the morning of the sixth of this month. As it happens, on the sixth I did see someone else. But by pure coincidence, and the worst luck, the people I encountered were the very men who had robbed the Bank of Etna.

Stormy had picked a stone, and I was in the process of taking it out of his shoe when the six men rode up. I was not expecting anything out of the ordinary from my encounter with them, so I was not nearly as vigilant as I should have been. As a result, I was caught off guard and knocked out.

Sally, I know this was a dumb, you might even say a tenderfoot, thing for me to do. And you know me better than that. You know that, normally, I am much more alert.

I suppose my only excuse is that I was tired from the travel. And to be honest, I wasn't in the best of spirits, due to the fact that I was on my way to Denver to lease our ranch. That is something I know we needed to do, but it wasn't something I was looking forward to.

Anyway, thanks to my own dumb poor judgment, I was knocked out. But the story gets even stranger, Sally, because when I came to, I realized that I was wearing the shirt of one of the men who had waylaid me. I didn't have time to wonder about it, though, because almost from the moment I came to, I was face-to-face with a posse from Etna.

It was then that I found out what the shirt was all about, because the posse, seeing me in that very shirt, assumed that I was one of the ones they were looking for. I was arrested, and taken into town.

I was certain that I would be able to prove my innocence, but because I had not encountered anyone during my time on the trail, I was unable to establish an alibi. The posse had not believed me when they picked me up, and neither did the jury. I was found guilty, not only of the robbery, but of the murder of the banker, a man named Rob Clark.

That brings us back to the opening line of this letter. As a result of the verdict, I was sentenced to death by hanging. And now, as I write this letter, I can hear them building the gallows out in the street.

Putting down the tablet and pencil, Smoke climbed up onto the bunk so he could look out through the high window. He couldn't actually see the gallows, though as it was now late afternoon, he could see its shadow against the side wall of the apothecary. The men had quit work for the day, but Smoke could tell from the projected shadow that they had completed the base of the gallows.

When Pearlie and Cal rode into Big Rock, Pearlie pointed to a buckboard and team that was parked in front of the telegraph office.

"Isn't that rig from Sugarloaf?"

"Yes," Cal said. "Smoke must be sending a telegram."

"Let's go surprise him," Pearlie suggested.

Dismounting alongside the buckboard, Pearlie and Cal stepped into the telegraph office. Rather than surprising Smoke, they were themselves surprised to see Sally there.

"Hello, Miss Sally," Cal said.

There was a look of concern on Sally's face when she turned, but that was replaced by a big smile the moment she saw Pearlie and Cal.

"Pearlie! Cal!" she said happily. Opening her arms, she embraced each of them in turn. "Oh, I'm so happy to see you. I am so glad you are back!"

"Where's Smoke?" Cal said. "We've got something for him."

The smile left Sally's face to be replaced, once more, by a look of concern.

"I don't know where he is," she said. "He is supposed to be in Denver, meeting with a land broker. He was going to send me a telegram to tell me that he had arrived safely, but I haven't heard anything."

"Well, maybe the telegraph lines are down," Pearlie suggested. "You know, this was an awful bad winter."

"The direct lines are down," Sally said. "But Cody was able to get a message through by relaying it through

Wichita. And If I can get through to Denver that way, you know he can get through to me."

Pearlie was quiet for a moment, then he nodded. "Yes, ma'am, I reckon if there was a way to send you a telegram, Smoke would figure it out," he said. "I was just tryin' to keep you from worryin' too much, that's all."

"You say you got through to Denver?" Cal asked.

"Yes. I sent a telegram to the broker, asking if Smoke had arrived. I'm waiting now for the reply."

Behind them, they heard the telegraph begin clacking. The telegrapher hurried over to the instrument, sat down in front of it, grabbed the key, then sent something back.

"Cody, is that my telegram?" Sally asked.

"Yes, ma'am, I believe it is," Cody replied.

The machine began clacking again, and Cody picked up a pencil and started recording the message on a little yellow tablet. The instrument continued for several seconds while Cody wrote; then the machine grew silent.

Once again, Cody put his hand on the key to send a message back. Then, clearing his throat, he tore the page from the tablet, stood up, and brought it over to Sally.

"I wish I had somethin' better to report, Miss Sally," Cody said as he handed the message to her.

HAVE NOT SEEN SMOKE JENSEN STOP EXPECTED HIM TWO DAYS AGO STOP WILL HAVE HIM SEND MESSAGE IF HE ARRIVES STOP

"Now I am beginning to get worried," Sally said.

"You want us to go look for him?" Pearlie asked.

"I don't want you to go without me," Sally said. "But I want to give it a couple more days. I would hate to be out looking for him, and not be here to get his telegram when it comes."

"All right," Pearlie said.

"Thank you, Cody," Sally called back to the telegrapher.

"Miss Sally, if anything comes for you in the next day or so, I promise I'll get it out to your ranch," Cody said.

"I appreciate that," Sally said. Then to Pearlie and Cal: "Well, I take it you two are back. Shall we go home?"

"We're back," Cal said. "And guess what we brung you."

"What you *brung* me?" Sally scolded.

"Uh, what we brought you?"

"That's better. And it doesn't matter what you brought me. I'm just happy to see the two of you back where you belong."

"Four hunnert dollars," Cal said.

"What?" Sally responded with a gasp, surprised by the comment.

"We brung . . . uh, that is, we brought you four hunnert dollars," Cal said. "To help save the ranch."

"Where on earth did you get . . . no, never mind, it doesn't matter where you got it. However you got it, it's your money. Please don't feel any obligation toward Sugarloaf."

"Miss Sally, you don't want to hurt our feelings, do you?" Pearlie asked.

"What? No, of course not."

"Well, then, you must know that we consider Sugarloaf our home too. I know we don't own any of it, or nothin' like that. But it is our home nonetheless. And like you said, this here money is our money, which means we can pretty much do with it as we please. Ain't that right?"

Sally sighed. She wasn't even going to consider the poor grammar.

"Yes," she said. "It's your money to do with as you like. And yes, Sugarloaf certainly is your home."

"Then, we want to give you this money to help save it."
"Thank you," Sally said. "I couldn't be more touched."

Smoke did not finish writing the letter the first day. For a while, he considered scrapping the entire letter, but realized that, while he was actually writing, it almost seemed as if he were with Sally. So, late in the afternoon of the second day, he picked up the tablet and continued the letter.

As I am sure you have learned by now, I did not get to Denver to see the broker, so I have not been able to rent out Sugarloaf. Maybe you can make all the arrangements by telegraph. Or maybe it would even be better for you to sell Sugarloaf. You should be able to get a lot more money than we owe on the ranch. Then you could move into town somewhere and live comfortably on the money you would get from the sale.

I know that right now, as you read this letter, money is probably the furthest thing from your mind. But it is one of the foremost things on my mind. If something like this had to happen, I wish it could have happened last year, or even the year before. The ranch was solvent then, and you would not have been as foolish as I was to risk so much on the greedy ambition of growing even larger. My only comfort now is in knowing that you are smart enough to be able to salvage what value there remains of the ranch.

I hope Pearlie and Cal return sometime soon. I think having them around will help you deal with this. Or maybe you will help them deal with it. For some reason, women seem to be stronger than men about such things.

I have been writing this letter for two days now, not because I am having a hard time in writing it, but because while I am writing it, I feel myself closer to you.

When Smoke heard the sound of construction halt for the day, he put the letter aside and, once more, climbed up onto his bunk to see what he could see. The sun was low in the west, and as it had done the day before, it projected the shadow of the gallows-in-progress onto the wall across the alley from the jail. Today he could see the base and the steps, and just the beginning of the gibbet.

On the third day, Smoke finished his letter.

Sally, I have faced death many times before, and just as I was not afraid then, I am not afraid now. You cannot spend your life in this magnificent country and not be aware that death is a part of life, or that there is something higher than we are. And because I believe in that higher power, I do not think this is the end. It is only a door from this life into whatever God has in store for me. If there is a balance sheet of my life, I am comfortable with the idea that I will be received into His Glory.

My only regret is that I did not have more time to spend with you. You, Sally, have been the purpose and the love of my life. Know that, even though you may not see me, I will find a way to be with you from now on.

Your loving husband,
Smoke

At about the same time Smoke finished his letter, the hammering and sawing stopped, and when he climbed up on his bunk to look at the shadow against the wall, he could see the entire gallows. The instrument of execution was complete, to include the gibbet and dangling rope. The hangman's noose was already tied.

Having faced death many times before, Smoke was convinced that he had come to an accommodation with it. But he was about to be hanged for something he did not do, and there was something about that prospect that bothered him even more than the actual dying. It wasn't just that he was going to be executed, though that was bad enough. It was that those who actually were guilty were getting away with it.

Smoke folded his letter and put it in the envelope Turnball had given him. He had just finished addressing it when Deputy Pike stepped up to the cell and looked in.

"Who'd you write that letter to?" Pike asked.

"I wrote it to my wife."

"Your wife, huh?" Pike said. He giggled. "Is your wife a good-lookin' woman? I mean, bein' as she's goin' to be a widder-woman, why, just maybe I'll go meet her."

"Why don't you do that?" Smoke said.

"Hah! You want me to go meet your widder?"

"Yes," Smoke said. "Tell her how much you enjoyed watching me die." Smoke smiled, a cold, hard smile. "Then I suggest you duck."

"Why? Is she goin' to hit me with a fryin' pan?"

"No. She is more likely to shoot you with a forty-four," Smoke said.

"Really?"

"Really."

"Well, we'll just see about that." Pike stuck his hand in

through the bars of the cell. "If you'll give me your letter, I'll see to it that it gets mailed."

"No, thanks."

"What do you mean no, thanks? Don't you want it mailed?"

"Not unless I'm dead."

"Well, don't you be worryin' none about that. You're goin' to be dead by a little after ten o'clock tomorrow mornin'."

"You can mail it then," Smoke said.

"Pike, get away from that cell and quit bothering the prisoner," Turnball called from his own desk.

"I was just . . ." Pike started.

"I don't care what you was just," Turnball said. "Just get away from the cell like I told you to."

"All right, Marshal, whatever you say," Pike replied.

That night, Deputy Pike was on duty. As it grew dark, he lit a kerosene lantern, but the little bubble of golden light that the lantern emitted barely managed to light the office. Although the cell was contiguous to the office, very little of the light from the lantern reached it. The cell, while not totally dark, was in deep shadows.

Just as the clock struck ten, Pike came over to the cell. Smoke was lying on the bunk with his hands laced beside his head. Because Pike was backlit by the lantern, Smoke could see him quite clearly. However, the dark shadows inside the cell made it more difficult for Pike to see Smoke.

"Hey, Jensen," Pike called. "Jensen, you awake in there?"

"I'm awake," Smoke replied, his low, rumbling voice floating back from the shadows.

"It's ten o'clock," Pike said. He giggled. "You know what that means, don't you? That means you only got twelve hours left to live."

Pike put his fist alongside his neck, representing a hangman's noose. Then he jerked his fist, tipped his head over to one side, and made a gagging sound in his throat.

"Shhhiiick!"

Laughing, Pike walked back into the office.

He came back at eleven. "Eleven hours," he said.

"Thanks so much for reminding me," Smoke said sarcastically.

"Oh, don't you worry none about that," Pike said. "I plan to come here ever' hour on the hour all night long. What's the good of hangin' somebody if you can't have a little fun with it?"

True to his word, Pike came back at midnight, and again at one. And each time, he told Smoke the time left with particular glee.

As it so happened, Smoke had a good view of the clock from his cell, so, just before two o'clock in the morning, he climbed up to the very top of the cell and hung on with feet and hands. As he expected, Deputy Pike came to the cell just as the clock was striking two. But because Smoke was in the shadows at the top of the cell, Pike didn't see him.

"Jensen?" Pike called. "Jensen, where are you?"

Smoke was in an awkward and uncomfortable position, and he didn't know how much longer he would be able to hold on. He watched Pike's face as the deputy studied the inside of the cell, and he could tell that Pike was both worried and confused.

"Where are you?" Pike asked again. "Where the hell did you go?"

Pike hurried back to get the key; then he returned and opened the door to step inside.

Smoke wasn't sure if he could have held on for another moment, but he managed to hold on until Pike was well inside the cell and clear of the door.

Then Smoke dropped down behind him.

"What the hell?" Pike shouted, turning around quickly to face Smoke. That was as far as he got. Before his brain had time to register what was going on, Smoke took him down with a powerful blow to the chin.

Working quickly, Smoke dragged the deputy over to the bunk. Then he pulled off the deputy's socks and stuffed them in his mouth to keep him from shouting the alarm after he left.

"Whew," Smoke said as he pulled the socks off Pike's smelly feet. "Those socks are pretty strong. Sorry about stuffing these in your mouth like this, Pike, but maybe you should think about washing your feet a little more often."

Smoke handcuffed the deputy to the bunk so he couldn't get rid of the socks. Then he closed and locked the door.

By then, Pike was conscious, and he lay on the bunk, glaring at Smoke with hate-filled eyes. He tried to talk, but could barely manage a squeak.

"Deputy Pike, it has been fun," Smoke said. "We'll have to do this again sometime."

Chapter Fourteen

Smoke retrieved his guns and saddlebags from the office. Then, almost as an afterthought, he took the red and black plaid shirt that had played such a role in his trial. After that, he let himself outside. The cool night breeze felt exceptionally refreshing to him, especially after several days of being cooped up in a cell.

As he stepped out into the street, he saw in actuality what he had only seen in shadow before now. The gallows was rather substantial, consisting of thirteen steps leading up to a platform that was about ten by ten. He didn't go up the steps for a closer examination, but he knew there would be a trapdoor at the center of the platform. Gabled over the top of the platform was the gibbet, and hanging from the gibbet was the rope and noose.

There was a sign in front of the gallows:

TO BE HUNG
AT TEN O'CLOCK OF THE MORNING
ON THE 15TH INSTANT
FOR THE MURDER OF ROBERT CLARK

KIRBY JENSEN

PUBLIC INVITED.

Taking out the pencil he had used to write his unsent letter to Sally, Smoke drew a large X across the sign. Then at the bottom he added:

HANGING CANCELLED

Chuckling to himself, Smoke hurried down to the livery stable. Although the night was moon-bright, it was very dark inside the stable where his horse was being kept.

He knew that Stormy was in here because he overheard Turnball telling someone that the town of Etna was going to sell Smoke's horse in order to pay for the expense of his trial and hanging.

As he moved down through the center corridor of the stable, he could smell straw and oats, as well as the manure, urine, and flesh of a dozen or more horses. The animals were being kept in stalls on either side of the center passage, but in the darkness of the building they were little more than large, looming, indecipherable shadows and shapes to him. He would have to depend upon Stormy to help him.

"Stormy?" Smoke called quietly. "Stormy, are you in here?"

Smoke heard a horse whicker in response, and going toward the sound, he found his horse with his head sticking out over the door of the stall.

"Good boy," Smoke said, rubbing his horse behind its ears. "Did you miss me?"

In response, Stormy nudged his nose against Smoke.

Smoke saw that his saddle was draped over the side of the stall. With a silent prayer of thanks for it being so convenient to him, he picked up the saddle and put it on his horse. Then, very quietly, he opened all the other stall doors in the stable and, clucking at the horses, called them out. Mounting Stormy, he then rode around to the corral and opened the gate. Within moments he had gathered a small herd of some thirty horses, and he started moving them out of town. He kept the herd going until he was at least two miles away. Then he pulled his pistol and fired into the air, causing the horses to break into a gallop.

The lead stallion started running in a direction that would take the herd farther away from Etna, and the others followed instinctively. Smoke was certain that after they tired of running, the herd would dissipate and the horses would probably return, one at a time, to the corral.

But for now they were in a panic, following the leader, and he knew it would be at least one day, maybe more, before the horses got back. He was certain that this wasn't every horse in town, but it represented a sizable number of them, enough to make the immediate raising of a posse difficult.

Once Smoke escaped from jail, he knew better than to go back home to Sugarloaf, or to even try to get in touch with Sally. There was no doubt in his mind but that Turnball would have notified Sheriff Carson back in Big Rock. And while Smoke and Carson were close friends, Carson was a man of great integrity, and Smoke's presence there under these circumstances would be very difficult for him.

The only way Smoke could avoid going back to jail, and keeping a date with the hangman, would be to find the real bank robbers and murderers. And it was that, his determination to find the real outlaws and clear his own name, that drove him now.

Tracking six riders on a trail that was a week old would be a task so daunting for most men that they would never even think to try. But Smoke wasn't most men, and he never gave the task before him a second thought. He had learned his tracking skills from a master tutor. The classes began during his days of living in the mountains with the man called Preacher,

"He's a good one to learn from," another mountain man once said to Smoke, speaking of Preacher. "Most anyone can track a fresh trail, but Preacher can follow a trail that is a month old. In fact, I've heard some folks say that he can track a fish through water, or a bird through the sky. And I ain't one to dispute 'em."

Now, as Smoke started on the trail of the bank robbers, the words of his tutor came back to him.

"Half of tracking is in knowin' where to look," Preacher told the young Smoke. "The other half is looking.

"Reading prints on a dirt road is easy. But if you know what you are doing, you can follow the trail no matter where it leads. Use every sense God gave you," Preacher explained. "Listen, look, touch, smell. Taste if you have to."

Smoke never was as good as Preacher, but if truth be told, he was second only to Preacher, and he could follow a cold trail better than just about anyone. Returning to the place where he had encountered the bank robbers, he managed to pick up their trail.

It was difficult, the trail being as old as it was, but he was helped by the fact that the robbers were trying to stay out of sight. Because of that, they avoided the main roads, and that made their trail stand out. The funny thing is, if they had stayed on the main roads, Smoke might not have been able to find them because their tracks would have been covered over, or so mixed in with the other travelers that he wouldn't be able to tell which was which.

But cutting a trail across fresh country the way they did led Smoke just as straight as if they had left him a map. Also, since they were isolated from the other traffic, Smoke was able to study each individual set of hoofprints. To the casual observer, all the prints would look alike, just the U shape of the horseshoes. But a closer examination showed that each set had its own peculiar identifying traits. That would be very helpful to him once they got back onto a major trail, for then he would be able to pick out the individual prints from among many others.

Tracking became even easier once he reached high country because there was still snow on the ground, and it was almost as if they were leaving him road signs.

Then, just on the other side of a large patch of snow, the riders went their separate ways. When that happened, Smoke had to choose which trail he was going to follow.

"What the hell?" Marshal Turnball said when he came into his office the next morning and found Deputy Pike gagged and handcuffed to the bunk and locked in the cell.

"Uhhnnn, uhhhnn," Pike grunted. He was unable to speak because of the socks that were stuffed in his mouth.

"Oh, shut up your moaning," Turnball said, his irritation showing in his voice. "Where are the damn keys?"

"Uhnnn, uhnnn," Pike grunted again.

"Oh, shut up," Turnball repeated.

Finding the keys lying on his desk, Turnball unlocked the cell door, then pulled the socks from Pike's mouth.

"Now, Deputy Pike, would you please tell me just what the hell happened?" Turnball asked as he started looking through the key ring for the one that would unlock the handcuffs.

Pike coughed and gagged for a moment after the socks were removed. "The son of a bitch got away!" he finally blurted out.

"I can see that, Pike," Turnball said. "The question is, how did he get away? When I left last night, he was locked in this cell. Now I come in here this morning and what do I find? Jensen? No! I find you all trussed up like a calf to be branded. Now I want to know how that happened."

"He jumped me," Pike said.

"He jumped you?"

"Yes, sir."

"You were outside, he was locked in the cell, and he jumped you?"

"I, uh, wasn't exactly outside the cell when he jumped me."

"Go on."

"Well, you see, I come into the cell," Pike said. He went on to explain how he had looked in the cell and, not seeing the prisoner, went in to investigate. He left out the fact that he had been harassing the prisoner every hour on the hour.

The front door to the jail opened then, and Syl Jones came in. Jones was the owner of the corral.

"Marshal, the horses is gone," Jones said.

"The horses? What horses?"

"Your horse, my horse, just about ever' horse in town. They're all gone."

"What the hell are you talking about? Gone? Gone where?"

"I don't know gone where. All I know is, when I come to work this mornin' the stable door was open, all the stalls was open, and the corral gate was open. They ain't one horse left."

"Jensen," Turnball said angrily.

"Jensen? Are you talkin' about Smoke Jensen? The fella we're goin' to hang this mornin'?" Jones had been a member of the jury that had convicted Smoke.

"Yes, that's exactly who I mean. The fella we was goin'

to hang this morning," Turnball said. He looked at Pike, the expression on his face showing his anger. "That is, we was goin' to hang him before Pike, here, just opened the door and let 'im go."

"You let 'im go? What the hell did you do that for?" Jones asked.

"Shut up, Jones," Pike growled. "You think I done it of a purpose?"

"Well, even if he did escape, why would he steal ever' horse in town?" Jones asked.

"He didn't steal them, he just ran them off," Turnball said. "He figured it would keep us from comin' after 'im."

"Oh, yeah, I guess that's right," Jones said. "Well, if he just run 'em off, like as not they'll all be back before the day's out."

"In the meantime, that gives him a full day's head start." Sighing audibly, Turnball ran his hand through his hair. "Damn you, Pike," he said.

Turnball started for the front door.

"Where you goin'?" Pike asked.

"To the telegraph office. There has to be some way to get a message out."

"Yes, we've got a line through to Omaha," James Cornett said. "Just got put back up yesterday."

"Could you send a message to the sheriff of Hinsdale County through Omaha?"

"Well, if they are connected to anyone, I suppose we can. We could go through Omaha to Wichita to Denver to . . ."

Turnball waved his hand. "I don't need you to build the telegraph line for me, Cornett. Just send the message."

"All right," Cornett replied. "What's the message?"

"I'll write it out for you," Turnball said as he began writing. "Actually, two messages, one to the sheriff of Hinsdale County and one to Big Rock, down in Rio Grande County."

Half an hour later, just after Turnball got through explaining to a disappointed crowd that there would be no hanging today, Cornett came into his office with a message.

"We heard back from the sheriff of Hinsdale County," Cornett said, handing the message to Turnball.

Turnball read it, then shook his head. "What have we gotten ourselves into?" he asked.

"What is it?" Pike asked.

Without a word, Turnball handed Pike the telegram.

ANY SUCH REWARD POSTER ON
KIRBY JENSEN AS MAY EXIST HAS LONG
BEEN RESCINDED STOP
KIRBY JENSEN IS ONE OF THE LEADING
CITIZENS OF THE STATE STOP IT IS HIGHLY
UNLIKELY THAT JENSEN WOULD
PARTICIPATE IN A BANK ROBBERY STOP
EXPECT INVESTIGATION FROM STATE ATTY
GENERAL OFFICE STOP GOVERNOR PITKIN
PERSONALLY INTERESTED IN CASE STOP

Cody Mitchell, the Western Union operator in Big Rock, Colorado, was sweeping the floor of his office when the instrument began clacking to get his attention. Putting the broom aside, he moved over to the table, sat down, and responded that he was ready to receive.

* * *

Cal was filling a bucket at the water pump when he saw a boy of about fifteen riding toward the house.

"Can I help you with somethin'?" Cal called out to him.

"This here's the Jensen spread, ain't it?" the boy replied.

"It is."

"I got a message for Mrs. Jensen from Mr. Mitchell."

"Mitchell?" Cal asked.

"Mr. Cody Mitchell, the telegrapher."

"Oh!" Cal said. He smiled broadly. "It must be from Smoke. Give the telegram to me, I'll take it to her."

The boy shook his head. "I ain't got no telegram. All I got is a message, and Mr. Mitchell says I'm to tell it to her personal."

"All right," Cal said, picking up the bucket. "Come on, I'll take you to her."

An hour after the message was delivered, Sally, Pearlie, and Cal were in Sheriff Carson's office.

"You didn't have to come into town, Miss Sally," Carson said. "I was goin' to come out there to see you."

"What's this all about, Sheriff?" Sally asked.

Sheriff Carson stroked his chin. "All I can tell you is what I heard from the marshal up in Etna. He said that they arrested Smoke for murder and bank robbery, and they tried him and found him guilty. He was supposed to hang this mornin', but he got away."

"Thank God," Sally said, breathing a sigh of relief.

"Yes," Carson said. "Well, he did get away, but it's my understanding that Marshal Turnball has sent word out all over the West sayin' Smoke is a wanted man."

"Sheriff, you know there is no way Smoke would hold up a bank, or murder someone," Sally said. "How could a fair jury find him guilty of such a thing?"

"I reckon they don't know him like we do," Carson said. "Sally, uh, they want me to arrest him if he comes back. I'm legally and morally bound to do it, so if he comes to the ranch first, you tell him to just keep on going and not to come into town."

"Don't worry, Sheriff," Sally said. "I don't think Smoke will come back until he has this mess all cleared up."

That night in the bunkhouse, Pearlie woke up in the middle of the night. When he awoke, he saw Cal sitting at the window, just staring outside.

"Damn, Cal, what time is it?" Pearlie asked from his bed.

"I don't know," Cal answered. "It's some after midnight, I reckon."

"What are you doin' up?"

"Can't sleep."

"You're thinking about Smoke, ain't you?"

"Yeah."

"Smoke will be all right. He can take care of himself, you know that."

"Yeah, I know it."

"And he'll find out who done this and get that set right too."

"Unless . . ." Cal answered, allowing the word to hang, pregnant with uncertainty.

"Unless what?"

Cal turned to look at Pearlie for the first time. "Pearlie, have you stopped to think that maybe Smoke, that is, maybe he . . ."

"Did it?" Pearlie responded.

Cal nodded his head, but said nothing. His eyes were wide, worried, and shining in the moonlight.

"Cal, believe me, I've known Smoke longer than you have. He didn't rob that bank and he didn't kill that banker."

"I mean, if he did, why, I wouldn't think no less of him," Cal said. "What with the winter we just come through, and the danger of him maybe losin' Sugarloaf an' all."

"He didn't do it," Pearlie said again.

"How can you be so sure?"

"I told you how I can be so sure. It's because I know him."

"Pearlie, you know how I come to be here, don't you? I mean, how I tried to rob Miss Sally that time? If it had been anyone else but her, I would of probably got away with it. Then, there's no tellin' where I would be now. I might even be a bank robber. But I ain't, 'cause she took me in."

"Yes, I know that."

"The point is, I ain't a thief. I mean, I ain't no normal thief, but I was pretty desperate then, so I done somethin' I never thought I would do. I could see how Smoke might do the same thing if he thought he had to."

"All right, Cal, do you want me to tell you how I know he didn't do this?"

"Yes."

"It's easy," Pearlie said. "The sheriff said there were six of 'em robbed the bank, right?"

"Right."

"If Smoke was going to rob a bank, he wouldn't need no five other men to help him get the job done. He would'a done it alone."

Cal paused for a minute; then he broke into a big smile.

"That's right!" he said. "He would'a done it alone,

wouldn't he? I mean, Smoke, there ain't no way he would need someone else to help him do a little thing like rob a bank."

"Are you satisfied now?"

"Yeah," Cal said. "Yeah, you're right. Smoke didn't rob that bank."

"So, you'll go to bed now and let me get some sleep?"

"Yeah," Cal said. "Good night, Pearlie."

"Good night, Cal."

Chapter Fifteen

It was just growing dark when Smoke rode into the little town of Dorena. He passed by a little cluster of houses that sat just on the edge of town and as he came alongside them, he could smell the aroma of someone frying chicken. That reminded him that he was hungry, not having eaten anything for the entire day.

Smoke had never been in Dorena before, but he had been in dozens of towns just like it, so there was a familiarity as he rode down the street, checking out the false-fronted buildings: the leather goods store, the mercantile, a gun shop, a feed store, an apothecary, and the saloon.

The saloon was called Big Kate's, and when Smoke stopped in front of it, he reached down into the bottom of his saddlebag, moved a leather flap to one side, and found what he was looking for. He had put one hundred dollars in the saddlebag before he left Sugarloaf, keeping it in a way that a casual examination of the pouch wouldn't find it. Fortunately, it had escaped detection when he was arrested and his horse and saddle were taken.

The smell of bacon told him that Big Kate's offered an opportunity for supper, so he went inside.

One of the amenities the customers could enjoy at

Big Kate's was a friendly game of cards. On the wall there was a sign that read: THIS IS AN HONEST GAMBLING ESTABLISHMENT—PLEASE REPORT ANY CHEATING TO THE MANAGEMENT.

In addition to the self-righteous claim of gambling integrity, the walls were also decorated with animal heads and pictures, including one of a reclining nude woman. There was no gilt-edged mirror, but there was an ample supply of decent whiskey, and several large jars of pickled eggs and sausages placed in convenient locations.

From a preliminary observation, Big Kate's appeared to be more than just a saloon. It was filled with working girls who all seemed to be attending to business. Smoke saw one of the girls taking a cowboy up the stairs with her.

The upstairs area didn't extend all the way to the front of the building. The main room, or saloon, was big, with exposed rafters below the high, peaked ceiling. There were a score or more customers present, standing at the bar talking with the girls and drinking, or sitting at the tables, playing cards.

A large, and very bosomy, woman came over to greet Smoke.

"Welcome to Big Kate's, cowboy," she said. "I don't believe I've seen you before. Are you new in town?"

"I am," Smoke answered. "I take it that you are . . ." He hesitated, then left out the descriptive word. "Kate?"

Big Kate laughed, a loud, guffawing laugh. "It's okay, honey, you can call me big. Hell, I've got mirrors and I ain't blind. Now, could I get you something to drink?"

"Yes," Smoke answered.

"Wine, beer, or whiskey?"

"Beer," Smoke said. "And something to eat, if you've got it."

"Beans and bacon is about it," Big Kate replied. "And cornbread."

"That'll be fine," Smoke said

"Kim, do keep the cowboy company while I get him something to drink," Big Kate said, adroitly putting Smoke with one of her girls.

Kim was heavily painted and showed the dissipation of her profession. There was no humor or life left to her eyes.

"You were in here last week, weren't you?" Kim asked. "Or was it last month?"

Smoke shook his head. "You've never seen me before," he said.

"Sure I have, honey," Kim answered in a bored, flat voice. "I've seen hundreds of you. You're all alike."

"I guess it might seem like that to you."

"Would you like to come upstairs with me?"

"I don't think so," Smoke said. He smiled. "I'm just going to have my dinner and play some cards. But I appreciate the invitation."

"Enjoy your dinner, cowboy," Kim said in a flat, expressionless voice that showed no disappointment in being turned down. Turning, she walked over to sit by the piano player.

The piano player wore a small, round derby hat and kept his sleeves up with garter belts. He was pounding out a rendition of "Little Joe the Wrangler," though the music was practically lost amidst the noise of a dozen or more conversations.

"What's the matter? You didn't like Kim?" Big Kate asked, returning with Smoke's beer.

"Kim was fine," Smoke said. "I've just got other things on my mind, that's all."

"It must be somethin' serious to turn down a chance to be with Kim. She's one of our most popular girls," Big

Kate said, laughing. "If you'll excuse me now, I see some more customers just came in and I'd better go greet them. Oh, there's a table over there. Your food will be right out."

"Thanks," Smoke said.

Ebenezer Dooley had stepped out through the back door to the outhouse to relieve himself. He was just coming back in when he saw Smoke Jensen talking with Big Kate.

What the hell? he thought. How the hell did he get out of jail?

Dooley backed out of the saloon before he was seen.

Kim brought Smoke another beer and supper, then left to ply her trade among some of the other customers. Smoke ate his supper, then, seeing a seat open up in a card game that was in progress, took the rest of his beer over to the table.

"You gents mind if I sit in?" he asked.

"We don't mind at all. Please, be our guest," one of the men said effusively, making a sweeping gesture. "The more money there is in a game, the better it is, I say."

"Thanks," Smoke said, taking the proffered chair.

Some might have thought it strange for Smoke to play a game of cards under the circumstances, the circumstances being that he was a man on the run. But he was also a man on the hunt, and he had learned, long ago, that the best way to get information was in casual conversation, rather than by the direct questioning of people. He knew that when someone started questioning people, seriously questioning them, the natural thing for them to do was to either be very evasive with their responses, or not say anything at all.

Smoke had already drawn his first hand before he saw the badge on the shirt of one of the other men who was playing.

"You the sheriff?" Smoke asked.

"Deputy," the young man answered with a broad smile. "The name is Clayton. Gideon Clayton. And you?"

"Kirby," Smoke replied, using his first name that no one ever used. Then, in a moment of inspiration, he decided to make that his last name. "Bill Kirby," he added.

For a moment, Smoke felt a sense of apprehension, and part of him wanted to just get up and leave. But he knew that doing something like that would create quite a bit of suspicion.

On the other hand, with Deputy Clayton being here, he might learn right away if any telegraph message of his escape had reached the sheriff's office. But when Deputy Clayton made no move toward him, nor gave any indication of being suspicious of him, Smoke knew that, for now, he was safe to continue his search.

To the casual observer it might appear that Smoke was so relaxed as to be off guard. But that wasn't the case, as his eyes were constantly flicking about, monitoring the room for any danger. And though he was engaged in convivial conversation with the others at the table, he was listening in on snatches of dozens of other conversations.

"I believe it is your bet," Deputy Clayton said to Smoke. Smoke missed the challenge when it was first issued because he was looking around the room to see if he could spot any familiar faces. "Kirby?" the deputy said again.

"I beg your pardon?"

"I said, I believe it is your bet," Clayton said.

"Oh, thank you," Smoke said. He looked at the pot, then down at his hand. He was showing one jack and two sixes. His down card was another jack. He had hoped to fill a full house with his last card, but pulled a three instead.

"Well?" Clayton asked.

Smoke could see why Clayton was anxious. The deputy had three queens showing.

"I fold," Smoke said, closing his cards.

Two of the other players folded as well, and two stayed, but the three queens won the pot.

"Thank you, gentlemen, thank you," Clayton said, chuckling as he raked in his winnings.

"Deputy Clayton, you have been uncommonly lucky tonight," one of the other men said good-naturedly. Smoke had gathered from the conversation around the table that the one speaking was Doc McGuire.

"I'll say I have," Clayton agreed. "I've won near a month's pay just sittin' right here at this table."

"What do you think, Beasley?" Doc asked one of the other players. "Will our boy Clayton here give up the deputy sheriffin' business and go into gambling full-time?"

"Ho, wouldn't I do that in a minute if I wasn't married?" Clayton replied.

"Where's Sheriff Fawcett tonight?" Beasley asked.

"The sheriff's taking the night off," Clayton said. "I'm in charge, so don't any of you give me any trouble or I'll throw you in jail," he teased. The others laughed.

"Where you from, Mr. Kirby?" Doc McGuire asked as he shuffled the cards.

"Down in Laplata County," Smoke lied.

"Did you folks have a hard winter down there?"

"Yes, very hard."

"I was reading an article in the Denver paper a few weeks ago," Clayton said. "According to the article this was the worst winter ever, and it was all over the West. Hundreds of thousands of cows were lost."

"It was a bad one all right," Beasley said as he dealt the cards. "Some folks think that bad weather only hurts the farmers and ranchers, but I can tell you as a merchant that it hurts us too. If the farmers and ranchers don't have any money to spend, we can't sell any of our goods."

"I reckon it was the winter that made those folks hold up the bank over in Etna," Smoke said, taking a chance in bringing up the subject.

"There was a bank robbery in Etna?" Beasley asked. "I hadn't heard that."

"Yes," Deputy Clayton said. "We didn't get word on it until yesterday. Six of 'em held up the bank and killed the banker."

"They killed the banker?" Beasley asked. "Wait, I know that banker. His name is Clark, I think."

"Yes, Rob Clark," Clayton said. "But I understand they caught one of the ones who did it."

"Good. I hope they hang the bastard," Beasley said. "From what I knew of him, Clark was a good man."

"Oh, I expect the fella that killed him is already hung by now," Clayton said.

"You haven't heard anything on any of the others, have you?" Smoke asked.

"No, as far as I know they're still on the run," Clayton said as he pulled in another winning hand.

Smoke won the next hand, which brought him back to even, and the way the cards were falling, he decided he had better stop now. When Clayton started to deal, Smoke waved him away.

"Are you out?"

"Yeah, I'd better quit while I have enough money left to pay for my hotel room," Smoke said, pushing away from the table and standing up. "I appreciate the game, gentlemen, but the cards haven't been that kind to me tonight. I think I'll just have a couple of drinks, then turn in."

Ebenezer Dooley was standing just across the street from the saloon, tucked into the shadows of the space between Lair's Furniture and Lathum's Feed and Seed stores. He had been there for just over an hour when he saw Smoke step outside.

"Well now, Mr. Jensen," Dooley said quietly. "It's time I settled a score with you, once and for all."

Dooley pulled his pistol and pointed it, but just as he did so, a wagon passed between him and Smoke. By the time the wagon had cleared, he saw Smoke going into the hotel.

"Damn!" he said, lowering his pistol.

Chapter Sixteen

The hotel clerk was reading a book when Smoke stepped up to the desk. He looked up.

"Yes, sir, can I help you?"

"I'd like a room."

"Would you prefer to be downstairs or upstairs?"

"Upstairs, overlooking the street if possible."

"Oh, I think I can do that for you," the clerk said. He turned the book around. "The room will be fifty cents."

Smoke gave him the half-dollar, then signed the book, registering as Bill Kirby.

The clerk turned the book back around, checked the name, then wrote the room number beside it. He took a key down from the board and handed it to Smoke.

"Go up the stairs, then back to your left. The room number is five; you'll see it right in front of you."

"Thanks," Smoke said, draping his saddlebags over his shoulder.

The stairs were bare wood, but the upstairs hallway was covered with a rose-colored carpet. The hallway was illuminated by wall-sconce lanterns that glowed dimly with low-burning flames, putting out just enough light to allow him to see where he was going.

The number 5 was tilted to one side, but Smoke didn't have any difficulty making it out. He unlocked the door, then went inside. The room was dark, illuminated only by the fact that he had left the door open and some light spilled in from the hall. He saw a kerosene lamp on the bedside table, as well as several matches.

Dooley was frustrated that Smoke had managed to go into the hotel before he was able to take a shot at him. He put his pistol back in his holster while he contemplated what to do next.

Dooley had a room in the hotel himself. Maybe the best thing to do would be to wait until much later, then sneak down the hall into Smoke's room and kill him in the middle of the night.

Dooley had just about decided to go back to the saloon and have a few drinks while he was waiting, when he saw a lantern light up in one of the windows facing the street on the second floor of the hotel. That had to be Smoke Jensen.

As it happened, the stable was just across the street from the hotel, so Dooley ran back to the alley, then down to the stable, coming in through the back door. Going to the stall where his horse was boarded and his saddle waited, he snaked his rifle from the saddle holster. Then, with rifle in hand, he climbed into the hayloft and hurried to the front to look across the street into the hotel. He smiled broadly when he saw that the shade was up and the lantern was lit. Just as he had thought it would be, the occupant of the room was Smoke Jensen.

He had an excellent view from the hayloft.

* * *

It was a little stuffy in the room, so Smoke walked over to the window, then raised it to catch the night breeze. That was when he saw a sudden flash of light in the hayloft over the livery across the street.

Instinctively, Smoke knew that he was seeing a muzzle flash even before he heard the gun report. Because of that, he was already pulling away from the window, even as the bullet was crashing through the glass and slamming into the wall on the opposite side of the room.

Smoke cursed himself for the foolish way he had exposed himself at the window. He knew better; he had just let his guard down. He reached up to extinguish the lantern, and as he did so, a second shot came crashing through the window.

He extinguished the lamp, and the room grew dark.

"Damn!" Dooley said aloud. He jacked another round into the chamber of his rifle and stared across the street into the open, but now dark, window of Smoke Jensen's room.

Dooley was very quiet, very still, and very observant for a long time, and it paid off. He saw the top of Jensen's head appear just above the windowsill. He fired a third time.

This bullet was closer than either one of the other two, so close that he could feel the concussion of the bullet. But this time he had seen the muzzle flash from across the way, so he had a very good idea of where the shooter was, and he fired back.

* * *

Dooley hadn't expected Jensen to return fire. For one thing, Dooley was well back into the loft, so he was convinced that he couldn't be seen at all. He hadn't counted on Jensen being able to use the muzzle flash of his rifle to locate his position.

The bullet from Jensen's pistol clipped just a little piece of his ear, and he cried out and slapped his hand to the shredded earlobe.

"You son of a bitch," he muttered under his breath.

"What was that?" Smoke heard someone shout.

"Gunshots. Sounded like they came from down by the . . ."

That was as far as the disembodied voice got before another shot crashed through the window.

"Get off the street!" another voice called. "Everyone, get off the street!"

Smoke heard the command, loud and authoritative, floating up from below. "Everyone, get inside!"

Smoke recognized the voice. It belonged to Deputy Clayton, the man he had been playing cards with but a few minutes earlier. On his hands and knees so as not to present a target, Smoke crept up to the open window and looked out again. He saw the deputy running up the street.

"Clayton, stay away!" he shouted down to him. Clayton headed for the livery stable with his pistol in his hand. "Clayton, no! Get back!"

Smoke's warning was not heeded. A third volley was fired from the livery hayloft, and Clayton fell facedown in the street.

With his pistol in his hand, Smoke climbed out of the window, scrambled to the edge of the porch, then dropped down onto the street. Running to Clayton's still form, he bent down to check on him. Clayton had been hit hard, and through the open wound in his chest, Smoke could hear the gurgling sound of his lungs sucking air and filling with blood.

"Damnit, Clayton, I told you to get down," Smoke scolded softly.

"It was my job," Clayton replied in a pained voice.

At that moment, another rifle shot was fired from the livery. The bullet hit the ground close by, then ricocheted away with a loud whine.

"He's still up there," Clayton said.

"Yeah, I know," Smoke said.

"What's going on?" someone shouted.

"What's all the shootin' about?" another asked.

"Get back!" Smoke yelled. "Do what the deputy told you! Get back!"

"Is the deputy dead?"

Another shot from the loft of the stable did what Clayton and Smoke had been unable to do. It forced all the curious onlookers away from the street and out of the line of fire.

Smoke fired back, shooting once into the dark maw of the hayloft. Then, taking Clayton's pistol and sticking it down in his belt, he ran to the water trough nearest the livery, diving behind it just as the man in the livery fired again. He heard the bullet hit the trough with a loud popping sound. He could hear the water bubbling through the bullet hole in the water trough, even as he got up and ran toward the door of the livery.

Smoke shot two more times to keep the shooter back. Then, when he reached the big, open double doors of the livery, he ran on through them so that he was inside.

Once inside, he moved quietly through the barn itself, looking up at the hayloft just overhead. Suddenly he felt little pieces of straw falling on him and he stopped, because he realized that someone had to be right over him. That's when he heard it, a quiet shuffling of feet. He fired twice, straight up, but was rewarded only with a shower of more bits and pieces of straw.

"That's six shots. You're out of bullets, you son of a bitch," a calm voice said.

Smoke looked over to his left to see a man standing in the open on the edge of the loft. It was one of the bank robbers.

"Well," Smoke said. "If it isn't the pockmarked droopy-eyed son of a bitch who set me up."

"How the hell did you get out of jail, Jensen?" he asked. "I figured they'd have you hung by now. I must confess that I was some surprised when I seen you come in the saloon tonight."

"You're going to shoot me, are you?" Smoke asked.

"Seems like the logical thing to do, don't you think?"

"What's your name?"

Dooley laughed. "What do you need to know my name for?"

"I don't know. Maybe because I'd like to know the name of the man that wants to kill me."

"It ain't just wantin' to, Jensen. I'm goin' to kill you. And to satisfy your curiosity, my name is Dooley. Ebenezer Dooley."

"Since you are in a sharing mood, Mr. Dooley, where are the others?" Smoke asked.

Dooly laughed. "You got some sand, Jensen," he said. "Worryin' about where the others are when I'm fixin' to shoot you dead."

"Where are they?"

"I don't know where they all went, but the Logan brothers was goin' to Bertrand. Not that it'll matter to you. You got 'ny prayers, now's the time to say them."

Slowly, and deliberately, the outlaw raised his rifle to his shoulder to take aim.

Smoke raised his pistol and fired.

Dooley got a surprised look on his face as he reached down and clasped his hands over the wound in his chest. He fell forward, tumbling over once in the air, then landing on his back in a pile of straw in the stall right under him. The horse whinnied and moved to one side of the stall, barely avoiding the falling body.

Smoke stepped into the stall and looked down at Dooley. The outlaw was gasping for breath, and bubbles of blood came from his mouth.

"How did you do that?" Dooley asked. "I counted six shots."

Smoke held out the pistol. "This is the deputy's gun," he said. "I borrowed it before I ran in here."

"I'll be go to hell," Dooley said, his voice strained with pain.

"I expect you will," Smoke said as Dooley drew his last breath.

Smoke saw that the horse was still pretty agitated, and he petted it on the neck to try and calm it down.

"I'll be damned," he said. "No wonder you are upset. You're his horse, aren't you?"

The horse continued to show its agitation.

"Don't worry, I'm not going to shoot you. You can't help it because your owner was such a bastard."

As Smoke continued to try and calm the horse, he saw a twenty-dollar bill lying in the straw over by the edge of the stall, just under the saddle.

"Hello, what's this?" he said, leaving the horse and

going over to retrieve the bill. That's when he saw another bill sticking out of the rifle sheath.

Smoke stuck his hand down into the rifle holster and felt a cloth bag. Pulling the bag out, he saw that it was marked Bank of Etna. There were five packets of bills in the bag, each packet wrapped by a band that said $1000. Four of the packets were full, and one was partially full.

Smoke looked back toward the door of the stable to make certain that he wasn't being watched; then he took the money bundles from the bag and stuck them inside his shirt. After that, he stuffed the empty bag back down into the rifle boot, then walked out into the street.

The street was still empty.

"It's all right, the shooter's dead!" Smoke called. "Someone get Doc McGuire to come have a look at the deputy!"

At his call, several people began appearing from inside the various buildings and houses that fronted the street. One of the first to show up was Doc McGuire, who, carrying his bag, hurried to the side of the fallen deputy. Kneeling beside the deputy, Doc McGuire put his stethoscope to the young man's chest. He listened for a moment, then, with his face glum, shook his head.

"He's dead," he said.

One of the others to hurry to the scene was the sheriff. The sheriff, who had gotten out of bed, was still tucking his shirt into his trousers as he came up. His badge gleamed in the moonlight.

"Damn," he said as he saw his deputy lying on the ground. "Anybody know who did this?"

"His name was Dooley. Ebenezer Dooley, and you'll find him in the barn," Smoke said.

"In the barn?" the sheriff said, pulling his pistol.

"It's all right. He's dead."

The sheriff looked at Smoke. "Did you kill him?"

"Yes."

"And who might you be?"

"The name's Kirby. Bill Kirby," Smoke said, continuing to use his alias.

"Tell me, Kirby, did you have a personal grudge with this fella?" Sheriff Fawcett asked.

"No."

"Then how come it was that you and him got into a shootin' war?"

"You'd have to ask Dooley that, Sheriff," Smoke said. "He's the one that started the shooting."

"What are you pickin' on him for, Sheriff?" one of the townspeople asked. "He's right, the man in the barn started the shootin' and Deputy Clayton come after him, only he got hisself kilt. Then this fella"—he pointed at Smoke—"went in after him. I seen it. I seen it all."

"Did you know this man?" Sheriff Fawcett asked Smoke.

"No."

"Then, how'd you know his name was Dooley?"

"He told me his name before he died."

Sheriff Fawcett had a handlebar mustache, and he curled the end of it for a moment. "Seems to me like I've heard that name before. There may be a wanted poster on him. Are you a bounty hunter?"

"I'm not a bounty hunter. I just happened to be here when this all started happening."

"Mr. Kirby would you be willing to stop by my office tomorrow and answer a few questions for me?"

"I don't mind," Smoke said.

"In the meantime, if some of you fellas would get these bodies over to the undertaker, I'll go see Mrs. Clayton and tell her about her husband." Sheriff Fawcett sighed. "I'd rather take a beating than do that."

Smoke hung around until the two bodies were moved; then he walked back across the street and into the hotel. The hotel clerk was standing at the front door when Smoke went inside.

"Mister, that's about the bravest thing I ever seen, the way you run into that barn like that. It was the dumbest too, but it sure was brave."

"You're half right," Smoke said with a little chuckle. "It was dumb."

When Smoke went up to his room, he took the money out of his shirt, counted it, then put it in his saddle bags. He'd counted 4,910 dollars, which was nearly half of what had been stolen. He wasn't exactly sure how he was going to handle it, but he had it in mind that, somehow, returning the money might help him prove his innocence.

But this was only half the money. For his plan to work, he would have to track down every remaining bank robber and retrieve whatever money was left.

Chapter Seventeen

The next morning Dooley's corpse was put on display in the front window of Laney's Hardware Store. He was propped up in a plain pine box, and was still wearing the same denim trousers and white shirt he had been wearing at the time of his death.

Dooley's eyes were open and opaque, and his mouth was drawn to one side as if in a sneer. When the viewers looked closely enough, they could see that, although the undertaker had made a notable effort, he had not been able to get rid of all the blood from the repaired bullet hole in the shirt.

A sign was hanging around the corpse's neck.

EBENEZER DOOLEY
THE MURDERER OF
DEPUTY GIDEON CLAYTON
SHOT AND KILLED
BY BILL KIRBY
ON THE SAME NIGHT

* * *

After the money was divided, the five remaining bank robbers went their separate ways. Dooley went off by himself, but the Logan brothers left together, and so did Fargo Masters and Ford DeLorian, who were first cousins.

Ford was relieving himself while Fargo remained mounted, his leg hooked around the saddle horn.

"Hey, Fargo," Ford called up from his squatting position. "You know what I been thinkin'?"

"Ha," Fargo teased. "I didn't even know you could think, let alone what you were thinkin'."

"I'm thinkin' it don't do no good to have this here money if we ain't got no place to spend it."

"Yeah, I've give that a little thought myself," Fargo replied.

Ford grabbed a handful of leaves and made use of them. "So, how about we go into the next town and spend a little of this money?" he said as he pulled his trousers back up.

"Sounds fine by me," Fargo replied. "Where is the closest town?"

"Closest town is Dorena," Ford said, "But we can't go there."

"Why not?" Fargo asked.

"'Cause that's where Dooley was goin'."

"So?"

"I thought he said it wouldn't be good for us to all go to the same place."

"We won't all be in the same place," Fargo said. "Just you'n me and Dooley."

"Yeah, you're right," Ford said as he remounted. "Ain't no reason he gets to go to the closest town and we got to ride over hell's half acre, just to find us a place to spend some money."

"That's what I was thinkin'. You been to Dorena before?" Fargo asked.

"Yeah, once, a long time ago."

"I've never been there. What's the best way to get there from here?" Fargo asked.

"It's just on the other side of that range of hills there," Ford said, pointing. "We should be there by noon."

"First thing I'm goin' to do when we get there is get me a big piece of apple pie," Ford said. "With cheese on top."

Fargo laughed. "You just give me an idea about what I aim to get me."

"What is that?" Ford asked.

"A cold piece of pie and a hot piece of ass," Fargo called back over his shoulder as he slapped his legs against the side of his horse, causing it to break into a trot.

Ford laughed, then urged his horse into a trot as well.

The sun was high in the sky as Fargo and Ford reached Dorena. A small, hand-painted sign on the outer edge of the town read:

Dorena
Population 515
Come Grow With Us

No railroad served the town, and its single street was dotted liberally with horse apples. At either end of the street, as well as in the middle, planks were laid from one side to the other to allow people to cross over when the street was filled with mud.

The buildings of the little town were as washed out and flyblown up close as they had seemed from some distance. The first structure they rode by was a blacksmith's shop.

TOOMEY'S BLACKSMITH SHOP

Ironwork Done.

Tree Stumps Blasted.

That was at the east end of town on the north side of the street. There, Ford and Fargo saw a tall and muscular man bent over the anvil, the ringing of his hammer audible above all else. Across the street from the blacksmith shop, on the south side of the street, was a butcher shop, then a general store and a bakery. Next were a couple of small houses, then a leather shop next door to an apothecary. A set of outside stairs climbed the left side of the drugstore to a small stoop that stuck out from the second floor. A sign, with a painted hand that had a finger pointing up, read:

Roy McGuire, M.D.

Next to the apothecary was the sheriff's office and jail, then the bank, a barbershop and bathhouse, then a hotel.

On the north side of the street, next to the blacksmith shop, was a gunsmith shop, then a newspaper office, then a café, then several houses, followed by a seamstress shop, then a stage depot, the Brown Dirt Saloon, several more houses, then the stable, which was directly across from the hotel.

Fargo pointed to the café. "There!" he said. "Let's go in there 'n get us somethin' good to eat."

"All right," Ford agreed. The two men cut their horses to the side of the street toward the café, then dismounted and tied them off at the hitching rail. When they stepped inside the building, some of the patrons reacted visibly to the filth and stench of the two visitors.

They found a table and sat down. A man and woman who were sitting at a table next to them got up and moved to another table.

"What you reckon got into them folks?" Ford asked.

"I guess they don't like our company," Fargo answered.

A man wearing an apron came up to them. "You gentlemen just coming into town, are you?" he asked.

"Yeah, and we're hungry as bears," Fargo said. "What you got to eat?"

"Oh, we have a lot of good things," the man replied. "But, uh, being as you just came in off the trail, perhaps you would enjoy your meal better if you cleaned up first? There is a bathhouse just across the street."

"Yeah, we seen it," Ford said. "But we're hungry. We'll eat first, then we'll go take us a bath."

"Go take a bath first," the waiter said. "Trust me, you will enjoy your meal much more."

"How do you know?" Ford asked.

"Because in your present condition, you are offensive to my other customers, and I don't intend to serve you until you have cleaned up."

"The hell you say," Ford replied angrily.

The waiter turned away from the table and started back toward the kitchen.

"Look here, mister, don't you walk away while I'm a'talkin' to you!" Ford called after him, reaching for his gun.

Fargo reached across and grabbed Ford's hand, preventing him from drawing.

"You don't want to do that, Ford," he said sternly, shaking his head.

"I ain't goin' to let no son of a bitch talk to me like that," Ford said angrily.

"Come on, let's go take a bath," Fargo said. "Our money ain't goin' to do us no good if we're in jail."

"You heard what . . ."

"Come on," Fargo said again, interrupting Ford's grumbling. "We'll board our horses, then take a bath."

As the two left the livery, they saw a crowd of people gathered in front of the hardware store, about halfway down the street.

"What do you reckon that's all about?" Fargo asked, pointing toward the crowd.

"I don't know," Ford said. "What do you say we go down there an' take a look?"

"All right," Fargo agreed.

The two men started down the street toward the hardware store, but stopped when they got close enough to see what everyone was looking at.

"I'll be damned," Ford said as he spit a stream of tobacco, then wiped the dribble from his chin. "That's ole Dooley up there in that pine box."

"It sure as hell is," Fargo replied.

"How'd he wind up there?" Ford asked.

"It tells you right there on the sign they got hangin' around his neck," Fargo said.

"Hell, Fargo, you know I can't read," Ford said. "What does the sign say?"

"It says he was kilt by a fella named Bill Kirby."

"Bill Kirby? I ain't never heard of no Bill Kirby, have you?"

Fargo shook his head. "Can't say as I have," he said.

"What for do you think this fella Kirby kilt 'im?"

"I don't know. Says on the sign that Dooley kilt a deputy sheriff, then this Kirby fella kilt him."

Ford studied the corpse for a long moment.

"What you lookin' at?" Fargo asked.

Ford chuckled. "Hell, the son of a bitch is even uglier dead than he was while he was alive."

Fargo laughed as well. "He is at that, ain't he?" He paused for a moment before he spoke again. "Wonder where at is his share of the money," Fargo said.

"He prob'ly spent it all already," Ford said.

"He couldn't of spent it this fast," Fargo insisted.

"Then he must'a hid it," Ford said.

"What do you say we hang around town long enough to find out just what happened?" Fargo suggested. He smiled. "Ha, the son of a bitch got most of the money; now he ain't even around to spend it. What do you say we find it and spend it for 'im?"

"Yeah," Ford agreed. "I would like that."

When Sally, Pearlie, and Cal rode into Etna, they saw a gallows in the middle of the street, just in front of the marshal's office. A rope was dangling from the gibbet, the noose at the end ominous-looking.

"That kind of gives you chills lookin' at it, don't it?" Cal said. "I mean, knowin' it was for Smoke."

"It wasn't used," Sally said, "so it doesn't bother me."

"Where do we start?" Pearlie asked.

"Why don't you two go on down to the saloon and see what you can find out?" Sally asked. "I'll check in the marshal's office."

"Uh, you want me'n Cal to go on down to the saloon?" Pearlie asked.

"Yes. Smoke always says you can find out more about what's going on in a saloon than you can from the local newspaper."

Pearlie smiled broadly. "Yes, ma'am, I've heard 'im say that lots of times. All right, me'n Cal will go on down there and see what we can find out. We'll all get together later," Pearlie added.

Pearlie and Cal continued to ride on down to the saloon, while Sally reined up in front of the office, dismounted, then went inside. A man with a badge was sitting at the desk, dealing poker hands to himself. He looked up as she entered.

"Somethin' I can do for you, little lady?" he asked with a leering grin.

"Are you Marshal Turnball?"

"No, I'm his deputy. The name is Pike."

"Where can I find Marshal Turnball?" Sally asked.

"What for do you need him?" Pike asked. "I told you, I'm his deputy." Pike moved around to the front of the desk, to stand uncomfortably close to Sally. "You want anything done . . . why, all you got to do is just ask."

"All right," Sally said. "I want you to tell me where I can find Marshal Turnball."

"I tell you what," Pike said, putting his hand on Sally's shoulder. "Maybe if you'd be nice to me, I'll be nice to you."

Pike moved his hand down to her breast.

Pearlie and Cal stepped up to the bar and ordered a beer apiece. When they were delivered, Pearlie blew some of the foam away, then took a long, Adam's apple-bobbing drink.

"You're pretty thirsty, cowboy," the bartender said.

"We rode a long way today," Pearlie answered.

"That'll make you thirsty all right," the bartender agreed.

"Say, we noticed the gallows out in the street as we came into town," Pearlie said. "You folks about to have a hangin'?"

"Well, we thought we was," the bartender said. "But the fella we was goin' to hang, a man by the name of Kirby Jensen, got away."

"How did he do that?"

The bartender laughed. "Hey, Marshal Turnball," the bartender called across the room. "Here's two fellas wantin' to know how Jensen got away."

"Ain't nobody's business how he got away," Turnball replied gruffly.

Pearlie and Cal turned toward the man who had answered the bartender. They saw a big man filling a chair that was tipped back against the wall. He was wearing a tan buckskin vest over a red shirt. The star of his office was nearly covered by the vest, though it could be seen.

Pearlie took his beer and started back to talk to the marshal. Cal followed him.

"Mind if we join you?" Pearlie asked when he reached the table.

"It's a free country," the marshal replied, taking in the empty chairs with a wave of his arm. "What can I do for you?"

"We're looking for Smoke Jensen," Pearlie said.

"Who?"

"Kirby Jensen," Pearlie clarified.

"Ha," Turnball said. "Ain't we all? What do you want him for?"

"We don't want him for nothin'," Cal said. "He's our friend."

"Your friend, huh? Well, mister, your friend robbed a bank and killed our banker."

"Was he caught in the act of robbin' the bank?" Pearlie asked.

"Near'bout," Turnball said.

Turnball explained how he and the posse found Smoke out on the prairie. "There was some of them empty wrappers, like's used to bind up money, on the ground around him, and they was marked 'Bank of Etna.' Besides which, he was still wearin' the same plaid shirt he was wearin' when he robbed the bank."

"Plaid shirt?" Cal said. He chuckled. "Smoke ain't got no plaid shirts. He don't even like plaid."

"Yeah? Well, he was wearin' one when he robbed the bank, and he was wearin' that same shirt when we caught him."

"Did he confess to robbin' the bank?" Pearlie asked.

"No." Turnball laughed, a scoffing kind of laugh. "He said he was set upon out on the prairie by the ones who actual done it, and one of 'em changed shirts with him."

"But you didn't believe him," Pearlie said. It was a statement, not a question.

"It wasn't just me that didn't believe him," Turnball said. "Your friend was tried legal, before a judge and jury, and found guilty."

"Did you think to send a telegram back to Rio Grande County to check with Sheriff Carson?" Pearlie asked.

"We couldn't. The telegraph line was down."

"If the line was down, how is it that you was able to send a telegram a few days ago sayin' that Smoke had escaped?"

Turnball squinted. "Are you fellas deputies to Sheriff Carson?"

"We ain't regular deputies, but we've been deputies from time to time," Pearlie said. "So I'll repeat my question.

How is it that you could send a telegram after he escaped, but you didn't think to send one to check on him?"

"They got a line put up that we was able to use," Turnball explained.

"If you had just waited, I think the sheriff would have told you that Smoke couldn't have done what you said he done."

"Let me ask you this," Turnball said. "Is it true that Jensen is bad in debt? That he's about to lose his ranch?"

"He owes some money, yes," Pearlie said. "But he wasn't about to lose the ranch. He was goin' to Denver to make arrangements to lease Sugarloaf out for the money that he needed."

"That's what you say. But sometimes folks change. Especially if they get desperate."

"How did Smoke escape?"

"What do you mean, how did he escape? He escaped, that's all. I had him in jail; then when I come back to the jail the next mornin', he was gone."

"Was there anyone guardin' him while he was in jail?" Pearlie asked.

"Yeah, my deputy was. Why?"

"A few minutes ago you said that Smoke robbed your bank and killed a banker. But you didn't say anything about him killin' your deputy."

"I didn't say that 'cause he didn't kill 'im," Turnball said.

"If Smoke is the killer you think he is, don't you think he would have killed the deputy when he was getting away?"

"What? I don't know," Turnball said. He was silent for a moment. "Maybe he would have."

"Marshal, we brung Mrs. Jensen with us," Cal said. "Would you like to meet her?"

"What do I want to meet her for?"

"She rode a long way to get here, Marshal," Pearlie said. "It wouldn't hurt you to meet her."

Turnball sighed and stroked his chin; then he nodded and reached for his hat.

"All right," he said. "I'll meet her. Where is she? At the hotel?"

"We left her down at your office," Cal said. "She might still be there."

"Oh, damn," Turnball said. "I hope she didn't tell Pike who she is."

"Pike?"

"Pike is my deputy," Turnball said. "He is as dumb as dirt, and he was . . . well, he was . . ."

"He was what?"

"He was ridin' Jensen pretty hard while he was in jail, carryin' on about how he was goin' to go back to Jensen's ranch and tell his widow first-hand what happened to him."

"That would be all the more reason for Smoke to kill your deputy, wouldn't it?" Pearlie said. "But he didn't do it, did he?"

"No, he didn't," Turnball said. "But now I'm worried about the woman bein' down there with Pike. There's no tellin' what that dumb son of a bitch might do if he knows who she is."

"Might do?" Pearlie asked.

"To Mrs. Jensen."

Pearlie and Cal looked at each other; then both laughed.

"What is it?" Turnball asked. "What's so funny?"

"What's funny is you worryin' about Miss Sally," Cal said.

* * *

When Pearlie, Cal, and Turnball stepped into Turnball's office a few minutes later, they saw Sally sitting at the desk, calmly dealing out hands of cards. She looked up and smiled.

"Hello, Pearlie, Cal," she said. She turned her smile toward Turnball. "And you must be Marshal Turnball," she said.

"Yes, ma'am, I am," Turnball said. "I'm sorry you had to wait here all alone. My deputy was supposed to be here."

"Oh, he is here," Sally said.

"He is? Where?"

"I'm afraid Mr. Pike was a bad boy," Sally said. "So I had to put him in jail."

Looking toward the jail cell for the first time, Turnball saw Pike, handcuffed to the bed. His socks had been stuffed into his mouth.

"I'm sorry about sticking his socks in his mouth like that," Sally said. "But his language was atrocious. I just didn't care to listen to it anymore."

Chapter Eighteen

Fargo and Ford were in adjacent bathtubs. They had agreed to spend some of their money on new duds, so a representative of the mercantile store came to the bathhouse to show some of the clothes the store carried. He was standing alongside the two tubs, displaying his shirts.

"Them's just ordinary work shirts," Ford said. "Ain't you got nothin' fancier than that?"

Like Fargo, Ford was wearing his hat, even though he was in the tub. And like Fargo, he was smoking a cigar.

"These are very good shirts, sir," the store clerk said defensively.

"I was just lookin' for somethin' a little fancier is all."

"We only had one dress shirt in stock," the clerk said. "And the merchants all went together to buy it and a suit of clothes for Deputy Clayton to wear for his funeral."

"Oh, yes, that's the man Bill Kirby shot, ain't it?" Fargo asked.

The clerk shook his head. "No, Mr. Kirby shot the man who shot the deputy. Dooley, his name was. Ebenezer Dooley."

"Do you know this here fella Bill Kirby?" Fargo asked. "Does he live here in town?"

"I don't know him. I believe he is just passing through," the clerk said. "He has a room down at the hotel."

"Hand me that bottle of whiskey," Ford said, pointing, and the clerk complied.

"Will you gentlemen be making a purchase then?" the clerk asked.

"Yeah," Fargo said. He pointed to the pile of dirty clothes they had been wearing. "I tell you what, you take them old ones, and leave us the new ones, and we'll call it an even trade."

The store clerk looked shocked. "I beg your pardon, sir?"

Fargo laughed out loud at his joke. "I was just funnin' you," he said. He reached down on the floor beside the tub and picked up a billfold, then took out some money and handed it to the clerk. "This here ought to do it."

"Yes, thank you," the clerk said.

"And you can also have the old clothes," Fargo said.

The clerk looked at the old clothes with an expression of distaste on his face. "You, uh, want me to take the old clothes?" he asked. "And do what with them, sir?"

"Do anything you want to with them," Fargo said. "Clean them up and wear them if you want to. Or burn them."

"Burn them, yes. Thank you, I'll do that," the clerk said. Looking around, he saw a stick and he used the stick to pick the clothes up, one item at a time. Then he dropped them into the paper in which the new clothes had been wrapped. "I'll take care of them for you," he said.

After the clerk very carefully and hygienically collected the old clothes, he wrapped them in the packing material, then left the bathhouse. Ford took a big drink of the whiskey, then tossed the bottle into an empty tub.

"Did you see the way he got into a piss soup when you

told him you wanted to trade even for them duds?" Ford asked, laughing out loud.

"Yeah," Fargo said, laughing with him. "He was so old-maidish the way he was handlin' them clothes, I should'a made him put them on and wear them out of here."

Ford lifted his arm and began rubbing the bar of soap against his armpit. "Hey, Fargo, how do you figure we ought to go about lookin' for Dooley's money?" he asked.

"We could start by goin' over to the hotel where he was stayin' at and lookin' through his room," Fargo suggested.

"Ha! Like they're goin' to let some strangers look through his room."

"We ain't strangers," Fargo said. "We're Dooley's brothers."

"What? No, we ain't," Ford said.

"We are if we say we are," Fargo said. "And who's going to know the difference?"

"Oh," Ford said. Then, as he understood what Fargo was saying, he smiled and nodded. "Oh!" he said again.

"Five hundred dollars?" Smoke said.

"Yes, sir," Sheriff Fawcett said. "Turns out I was right. I had heard Dooley's name before. There's a reward poster on my wall right now offerin' five hundred dollars for anyone who kills or captures him. By rights, that money should go to you. Unless you have something against taking bounty money."

"No, believe me, I don't have anything against it," Smoke said.

"Well, then, if you hang around town for another twenty-four hours, I'll have authorization from the governor's office to pay you the reward," the sheriff said.

"Thanks." Smoke smiled. "You've got a nice, friendly

town here. I don't mind staying another twenty-four hours."

Ford belched loudly as he finished eating. A plate filled with denuded chicken bones told the story of the meal he had just consumed. In addition to fried chicken, mashed potatoes, biscuits, and gravy, he had also eaten two large pieces of apple pie, each piece topped by melted cheese.

"Let's go get drunk," he suggested.

"Not yet," Fargo said. "First things first."

"Yeah? What could possibly come before getting drunk?"

"Finding the money," Fargo said.

"Oh, yeah. So, where do we start?"

"We start at the hotel."

"Will that be all, gentlemen?" the waiter asked, approaching their table then.

"Yeah."

"And don't you both look so nice now that you are all cleaned up?" the waiter said obsequiously. Using a towel, he bent over Ford and began to brush at his shirt.

"Here? What are you doing?" Ford said in an irritable tone of voice.

"I'm just brushing away a few of the crumbs," the waiter said. "It is part of the service one performs when one is in a position to receive gratuities."

"Receive what?" Ford asked.

"Gratuities."

"What is that?"

"Tips?" the waiter tried.

Ford shook his head. "I don't know what you are talking about."

"Oh, well, then, let me explain, sir," the waiter said. "It

is customary in a place like this that when one provides a service that is satisfactory, the customer will leave a gratuity, that is, leave some money as a"—the waiter struggled for the word—"gift, as a token of his appreciation for that service."

"What you are sayin' is, you expect us to give you some money above the cost of the meal," Fargo said. "Is that it?"

The waiter broke into a wide smile. "Yes, sir. I'm glad you understand, sir. Ten percent is customary."

"A gratuity?"

"Yes, sir."

"But that's not part of the bill, is it? I mean, if we don't leave you anything, that's not against the law?" Fargo asked.

"Oh, no, sir, not at all. That's why it is called a gratuity."

"Well, if the law don't say I've got to, I ain't goin' to," Fargo said. "Come on, Ford, we've got work to do," he added.

"Good-bye, gentlemen," the waiter said with a forced smile. He watched them until they stepped out into the street; then the smile left his face. "You cheap bastards," he added under his breath.

Fargo and Ford were standing in front of the registration desk at the hotel.

"Would you tell me what room Mr. Ebenezer Dooley is a'stayin' in?" Fargo asked. "He's our brother."

The clerk blinked a few times in surprise.

"I beg your pardon," he said. "Who are you asking for?"

"Mr. Ebenezer Dooley," Fargo said. "We was all supposed to meet up here in this hotel today, and we figured he'd be down here in the lobby waitin' for us by now, but he ain't here." Fargo chuckled. "Course, as lazy as ole Eb is, like as not he's lyin' up there sleepin' like a log."

"Oh," the clerk said. "Oh, dear, this is very awkward."

"Ain't nothin' awkward about it," Fargo said. "He's our brother, and he's expectin' us. Tell you what, just give me the key and we'll go wake him up our ownselves."

"You haven't heard, have you?"

"We ain't heard what?" Fargo replied, playing out his role. "What are you talkin' about? Look, just give us the key so we can go wake up our brother and then we can get on our way."

The hotel clerk shook his head. "I'm talking about your br . . . uh, about Mr. Dooley. I can't believe you haven't heard yet."

"What's there to hear?"

"I'm sorry to have to tell you gentlemen this, but Mr. Dooley was killed last night."

"Kilt? Did you hear that, Ford? Our brother was kilt," Fargo said, feigning shock and concern.

"That's real bad," Ford said, though neither the expression in his voice nor his face reflected his words.

"How was he kilt? What happened?" Fargo asked the hotel clerk.

"He was involved in a shoot-out," the clerk answered. "It seems that your brother killed our deputy sheriff; then he was killed himself."

Fargo pinched the bridge of his nose and shook his head. "Oh," he said. "Mama ain't going to like this, is she, Ford."

"No," Ford said, his voice still flat and expressionless. "She ain't goin' to like it."

"You can, uh, view your brother down the street if you'd like," the hotel clerk said. "His remains are on display in the window of the hardware store."

"What? What kind of town is this that they would put our brother in the window for ever'one to gape at?" Fargo asked.

"Believe me, sir, it wasn't my doing," the clerk said, frightened. He held up his hands and backed away, as if distancing himself from the issue.

"Where at's our brother's things?" Fargo asked. "We'll just get them and be on our way."

"Your brother's things?"

"His saddlebags, or suitcase, or anything he might have had with him. I want to take 'em back to Mama. You got 'em down here?"

"No, they are still in the room. I'm waiting for the sheriff to tell me it is all right to take them out."

"What's the sheriff got to do with it? I told you, we're his brothers. If Brother Eb's still got some things in his room, then we're the ones should get them, not the sheriff."

"Well, I don't know," the clerk said. "I'm not sure about this."

"Just give me the key to his room," Fargo said, more forcefully this time. "We'll go up there and have a look around our ownselves."

"Sir, how do I know you are his brother?"

"How do you know? 'Cause I told you I am his brother."

"Just the fact that you tell me that doesn't validate it."

"Doesn't what?"

"Doesn't prove it."

"Well, hell, why didn't you say you needed proof? Ford, tell him I'm Dooley's brother."

"Yes, sir, he's Dooley's brother all right," Ford said.

"And Ford is his brother too," Fargo said. "So there, you've got all the proof you need."

"That's not really proof, that's just the two of you vouching for each other," the clerk said. "Maybe we should wait for the sheriff. I could send for him if you like."

"Tell you what," Fargo said. "My brother had a drooping eye right here." Fargo put his hand over his right eye. "Now, how would I know that if I wasn't actual his brother?"

The clerk sighed. The two men were getting a little belligerent with him and they were frightening-looking to begin with. What was he protecting anyway? As far as he knew, there was nothing up there but a set of saddlebags anyway.

The clerk took a key from the board and handed it to Fargo. "Very well, Mr. Dooley. This goes against my better judgment, but go on up there and look around if you must."

"Thanks," Fargo said.

Fargo took the key; then he and Ford went up to the room. Dooley's saddlebags were hanging over a hook that stuck out from the wall.

Fargo grabbed the bags and dumped the contents onto the bed. One shirt, one pair of denim trousers, a pair of socks, and a pair of long underwear tumbled out.

"You pull out all them drawers and have a look," Fargo ordered, and Ford started pulling out the drawers from the single chest.

Finding nothing, Fargo stripped the bed, then turned the straw-stuffed mattress upside down.

"Nothin' here," Fargo said angrily. "Not a damn thing!"

Ford started to put the drawers back in the chest.

"What are you doin'?"

"Puttin' these back."

"To hell with 'em, just leave 'em," Fargo said. "We can't be wastin' no more time here."

When the two men came back downstairs, the clerk

looked up. He was surprised to see that they weren't carrying anything with them.

"You didn't find his saddlebags?" he asked.

"We found 'em, but there weren't nothin' there that Mama would want," Fargo said as they left.

"What'll we do now?" Ford asked when the two men went out into the street.

"I don't know," Fargo said, taking his hat off and running his hand through his hair. "I figured for sure he would have had the money hid out in his room somewhere," Fargo said.

"Maybe he had it with him, and the undertaker took it," Ford suggested.

"Good idea. Let's go down there and talk to him," Fargo said.

"You think the undertaker would keep the money if he found it?" Ford asked.

"We'll soon find out."

Chapter Nineteen

Gene Prufrock, the undertaker, had done nothing to prepare the outlaw's body but wash the shirt, then put him in a pine box. He didn't like the idea of making a public show of the dead, no matter how despicable a person he might have been. So when the sheriff asked him to stand Dooley's body up in the hardware store window, Prufrock tried to talk him out of it. But the sheriff prevailed, and Dooley's body was now on display.

It was a different story with Gideon Clayton, though. The young deputy had been very popular among the citizens of the town, and Prufrock was taking his time to do as good a job as he possibly could. Several of the merchants had gotten together to buy a special coffin for Clayton. It was finished with a highly polished black lacquer and fitted with silver adornments. Those same merchants had also bought him a suit, so that Gideon Clayton's body lay on Prufrock's preparation table, dressed in a suit and tie that he had never worn in life. The undertaker made the final touches, combing Clayton's hair and powdering and rouging his cheeks.

Prufrock had just stepped back to admire his work when he was suddenly surprised by the entry of two men.

"Is there something I can do for you gentlemen?" Prufrock asked.

"Yeah, we want to ask you some questions," Fargo said.

"Could the questions wait? As you can see, I'm working on a subject."

"Is that what you call them? Subjects? Why don't you just call them what they are? Dead meat?" Ford asked with a laugh.

"I'm sorry, sir, but I do not find your joke at all funny. I believe, very strongly, in maintaining the dignity of the departed," Prufrock said.

"I hear that when somebody dies, you take all the blood out of them," Ford said. "Is that true."

"Yes."

"What do you do that for?"

"So we can replace the blood with embalming flood. It preserves the body."

"What do you do with the blood?"

"We dispose of it," Prufrock said impatiently. "Gentlemen, please, I don't like people back here. Is there something I can do for you?"

"Who is this fella you're workin' on here?" Fargo asked, pointing to the body on the table. "Was he rich or somethin'?"

"No. Why would you think he is rich?"

"Well, look at him. He's all decked out in a new suit. And I'm lookin' at that real pretty coffin over there and figurin' you're about to put him in it. Is that right?"

"That's right."

"Then he must'a been rich."

"He wasn't rich, he was just well respected. He was our deputy sheriff."

"Your deputy sheriff, huh? So what you are saying is that this is the man our brother killed."

Prufrock gasped. "Good heavens! Mr. Dooley is your brother?"

"Yeah," Fargo said.

The mortuary was in the same building as the hardware store, but behind it. Fargo pointed toward the front. "The man you have standin' up in that window out there, showin' him off like a trussed-up hog, is our brother. Is that what you mean when you say you like to maintain the dignity of the departed? Our brother is a departed, ain't he? Where at's his dignity?"

"I . . . I'm sorry. I don't think anyone knew that he had kin in town."

"We just come into town this mornin'," Fargo said, indicating himself and Ford. "Didn't find out about our brother until we saw him standin' there in that store window for all the world to see."

"I'm sorry about your brother," Prufrock said.

"Yes, well, like I say, he was our brother. So that means that anything you found on him is rightly our'n."

"I beg your pardon?" Prufrock said, surprised by the sudden change in the direction of the conversation.

"His belongin's," Fargo said. "Ever'thin' he had on him is rightly our'n now. Well, 'cept he can keep them clothes on he's a'wearin'. Wouldn't want him to have to show up in hell butt naked."

Both Fargo and Ford laughed.

"That'd be funny all right," Ford said. "Ole Dooley walkin' around in hell naked as a jaybird."

"Dooley?" Prufrock said.

"What?"

"You called him Dooley."

"Well, hell, that's his name," Ford said. "What else am I supposed to call him?"

"It's just that, within the family, people normally use first names."

"Yeah, well, Eb, bein' the oldest, was just always called Dooley," Fargo said, trying to smooth over Ford's mistake. "Now what about his belongings? Do you have any of 'em here?"

"Well, of course there's his gun and his boots," Prufrock said. "Only other thing he had was the clothes he is wearing. But of course, you have already indicated that you don't want those."

"What about the money?"

"Yes, I'm glad you brought that up," Prufrock said. "That will be five dollars."

"Five dollars? That's all he had on 'im, was five dollars?" Fargo asked.

"Oh, no, you misunderstand. He had less than one dollar on him. The five dollars is what you owe me."

Fargo looked confused. "Why the hell should I owe you anything?"

"You did say that he was your brother, did you not? That means that someone owes me for the preparation of his body. As you two gentlemen are his next of kin, you are responsible for his funeral."

"Far as I'm concerned, he ain't goin' to have no funeral," Fargo said. "We may be his next of kin, but you ain't goin' to get no money from us."

"Then, what do you propose that I do about burying your brother?"

"What would you do about buryin' him if I hadn't'a come along today?"

"He would be declared an indigent, and I would collect the fee from the town council. Of course, that would also mean that he will be buried in a pauper's grave."

"That's fine with me. Go ahead and get your money from the town," Fargo said. "Come on, Ford, let's go."

"Aren't you even interested in when and where he is to be buried?" Prufrock called out as Fargo and Ford left the mortuary.

"No," Fargo yelled back over his shoulder.

"My word," Prufrock said quietly as the men left.

"The only place we ain't looked yet is the stable," Ford said. "Are we goin' to tell the fella watchin' the stable that Dooley was our brother?"

"No," Fargo said. "If Dooley owes any money for boardin' his horse, the son of a bitch might try to make us pay."

"Then how are we goin' to look?"

"We'll just have to find another way," Fargo replied.

Fargo and Ford hung around the stable until they saw the stable attendant go into the corral to start putting out feed for the outside horses. Then the men slipped into the barn.

"How will we find what stall he was in?" Ford asked.

"You know his horse, don't you?"

"Yeah, sure I know his horse."

"We'll just look around until we see whichever horse is his."

The two men started looking into the stalls. Then, at the fifth stall they examined, Ford said, "There he is. I'd recognize that horse just about anywhere."

Opening the door, they stepped inside; then Fargo picked up a pitchfork and handed it Ford. "Get to work," he said.

"Get to work doin' what? What's this here pitchfork for?"

"Start muckin' around in the straw, make sure he don't have it hid there."

"Yeah, well, while I'm shovelin' straw and shit, what are you going to do?"

"I'm going to look at his saddle and blanket roll."

"How come you get to look in his saddle, while I have to muck around in the straw and horseshit?"

"That's just the way it is," Fargo said.

Grumbling, Ford began tossing the straw aside while Fargo examined the saddle. Finding nothing there, he unrolled the blanket. When his search of the blanket turned up nothing, he stuck his hand down into the empty rifle sheath.

"Ha!" he said happily. "I feel somethin' here! I think this is it!"

Ford tossed the pitchfork aside and hurried over to watch Fargo as he retrieved a bag. But as soon as he brought the bag out for a closer examination, his smile changed to a frown.

"What the hell?" he said. "The bag is empty. There ain't no money here!"

"Well, where is it?" Ford asked. "Somebody's got it. He wouldn't of just kept an empty bag."

"Bill Kirby," Fargo said.

"Who?"

"The man they say shot Dooley. His name is Bill Kirby. And I'd bet you a hunnert dollars to a horseshoe that he's the one that got the money."

"So what do we do now?"

"We find the son of a bitch," he said.

Chapter Twenty

When Fargo woke up the next morning, he saw that he was in one of the rooms upstairs over Big Kate's saloon. There was a whore sleeping beside him and as he looked at her in the harsh light of day, he marveled at how different she looked now from the way he'd thought she looked last night. There was a large and disfiguring scar on one cheek. She was missing three teeth, and her breasts were misshapen and laced with blue veins.

"Damn," he said to himself. "How'd you get so ugly so fast? I must'a been pretty damn drunk last night."

Turning the covers back, he stepped out on the floor, put on his hat, and then, totally naked except for the hat, walked over to the window and looked at the back of the building behind the saloon. Feeling the need to urinate, he lifted the window and let go, watching as a golden arc curved down. A cat, picking through the garbage below, was caught in the stream and, letting out a screech, started running down the alley.

"Ha!" Fargo laughed out loud.

At that moment the door to the room opened and Ford came in.

"Son of a bitch!" Ford DeLorian said. "I seen 'im! I seen 'im when he come out of the sheriff's office."

"You seen who?" Fargo asked.

"I seen the fella that kilt ole Dooley."

"You seen Kirby?"

Ford smiled broadly. "Yeah, I seen 'im," he said. "Only his name ain't Kirby."

"What do you mean, his name ain't Kirby?"

"I mean his name ain't Kirby 'cause it's Jensen. He's the same fella that we put Logan's shirt on," Ford said. "Smoke Jensen, Dooley said his name was then. You recollect him, don't you, Fargo? He's a big man."

"Yes, I recollect him all right," Fargo said. "But how do you know he's the one that kilt Dooley?"

"Well, he's the one they give the reward for doin' it," Ford said. "They was talkin' about it downstairs, how Kirby was goin' to get a reward from the sheriff this mornin'. That's why I went down there so I could see what he looked like."

"You went down to the sheriff's office?"

"Yeah. I was out workin' this mornin', while you was in here layin' up with the whore."

"Well, you had her first. If you hadn't been so tight about it, we could'a each had our own whore 'stead of sharin' one."

"Is she still asleep?" Ford asked, looking toward the bed.

"Yeah, she's either asleep or passed out," Fargo replied.

"She did drink a lot last night," Ford said.

"She couldn't of drunk as much as we did. Otherwise, we wouldn't of brought her up here. Did you get a good look at her? She is one ugly woman."

"Yeah, well, me'n you ain't exactly what you would call good-lookin'," Ford replied. "Damn, Fargo, you just goin' to stand there naked all day?"

"Oh, yeah," Fargo said. "I guess I'd better get dressed."

"You know what I don't understand?" Ford asked as Fargo began pulling on his long underwear. "I don't understand what Jensen's doin' here. How come he ain't in jail?"

"He must'a broke out."

"Yeah, well, that's the trouble with jails these days," Ford said. "Hell, a citizen can't even count on 'em to keep the outlaws locked up."

"Are you sure it was Jensen you saw?"

"Yeah, I'm sure. And if you don't believe me, you can see for yourself. He's downstairs right now. But you better hurry, 'cause he ain't goin' to be there long."

"How do you know?"

"'Cause I heard him askin' someone how to get to Bertrand."

Fargo look up sharply. "Bertrand, you say?"

"Yeah."

"That's where the Logans was goin'."

"Yeah, that's what I was thinkin' too," Ford said. "You reckon Jensen is goin' after them?"

"Of course he is. Damn, you know what I think the son of a bitch is doin'?"

"No, what?"

"Well, what he is plannin' on doin' is runnin' us down and killin' us one at a time," Fargo said.

"For revenge?"

"Probably some revenge," Fargo agreed. "But more'n likely, it's to get his hands on the money that we stole."

"Damn! That mean he plans to kill us, don't it?"

"Yeah," Fargo replied. "Unless we kill him first."

"How we goin' to do that? We can't just walk downstairs and shoot him where he's sittin'."

"No, but if he's goin' to Bertrand, we can set up an ambush along the way."

As Smoke rode out of Dorena, he thought about the reward money he had received from killing Ebenezer Dooley. Five hundred dollars was still quite a way from having enough money to pay off the note on his ranch, but it was a start. If there had been a reward for Dooley, maybe there was a reward on the others. If each of them was worth five hundred dollars, finding them all would be worth three thousand dollars. Three thousand dollars would not only pay off the note on his ranch, it would give him a little operating capital to start the next year with.

Smoke had never been a bounty hunter, had never even considered it. But this was a different situation from hunting men just for the bounty. He needed to find each of these men in order to prove that he was innocent of the bank robbery in Etna.

On the first night on their way back to Sugarloaf Ranch, Sally, Pearlie, and Cal made camp on the trail. They found a place next to a fast-flowing spring of clear water where there was abundant wood for their fire and grass for the horses. Cal had gathered the wood, Pearlie had made the fire, and now Sally was cooking their supper.

Pearlie started laughing.

"What ever are you laughing about?" Sally asked.

"I was thinkin' of the way you had the deputy all trussed up and gagged like that."

"Yeah," Cal said. "And what was real funny was the

way the marshal was laughin' at it. He said Smoke done the same thing to him."

"*Did* the same thing," Sally corrected.

"Yeah," Cal said. "But you have to admit, whether he done it or did it, it was funny, especially you doin' it too."

"He had such a dejected look about him that I almost felt sorry for him," Sally said.

The others laughed again, then Cal inhaled deeply. The aroma of Sally's cooking permeated the camp.

"They ain't nothin' no better'n bacon and beans when you're on the trail," Cal said as he walked over to examine the contents of the skillet that was sitting on a base of rocks over the open fire. A Dutch oven of biscuits was cooking nearby. "It sure makes a body hungry."

"Cal, you are incorrigible," Sally said, shaking her head. "What you mean is, there isn't *anything* better than bacon and beans," she said, correcting him.

"Yes, ma'am, I reckon that is what I meant," Cal said contritely.

"And when have you not been hungry?" she added with a chuckle.

"Well, you're right about that, Miss Sally," Cal said. "But there ain't . . . isn't," he corrected, "anything any better than bacon and beans cooked out on the trail."

"'Ceptin' maybe bear claws," Pearlie said. "Too bad you can't make us a batch of them out on the trail."

Sally smiled. "Well, maybe I will make some tomorrow night," she suggested.

Pearlie smiled broadly. "That would be . . ."

"Help me, somebody," a voice called, interrupting Pearlie in mid-sentence.

"What was that?" Sally asked.

"Help me," the voice called again.

"Can anyone see him?" Cal asked, looking all around them.

"Who is it? Who's out there?" Pearlie called. He pulled his pistol and cocked it. "Answer up. Who's out there?"

"Don't shoot," the voice called. "I ain't got no gun."

"Come toward the camp," Pearlie said. "Come slow, and with your hands up in the air, so we can see you as you come in."

"I'm comin'," the man's voice answered.

The three campers looked toward the sound of the voice until a man materialized in the darkness. As he came toward them, he kept his hands raised over his head, just as Pearlie had ordered.

"That food sure smells awful good," he said. "It's been near a week since I've et 'nything other'n some roots and bugs."

"Who are you?" Sally asked.

"The name is Yancey, ma'am," the man said. "Buford Yancey." His hands were still raised.

"You can put your hands down, Mr. Yancey," Sally said. "And you are welcome to some of our beans."

"Thank you, ma'am, that's mighty decent of you," Yancey said.

"What happened to your horse?" Cal asked.

"He stumbled and broke his leg," Yancey said. "I had to put him down."

"How'd you do that? You don't have a gun," Pearlie said.

"Oh," Yancey replied. "Well, I, uh, lost my gun. It must'a fell out of my holster. Uh, if you don't mind, I'm goin' to go over there an' get me a drink of water."

Yancey went over to the side of the stream, lay on his

stomach, stuck his mouth down into the water, and drank deeply.

A few minutes later Sally took the food off the fire, then distributed it to the others. Pearlie noticed that she took less for herself than she gave anyone else.

After they had eaten, Pearlie found a moment to talk to Sally without being overheard.

"Miss Sally, what do you aim to do about this man?" he asked.

"Do? What do you mean what do I aim to do about him?"

"What I mean is, he's eaten. Don't you think it's time to send him on his way?"

"Look at the man," Sally said. "He's half dead. We can't just send him away."

"Well, what do you plan to do with him?"

Sally sighed. "I don't know exactly," she said. "As far as I know, the closest town is still Etna. I guess we should take him back there."

"That'll make it two extra days before we get back to the ranch," Pearlie said.

"I realize that, but it can't be helped."

"So that means you're going to let him spend the night here with us?"

"Pearlie, I told you, we can't just run him off," Sally insisted.

"I don't like it. There's somethin' about him that I don't trust."

"I'll tell you what," Sally suggested. "We can take turns staying awake all night. That way, someone will always be watching him. Do you think that would make you feel better?"

"Yes, ma'am," Pearlie said. "I think that would be a good idea."

"All right, I'll take the first watch. I'll stay awake until midnight. You take the second watch, from midnight to four, and we'll get Cal to take the watch from four until dawn."

"You know your problem, Miss Sally? Your problem is you are too decent to people," Pearlie said. "Your first notion is to just take ever'one at their word. But that hasn't been my experience."

"Pearlie?" Sally said. She put her hand on his shoulder and gently shook him. "Pearlie?"

"What?" Pearlie asked groggily.

"It's your time on watch," Sally said.

"Oh," Pearlie groaned.

Sally chuckled. "Don't blame me. You said we shouldn't trust our visitor, remember?"

"Yes, ma'am, I remember," Pearlie said. He sat up and stretched, then reached for his boots. He nodded toward Yancey, who was wrapped up in a spare blanket. "Has he been quiet?"

"Sleeping like a log," Sally replied.

"It don't seem—"

"It doesn't seem," Sally corrected.

"Yes, ma'am. It doesn't seem fair that he gets to sleep all night, while we have to take turns lookin' out for him."

"Don't forget to wake Cal at four," Sally said.

During Pearlie's watch he sat very still, just listening to the snap and pop of the burning wood. For the first hour he stared into the fire. He looked at the little line of blue flame that started right at the base of the wood, watching as the blue turned to orange, then yellow, and finally into twisting ropes of white smoke as it streamed up from the fire. Orange sparks from the fire rode the heat column high into the night sky, where they added their tiny, red glow to the blue pinpoints of the stars.

Pearlie didn't know when he fell asleep, but he did know when he woke up. He woke up when he heard the metallic click of a pistol being cocked. Opening his eyes, he saw Buford Yancey standing in front of him, holding a pistol that was pointed directly at him.

"I figured if I stayed awake long enough, I'd catch one of you asleep," Yancey said.

"Where did you get the pistol?" Pearlie asked.

Yancey pointed to one of the two bedrolls.

"The boy over there had it lying on the ground alongside him. It wasn't hard to get. No harder than it's goin' to be for me to take one of them horses."

"You don't need to do that," Pearlie said. "Miss Sally was plannin' on us takin' you into Etna tomorrow. She figured you could get back on your feet there."

"Ha!" Yancey said, laughing out loud. "Now that would be a fine thing, wouldn't it? For you to take me back into Etna, after I just robbed the bank there little more'n a week ago."

"You?" Pearlie said. "You are the one who robbed the bank?"

"Yeah, me'n some pards," Yancey said. "Only they ain't much my pards now. The stole my share of the money from me."

"Was one of your pards Smoke Jensen?" Pearlie asked.

"Who? No, he ain't . . . wait a minute," Yancey said. "I think Jensen was the name of the fella we put Curt's plaid shirt on. Leastwise, that's what Dooley said his name was."

"So you admit you framed him?"

"Slick as a whistle," Yancey said with a laugh.

"Thank you, Mr. Yancey," Sally's voice said. "I will expect you to tell Marshal Turnbull that."

"What the hell?" Yancey said, spinning around quickly, only to see Sally holding her pistol on him.

"Drop your gun," Sally ordered.

Yancey smiled. "You think I'm going quake in my boots and drop my gun just because some woman's holding a pistol on me? Why, you'd probably pee in your pants if you even shot that thing." Yancey reached for her gun. "Why don't you just hand that over to me before you hurt yourself?"

Sally fired, and the tip of Yancey's little finger turned to blood and shredded flesh.

"Oww!" Yancey shouted, dropping his gun and grabbing his hand. "What the hell? You shot my finger off."

"Just the tip of it," Sally replied. "And I chose your little finger because I figure you use it less. It could be worse."

"Are you trying to tell me that you aimed at my little finger? That it wasn't no accident that you hit it?"

"Miss Sally always hits what she aims at," Pearlie said, picking up the pistol Yancey dropped.

"Get over there and sit down," Sally ordered.

"Miss Sally, I'm sorry about this," Pearlie apologized. "I must've fallen asleep. The next thing I knew, he was holding a gun on me."

"That's all right," Sally answered. "I'm sorry I didn't pay more attention to you. You said there was something about him you didn't trust. It turns out that you were right."

Chapter Twenty-one

Ford lay on top of a flat rock, looking back along the trail over which he and Fargo had just come.

"Do you see him?" Fargo asked.

"Yeah, he's back there, comin' along big as you please. He's trailin' us, Fargo. I mean he's stickin' to us like stink on shit. We can't get rid of him."

"I don't want to get rid of him," Fargo said.

"What do you mean you don't want to get rid of him? You said yourself that you thought he was trackin' down ever'one of us to kill us."

"Why did I suggest that we come through Diablo Pass? It's twenty miles farther to Bertrand this way than it would have been by going through McKenzie Pass."

"I thought it was to throw him off our trail," Ford said.

"No. It was to get him to come through here. I can't believe the son of a bitch was dumb enough to take the bait. We're playin' him like you'd play a fish."

"If you say so," Ford said, though it was clear that he still didn't understand what Fargo had in mind.

"Think about it, Ford," Fargo said. "This is the perfect place to set up an ambush. I'll stay on this side of the pass, you go on the other side. When he gets between us, we'll open up on him. We'll have him in a cross fire."

"Why do I have to go over the other side?" Ford asked. "That means I've got to climb down, go over, then climb back up."

"Want the money he took from Dooley, don't you?"

"Yeah."

"Then just do what I tell you without all the belly-aching."

"All right," Ford answered. "But after all this trouble, he better be carryin' that money with him, is all I can say."

"He's got the money," Fargo said. "It couldn't be anywhere else. But even if he didn't have it, we'd have to kill the son of a bitch before he killed us. Remember?"

"Yeah," Ford said. "I remember. All right, I'll go over to the other side."

"Get a move on it. Looks like he's comin' along pretty steady," Fargo ordered.

Smoke had noticed the hoofprints shortly after he left Dorena. Because he had identified each set of prints from his original tracking, he recognized these prints as belonging to two of the bank robbers.

Smoke was actually going to Bertrand to follow up on Dooley's declaration that two of the robbers had gone there. He had not expected to cut the trail of two of the very people he had been tracking.

Could these tracks belong to the Logan brothers? At first he thought they might. Dooley had told him they were in Bertrand, but clearly, these tracks were fresh. In fact, they were made within the last hour. If they belonged to the Logan brothers, what were they doing out here? Especially if they were holed up in Bertrand? These tracks didn't seem to be going to Bertrand, or at least, if they were going there, they weren't going by the most direct route.

As a result of having come across the fresh hoofprints, Smoke's journey to Bertrand changed from a normal ride to one of intense tracking. But within an hour after he first came across the trail, he realized, with some surprise, that they weren't trying to cover their tracks. On the contrary, it was almost as if they were going out of their way to invite him to come after them.

Why would they do that? he wondered.

Then, as he contemplated the question, the answer came to him.

They wanted him to find them, and they wanted him to find them so they could kill him. They must have been in Dorena while he was there. That meant that they probably knew that he killed Dooley. They probably also knew that he took Dooley's share of the loot.

Smoke saw that the trail was leading to a narrow draw just ahead of him. He had never been in this exact spot before, but he had been in dozens of places just like this, and he knew what to expect.

He stopped at the mouth of the draw and took a drink from his canteen while he studied the twists and turns of the constricted canyon. If the two men he was following were going to set up an ambush, this would be the place for them to do it.

Smoke pulled his long gun out of the saddle holster; then he started walking into the draw, leading his horse. Stormy's hooves fell sharply on the stone floor and echoed loudly back from both sides of the narrow pass. The draw made a forty-five-degree turn to the left just in front of him, so he stopped. Right before he got to the turn, he slapped Stormy on the rump and sent him on through.

Stormy galloped ahead, his hooves clattering loudly on the rocky floor of the canyon.

"Ford, get ready!" Fargo shouted. "I can hear him a 'comin'!"

"I see 'im!" Ford shouted back.

The canyon exploded with the sound of gunfire as Ford and Fargo began shooting from opposite sides. Their bullets whizzed harmlessly over the empty saddle of the horse, raising sparks as they hit the rocky ground, then ricocheted off the opposite wall, echoing and reechoing in a cacophony of whines and shrieks.

"Son of a bitch!" Ford shouted. "Did we get him? We must've got him! I don't think I saw nobody on the horse!"

"I don't know," Fargo replied. "I didn't see him go down. Look on the ground. Do you see him anywhere?"

"No," Ford replied. "I don't see him. Where is the son of a bitch?"

From his position just around the corner from the turn, Smoke looked toward the sound of the voices, locating one of the two ambushers about a third of the way up the north wall of the canyon. The man was squeezed in between the wall itself and a rock outcropping that provided him with a natural cover.

"Fargo, where is he?"

The one who called out this time was not the one he had located, so looking on the opposite side of the draw, toward the sound of this voice, Smoke saw a shadow move.

Smoke smiled. Now he had both of them located, and he not only knew where they were, he knew who they were. At least, he knew their first names.

"Fargo? Ford?" he called. "I'm right here. If you're looking for me, why don't you two come on down?"

"You know our names?" Ford called down to him. "Hey, Fargo, the son of a bitch knows our names! How does he know our names?"

"Oh, I know all about you two boys," Smoke called back. "I know that you robbed the bank back in Etna. I know that you killed the banker."

"Weren't us that killed the banker," Ford called back. "It was Ebenezer Dooley and Curt and Trace Logan that done that. We was across the street from the bank."

"Ford, will you shut the hell up?" Fargo called across the canyon.

"Dooley cheated the rest of you, didn't he?" Smoke called. "There was ten thousand dollars taken from the bank, but he kept half of it."

"How do you know he kept half the money?" Fargo called down to him.

"Well, now, how do you think I know, Fargo?"

"You took it, didn't you? You've got the money with you right now."

"That's right," Smoke said.

"You son of a bitch!" Fargo said. "By rights, that's our money."

Smoke laughed. "It's not your money. It belongs to anyone who can hold onto it. And right now I'm holding onto it. You know what I'm going to do now?"

"What's that?"

"I'm going to take *your* money," Smoke said.

"The hell you are," Fargo replied. "You might'a noticed, mister, they's two of us and they's only one of you."

All the while Smoke was keeping Fargo engaged in conversation, he was studying the rock face of the wall just behind the outlaw. Then he began firing. His rifle boomed loudly, the thunder of the detonating cartridges picking up resonance through the canyon and doubling and redoubling in intensity. Smoke wasn't even trying to aim at Fargo, but was, instead, taking advantage of the position in which his would-be assailant had placed himself.

Smoke fired several rounds, knowing that the bullets were splattering against the rock wall behind his target, fragmenting into deadly missiles.

"Ouch! You son of a bitch, quit it! Quit your shootin' like that!" Fargo shouted.

As Smoke figured it would, the ricocheting bullets made Fargo's position untenable and Fargo, screaming in anger, stepped from behind the rock. He raised his rifle to shoot at Smoke, but Smoke fired first.

Fargo dropped his rifle and grabbed his chest. He stood there for a moment, then pitched forward, falling at least fifty feet to the rocky bottom of the canyon.

"Fargo?" Ford shouted. "Fargo?"

"He's dead, Ford," Smoke shouted. "It's just you and me now."

Smoke watched the spot where he knew Ford was hiding, hoping to see him, but Ford didn't show himself. Smoke took a couple of shots, thinking it might force him out as it did Fargo, but he neither saw nor heard anything except the dying echoes of his own gunshots.

"Ford? Ford, are you up there?"

Then, unexpectedly, Smoke heard the sound of hoofbeats.

Damn! he thought. He should have realized that they would have their horses on the other side. Ford had slipped away.

Smoke started to step around the turn, then halted. Ford could have sent his empty horse galloping up the trail, just to fool him.

He looked cautiously around the corner, then saw that his caution, though prudent, was not necessary. Ford was galloping away.

Smoke also saw Stormy standing quietly at the far end of the draw. He whistled and Stormy ducked his head, then came trotting back up the draw toward him.

A second horse joined Stormy, and Smoke realized that it must be Fargo's horse.

In a saddlebag on Fargo's horse, Smoke found a packet of bills bundled up in a paper wrapper. The name of the bank was printed on the wrapper, along with the notation that the wrapper held one thousand dollars.

The bills were so loosely packed within the wrapper that Smoke knew there was considerably less than one thousand dollars, which, he knew, had been Fargo's share of the take.

Smoke put the roll in his saddlebag where he was keeping the money he had taken from Dooley. After that, he led the horse over to Fargo's body.

"Sorry to have to do this to you, horse," Smoke said as he lifted Fargo up and draped him over the saddle. "I know this is none of your doing, but we can't just leave him out here."

Marshal Turnball, with his chair tipped back and his feet propped up on the railing, was ensconced in his usual place in front of Dunnigan's Store. He was rolling a cigarette and paying particular attention to the task at hand when he felt Billy Frakes's hand on his shoulder.

"That's one of 'em," Billy said.

"What?"

"That's one of the bank robbers," Billy said excitedly.

"He was one of the fellers that was in front of Sikes Leather Goods lookin' at the boots when the bank was robbed."

When Turnball looked in the direction Billy Frakes had pointed, he saw four people coming toward him. There were four people, but only three horses. The woman, whom he recognized as Sally Jensen, was riding double with Cal, the younger and smaller of the two men who had come to Etna to see about her husband.

The fourth person, the one Frakes had pointed out, was riding alone. He also had a rope looped around his neck, and riding next to him, holding onto the other end of the rope, was Pearlie.

"Damn," Turnball said with a long-suffering sigh. "I thought they had left town."

Turnball tipped his chair forward and stood up.

"Maybe they come back to bring the bank robber," Frakes said.

"You're sure that fella with them is one of the bank robbers?"

"I was standin' not more'n twenty feet from him when it all happened," Frakes said. "And I got a good look at him 'cause he wasn't wearin' no mask like the ones that went into the bank. But he was waitin' outside and, when the robbers rode out of town, all of 'em shootin' and such, he was ridin' along with 'em, shootin' his gun and screamin' like a wild Indian."

The riders, seeing Turnball standing on the porch in front of Dunnigan's Store, headed his way.

"Mrs. Jensen," Turnball said politely, touching the brim of his hat. "Gents," he said to the others.

"Marshal," Sally replied.

"Who have you got here?" Turnball asked.

"This man's name is Buford Yancey," Sally said.

"Yancey has something to tell you," Sally said.

"Arrest this woman, Marshal," Yancey said. He held up his little finger, which was covered by a bandage. The bandage was reddish brown with dried blood. "She shot my finger off."

"You're lucky she didn't shoot something else off," Pearlie said. "Now tell the marshal what you told us."

"I don't know what you're talkin' about," Yancey said. "I ain't got nothin' to say."

"Are you sure about that?" Pearlie asked as he gave a hard jerk on the rope.

"Easy there," Yancey said fearfully. "You could break my neck, messin' around like that."

"Get down off my horse, Yancey," Cal said.

Scowling, Yancey got down.

"You're goin' to tell the marshal what you told us, or I aim to drag you from one end of this street to the other," Pearlie said, backing his horse up and putting some pressure on Yancey's neck.

"All right, all right," Yancey said. "I'll talk to him."

"You was one of them, wasn't you?" Frakes said. "You was one of the bank robbers. I seen you."

Yancey looked over at Sally. "I don't reckon I need to say much," he said. "The boy here's done said it for me."

"He hasn't said it all," Sally said.

"You got more to say, Yancey?" Turnball asked.

"I wasn't one of 'em what went inside," Yancey said. "Like the boy here said, he seen me standin' in front of the store across the street from the bank. I didn't go inside."

"What about the others? The ones who did stay inside? Who was they?" Turnball asked.

Yancey thought for a moment, then he nodded. "Yeah," he said. "Hell, yeah, you want to know who they was, I'll tell you. Ain't no need in coverin' up for them. Them sons of bitches stole my share of the money, and you better believe I don't intend to go to jail while they're wanderin' around free."

"First, Mr. Yancey, tell them who was not with you," Sally demanded.

"Who was not with me?" Yancey replied, a little confused by Sally's remark. Then, realizing what she was saying, he nodded. "Oh, yeah, I know what you mean. You're talkin' about Jensen," Yancey said. Yancey looked back at the marshal. "Jensen wasn't with us. He wasn't no part of the robbin' of the bank."

"What do you mean he wasn't with you? I saw him," Turnball said. "We all saw him. Nobody is likely to miss that shirt he was wearing."

"Yeah, that was Dooley's idea," Yancey said. "We put Curt Logan's shirt on him. Then we dropped a couple of them paper things that was wrapped around the money by him. We seen you and the posse when you found him. You took the bait like a rat takin' cheese." Yancey laughed. "Dooley's an evil son of a bitch, but he sure is smart."

"Dooley," Turnball said. "Would that be Ebenezer Dooley?"

The smile left Yancey's face. "Yeah, Ebenezer Dooley. He was the one behind it all, and he's the one that stole from me. I tell you true, I hope you catch him."

"We don't have to catch him," Turnball said. "He's dead."

"He's dead? The hell you say," Yancey said.

"It came in by telegram," Turnball said. "He was shot by a man named Kirby."

"Kirby?" Sally said.

"That's the name that was on the telegram," Turnball said. "Seems that Dooley shot the deputy sheriff over in Dorena, and this fella Kirby shot Dooley."

"This man Kirby," Sally said. "Is he another deputy, or something?"

"Not unless it's someone they've put on recently," Turnball said. "I've never heard of him."

"I see."

"Come on, Yancey," Turnball said. "Oh, and Mrs. Jensen, you might want to come down to the jail with me."

"Why?" Sally asked.

Turnball chuckled. "Don't worry, I ain't arrestin' you or nothin'. But I've got a feelin' that there's a reward out on Yancey. I thought you might be interested in it if there was."

"You thought right, Marshal. I would be very interested in it," Sally said.

Deputy Pike was standing by the stove, pouring himself a cup of coffee, when he heard the door open.

"You want some coff . . . ," Pike began, speaking before he turned around. He stopped in mid-sentence when he saw that Turnball had a prisoner. "Who is this?" he asked.

"This is one of the bank robbers," Turnball said. "Put him in jail."

"Yes, sir!" Pike said. "Come on, you, we've got just the place for you." Grabbing the key from a wall hook, Pike took the prisoner back to the cell, opened the door, and pushed him in. "Where'd you catch 'im?" Pike asked as he closed the door.

"I didn't catch him," Turnball answered. "She did."

"What?" Pike asked. Turning back again, he saw Jensen's wife and the two men who were traveling with her. "You!" he said. "What are you doing here?"

"Why, Mr. Pike," Sally said. "Aren't you happy to see me?"

"I'd be happy if I never saw you again," Pike said.

Turnball chuckled. "Don't worry. I won't let her throw you in jail again."

"She tricked me," Pike said.

"Yeah, I'm sure," Turnball said. He began going through several circulars. Then finding what he was looking for, he held it up for Sally. "I was right. Mr. Yancey is worth five hundred dollars."

"You said somethin' about the town offerin' two hundred and fifty dollars as well?" Pearlie said.

"I did say that, didn't I? Mrs. Jensen, it looks like you'll be getting out of here with seven hundred and fifty dollars. That ought to make you feel a little better about us."

"I'll feel much better when you send out telegrams informing everyone that my husband is no longer wanted for bank robbery and murder."

"Yes, ma'am, all the lines are open now, so I'll do that right away," he said.

"Do you think there was a reward for Ebenezer Dooley?"

"I'm sure there was."

"Good."

"Why do you say good? He's already been killed."

"I said good because I'm sure Smoke is the one who killed him."

Turnball shook his head. "No, ma'am. I told you, it was somebody named Kirby." Then he stopped. "Wait a minute. Your husband's name is Kirby, isn't it? Kirby Jensen."

"Yes."

"Do you really think it was him?"

"If Smoke was found guilty for something he didn't do,

I've no doubt but that he is hunting down the bank robbers right now in order to clear his name."

"Well, I tell you what, Mrs. Jensen. If your husband is the one who took care of Dooley, and he can have the sheriff of Dorena vouch for him, we'll be sending on another two hundred fifty dollars reward on him as well."

"Thank you," Sally said. "When will I get the reward due me?"

"I'll get a telegram off to Denver today. I figure by tomorrow we'll have authorization back. You should get all your money then."

"Hey, Marshal, if you're through talkin' about how much money you're goin' to give this woman for shootin' my little finger off, maybe you'll get the doctor to come take a look at it," Yancey called from his cell.

"Looks to me like Mrs. Jensen did a pretty good job of doctorin'," Turnball said.

"I know my rights," Yancey insisted. "I'm your prisoner. That means I got a right to have a doctor treat me."

"All right, I'll get the doc down here for you," Turnball said. "I ought to tell you, though, he likes to amputate. More'n likely he'll chop that finger clean off. Maybe even your hand."

"What?" Yancey gasped. He stepped back away from the bars. "Uh, no, never mind. She done a good enough job on me. I won't be needin' no doctor."

"I didn't think you would," Turnball said.

Pearlie and Cal were laughing at Yancey as they left the marshal's office.

"You know what, Miss Sally? With your reward money and what we have, there's almost enough money to save Sugarloaf right there," Pearlie said.

"Yes, there is."

"I tell you this. The trip back home tomorrow is going to be a lot more joyful than it was when we started out yesterday," Cal said.

"It would be if we were going back home. But we aren't going to Sugarloaf yet," Sally said.

"Where are we going?"

"We're going to find Smoke."

"How are we going to find him? I mean, where will we start?" Cal asked.

"We'll start in Dorena," Sally said. "First thing tomorrow, after we collect the reward money."

"Do you think Smoke is the one who killed Dooley?" Cal asked.

"I'd bet a thousand dollars he was," Sally said.

Chapter Twenty-two

Smoke looked back over his shoulder as he led the horse across the swiftly running stream. The horse was carrying Fargo's body, belly down, across his back. The horse smelled death and he didn't like it one little bit.

Stormy and Fargo's horse kicked up sheets of silver spray as they trotted through the stream. Smoke paused to give them an opportunity to drink. Smoke's horse, Stormy, was a smart horse and knew from experience that he should take every opportunity to drink when he could. He put his lips to the water and drank deeply, but Fargo's horse just tossed its head nervously. The horse was obviously anxious to get to where it was going so it could rid itself of its gruesome cargo.

Smoke reached over and patted Fargo's horse on the neck a few times.

"Hang on just a little longer, horse," Smoke said gently. "If what they told me back in Dorena is right, it won't be much longer, then you'll be rid of your burden."

The horse whickered, as if indicating that it understood.

"Come on," Smoke said when Stormy had drunk his fill. "Let's be on our way."

* * *

Sheriff Fawcett was sitting at his desk with a kerosene lantern spread out before him. He was cleaning the mantle when Sally, Pearlie, and Cal stepped through the door. Seeing a beautiful woman coming into his office, the sheriff smiled and stood.

"Yes, ma'am," he said. "Is there something I can do for you?"

"I hope you can help me find my husband," Sally said.

The smile left, to be replaced by a troubled frown. "Is he missing?"

"Well, not missing in that he is lost," Sally said. She smiled to ease his concern. "He is missing in that I don't know where he is."

"You think he is here in Dorena?"

"I think he has been here," Sally said. "His name is Kirby Jensen, though most people call him Smoke."

"Jensen?" Sheriff Fawcett said. "Jensen? Wait a minute. I just heard something about someone with that name." He walked over to a table that was up against the wall and started shuffling papers around. He picked up a yellow sheet of the kind that was used for telegrams. "Here it is," he said. He read the message; then his face grew very concerned and he looked up at Sally.

"Did you say Jensen was your husband?"

"Yes. My name is Sally Jensen."

"And you are looking for him?"

"I am."

Sheriff Fawcett shook his head and sighed. "Well, evidently, so is every lawman in Colorado," he said. He held up the paper. "According to this, he is an escaped prisoner, convicted of murder and robbery."

"No, he ain't!" Cal shouted in a bellicose voice.

"Cal," Sally said, holding up her hand as if to calm him down, "it's all right." She maintained her composure as she smiled at the sheriff. "What my young friend is trying to say is that the wanted notice has been rescinded."

"It's been what?"

"It has been canceled," Sally explained. "Marshal Turnball, back in Etna, sent out telegrams rescinding the notification that my husband was a wanted man."

"Why would he do that?"

"'Cause Smoke wasn't guilty, that's why," Cal said, his voice holding as much challenge as it had earlier.

"It seems that one of the bank robbers was caught," Sally said.

"Ha! It wasn't the law that caught him. Tell the sheriff who it was that caught 'im, Miss Sally," Pearlie said.

"She caught him," Cal answered, pointing proudly to Sally. "She caught 'im, and we took him in and got a reward for him."

"His name was Buford Yancey," Sally said.

Sheriff Fawcett nodded. "Yancey," he said. "Buford Yancey. Yes, I've heard that name. He's a pretty rough customer, all right."

"He ain't so rough now," Cal said. "He's over in Etna behind bars."

"And he has not only confessed to the robbery," Sally said, "he has also confessed that my husband was not involved. The actual bank robbers framed him so people would think he was guilty."

"And you say that word has been sent out to all the law agencies around the state calling back the wanted notice?" Sheriff Fawcett asked.

"He was supposed to have sent word out by telegraph," Sally said.

Again, Fawcett began looking through all the papers on

his desk. After a moment or two of fruitless search, he shook his head.

"I'm sorry. There's nothing here."

"What about your telegraph service? Is your line still up?"

"As far as I know it is," Fawcett answered. "If you'd like, Mrs. Jensen, we could walk down to the telegraph and check this out."

Sally nodded. "Yes, thank you, I would like that," she said.

The four walked from the sheriff's office down to the Western Union office. The group was unremarkable enough that no one paid them any particular attention as they passed by, other than to take a second glance at the very pretty woman who was obviously a stranger in town.

The little bell on the door of the Western Union office caused the telegrapher to look up. He stood when he saw the sheriff, and smiled when he saw the pretty woman with him.

"Can I help you, Sheriff?"

"Danny, have you got any telegrams you haven't brought down to my office yet?" Sheriff Fawcett asked.

"As a matter of fact, I have," the telegrapher said. "I didn't think there was any rush to it, so I hadn't gotten around to it yet."

The telegrapher picked up a message from his desk, then handed it to Sheriff Fawcett. Fawcett read it, then nodded.

"You're right, Mrs. Jensen," he said. "Your husband is no longer wanted."

"Except by me," Sally said. "I have to find him. You see, he doesn't know that he is no longer a wanted man."

"I see. And you are afraid of what he might do while he thinks he is wanted?"

"I'm sure that whatever he does will be justified by the law," Sally said. "For example, I am sure that he killed a man called Ebenezer Dooley right here in your town."

Sheriff Fawcett shook his head. "No, that was a man named Kirby. We have eyewitnesses who say they saw Bill Kirby engage Ebenezer Dooley . . . in self-defense, I hasten to add . . . and shoot him down."

"Was he a big man with broad shoulders, a narrow waist, blue eyes?"

"Well, yes, that sounds like him, all right," Sheriff Fawcett said.

"That's him."

"So his name isn't Kirby?" Sheriff Fawcett asked. Then he stopped in mid-sentence and chuckled. "Wait a minute, I get it now. He's calling himself Kirby from Kirby Jensen, right?"

"That's right," Sally said. "Did you say you paid him a reward?"

"Yes. Dooley had a five-hundred-dollar reward on him."

"Seven hundred fifty," Sally corrected.

"No ma'am, it was only five hundred," Sheriff Fawcett said.

"Dooley was one of the bank robbers," Sally explained. "The town of Etna added two hundred fifty dollars to the reward."

"Uh, Mrs. Jensen, if you are asking me to pay the additional two hundred fifty dollars, I got no authority to do that," the sheriff said.

"I don't need the money from you, just your verification that my husband is the one who killed Dooley."

"Well, uh, I don't know as I could actually . . ." Fawcett began, but Sally interrupted him.

"Is this the man?" she asked. She was holding an open

locket in her hand, and Fawcett leaned down to look at the picture. He studied it for a moment, then nodded.

"Yes, ma'am, that's him all right," he said.

"You'll write the letter validating that he is the one who killed Dooley?"

"Yes, ma'am, I'll be glad to do that," the sheriff said. He smiled. "I'll do better than that. Danny," he called to the telegrapher.

"Yes, Sheriff?"

"Send a telegram to the city marshal in Etna, Colorado," he said. "In the message, say that Kirby Jensen is the man who killed Ebenezer Dooley. As this was a justifiable killing, there are no charges against Jensen, and he was paid a reward for bringing Dooley to justice. Then put my name to it."

"Yes, sir," the telegrapher said as he sat down to his instrument.

"You know," the sheriff said with a smile. "Now that I know who you are talking about, I think I might even be able to help you find him. At least, I can tell you where he went from here."

"Where?"

"Bertrand," the sheriff answered.

"How far is it to Bertrand?"

"Well, there are two ways to go. Some folks go through Diablo Pass because the pass isn't quite as high. But most folks go through McKenzie Pass, which is about ten miles closer."

"Thanks," Sally said.

Chapter Twenty-three

After several hours of riding on a bumping, rattling, jerking, and dusty stagecoach, the first view of Bertrand could be quite disconcerting to its passengers. Especially to someone who had never seen the town before. Experienced passengers were often called upon to point out the town, for from the top of the pass it looked like nothing more than a small cluster of the brown hummocks and hills common to this country.

Five years after founding the town, a saloon keeper named John Bertrand was shot down in the street of his own town. The drunken drifter who killed him was lynched within an hour of his foul deed. Now, without the entrepreneurial spirit of its founder, the little town was dying, bypassed by the railroad and visited by the stagecoach but two times per week. Its only connection to the outside world was a telegraph wire, and though it was recently restrung, even it had been down for most of the winter.

Smoke stopped on a ridge just above the road leading into Bertrand. He took a swallow from his canteen and watched the stage as it started down from the pass into the town. Then, corking the canteen, he slapped his legs against the side of his horse and sloped down the long ridge, leading the horse over which Fargo's body had been thrown.

Smoke was somewhat farther away from town than the coach, but he knew he would beat it there because he was riding down the side of the ridge, whereas the coach had to stay on the road, which had many cutbacks as it came down from the top of the pass.

Smoke passed by a sign that read: WELCOME TO BERTRAND. Behind it, another sign said: THE JEWEL OF COLORADO.

Smoke wasn't at all sure that the person who wrote that sign was talking about the same town he was riding into about then. He didn't see much about the little town that would classify it as the "Jewel of Colorado."

Two dirt roads formed a cross in the middle of the high desert country. The town consisted of a handful of small shotgun houses, and a line of business buildings, all false-fronted, none painted. The saloon was partially painted, though, with LUCKY NUGGET painted in red high on its own false front.

As he rode into town, the fact that he was bringing in a corpse caused him to be the center of attention. Several people, seeing him, began to drift down the street with him to see where he was going.

Smoke was heading for one particular building, identified by black letters on a white board sign that said:

TATUM OWENS, *Sheriff.*
Bertrand, Colorado.

By the time he reached the front of the sheriff's office, more than twenty people had gathered around. Even the sheriff had come out of his office, summoned by someone who had run ahead to tell him about the strange sight of someone riding into town bringing with him a dead body.

As Smoke dismounted and tied Fargo's horse to the hitching rail, Sheriff Owens lit his pipe.

"Did you kill 'im?" the sheriff asked around the puffs that were necessary to get his pipe started.

"I did."

"I figure you must think you had a good reason to kill 'im," the sheriff said. "Otherwise, you would have left him."

"He was trying to kill me," Smoke said.

"Sounds like reason enough," Sheriff Owens said. "And if there ain't nobody to back you up, there ain't nobody here to say any different. What you plannin' on doin' with him?"

"I figured the sheriff's office was as good a place as any to leave him," Smoke replied.

"Would you happen to know his name?"

"I don't know his last name. But I heard him called Fargo," Smoke said. "He robbed a bank in Etna," Smoke added.

The sheriff nodded. "Ah, then that would be Fargo Masters."

Smoke looked up in surprise.

"How do you know that?" he asked.

The sheriff nodded. "The telegraph is up again, and word come through this mornin' tellin' about the robbery. It also named all the robbers, and put out a reward of two hundred fifty dollars for each one of them. That means you've got money comin', if we can prove this is who you say he is."

"What if I show you the money he had on him?" Smoke asked.

"You got the money from him?"

Smoke nodded. "From him, and from Ebenezer Dooley."

"If you've got the money, I'd say that's pretty good proof."

"Sheriff, what do you want me to do with the body?" a tall, skinny man asked. His long black coat and high-topped hat identified him as an undertaker.

"Find a pine box for him," the sheriff said. "If nobody claims him within a few days, you can bury him."

"Is the town going to pay?"

"Five dollars, Posey," the sheriff said. "Same as with any indigent."

"Sometimes the town don't pay," Posey complained as he took the horse by the reins and started leading it down the street to the mortuary.

"I admit we're late sometimes," Owens called after Posey. "But when you get down to it, we've always paid."

Having satisfied their curiosity as to who the corpse was, most of the gathered townspeople began moving away. The coach that Smoke had seen several minutes earlier was just arriving in town now, and it pulled to a stop at the stage depot, which was next to the sheriff's office.

"Hey, Walt, how was your trip?" the sheriff called up to the driver.

"The trip was fine, no problems," Walt replied as he set the brake and tied off the reins of his six-horse team. "Folks, this is Bertrand!" he called down.

The door to the coach opened and the passengers stepped outside. One of them glanced over toward the sheriff, then seeing Smoke, smiled broadly.

"Why, Smoke Jensen!" the passenger called over to

him. "What are you doin' here? You're a long way from home, aren't you?"

Smoke knew the passenger only as Charley. Charley was a salesman who from time to time had come into Longmont's Saloon when he was in Big Rock.

Smoke considered pretending that he didn't know what the passenger was talking about, but decided it would be less noticeable to just respond and get it over with.

"Hello, Charley," Smoke said. "I haven't seen you in a while."

"No, Big Rock isn't my territory anymore," Charley replied. "But I sure had me some friends over there. Listen, when you get back over there, you tell Louie Longmont and Sheriff Carson that ole Charley Dunn said hi, will you?"

"Sure, Charley, I'll do that," Smoke replied. He was aware that Sheriff Owens was staring hard at him.

"You're Smoke Jensen?" the sheriff asked. "Is your real name Kirby Jensen?"

"Yes," Smoke said. He poised for action. He didn't want to kill the sheriff, but he wasn't going to go back to jail either. Especially for a crime he didn't commit.

"Oh, then you must've already got the word. Otherwise, you'd still be running."

"I've already got the word?" Smoke asked. "Got what word?"

"Why, that you've been cleared," the sheriff said. "That message that come in this morning also canceled the wanted notice that went out on you." Owens laughed. "But, since we didn't have a telegraph line through to anyplace else until just the other day, we wasn't gettin' much news anyway. I found out that you was wanted and not wanted on the same day."

Smoke smiled broadly. "Well, that's good to know, Sheriff," he said.

"So, what are you going to do now? Go back home?" Sheriff Owens asked.

Smoke shook his head. "You say there is a two-hundred-fifty-dollar reward for every one who took part in the bank robbery?"

"That's right."

"That's good to know," Smoke said. He smiled. "It's also good to know that I don't have to worry about you wanting to lock me up while I go about my business."

"What business?"

"Finding the other bank robbers."

Bidding the sheriff good-bye, Smoke started toward the saloon, as much to slake his thirst as to find out more information. He tied his horse off in front, then on a whim, took the plaid shirt out of his saddlebag and put it on.

Pulling his pistol from its holster, Smoke spun the cylinder to check the loads, then replaced the pistol loosely and went inside. He had long had a way of entering a saloon, stepping in through the door, then moving quickly to one side to put his back against the wall as he studied all the patrons. Over the years he had made a number of friends, but it seemed that for every friend he made, he had made an enemy as well. And a lot of those enemies would like nothing better than to kill him, if they could. He didn't figure on making it easy for them.

As Smoke stood there in the saloon with his eyes adjusting to the shadows, he saw one of the men he was looking for. He might not have even noticed him had the man not been wearing the shirt Smoke was wearing when the men jumped him. It was a shirt that Sally had mended when Smoke tore it on a nail in the barn.

As Smoke thought about it, he began to get angrier and

angrier. He was not only angry with the man for being one of those who framed him, he was angry because the man was wearing a shirt that Sally's own hands had mended and washed.

What right did that son of a bitch have to be wearing, next to his foul body, something that Sally had touched?

The man was talking to a bar girl, and so engaged was he that he noticed neither Smoke's entrance, nor his crossing the open floor to step up next to him.

"Would you be Curt or Trace Logan?" Smoke asked.

"I'm Curt. Do I know you?"

"Let's just say that's my shirt you are wearing," Smoke said.

"What?" the man replied. For a moment he was confused; then, perhaps because Smoke was wearing the very shirt he had been wearing, he realized who Smoke was. Smoke saw the realization in the man's eyes, though he continued to protest.

"What do you mean I'm wearing your shirt? I don't know what are you talking about."

"You know what I'm talking about," Smoke said. "You, your brother, and four others set me up to take the blame for a bank you robbed in Etna. I've already taken care of two of your friends. You and Trace are next. Where is Trace, by the way?"

Curt's eyes widened, then he turned toward the bartender. "Bartender, send somebody for the sheriff," he said. "This man is an escaped convict."

"Go ahead, send somebody for the sheriff," Smoke said. "I just left his office." Smoke gave a cold, calculating smile. "I'd like him to come down here and take charge. According to the sheriff, Curt Logan is worth two hundred fifty dollars to me."

The bartender looked back and forth between the two men, not knowing who to believe.

"Dan, this man is Smoke Jensen," someone called out from the door. Although Smoke didn't realize it, Charley, the salesman, had followed him to the saloon from the sheriff's office, and was now standing just a few feet away. "I've known Mr. Jensen for years, and I'll vouch for him. And I was just down at the sheriff's office while Jensen and the sheriff were talking. Jensen's telling the truth. This man," he said, pointing toward Curt, "is lying."

"You're crazy," Logan said.

"I don't know that he is so crazy," the bartender said to Logan. "I've been wonderin' where you and your brother got all the money you two been throwing around ever since you come to town. Besides which, Jensen is wearing a shirt just like the shirt your brother is wearing. To me, that means that the story he's tellin' makes sense."

"We . . . we sold some cows, that's where we got the money. And the shirt's just a coincidence."

"Where is your brother?" Smoke asked.

Suddenly Curt went for his pistol. Smoke drew his as well, but rather than shooting him, he brought it down hard on the top of his head.

Logan went down like a sack of feed.

Smoke stared at the man on the floor. "Do you have any idea where his brother is?"

"Yeah, I know. He's upstairs," the bartender said. "Like I told you, they been spendin' money like it was water. He and this one have been keepin' the girls plumb wore out ever since they got here."

"Which room is he in?"

"Well, he's with Becky, so that'd be the second room on your left when you reach the head of the stairs. And you better watch out for Becky too. She's some taken with him now, I think. Though to be truthful, I think it's more his money than it is him."

"Thanks."

The altercation at the bar had caught the attention of all the others in the saloon, and now all conversation stopped as they watched Smoke walk up the stairs to the second floor.

When Smoke reached the room at the top of the stairs, he stopped in front of the door, then raised his foot and kicked it open.

Becky screamed, and Trace called out in anger and alarm.

"What the hell do you mean barging in here?" he shouted.

"Get up and get your clothes on," Smoke said. "There's a two-hundred-and-fifty-dollar reward out for you for robbing a bank, and I aim to collect it. I'm taking you down to the sheriff."

"The hell you are."

Smoke should have been more observant. If he had been, he would have noticed that Trace had a gun in the bed with him. From nowhere, it seemed, a pistol appeared in the outlaw's hand.

Trace got off the first shot, and Smoke could almost feel the wind as the bullet buzzed by him and slammed into the door frame.

Smoke returned fire and saw a black hole suddenly appear in Trace's throat, followed by a gushing of blood. The outlaw's eyes went wide, and he dropped the gun and grabbed his throat as if he could stop the bleeding. He fell back against the headboard as his eyes grew dim.

Becky's screaming grew louder and more piercing.

"You killed him! You killed him!" Becky shouted. She

picked up the outlaw's gun and, pointing it at Smoke, fired at him.

Becky's action surprised him even more than the fact that Trace had had the gun in bed with him. Stepping quickly toward her, he stuck his hand down to grab the gun, just as she pulled the trigger again. The hammer snapped painfully against the little web of skin between Smoke's thumb and forefinger. It brought blood, but it didn't hit the firing pin, so the gun didn't go off.

Smoke jerked the pistol away from Becky, then threw it through the window. Then, just to make certain there were no other hidden weapons, he picked up one side of the bed and turned it up on its end, dumping Trace's body and the naked bar girl out on the floor.

Becky curled up into a fetal position and began crying. Smoke looked at her for a moment, then left the room. When Smoke reappeared at the top of the stairs, he saw that everyone in the saloon was looking up to see how the drama had played out. They watched in silence as he descended the stairs; then several rushed toward him to congratulate him.

Smoke smiled back and nodded at them, but he was very subdued about it. He didn't consider killing a man to be anything you should be congratulated for. Looking toward the floor, he saw that Curt Logan was gone. Silently, he cursed himself for not tying him up before he went upstairs.

"Where did he go?" he asked.

The bartender looked toward the floor where Curt Logan had been lying, and was genuinely surprised to see that he was no longer there.

"I . . . I don't know," the bartender said. "We was all lookin' upstairs to see what was goin' to happen. I reckon he must've left when nobody was payin' attention to him."

"That's real brotherly love for Curt to leave and let Trace face me alone," Smoke said.

He walked over to the bar. "I'll have a beer," he said.

"Yes, sir, and it's on the house," the bartender replied. As the bartender took an empty mug down to the beer barrel to fill it, Smoke happened to glance toward the mirror that was behind the bar. That was when he got a quick glimpse of the reflection of Curt Logan just outside the front window. The outlaw had a gun in his hand, and he appeared to be sneaking up toward the front door.

When Smoke leaned over the bar for a better look, he happened to see the double-barrel, ten-gauge, sawed-off Greener shotgun that the bartender kept handy. Picking it up, Smoke pulled both hammers back, then turned toward the door just as Curt Logan came through the batwings with his pistol in his hand.

"You son of a bitch!" Logan shouted, shooting toward Smoke. His bullet crashed into one of the many bottles that sat in front of the mirror, shattering the bottle and sending up a spray of amber liquid. The other customers at the bar, suddenly finding themselves in the line of fire, dived to the floor and scooted toward the nearest tables.

Smoke pulled both triggers on the shotgun and it boomed loudly, filling the saloon with smoke. Curt Logan was slammed back against the batwing doors with such force as to tear them off the hinges. He landed on his back at the far side of the boardwalk with his head halfway down the steps just as Sheriff Owens, drawn by the sound of the first shots, was arriving.

When Owens came into the saloon, he saw Smoke standing at the bar, still holding the Greener. Twin wisps of smoke curled up from the two barrels.

The sheriff looked back through the broken door at the body lying on the porch; then he stepped up to the bar.

"Give me a beer, Dan," he said.

Dan drew the beer, then with shaking hands, held it toward the sheriff.

"Better let me take that before you spill all of it," the sheriff said, taking the beer. He blew the foam off, and took a drink before he spoke to Smoke, who by now had put the shotgun down and picked up his own beer.

"Let me guess," the sheriff said. "You've just earned yourself another two hundred fifty dollars."

"Five hundred," Smoke replied. "That's Curt Logan. His brother Trace is upstairs."

Suddenly there was a commotion at the door and, as fast as thought, Smoke drew his gun and turned toward the sound.

"Hello, Smoke," Sally said. "How've you been?"

Sally had a gun in her hand, having just used it as a club. Ford DeLorian was lying facedown on the floor, unconscious. His right arm was stretched out before him, his fingers wrapped around a pistol.

Pearlie bent down and took the pistol from Ford's hand.

Cal came in right behind Sally and Pearlie, and Sally came over quickly to embrace Smoke.

"Sheriff Owens, this is my wife, Sally."

"Sheriff," Sally said, smiling sweetly. "I hope your aren't planning on arresting my husband for bank robbery. Because I'm here to tell you that he has been cleared."

"Yes, ma'am, I know that," Sheriff Owens said. "I was just tellin' him that the state owes him seven hundred fifty dollars."

"Make that a thousand dollars," Smoke said, nodding toward the man who was just beginning to regain consciousness. "His name is Ford DeLorian."

"I guess that explains why he was planning to shoot

you," Sheriff Owens said. "All right, I stand corrected. The state owes you one thousand dollars."

"No," Sally said. "You were right the first time. It's just seven hundred fifty."

"What are you talking about?" Smoke asked. "He was one of the bank robbers, and there is a two-hundred-fifty-dollar reward for each of them."

"I know," Sally said. She smiled at Smoke. "But this two hundred and fifty dollars is mine."

As Ford came to, he looked around in confusion, wondering what everyone was laughing at.

RAMPAGE OF THE MOUNTAIN MAN

Chapter One

Willow Creek, Colorado

A heavy, booming thunder rolled over the breaks, and gray veils of rain hung down from ominous, black clouds that crowded the hills. Though it had not yet reached him, the storm was moving quickly, and Smoke Jensen took a poncho from his saddlebag and slipped it on to be prepared for the impending downpour.

Smoke was on his way to Denver, and he was butt-sore from riding. Looking to hunker down from the approaching storm, he saw the little town of Willow Creek rising before him. The town had no more than half-a-dozen commercial buildings, and about three dozen houses.

Smoke leaned forward and patted his horse on the neck.

"What do you say that we find us a place to ride this storm out?" Smoke asked his horse. Often on long, lonely rides, Smoke wanted to hear a human voice, even if it was his own. Talking to his horse provided him with an excuse for talking aloud, without really talking to himself.

"A livery for you, and maybe supper and a beer for me," he continued in his one-sided conversation.

The first few drops of rain had just started when Smoke

rode in through the big open door of the Jim Bob Corral. His nostrils were assailed with the pungent but familiar smell of hay, horseflesh, and horse manure. To a city person the odor might be unpleasant, but to Smoke, the aroma was almost comforting. Smoke took off his poncho and rolled it up. He had just finished tying it back onto his saddle when a boy of about sixteen appeared, having come from somewhere deep in the shadows of the barn.

"You wantin' to board your horse here, mister?" the boy asked.

"Yes," Smoke answered. "Find a dry place for him, rub him down, and give him oats." Smoke gave the boy a dollar.

"How long?" the boy asked.

"Just tonight."

"Then it's only a quarter," the boy said. "I'll get your change."

"You keep the change," Smoke said. "Just take extra care of my horse."

A broad smile spread across the boy's face. "Mister, the folks stayin' over to the Dunn Hotel won't be gettin' no better treatment than this here horse."

"I appreciate that," Smoke said.

Smoke looked across the street at the saloon.

"Do they serve food in the saloon?" he asked.

"Yes, sir, and it's good food too," the boy said. "My ma cooks there."

Smoke smiled. "Then I know I will enjoy it."

The rain was coming down pretty steadily now as Smoke hurried across the street for the saloon. Stepping inside, he took off his hat, then poured water from the crown as he looked around. For a town so small, the saloon was surprisingly full. It even had a piano, at which a piano player was grinding away in the back.

More than half the patrons in the saloon turned to look at him, and as they realized he was not a local, even more turned to see who the stranger was in their midst.

The barkeep moved toward him when Smoke stepped up to the bar.

"Hope you ain't put out none by ever'one lookin' at you, but we don't get a lot of visitors here, especially on a night like this."

"A night like this is what drove me here," Smoke replied.

The bartender chuckled. "Yes, sir, I see what you mean. What's your pleasure?"

"I'd like a beer."

"Yes, sir, one beer comin' up."

A moment later, the bartender put a mug of golden beer with a frothy head in front of Smoke. Smoke blew off some of the head, then took a long swallow. After a full day of riding, the beer tasted very good to him and he took another deep drink before he turned his back to the bar to have a look around the place that called itself The Gilded Lily.

A card game was going on in the corner and Smoke watched it for a few minutes while he drank his beer.

Smoke's peripheral vision caught someone coming in through the back door, and turning, he saw a tall, broad-shouldered man, wearing a badge. Because he had just come in from the rain, water was dripping from the lawman's sweeping mustache.

"I'm lookin' for a man named Emerson Pardeen," the man said.

One of the cardplayers stood up slowly, then turned to face the man with the badge.

"I'm Emerson Pardeen. Who the hell are you?"

"The name is Buck Wheeler. *Marshal* Buck Wheeler," he added, coming down hard on the word "Marshal."

"Yeah? Well, what do you want with me?"

"I'm taking you back to Dodge City to stand trial for the murder of Jason Tibbs."

"Dodge City is in Kansas, this is Colorado. You got no jurisdiction here."

"Maybe I should've told you I'm a United States marshal," Wheeler added. "I've got jurisdiction everywhere."

"Yeah? Well, Mr. United States Marshal Buck Wheeler, I ain't goin' back to Dodge City with you," Pardeen said.

"Oh, you're going back all right," Wheeler said. "Either sitting in your saddle, or belly-down over it."

Realizing that a gunfight was very likely, the others who had been sitting at the table jumped up and moved out of the way, a couple of them moving so quickly that their chairs fell over.

The marshal pulled his gun and pointed it at Pardeen. "Now, shuck out of that gunbelt, slow and easy-like," he ordered.

Pardeen shook his head. "No, I don't think so. I think maybe I'm just goin' to call you on this one."

"Whatever you say, Pardeen. Whatever you say," the marshal replied.

Smoke, like the others, was watching the drama unfold, when he heard a soft squeaking sound as if weight were being put down on a loose board. The sound caused him to look up toward the top of the stairs. When he did so, he saw a man standing there, aiming a shotgun at the back of the marshal.

"Marshal, there's a gun at your back!" Smoke shouted. Concurrent with Smoke's warning, the man wielding the shotgun turned it toward Smoke.

"You sorry son of a bitch!" he shouted.

Smoke had no choice then. He dropped his beer and pulled his pistol, firing just as the man at the top of the stairs squeezed his own trigger. The shotgun boomed loudly. The heavy charge of buckshot tore a large hole in the top and side of the bar, right where Smoke had been standing. Some of the shot hit the whiskey bottles in front of the mirror, and one of the nude statues behind the bar. Like shrapnel from an exploding bomb, pieces of glass flew everywhere. The mirror fell except for a few jagged shards, which hung in place where the mirror had been, reflecting distorted images of the dramatic scene playing out before it.

Smoke's single shot had not missed, and the man with the shotgun dropped his weapon. His eyes rolled up in his head and he fell, twisting around so that he slid down the stairs on his back and headfirst, following his clattering shotgun to the ground floor. The wielder of the shotgun lay at the foot of the stairs, with his head on the floor and his legs splayed apart stretching back up the bottom four steps. His sightless eyes were open and staring up toward the ceiling.

The sound of the two gunshots had riveted everyone's attention on that exchange, and while their attention was diverted from him, Pardeen took the opportunity to go for his own gun. Suddenly, the saloon was filled with the roar of another gunshot as Pardeen fired at the marshal who had confronted him.

Marshal Wheeler had made the fatal mistake of being diverted by the gunplay between Smoke and the shotgun shooter. Pardeen's bullet struck the marshal in the forehead and the impact of it knocked him back on a nearby table. The marshal lay belly-up on the table with his head hanging down on the far side while blood dripped from the hole in his forehead to form a puddle below him. His gun fell from his lifeless hand and clattered to the floor. Pardeen then swung his pistol toward Smoke.

"Mister, this isn't my fight," Smoke said. "We can end it here and now." Smoke put his pistol back in its holster.

As he realized that he now had the advantage, a big smile spread across Pardeen's face. "Oh, it's goin' to end all right," Pardeen said. "'Cause I aim to end it right now." Pardeen cocked his pistol.

Those who were looking on in morbid fascination were surprised by what happened next, because even as Pardeen was cocking his pistol, Smoke drew and fired. His bullet caught Pardeen in the center of his chest and Pardeen went down. He sat up, then clutched his hand over the wound as blood spilled between his fingers.

"How the hell did you do that?" he asked. He coughed once—then he fell back dead.

"What's goin' on in here?" a voice asked. "What's all the shootin'?"

When Smoke turned toward the sound of the voice, he saw a man dripping water onto the floor as he stood just inside the open door. Because the man was standing in the shadows, Smoke couldn't quite make out his features.

"Step into the light so I can see you," Smoke said.

"Mister, do you know who you are talking to?" the man in the door asked.

Smoke pulled the hammer back, and his pistol made a deadly metallic click as the sear engaged the cylinder. "Doesn't much matter who I'm talking to. In about one second you'll be dead if you don't step into the light."

This time the man moved as ordered. Doing so enabled Smoke to see the badge on the man's shirt, and he let the hammer down on his pistol, then dropped it back into his holster.

"Sorry, Sheriff," Smoke said. "I didn't know you were the law."

"What happened here?"

"I'll tell you what happened," one of the other card-players said.

"Who are you?"

"The name is Corbett." Corbett pointed to Smoke. "This here fella just kilt three men. He kilt the marshal, Eddie Phillips, and Emerson Pardeen."

The sheriff made a grunting sound. "Now you tell me, Corbett, just why would this fella kill the marshal *and* Pardeen? Marshal Wheeler stopped by my office not ten minutes ago to tell me he was here to arrest Pardeen, so I know it isn't very likely that Marshal Wheeler and Pardeen would be on the same side in this fracas."

"Hell, Sheriff, I don't know why he done it. Maybe you need to ask him."

"All right, I'll ask him," the sheriff said. "Did you kill all three of these men, mister?"

"No. I only killed two of them," Smoke replied.

Inexplicably, the sheriff chuckled. "I see. You just killed two of them. So that makes you what? One-third innocent?"

"One-hundred-percent innocent," Smoke replied. "I only killed the ones who were trying to kill me. And in my book that is self-defense."

"He's lyin', Sheriff," Corbett said. "He kilt Phillips and Pardeen in cold blood."

"Oh, so now you are saying he only killed two of them?"

"In cold blood, yes," Corbett said.

"Corbett is the one who is lyin', Sheriff," the bartender

said. "This fella is telling the truth. Eddie Phillips shot first. He was standin' up there at the head of the stairs holdin' a scattergun pointed at the marshal's back. This fella shouted a warnin' to the marshal, and Phillips turned the gun on him. Take a look at the bar here, and you'll see what I'm talkin' about. Hell, it was a wonder I wasn't kilt my ownself. Then Pardeen kilt Marshal Wheeler and swung his gun around toward this fella, tellin' him he was fixin' to kill him too. And what happened then, you ain't goin' to believe."

"Try me," the sheriff said.

"Well, sir, this here fella had already put his gun away. Pardeen had the drop on him, and was pullin' back the hammer when this fella drew and shot him. Damn'dest thing I ever seen."

The sheriff stroked his chin as he looked at Smoke. "Is what he saying true?"

Smoke nodded. "It's like the barkeep said. Pardeen was about to shoot me."

"Pardeen wasn't about to shoot him," Corbett said. "He was just goin' to hold him for killin' Phillips and the marshal."

"Hold him?"

"Yeah, Pardeen was goin' to hold him until you got here," Corbett said.

Several in the saloon laughed then.

"Tell you what, Sheriff. You arrest him, I'll testify against him at his trial."

"Corbett," the sheriff said. "I'm not aware that there is any paper out on you, but that might be because I haven't looked hard enough."

Corbett's eyes narrowed. "You ain't goin' to find any

paper on me, Sheriff. The one you should arrest is this fella."

The sheriff looked around the saloon at the other patrons, who were still watching the drama.

"Anyone in here back up what Corbett is saying?" the sheriff asked.

Several responded at once.

"He ain't tellin' it the way I seen it," one of the other customers said. "I seen it the same way the bartender told it."

"That's the way it looked to me, too," another said.

"Yeah, ever' word the bartender said is the gospel."

The sheriff held up his hand. "So what I'm hearin' is, nobody backs up Corbett's version of the story?"

Everyone was quiet, and the sheriff looked at Corbett. "Looks like a clear case of self-defense to me," he said.

Corbett looked at Smoke. "Pardeen was my friend," he said. "I don't like the way you shot him down like that. Maybe I'll just settle the score myself."

"No!" the sheriff said. "There's been enough killin' for one night."

"What's your name, mister?" Corbett asked.

"Jensen. Kirby Jensen. But most folks just call me Smoke."

There was a collective gasp from everyone in the saloon.

"Smoke Jensen," one unidentified speaker said. "No wonder he could do what he done. Ain't nobody nowhere no faster'n Smoke Jensen."

"Are you the Smoke Jensen from over by Big Rock?" the sheriff asked. "That Smoke Jensen?"

"I have a ranch just outside Big Rock, yes," Smoke replied. He knew that the sheriff was trying to determine if he was *the* Smoke Jensen, but humility prevented him from elaborating.

"I'll be damned," the sheriff said. "What are you doing in Willow Creek?"

"I'm just passing through, on my way to Denver," Smoke said.

The sheriff looked over at Corbett, who had also recognized the name.

"Corbett, you still want to settle accounts with this fella?"

Corbett stroked his chin nervously. "Uh, no, Sheriff, it's like you said, there's been enough killin' for one night."

Corbett pointed at Smoke. "But I think maybe you ought to know that Pardeen has a brother named Quince. He ain't goin' to like it that you kilt Emerson, and one of these days you'n him are goin' to run across each other." Corbett smiled, a dry, humorless smile. "And when you two do run into each other, well, I would like to be there to see it."

"That wouldn't be a threat now, would it, Corbett?" the sheriff asked.

"No threat," Corbett said. "Just a friendly warnin', so to speak."

"There ain't nothin' about you friendly," the sheriff said. "If I was you, Corbett, I'd leave town right now."

"In case you ain't noticed, Sheriff, there's a storm goin' on out there," Corbett said.

"Because I'm going to go back to my office and look for a dodger on you," the sheriff continued, as if he had not even heard Corbett. "And if I can't find one, I may just come back and arrest you anyway."

Corbett glared at Smoke and the sheriff for a moment longer. Then he picked up his hat and started toward the door. "I'll be goin' now."

"Wait!" the sheriff called after him.

Corbett stopped and looked back.

"What about your pards?" The sheriff asked, pointing at Pardeen and Phillips.

"What about 'em?" Corbett replied.

"Are you just goin' to walk out and leave them layin' here? Aren't you going to wait until the undertaker comes so you can make burial arrangements?" the sheriff asked.

"Hell, they ain't either one of 'em my kin. That means they ain't my responsibility," Corbett said. "Just put 'em anywhere."

"I see. Friendship don't mean that much to you, does it?" the sheriff asked.

"They was my friends when they was alive. They're dead," Corbett said as if, somehow, that justified his indifference to them. He pushed through the batwing doors and walked out into the pouring rain.

"Are you planning on staying in town for long, Mr. Jensen?" the sheriff asked.

"The name's Smoke, Sheriff," Smoke said in a friendly tone. "I had only planned to stay the night, just long enough to ride out the storm. But I reckon I can stay a bit longer if you think that's necessary."

The sheriff looked at the bodies still lying on the saloon floor. "No," he said, shaking his head. "There are enough witnesses here to verify what happened. I see no need for getting a judge to come this far just for an inquest that we know how it's going to turn out."

"If you do need me for anything, just get in touch with Sheriff Carson in Big Rock."

"I'm sure there won't be a need for that," the sheriff replied. "Oh, but Smoke, there's one thing Corbett said that you should take to heart."

"What's that?"

"Quince Pardeen. Do you know him?"

Smoke shook his head. "I've heard his name, but I can't say that I know him."

"He's good with a gun, but that ain't the thing that makes him so dangerous. What makes him dangerous is the fact that he is a killer, and he don't particular care how he kills. You look out for him."

"I will, Sheriff," Smoke replied. "And thanks for the warning."

Chapter Two

Denver wasn't the largest city Smoke had ever seen, but it was the largest city in Colorado and as Smoke rode down Wynkoop Street, he had to maneuver his horse from side to side in order to negotiate his way through the heavy traffic of coaches, carriages, and wagons.

There was a large banner stretched across the street, and looking up, Smoke smiled when he saw the name on it.

COLORADO HONORS MATT JENSEN

This was a proud moment for Smoke, having Matt honored by the State of Colorado.

As a young boy, Matt Cavanaugh had run away from an orphanage, and would have died had Smoke not found him shivering in a snowbank in the mountains. Smoke took him to his cabin and nursed him back to health.

It had been Smoke's intention to keep the boy around only until he had recovered, but Matt wound up staying with Smoke until he reached manhood. During the time Matt lived with Smoke, he became Smoke's student, learning everything from Smoke that Smoke had learned from Preacher many years earlier, including the most important lesson of all, how to be a man of honor.

By the time Matt reached the age of eighteen, he was skilled in everything from the use of weapons to fighting to tracking, hunting, and camping. Feeling that the time was right, he left to go on his own. Smoke did not have the slightest hesitancy over letting him leave because Matt had become one of the most capable young men Smoke had ever seen.

Just before Matt left, he surprised Smoke by asking permission to take Smoke's last name as his own. Smoke was not only honored by the request, he was touched, and to this day there was a bond between them that was as close as any familial bond could be.*

Smoke and Matt had shared their time together long before Smoke married Sally, and long before his two most loyal hands, Pearlie and Cal, had come to work at Sugarloaf. But Sally understood the bond between Smoke and Matt, and it was she who suggested that Smoke go to Denver for the ceremony.

After getting a room at the hotel, Smoke took a bath and put on a suit, then went downstairs and walked through the lobby to a large ballroom that was being used as a reception hall. Through the open door of the room, he could see several well-dressed men and women standing around, laughing and talking.

A large man was standing near the open door, looking out into the lobby. By the man's demeanor and by the expression on his face, Smoke could see that he was not a guest of the reception, but was a guard. The guard came toward Smoke, shaking his head and with his hand extended.

* *The Last Mountain Man*

"Sir, this is a closed reception," the guard said.

"That's good," Smoke said. "It shouldn't be open for just anyone. Why, there's no telling what kind of disreputable figure might try to come in."

"You don't understand, sir," the guard said. "I'm talking about you. You can't come in here."

"Wait a minute. Are you calling me a disreputable figure?"

"No, sir, I'm just telling you that this is a closed reception and unless you have a personal invitation from the governor, you cannot come in."

"Well, the gentleman being honored and I are old friends," Smoke said.

"Do you have an invitation?"

"No."

The guard smiled triumphantly. "Well, if you were old friends, you would have an invitation now, wouldn't you? I'm sorry, sir, but you can't come in. I'm going to have to ask you to leave."

"Why don't we just ask the man being honored?" Smoke suggested. He started into the room.

"Sir, if you don't leave now, I am going to personally throw you out of here!"

Smoke looked at the guard. The guard was a big man and it was obvious that he could handle himself. But at the same time Smoke was looking the guard over, the guard was taking stock of Smoke, and Smoke could see by the expression on his face that he wasn't looking forward to any encounter with someone Smoke's size.

Smoke sighed. The guard was just doing his job.

"All right," Smoke said. "I don't want to cause any trouble." He pointed to the lobby. "I'll wait out here. I would appreciate it, though, if you would tell Matt Jensen that Smoke is here."

At that moment, the governor happened to glance over toward the door and saw Smoke standing in the door. Breaking into a wide smile, the governor came over to extend a personal greeting.

"Smoke Jensen," Governor John Long Routt said, extending his hand. "How good to see you."

"Hello, John," Smoke replied, returning the smile.

"Governor, this man doesn't have an invitation," the guard said.

"Really? Well, don't worry about it, Mitchell," the governor said. "Mr. Jensen and I are old friends."

"Oh. Mr. Jensen, I'm sorry I didn't know. I hope you don't take offense."

"Don't be sorry, my friend," Smoke said. "You were just doing your job. And, if I may say so, you were doing it quite well."

"Uh, yes, sir. Thank you, sir. But you should'a said you were a friend of the governor. You said you were a friend of the man being honored."

"Indeed he is, Mitchell," Governor Routt said. "In fact, he is much more than a friend. Perhaps you didn't catch his last name. It is Jensen."

"Jensen? Oh, you mean like Matt Jensen, the man getting the award tonight?"

"Yes," Governor Routt said. "Come with me, Smoke, I'm sure Matt is looking for you."

Smoke shook his head. "I doubt it," he said. "I didn't tell him I was coming. I wanted to surprise him."

"Oh. Well, that is even better. Come along."

Smoke followed the governor through a cloud of aromatic tobacco and pipe smoke. He saw Matt before Matt saw him. It was easy to pick Matt out from the crowd. His young protégé stood over six feet tall with broad shoulders and narrow hips. His blond hair seemed even more yellow than Smoke remembered.

Matt didn't see Smoke right away, because he had his back turned and he was surrounded by almost half-a-dozen very beautiful women, each woman vying for his attention. As Smoke approached, the women broke out into laughter over some story Matt was telling.

"You always were able to spin a good yarn," Smoke said.

Recognizing Smoke's voice, Matt turned toward his mentor with a broad smile on his face.

"Smoke! What are you doing here?"

"You are getting an award from the governor, aren't you?" Smoke replied. "I had to be here."

Matt took Smoke's hand in his and the two shook hands and clasped each other on the shoulder.

"Ladies, this is Smoke Jensen," Matt said.

"Did you say Jensen?" one of the women asked.

"I sure did."

"Is he your brother?" another asked.

Matt nodded. "Yes, indeed," Matt said. "Smoke is my brother."

There was a dinner after the reception, and though Smoke offered to leave, he was persuaded to stay when he learned that the governor had made special arrangements for him at the head table. When all were seated, Governor Routt tapped his spoon on the crystal goblet. The clear ringing sound could be heard above all the laughter and conversation, and it had the desired effect of silencing the guests.

"Ladies and gentlemen, it is my distinct honor and

privilege tonight to host this banquet in honor of Matthew Jensen, one of Colorado's leading citizens.

"Last winter during an attempted train robbery, some bandits killed both the engineer and the fireman of the Midnight Flyer. Now, the dead man's throttle is supposed to stop the train anytime the engineer is incapacitated, but it failed, and rather than stopping the train as the bandits planned, their action caused a runaway train. Matt Jensen was a passenger on that train. And while he knew nothing about the attempted holdup, he did realize, rather quickly, that the train was in great danger. He knew also that, somehow, he would have to get to the engine.

"The only way for him to get to the engine, was to crawl along the top of the swaying, ice-covered cars on a train that was speeding through the dark at sixty miles per hour. Matt finally managed to reach the engine and stop the train, just before it rounded a sharp turn. Had he not succeeded, the speed they were traveling would have sent the train, and all one hundred thirty-one passengers, over the side of a mountain to a sure and certain death."

The governor paused in his speech long enough to enable the crowd to react with exclamations of awe and wonder at Matt's skill and bravery. The crowd did just as he expected, and the governor waited until it was quiet again before he continued with his proclamation.

"And now, as governor of the State of Colorado, I hereby issue this proclamation declaring this day to be officially entered into the state historical records as Matthew Jensen Day."

The presentation was greeted with applause and cheers for Matt, who despite the shouts of "Speech!" managed only to mumble his thanks.

Following the reception and dinner, Smoke was surprised by the number of people who, after congratulating Matt, came to shake *his* hand.

At breakfast the next morning, Smoke commented on his surprise over the number of people who had made a special effort to greet him.

"You shouldn't be surprised," Matt replied. "Surely you know that you are one of the best-known men in the entire state of Colorado. Why, if you ran for governor today, I've no doubt but that you would be elected."

Smoke chuckled. "Don't tell John that," he said. "Though he has no need to worry. I have no intention of ever entering politics. But maybe you should. You are getting quite an enviable reputation yourself, and you are still young enough—why, you could have a very successful political career."

"Thanks, but no, thanks," Matt replied, clearly uncomfortable with any such suggestion. Clearing his throat, he changed the subject. "How is Sally?"

"Sally sends her love."

"You tell her that I send mine as well," Matt said.

"I'll do that," Smoke said, putting some money on the table as he stood.

"No," Matt said resolutely. He picked the money up and gave it back. "I'm buying breakfast."

Smoke pocketed the money and laughed. "All right," he said. "But don't you think for one moment that a measly breakfast is going to pay me back for all the meals I furnished you when you were a snot-nosed kid."

Matt laughed as well and walked to the door with his friend. It was always like this when the two encountered each other. Matt had never made an effort to dissuade Smoke from going, nor had he ever put forth an offer to join him. Each man was supremely confident in his own life, and in the absolute certainty that their friendship would remain strong despite lengthy and distant separation.

"Smoke?" Matt called as Smoke mounted his horse.

Smoke swung into the saddle, then patted his horse on the neck before he responded.

"Yes?"

"You take care, you hear? You're the only family I have."

Smoke touched the brim of his hat and nodded. "I'll do that, Matt," he replied.

As Smoke reached the outskirts of Denver, he had to stop at the railroad tracks to wait for a train to pass. He sat in his saddle and watched the windows slide by, nodding at a couple of the passengers who had nodded at him.

One of the passengers on the train was Trent Williams, and though Williams did not acknowledge the cowboy who sat on his horse alongside the track, he did see him. Then, just after they passed the cowboy, Williams heard the hiss and squeal of the brakes. As the train started to slow, Williams took an envelope from his inside jacket pocket and pulled a well-read letter from the envelope, opened it, then read it again.

Dear Mr. Williams,

Your offer to buy fifty-one per cent of the Miners Bank and Trust has been received, and our board asks that you come to Denver to present your proposal in person.

We are in agreement that we would like to have

you run our bank, but there is some concern as to whether we should turn over absolute control to one man, as would be the case if you were to acquire fifty-one per cent of the stock. We look forward to meeting you, and to discussing at length the details of the sale. Please advise us when you will arrive. I will meet you at the depot to take you to the bank, where the board meeting will take place. In order that you may recognize me, I will be wearing a red feather in the band of my hat.

Sincerely,
Vernon Bess

Williams put the letter away as the train screeched to a halt. When he stepped out onto the platform, he saw a man wearing a hat with a red feather in the band.

"Mr. Bess?" he asked.

The man smiled and extended his hand. "Yes, you are Mr. Williams, I presume?"

"I am."

"I have a carriage here," Bess said. "The board meeting will be held at ten o'clock this morning. Do you have luggage?"

"I do, yes."

Bess made a motion toward the driver of the carriage, and the driver went to retrieve Williams's luggage.

"I think you will have no trouble with the board. As president of the Bank of Salcedo in Wyoming, you have just the kind of experience that can make a success of our bank. Although I must say that at first the board members were a little put off by your insistence on owning fifty-one percent. I think you will have to explain why you feel that is necessary."

"It is absolutely necessary if I am to make a success of the bank," Williams said.

"I'm sure you will be able to make your case satisfactorily," Bess replied.

The board, which was made up of investors and businessmen from Denver, had gathered at the bank for the meeting and they greeted Vernon Bess when he arrived.

"Gentlemen of the board, it is my pleasure to introduce Mr. Trent Williams. As you know, Mr. Williams is president of the Bank of Salcedo. I have done research on that bank and find that it is one of the most successful and fiscally sound banks in all of Wyoming. I believe him to be just the man we are looking for."

Williams acknowledged the introduction, then spoke to the board for a few minutes about his plans for the bank. Then he asked if there were any questions.

"Mr. Williams, why do you insist on buying fifty-one percent of our bank?" one of the board members asked.

"If I am going to make this bank successful, I must have total freedom of operation," Williams explained. "With fifty-one percent, I will not have to be bound by any restrictions placed on me by the board."

"So, what you are saying is that you want to make us irrelevant."

"Well, I wouldn't put it quite that way," Williams replied. "I will, of course, be open to any suggestions the board might have."

"I don't know if I can go along with that. After all, I have a lot of money invested in this bank. What if you are wrong and the bank fails?"

"I will have a lot more money invested than you,"

Williams said. "That means I have even more incentive than you to make the bank succeed."

"Elmer, think about it," Bess said to the hesitant board member. "He's not going to invest fifty thousand dollars, then let the bank fail."

"I agree," one of the other board members said. "If Mr. Williams needs freedom of action to save the bank, I say let's give it to him. God knows we haven't been doing very well ourselves. And this way, we'll be able to recoup some of our money while still maintaining an investment. If he succeeds in making the bank successful, we will congratulate ourselves for having made such a sound decision."

"All right," said Elmer. "I just wanted to ask the question, that's all. How soon can we expect the fifty thousand dollars?" he asked Williams.

"I will have to return to Salcedo and put my affairs in order there," Williams said. "It would not be fair to my employers to leave without giving adequate notice."

"An honorable thing for you to do," Bess said. "All the more reason I believe we should accept the proposal. I now call for a vote."

The board voted to accept the proposal, with even Elmer voting "aye." Williams accepted the congratulations of the board, then left the bank to walk down to the hotel. Before getting a room at the hotel, he stopped at the Western Union Office to send a telegram.

UNDERSTAND YOU HAVE NEED FOR
CATTLE STOP PLEASE ADVISE ME
OF BEST PRICE PER HEAD STOP
REPLY TRENT WILLIAMS SALCEDO
WYOMING TERRITORY STOP

Chapter Three

Smoke had been home for two weeks when he was awakened one morning by the aroma of breakfast cooking. When he got dressed and went into the kitchen, he saw that Sally was preparing a veritable feast: eggs, bacon, biscuits, gravy, and fresh-baked bear claws. Pearlie and Cal were already in the dining room, drinking coffee and looking on hungrily.

"You boys are up early," Smoke said, speaking to his two longtime and most loyal hands.

"How could I sleep with Pealie's stomach growlin' so?" Cal asked.

"Oh? Was your stomach growling, Pearlie?" Smoke teased.

"How could it not be?" Pearlie replied. "There I was, sleepin' out there in the bunkhouse all peaceful like, when all of a sudden I started smellin' the most wonderful smells. You doggone right my stomach started growlin'."

"So, me'n Pearlie come in here and seen Miz Sally just cookin' away," Cal said.

"So, Miz Sally, ain't it about ready?" Pearlie asked. "All them smells got me so hungry I can't hardly stand it."

Sally sighed. “Pearlie, I swear, your grammar is so atrocious that it makes me cringe.”

“Well, yes’m, I mean bein’ as you was a schoolmarm ’n all a’fore you and Smoke married up, well, I reckon it’d be only natural that you wouldn’t think I talk all that good,” Pearlie said.

Sally put her hands over her ears. “Ahhh!” she said. “Smoke, shoot him! Shoot him right now before he says another word!”

“No, ma’am!” Pearlie said. “Leastwise, not till I’ve et some of this here breakfast.”

Sally laughed, and shook her head. “You are incorrigible,” she said.

“Yes’m, I reckon I am,” Pearlie said. “I’m hungry too.”

“Go sit at the table, all of you. I’ll bring it to you.”

After the huge breakfast, when Smoke finished his coffee, Sally jumped up from the table and refilled his cup.

“You’re being awfully nice, Sally,” Smoke said.

“Can’t I be nice to my husband if I feel like it?” Sally replied with a sweet smile.

“You’ll get no argument from me,” Smoke said, returning the smile.

“I swear, Miz Sally, if this ain’t about the best breakfast I done ever et anywhere,” Pearlie said.

“Ha!” Cal said. “It’s come to my mind, Pearlie, that anything you eat is the best thing you ever ate.”

“Well, yeah, I do like to eat, there ain’t no denyin’ that. But this here breakfast is particular good.”

Cal nodded. “I’ll have to agree with you on that. Why the big feed, Miz Sally?”

“No particular reason,” Sally answered.

Smoke stared at his wife over the rim of his coffee cup. Seeing his intense stare, Sally looked away.

"Another bear claw, darling?" she asked.

"What is it, Sally?" Smoke asked. "What is going on?"

"What makes you think something is going on?"

"Because I know you, Sally. We're married, remember?"

"All right, I'll tell you," Sally replied.

Sally poured herself a cup of coffee, then sat back down before she went on.

"Do you remember the big winter freeze we had a couple of years ago? We lost over eighty percent of our herd. Do you remember that?"

"Of course I remember that," Smoke said. "We not only lost our herd, we almost lost Sugarloaf."

Sally reached back to the sideboard and got a small book, which she slid across the table to Smoke.

"What is that?" Smoke asked.

"It's the *Farmer's Almanac,*" Sally said. "According to the *Almanac,* this winter is going to be as bad as that one was."

"Oh, that's bad," Pearlie said. "That's really bad."

"And that's why the big breakfast?" Smoke asked. "We are celebrating the fact that we are going to have another bad winter?"

Sally shook her head. "No, we are celebrating the fact that a bad winter isn't going to be as big a problem for us this year."

Smoke drummed his fingers on the table. "What makes you think it won't be a problem?"

"After that last big freeze, you built shelter areas, remember?"

"Of course I remember. But we can only shelter about half of our herd."

"That's all we'll need to shelter," Sally said.

"Sally, it won't put Sugarloaf in danger like the last freeze-up, but do you have any idea how much money it would cost us to lose three thousand head."

"Just over one hundred thousand dollars," Sally said easily.

"What?"

"It would cost us just over one hundred thousand dollars to lose three thousand head. But we won't lose them if we sell them," Sally said.

Smoke shook his head. "You might be right, but if everyone is in the same situation, we won't be able to sell them."

"I know where we can sell them," Sally said.

"Where?"

"We can sell them to Mr. Colin Abernathy."

Smoke shook his head in confusion. "I don't know anyone named Colin Abernathy. He's not a local rancher. Is he an absentee owner?"

"Mr. Abernathy is the Indian agent for all the Cheyenne in Wyoming Territory. He needs the beef to get the Indians through the winter."

"Wait a minute. Did you say all the Cheyenne in Wyoming?"

"Yes, and to be honest, that is the fly in the ointment," Sally said. "Mr. Abernathy will only pay for them when they are delivered to the procurement center. That means we'll have to drive three thousand head to Sorento, where we will deliver them to Cephus Malone."

"I thought you said Colin Abernathy. Who is Cephus Malone?"

"Malone works for Abernathy."

"I see. And where is Sorento?"

"It's in Wyoming Territory, near the town of Laramie."

"Whoa, that's almost five hundred miles. You are proposing that we drive three thousand head five hundred miles? Sally, darlin', I know you mean well, but think about it. It would take us a month to get there, and you say that it is just a fly in the ointment. That's a pretty big fly, don't you think?"

"It is, I suppose," Sally said. "But when you think about it, we will have a pretty big fly swat." Sally smiled sweetly at her husband.

"What do you mean, we'll have a pretty big fly swat?"

"Mr. Abernathy is paying thirty-five dollars a head at delivery."

"Thirty-five dollars a head?" Smoke said in surprise. "Why, that's . . . ."

"That's one hundred and five thousand dollars," Sally said, finishing Smoke's sentence.

Pearlie dropped his fork and stared across the table at Sally. Cal laughed out loud.

"Pearlie, that's the first time I ever seen anything stop you eatin' in mid-chew," Cal said.

"Miz Sally, did you . . ." Pearlie began, then remembering that his mouth was full, finished chewing and swallowed before he returned to his question. "Did you just say one hunnert'n five thousand dollars?"

"I did say that," Sally said. She smiled at Smoke. "That's why I was able to answer your question as to how much it would cost us to lose three thousand head."

"Lord, I've never seen that much money. I ain't never even heard of that much money," Cal said.

"You haven't said anything, Smoke," Sally said. She took a sip of coffee and stared at her husband over the rim of the cup. "What's the matter? Has the cat got your tongue?"

"That's a lot of money," Smoke said. "And you are

right, that is one big fly swat. Something like that would be worth going all the way to Sorento."

"Smoke, do you really think we can drive that many cows all the way to Sorento?" Pearlie asked.

"Looks like we don't have any choice," Smoke said, smiling at Sally. "The boss has spoken."

"Lord, just us?" Cal asked.

Smoke chuckled. "What's the matter, Cal? Don't you think we can do it?"

"I—I reckon so, if you say we can," Cal said, though it was obvious he was unconvinced.

Smoke laughed again. "Don't worry, we'll get some men to help us: drovers, a blacksmith, a cook."

"You won't need a cook," Sally said.

"No cook? Miz Sally, you don't aim for us to make a drive like that on nothin' but beef jerky, do you?" Pearlie asked.

"No, I expect you to make the drive on bacon and beans, biscuits and cornbread, ham and fried potatoes, some roast beef, steak from time to time, apple pie, and . . . maybe a few bear claws."

"Lord a'mercy, you're goin' with us?"

"No," Smoke said.

"Yes," Sally said at the same time.

"Sally, this isn't some picnic in the country," Smoke said. "I'm not going to let you go."

Sally stared at Smoke with her eyes flashing. "Smoke Jensen. Did you just say what I thought you said? Did you say you aren't going to *let* me go?"

"I, uh . . ." Smoke began, but he stammered to a stop in mid-sentence.

"Cal, if you would be so kind as to hitch up the team, I'll take a wagon into town and pick up all the possibles we're going to need for the drive," Sally said.

Cal looked at Smoke.

Smoke smiled, and shook his head. "Well, do what the lady says," he said. "Maybe a few bear claws would taste good out on the trail."

"Yes, sir!" Cal said with pleasure.

"I'll help you with the team," Pearlie said, following Cal outside.

"I thought you might see it my way," Sally said after the two young men were gone.

"I haven't seen it your way," Smoke said.

"Oh? Kirby Jensen, are you telling me you are going to stop me from going?"

Sally used Smoke's real name, a sign that she meant business.

"No, hold on now," Smoke said, raising his hands in defense. "I said I haven't seen it your way. I didn't say you weren't going."

Sally smiled. "I didn't think you would actually try to stop me."

"I won't do that," Smoke said. "But if there comes a gully-gusher and you're trying to drive the chuck wagon hub-deep through water and mud, I don't want to hear the slightest complaint from you."

Sally leaned into Smoke and looked flirtatiously into his eyes.

"Why, Smoke, darling," she said. "Do I ever complain?"

Chapter Four

Even as Pearlie and Cal were hitching up the wagon for Sally to drive into town, several hundred miles north, in the little town of Salcedo in Wyoming Territory, Trent Williams was awakened from a sound sleep by a loud knock on his hotel room door.

"Mr. Williams? Mr. Williams, sir?"

"Yes?" Williams answered in a voice that was groggy with sleep.

"It is seven o'clock, Mr. Williams. You left word with the desk that you were to be awakened at seven sharp."

"All right, all right, I'm awake," Williams said. "Quit pounding on the door."

"Yes, sir," the chagrined voice said from outside Williams's hotel room.

Trent Williams lived in the hotel. As president of the Bank of Salcedo, Williams could afford to live anywhere he wanted, but he preferred a hotel room to a house or an apartment in a boardinghouse. Life was just simpler living in a hotel.

A slight morning breeze filled the muslin curtains and lifted them out over the wide-planked floor. Getting out of bed, Williams padded barefoot over to the window and looked down on the town, which was just beginning to awaken. The morning's enterprise had already begun. Water was being heated behind the laundry and boxes were being stacked behind the grocery store. A team of four big horses pulled a fully loaded freight wagon down the main street.

From somewhere, Williams could smell bacon frying and his stomach growled, reminding him that he was hungry. He splashed some water in the basin, washed his face and hands, then got dressed and went downstairs. There were a couple of people in the lobby, one napping in one of the chairs, the other reading a newspaper. Neither of them paid any attention to Williams as he left the hotel.

The morning sun was bright, but not yet hot. The sky was clear and the air was clean, and as he walked toward the café he could hear the sounds of commerce: the ring of a blacksmith's hammer, a carpenter's saw, and the rattle of working wagons. That was in contrast to last night's sounds of breaking liquor bottles, out-of-tune pianos, loud laughter, and boisterous conversations. How different the tenor of a town was during the business of morning and the play of evening.

Several of the town's citizens doffed their hats in respect to Williams as he passed them on the street. Williams nodded in return, but because of his station in the town, he did not doff his own hat.

"Good morning, Mr. Williams," the owner of the café said as Williams stepped inside. Eric Jordan held a folded newspaper out toward Williams. "Your table is ready for you, sir, and the coffee is hot."

Williams grunted in reply, then took the paper and walked over to his table. Even as he was sitting down, a waiter appeared and poured the coffee for him.

"Your usual, Mr. Williams?" the waiter asked.

"Of course my usual. Bacon, eggs, fried potatoes, biscuits and gravy," Williams replied. "Have I ever varied my order?"

"No, sir."

"Then don't waste my time asking foolish questions," Williams said. "Just get my breakfast out here."

"Right away, sir," the waiter answered.

Half an hour later, Williams was just finishing his breakfast when a man stepped up to his table. The man needed a shave and a bath. His clothes hung in rags from his body.

"You are in my light," Williams said. "Move."

Obligingly, the man stepped to one side. "Sorry, Mr. Williams. Didn't mean no offense," the man said.

"What do you want, Percy?"

Williams asked the question without so much as looking at the man, concentrating instead on his breakfast.

Percy ran his hand across the stubble of his beard. "Well, sir, Mr. Williams, you said I was to bring you a telegram if it come."

"That's right."

"Well, sir, it's come," Percy said. "It come this mornin'."

Williams stuck his hand out.

"Yes, sir, it come this mornin' and I got it first thing and brung it over to you," Percy said, making no effort to hand over the telegram.

Williams grunted, then reached into his pocket and pulled out a quarter. He gave it Percy. "Will this compensate you for your trouble?"

"Yes, sir!" Percy said brightly. "Thank you, Mr. Williams."

"The telegram?"

"Oh, yes, sir. Here it is," Percy said, handing the little envelope to Williams. "You want me to hang around so's you can answer it?"

"No," Williams replied. "That won't be necessary."

"If you need me to run any more errands for you, I'll be glad to do it, Mr. Williams. Whatever you want, why, you just let me know and I'll do it for you," Percy said.

"What I want is for you to go away, Percy," Williams said, making a motion with his hand. "You smell and you are disturbing my breakfast."

"Yes, sir," Percy said, turning toward the door. "But if you need any more errands run, well, you know where I'll be."

"Yes, I know where you will be," Williams replied. "Like as not you'll be passed out on the floor of Duffy's saloon."

The smile left Percy's face, to be replaced by an expression of hurt. "There's no need for you to talk to me like that," Percy said. "Just 'cause I got no money or no place to live, that don't mean I ain't a person."

Williams opened the envelope without answering and, realizing that Williams was no longer paying any attention to him, Percy turned and walked away.

Williams read the telegram.

PER YOUR INQUIRY INDIAN AGENCY DOES REQUIRE BEEF STOP WILL PAY THIRTY-FIVE DOLLARS PER HEAD PAYABLE ON DELIVERY TO SORENTO STOP

Williams folded the telegram and put it away, then, smiling, began drumming his fingers on the table.

"Good news, sir?" the proprietor of the café asked.

"Yes, Mr. Jordan, it is very good news."

"About the bank?"

"Uh, in a manner of speaking, I suppose you could say that it is about the bank," Williams said. "Although I do have a life other than as president of the bank," he added.

"Yes, sir, I'm sure that you do," Jordan replied. "But

you are a very conscientious man, Mr. Williams. All the stockholders insist that the bank has prospered because of you. The bank is very fortunate to have you. Indeed the town of Salcedo is fortunate to have you."

"Well, thank you, Mr. Jordan," Williams said. "I appreciate that."

"More coffee?"

"No, I'll just finish this cup, then be on my way."

"Very good, sir," Jordan said. "Just call me if you need anything."

Williams nodded, then took a swallow of his coffee and looked once more at the telegram. Jordan had asked if this news concerned the bank. It did concern a bank, just not this bank. If everything worked out right—and he saw no reason why it would not—he would soon own his own bank.

When Williams read in the paper that all the Indians had been ordered onto reservations, he realized that feeding them would become the responsibility of the U.S. government. He also realized that that would require a lot of beef, and the moment he realized that, he knew that he had found the way to pay for the bank he wanted to buy. All someone had to do in order to make a lot of money was be in position to make that beef available to the U.S. government.

Williams was not a rancher, but that didn't mean he couldn't come up with enough cattle to negotiate a profitable deal with the U.S. government. Last month he had bought a demand mortgage from the bank. That mortgage, for one thousand dollars, was due two weeks from today.

Twice before, Jason Adams, owner of Backtrail Ranch, had arranged an extension on his loan. No doubt he would attempt to do so again, but this time it would not be the bank he was dealing with. By buying the note, which was a perfectly legitimate business arrangement, Williams would be able to force Adams to deal directly with him.

What made the deal particularly attractive as far as Williams was concerned was that he would not have to deal with the board of directors. He could, and he would, make his own arrangements with regard to the note. And those arrangements could be quite lucrative.

Williams had Adams over a barrel. If Adams wanted to save his ranch, he was going to have to pay off the note. And the only way he could pay off the note would be by forfeiting his two thousand head of cattle. Williams chuckled as he did the math. By settling the loan, he would be paying one thousand dollars for two thousand head of cattle. That came out to fifty cents a head. He would then sell those same cows at thirty-five dollars a head. That would be a pure profit of sixty-nine thousand dollars. That was more than enough to buy the Miners Bank. Yes, sir, the arrangements would be quite lucrative indeed.

As Williams walked from the restaurant to the bank, he stopped at the barbershop for his weekly tonsorial appointment. The barber, Earl Cook, was sitting in his chair reading the newspaper when Williams walked in. Hopping up quickly, he made a point of brushing out the chair before holding his arm out in invitation.

"Good morning, Mr. Williams," Cook said. "Here it is, nine o'clock on Tuesday morning, and you are here, punctual as usual."

"I consider punctuality to be the hallmark of any businessman," Williams said as he sat in the chair. "I only wish the bank customers were as punctual in the payment of their debts."

"Indeed, indeed," Cook said as he draped the cover over Williams. "You will want a shave, I suppose?"

"Yes," Williams said, leaning back as Cook lowered the back of the chair.

Cook made lather, then began applying it to Williams's chin. "Jason Adams was in here earlier this morning."

"Adams was here? What for?"

"Why, for a shave and a haircut," Cook replied. Cook chuckled. "Wearing a suit, he is, and with a fresh shave and a haircut, he is quite dapper-looking if I do say so."

"Hmmph," Williams said. "You'd think he would have better things to do with his money."

"I expect he'll be dropping in to see you later today," Cook said. He began applying lather to the lower part of Williams's face. "I expect he just wanted to make a good impression."

"He could have saved his time and his money," Williams replied. "I'm afraid I won't be able to extend his loan any longer. I wish I could do something for him, I truly do. But he has already had two extensions, and I am running a business."

"I understand," Cook said as he drew the razor across Williams's face. "It's just that Jason and his wife, Millie, are such good people, pillars of the church, always first to volunteer to help someone when help is needed."

"Now, Mr. Cook, if I ran the bank with my heart instead of my head, where would we be? You are a stockholder, are you not?"

Cook chuckled. "You've got me there, Mr. Williams. As I told you, we are very lucky to have a man with your business sense. And you are right, you can't run a bank with your heart."

Williams sighed. "Well, I must confess that I am being disingenuous with you. I too have been worried about Jason Adams, so I have done something that I might regret."

"What is that?"

"I bought his note from the bank," Williams said.

Cook raised up to look at him. "You bought Jason's note? Why would you do that?"

"Because in all good conscience, I cannot allow the bank to extend his note any longer. However, as the personal holder of his note, I believe I can work out some way with Mr. Adams that will allow him to keep his ranch. That is, if he is willing to work with me."

"You are a good man, Mr. Williams," Cook said as he resumed shaving the banker. "Yes, sir, you are a good man."

"Of course, Jason may not like what I am offering him," Williams said. "It's going to be harsh, but it's the only way he will be able to save his ranch. And after all, it is better to swallow a bitter pill than to lose the entire ranch."

"That's true all right," Cook said as he continued to cut the hair. "Sometimes a fella just has to bite the bullet."

Half an hour later, Williams was in his office in the back of the bank when Ron Gilbert, his head teller, knocked on the door.

"Yes, Gilbert, what is it?"

"Mr. Williams, Mr. Jason Adams is here to see you," Gilbert said.

"Is he here to pay his note, or to ask for an extension?"

"From the expression on his face, he is here to ask for an extension, I believe," Gilbert said.

"That is a shame," Williams said. Williams projected an image of concern and compassion, though in truth he could scarcely contain his joy over the fact that everything was going exactly as he had planned.

"Send him in," Williams said.

Adams came in and stood nervously just inside the

door. He was, as Cook had described, wearing a suit and was freshly shaved and trimmed. It was obvious that he was going all out to make as positive an appearance as he possibly could.

"Good morning, Jason," Williams said, smiling at the rancher. "Please, come in, have a seat. How is Millie?"

"My wife is fine, thank you for your concern," Adams replied nervously.

"And your two boys? They must be a head taller than they were the last time I saw them."

Adams nodded. "Yes, sir, they've grown quite a bit."

"Well, I hope everything is fine with you. What brings you to town, Jason? What can I do for you?"

"I'm here to talk about my loan."

"You are a little early, aren't you? Your loan isn't due for a couple of weeks."

Adams looked surprised. "You can remember when my loan is due?"

Williams cleared his throat. It wouldn't be good to show that he was taking a particular interest in Jason Adams's loan.

"Well, when I heard you were in town today, I thought it might have something to do with your loan," Williams said. He forced a laugh. "I didn't think you would stop by just to pass the time of day."

"Oh, no, sir, no, sir," Adams said. "I would never waste your time like that."

Williams rubbed his hands together.

"So, you want to pay your loan off, do you?" Williams asked cheerfully. He knew that Jason had no intention of paying off the loan. In fact, he didn't want him to pay off the loan.

Adams's lips drew into a tight line. "Uh, no, sir, I'm

afraid I can't do that," he said. "I'm going to have to ask for another extension."

"Oh," Williams said. "Oh, that's too bad. Yes, sir, that is too bad." Williams shook his head. "Is there any chance you will be able to pay it off by the time it is due?"

"No, sir," Adams said. "I'm sorry, Mr. Williams, I truly am. But I'm not going to be able to pay the loan off."

"Mr. Adams, for your sake, and for the sake of your family, I was really hoping that this time you would be able to pay the note off," Williams said as he stroked his chin. "You see, I'm afraid that it isn't going to be possible to give you another extension."

"Not—not possible?" Adams asked, obviously crestfallen by the information. "Are you saying you won't extend the note?"

"I'm really sorry, Mr. Adams," Williams said. "I wish I could extend your loan again, I really do. But my hands are tied. I have an obligation, not only to the stockholders of this bank, but also the depositors."

"I see," Adams said. "What—what is going to hap-pen now?"

"Well, I'm afraid that you are going to lose your ranch."

Adams shook his head. "No, you can't take the ranch away from me," he said. "You can't! That's my home. That's the only place me'n Millie has ever lived. Both our kids was born there. Please, there must be some other way out of this rather than forcin' me to lose my ranch."

"I'm sorry, I wish I could help you," Williams said. "But I'm afraid there's nothing I can do. Please try to understand, my hands are tied."

"What . . . what am I going to tell Millie?" Adams asked, barely managing to keep control of his emotions.

Williams drummed his fingers on the table as if in

deep thought. Then he ran his hands through his hair. "There is—one—way," Williams said. "I'm not sure you will want to go along with it."

"What do you mean I won't want to go along with it? If there is a way, any way . . ." Adams's desperate plea trailed off.

"After all, I suppose that, for you, the most important thing would be to save your ranch, am I right? I mean, it is your home."

"Yes. I'd do anything to save it."

"Then I do have an idea. It isn't something that I want to do, but under the circumstances, I'll do it for you," Williams said. "I'll buy the note from the bank. Then you would owe me, and not the bank."

"And you would give me an extension?"

Williams chuckled and held out his hands. "No, no, don't misunderstand. There is no way I could afford to do something like that," Williams said. "But what I will do is mark the note paid in full in exchange for your cattle."

"My cattle? How many of my cattle?"

"All of them."

"What? No, I couldn't do that. Why, I have two thousand head," Adams said. "I couldn't possibly let you have two thousand head of cattle for one thousand dollars."

"Consider this, Mr. Adams," Williams said. "The note you signed with the bank was for your ranch and all livestock and improvements. So you are faced with this choice. Let the bank foreclose and lose everything, including your cattle, or settle with me for your cattle, and keep your ranch."

"I couldn't possibly do that," Adams said. Suddenly, he smiled. "But I could sell enough of my cattle to pay the note."

"No, you can't do that," Williams said.

"What do you mean I can't do that? Of course I can. I don't know why I didn't think of it earlier."

"If you sell those cattle, Mr. Adams, you will go to jail."

"What are you talking about? Why would I go to jail?"

"Remember, your loan note was for the ranch, livestock, and all accoutrements," Williams said. "That means you have your cattle mortgaged, and there is a law against selling mortgaged property."

"I—I didn't know that," Adams said in a defeated tone.

"Now you do know. So the choice is this, Mr. Adams. Either turn over all your cattle to me, in exchange for a release from debt, or I will be forced to foreclose on your ranch and your cattle." Gone was the silken, cajoling demeanor in Williams's voice. He was now speaking in a cold, clipped, and demanding voice.

"I—I suppose when you put it that way, I really have no choice," Adams said.

Sensing victory, Williams eased up a bit. "Mr. Adams, the truth is, I've gone way out on a limb for you on this. I probably shouldn't have done so, but I've already bought the note. It was the only way I could think of to save your ranch."

"I see," Adams said.

Williams opened the drawer of his desk and pulled out a paper.

"We can take care of this right now if you want to," he said. "Sign this paper turning your cattle over to me, and I'll release the lien on your ranch."

Williams slid the paper across to Adams, then handed him a pen. Adams held the pen poised over the line for his signature for a moment, but he didn't sign.

"What's wrong?"

"I've got two more weeks," he said.

Williams chuckled. "Mr. Adams, you've had two years to settle this debt and you've been unable to do so. What makes you think you can do it in two more weeks?"

"I can't settle in two more weeks," he said. "But before I do something like this, I need to discuss it with Millie."

"I see," Williams said. "And your wife makes all your decisions for you, does she?"

"No, sir. But we do make them together," Adams replied.

Williams sighed. "All right, Mr. Adams, discuss this with your wife if you must. But make certain she understands all the ramifications of it. Because if you don't accept this offer before the two weeks are up, the deal will be taken off the table. I'm afraid then that I will be forced to exercise every clause of the loan agreement. And that means, Mr. Adams, that you will not only forfeit your cattle, you will lose your ranch as well."

"Yes, sir, I understand," Adams said. "And I appreciate what you are doing for me, Mr. Williams, really I do. It's just that I'm going to have to bring my wife around."

"Very well. Give her my best," Williams said.

"I will. And thank you again, sir."

After Adams left, Williams walked over to his window to watch as the rancher climbed up into his buckboard, then drove away. Two thousand head at fifty cents a head, for which he would get thirty-five dollars a head. Yes, sir, this was going to work out just fine.

Chapter Five

Big Rock, Colorado

As the two cowboys dismounted in front of a saddle store, one of them rubbed his behind.

"Damn, that's the hardest, most uncomfortable saddle I ever sat in," he said. "I'll be glad to get mine back."

Don't know why you brung it in to get repaired anyway," the other cowboy said as they tied off their horses at the hitching rail. "As far as I could see, there wasn't that much wrong with it."

"The fender was tore."

"Well, hell, it don't hurt nothin' to have a tore fender. All a fender does is make a saddle look good. Don't have nothin' to do with the way it sits."

"Maybe it don't mean nothin' to somebody like you. But I'm particular about my saddle. You can ask anyone and they'll tell you that LeRoy Butrum is particular about his saddle."

"Yeah, if you ask me, you're old-maid particular," the other cowboy said.

"And you don't never care what yours is like. I swear, Hank, if I hadn't been around when you was born, I wouldn't even believe you was my brother."

The two men stepped up onto the porch, then pushed the door open to go inside. The store smelled of leather, saddle soap, and neat's-foot oil. There was one particularly handsome saddle on display.

"Lookie here," LeRoy said, rubbing his hand over the saddle. "He's got my saddle out here for the whole world to see."

"Did he fix the fender?" Hank asked.

LeRoy put his hand on the piece of leather that was attached to the stirrup strap.

"Yep, here it is, as good as new," he said.

The proprietor came up front then and, seeing the two cowboys standing by the saddle, nodded at them.

"Boys," he said.

"Mr. Pogue," Hank replied.

"Tell me, Mr. Pogue, why you got my saddle out front like this?" LeRoy asked. Then he smiled. "Prob'ly 'cause it's the prettiest saddle in town, huh?"

"Not exactly," Pogue said. "I had it out here to sell it."

"To sell it?" LeRoy responded loudly. "What the hell do you mean you had it out here to sell it? Mister, this here ain't your saddle to sell."

"You said you would pick it up within a week," Pogue replied. "It's been a month."

"Yeah, well, I didn't have the money then. But I'm here to pick it up now."

"Good, that will make both of us happy," Pogue said.

LeRoy gave Pogue a five-dollar bill. Pogue just stared at it for a moment.

"What is this for?" he asked.

"What do you mean, what is this for? This here is for the work you done on the saddle."

"That will be twenty-five dollars," Pogue said.

"What?" LeRoy and Hank shouted as one.

"The cost of the repair to your saddle is twenty-five dollars."

"The hell you say!" LeRoy replied. "Mister, you can get a brand-new saddle for twenty-five dollars."

"Not like this one."

"Well, you didn't make this one, and I already paid for it once. All you done was put on a new fender."

"And I'm chargin' you twenty-five dollars for that," Pogue said.

"You can charge all you want, I ain't payin' it," LeRoy said angrily. "Just take the damn thing off."

"That'll be ten dollars," Pogue said.

"Ten dollars? What for? I told you to just take it off. I don't want it," LeRoy said.

"The ten dollars is for the aggravation," Pogue said.

"I ain't payin' you no ten dollars for nothin'," LeRoy said. He jerked the fancy leatherwork fender off the stirrup strap and tossed it toward Pogue. "There, I done the work for you. Come on, Hank, let's go."

LeRoy put the saddle up onto his shoulder and started toward the door.

"Stop!" Pogue called at them. "You're stealing that saddle."

"You can't steal what's already yours," LeRoy said without looking back toward Pogue.

Fortunately, Hank was looking toward Pogue, because he saw the saddle-shop proprietor hurry toward the counter and reach for a shotgun. Quickly, Hank's pistol was in his hand, pointing toward Pogue.

"Don't you try nothin' dumb now, Mr. Pogue," Hank cautioned.

"You are stealing that saddle."

"We ain't stealin' it," LeRoy said. "Soon's I get ten

dollars, I'll come back and pay you, even though I don't think I ought to have to."

"Help! Someone, help!" Pogue started shouting. "I'm being robbed!"

LeRoy put the saddle down while he started removing the old saddle from the horse he had ridden.

"Help! Sheriff! Help!" Pogue continued to shout.

"Will you shut up?" Hank yelled at Pogue.

Both men were stopped then by the sound of a pistol being cocked. Turning, they saw one of the deputies standing out in the road, pointing his gun at them.

"What's going on here?" the deputy asked.

"Thank God someone answered my call," Pogue said. He pointed at the Butrum brothers. "These men are stealing this saddle."

"I ain't stealin' it," LeRoy said. "This here saddle belongs to me."

"You brought it in for repair, and you did not pay for the repair," Pogue said. "According to the law, until you pay for the repair, the saddle belongs to me."

"I undid the repair," LeRoy said.

"That doesn't matter. I already did the work."

"I think you two boys better come with me," the deputy said.

"Come on, Deputy, this here is just a misunderstandin', that's all," LeRoy said. He reached for his saddle.

"No, leave the saddle and come with me. Both of you."

Pogue waited until the deputy had them halfway to the jail before he stepped outside to retrieve the saddle.

"Will you lookie there?" LeRoy muttered. "That son of a bitch got my saddle."

"It isn't your saddle until you have satisfied the debt owed against it," the deputy said.

* * *

Neither Sally, Pearlie, nor Cal were aware of the drama that had just played out at the saddle shop when they rolled into town later that morning. Big Rock was a busy place with two trains at the depot, one passenger and one freight. The passenger train was taking on passengers for its run to the east, and even though the engineer was at rest, the fireman wasn't. He was working hard, stoking the fire to keep the steam pressure up.

In contrast to the fireman's toil, the engineer was leaning out the window of the highly polished green and brass locomotive, smoking a curved-stem pipe as he watched the activity on the depot platform. He was serene in the power and prestige of his position.

Passenger trains were called "varnish" by railroad people because, unlike the roughly painted freight cars, the passenger cars were generally beautifully finished. The conductor stood beside the string of varnished cars, keeping a close check of the time. The freight train was sitting over on the sidetrack, its hissing relief valve opening and closing as the steam pressure was maintained. The "varnish" had priority over the main line, and not until it departed would the freight be allowed to move back onto the high iron in order to continue its travel west.

Two stagecoaches and half-a-dozen carriages were also sitting at the depot, either having just delivered or waiting for train passengers. Out in the street behind the depot, a horse-drawn streetcar rumbled by.

This was what greeted Sally, Pearlie, and Cal as the three came into town to buy supplies. Sally was driving a large wagon and Pearlie and Cal were mounted, but riding slowly to keep pace with the wagon.

"Whoo-ee, this sure is a busy place this morning," Cal said as he saw three loaded freight wagons rumbling by.

"It always gets busy when a train is here," Sally said.

"Miz Sally, you know what we ought to do?" Pearlie asked. "We ought to make arrangements with the railroad to carry the cattle up to Sorento. That way we wouldn't have to drive 'em none."

"My goodness, Pearlie, do you have any idea how many cars it would take to move three thousand cattle?" Sally asked.

"No, I don't."

"Well, if you could get thirty cows to a car, it would take a hundred cars," Sally said. "That would be at least five trains. And because there is no track direct from here to Sorento, the trains would have to go almost a thousand miles to get there. That means it would take nearly as long to ship them up by train as it would to drive them . . . and the shipping cost would eat up about a quarter of the gross."

"How'd you come up with all that?" Pearlie asked. "You're awfully smart to figure all that out."

Cal laughed. "Maybe if you would think about something other than eatin' all the time, you would be able to come up with things like that too."

"What are you talkin' about?" Pearlie replied. "You didn't know none of that stuff neither."

"Yes, I did."

"Did not."

"Did too."

Sally stopped the wagon and the two young cowboys halted their horses. They sat in the middle of the street while traffic passed back and forth around them, paying little attention to them.

"Boys," Sally said, scolding them. "Would you please

stop arguing? I've got business to attend to, and you do as well. Remember, Smoke wanted you to find some drovers who are willing to make the drive with us. You do understand that, don't you?"

Pearlie and Cal looked at each other for a moment. Pearlie was the first to speak.

"Yes, ma'am, we understand. It's just that we were wonderin' . . ." He let the sentence hang.

"You were wondering what?" Sally asked. "What's wrong?"

"Miz Sally, that seems to me like an awful big responsibility for me'n Cal to handle," Pearlie said. "I mean, they're goin' to be workin' for Smoke. Seems like he should be hirin' 'em. What if we don't get the right kind of men?"

"Pearlie, you are going to be the foreman, and Cal, you are going to be right under him. Everyone we hire will be working for the two of you, just like they are working for Smoke and me. You've been around Sugarloaf for a long time now. You know what kind of men will be good for the job."

"But . . ." Pearlie began.

"But nothing," Sally said. "Smoke has every confidence in the world in the two of you, and so do I. Now, go hire us some good men. You can do that, can't you?"

Pearlie nodded. "Yes, ma'am," he said. "Yes, ma'am, I reckon we can do that. Right, Cal?"

Cal nodded solemnly. "Yes," he agreed. "We'll get men you'n Smoke will be proud of."

"I know you will," Sally said. She slapped the reins against the backs of the team and the mules strained into the harness, pulling the wagon forward.

"When you've hired the men, come down to the general store," Sally called back over her shoulder as she drove away. "I should have the wagon loaded by then."

"Yes, ma'am," Pearlie replied. "Come on, Cal, let's me'n you go get us some cowboys."

"You got 'ny idea where we should start?" Cal asked.

"Not directly. But town's a busy place today. I'm sure we'll run into someone, somewhere," Pearlie replied.

Chapter Six

As the two cowboys rode down to the opposite end of town, they saw a fistfight in progress in the street in front of the livery. One of the combatants was a soldier in uniform. He was wearing sergeant's stripes on his sleeves.

The other combatant was a civilian. The civilian was much younger than the soldier, but he was nearly as big, and he was more than holding his own.

As the cowboys got closer, they saw that the civilian was Mike Kennedy. Kennedy worked for the livery stable as a hostler and as an apprentice blacksmith. Mike was about the same age as Cal, and, in fact, the two were good friends. Mike was younger and smaller than the sergeant, but he was strong and whatever it was that started the fight had filled him with resolve. At first there had been a sly smirk on the sergeant's face.

"Boy, I'm goin' to play with you for a bit," the sergeant said. "Then I'm going to hurt you, and I'm going to hurt you bad."

But Mike was proving to be a little more than the sergeant expected. The sergeant swung hard with a roundhouse right, but Mike, who was quick and agile, ducked under the swing, then countered with a left jab to the sergeant's nose. It was considerably more than a light jab, because the soldier's nose went flat, then almost immediately begin to swell. The sergeant let out a bellow of pain as a trickle of blood started down across his mustache.

"Why, you snot-nosed kid!" the sergeant shouted. "I'm going to knock your block off!" He swung with another roundhouse right, missing again, and this time Mike caught him with a right hook to the chin. The hook rocked the sergeant back, but it didn't knock him down.

By now a rather substantial crowd had gathered to watch the fight, and everyone was rooting for their champion. To the surprise of both Cal and Pearlie, there seemed to be about as many soldiers cheering for Mike as there were supporting the soldier.

Mike scored with two more sharp jabs, and it was now obvious that the sergeant was on his last legs. He was stumbling about, barely able to stay on his feet. Mike had set him up for the finishing blow when one of the soldiers who had been supporting the sergeant suddenly grabbed the boy from behind. With his arms pinned, Mike was an easy target for the roundhouse right that, until now, had missed.

The sergeant connected and Mike's knees buckled, but he didn't go down. Pearlie slid down from his horse and before the sergeant could throw another punch, Pearlie brought the butt of his pistol down on the head of the man who had grabbed Mike. The man collapsed like a sack of potatoes and, though Pearlie and Cal were prepared to have to defend the action if need be, Pearlie found himself cheered by the crowd, civilian and soldier alike.

With his arms now free, Mike was able to finish the fight with two more blows, setting his man up with a hard left jab, then dropping him with an even harder right cross.

With the fight over and nothing to hold the spectators'

interest, the crowd broke up. Several of the soldiers dragged their beaten comrade away with them, leaving Mike standing in the middle of the street, breathing hard from the exertion.

It wasn't until that moment that Pearlie realized the fight hadn't been as one-sided as he had thought. Mike had a cut lip and a swollen eye. The boy walked over to the watering trough and dipped his handkerchief into the water.

"Here, let me do that," Cal said, taking Mike's handkerchief and dabbing lightly at his lip.

"Thanks, Cal," Mike said.

"What was the fight about?"

"The soldier took some oats from Mr. Lambert's livery. When I told him he had to pay for them, he called me a liar. One thing led to another and the next thing you know, we was fightin'."

"Kennedy, you're fired!" a man said, coming up to them then.

"Mr. Lambert, that soldier was stealin' oats from you."

"He said he wasn't," Lambert said.

"He was, I seen him do it."

Lambert shook his head. "Well, that don't matter none anyway," he said. "What's a nickel's worth of oats? You get the army mad, we won't get none of their business. All for a nickel's worth of oats? It just ain't good business, boy," Lambert said. "'Bout the only way I can make up for it now is to fire you."

"But Mr. Lambert, I need the job," Mike said.

"Sorry, boy, but business is business. Besides, this ain't the first time you've got into a fight. And I told you last time I wasn't goin' to put up with no more of it. You're fired."

A couple of the soldiers overheard the conversation, and they came back up to talk to the livery owner.

"Mr. Lambert, don't take it out on the boy," one of the soldiers said. "I don't know whether Sergeant Caviness stole any oats or not, but I do know that Caviness is a hothead, and he hit the boy first."

Lambert waved his hand. "Well, he wouldn't have hit Kennedy if the boy hadn't done somethin' to provoke him. He's fired, and that's it."

Lambert turned and started striding purposefully back to the livery.

"I'm sorry," one of the soldiers said. "It ain't right that you get fired for somethin' Caviness done."

"Ahh, don't worry about it," Mike said. "Truth is, I think Mr. Lambert was lookin' for an excuse to fire me anyway. I know he's been complainin' about how much it costs to keep me on."

"Yeah, well at least you taught Sergeant Caviness a lesson," the other of the two soldiers said. "He's a bully who hides behind his stripes. He knows that none of the soldiers he picks on can fight back without windin' up in the stockade. That's why there was so many of 'em cheerin' for you."

"I welcome the support," Mike said. "But I still lost the job."

"Pearlie, what do you think?" Cal asked.

Pearlie nodded. "I think yes," he said.

"What are you two talking about?" Mike asked.

"You're goin' to be lookin' for another job, right?" Pearlie asked.

"Yeah, I reckon I will be," Mike answered.

"How'd you like to come work for the Sugarloaf?"

"What?" Mike asked, brightening considerably at the offer. "Are you serious?"

"Yes, I'm serious."

"Do you think Mr. Jensen would hire me?"

"We're hirin' you," Pearlie said.

"You?"

Cal nodded. "We're fixin' to drive a herd of cows up to Wyoming," he said. "Smoke sent us into town to hire some men. If you want the job, it's yours."

"Yes, sir, I want the job!" Mike said excitedly. "You better believe I want it."

"Good. Now we just need to find five more men."

"Three," one of the soldiers said.

"What do you mean I only need three more?" Pearlie asked.

"My name is Andy Wilson," the soldier said. He pointed to the other soldier. "This here is Dooley Thomas. We'd be happy to come work for you if you'll have us."

Pearlie shook his head. "Huh-uh," he said. "I'm afraid not."

"Why not? We're good workers," Andy replied.

"You're also in the army. I ain't goin' to hire no deserters, and I know Smoke won't."

Andy smiled broadly. "Well if that's the only problem, then it ain't a problem," he said.

"And why isn't it a problem?"

"'Cause we ain't deserters," Andy said. "Get your paper out, Dooley," Andy said to his friend. As Dooley pulled out a piece of paper from his back pocket, Andy did the same. He showed the paper to Pearlie.

"What is this?"

"These here is our discharge papers," Andy said. "Me'n Dooley has done served our time, and we got ourselves mustered out this mornin'. We're still wearin' uniforms 'cause we ain't got us no civilian clothes yet."

Pearlie read both papers, then he looked at Andy "According to this paper you're from Cincinnati, and Dooley here is from Boston."

"Yes, sir, that's right."

"What did you do before you come into the army?" Pearlie asked.

"Well, sir, I worked down on the river docks, loadin' and unloadin' boats," Andy said.

"I worked in a factory making bricks," Dooley said.

"A dockworker and a brick maker," Pearlie said. "There won't be much call for loadin' boats or makin' bricks during this drive."

"Wasn't much call for loadin' boats or makin' bricks in the army either," Andy said. "But we both learned to soldier."

"I need cowboys. Do either of you know anything about cows?"

"They give milk," Dooley said.

"Horses can give milk," Cal said.

"Well, I can tell the difference between a cow and a horse," Dooley said.

Pearlie looked surprised for a moment; then he laughed out loud.

"Well, I'll give you credit for honesty," he said. He stroked his chin. "I reckon anyone who can learn how to soldier can learn how to cowboy. All right, you two go with Mike. Mike, get your tack and go down to the general store. Miz Sally is down there getting supplies. You can help her load the wagon."

"Who is Miz Sally?" Dooley asked. "How will we recognize her?"

"She's the boss's wife," Mike said. "And don't you be worryin' none about recognizing her. She'll be about the prettiest woman in town. I know what she looks like."

Chapter Seven

Pearlie and Cal watched as the three men walked down toward the general store.

"You think they'll work out all right?" Cal asked.

"I don't know why not. Like I said, they learned how to soldier. And I like the way they took up for Mike like that."

"Yeah," Cal said. "I liked that, too."

A couple of minutes later, Pearlie and Cal tied their horses off in front of the Longmont Saloon, then stepped inside.

"Pearlie, Cal," Louis Longmont called to them from behind the bar. "It's good to see you boys. Is Smoke with you today?"

"No, sir, Mr. Longmont, he's still out at the ranch," Pearlie answered.

Longmont smiled. "Well, that's all right. You boys are always welcome, with or without Smoke. What'll it be?"

"Two beers," Pearlie said.

"And I'll have the same," Cal added.

Longmont chuckled as he drew four mugs, then set them in front of the two boys. "Cal, wasn't that long ago you wasn't old enough to drink beer. I remember Miz

Sally tellin' me what she'd do to me if she caught me servin' you one."

"I'm old enough now," Cal said.

"Yeah, that's why I put them in front of you. No way I'd go against Miz Sally otherwise. So, how are things goin' out at Sugarloaf?"

"We're lookin' to hire three good men," Pearlie said.

Longmont looked surprised. "Really? It's mid-fall. Most ranches lay off at the end of summer. What are you doin' out at Sugarloaf that you need more men?"

"We're drivin' a herd up into Wyoming," Cal said.

"Oh, I see. So you're lookin' to hire someone next spring," Longmont said.

"No, not in the spring—we want someone now," Pearlie said.

"Why would you want someone now? Why not wait until you actually drive the herd?"

"'Cause we're driving the herd up now," Cal said.

"What? This late in the year? Why, that's crazy. Why would Smoke do somethin' like that?"

"'Cause Miz Sally has got it in her mind that we're goin' to have another winter kind'a like that one we had a couple years back when there was that big freeze-out," Cal said. "So, we're sellin' off half the herd to the U.S. government so's they can provide beef for the Indians. Only, the government won't pay for the beef until we deliver it to them."

Longmont nodded. "Yeah, I guess I can see why you would want to drive a herd north. I guess my question now is, can you do it?"

"I think we can if we have good men with us," Pearlie said. "You said a lot of cowboys have been laid off for the winter, right?"

"Yes."

"What about Billy Cantrell? He was riding for the

Double Tree. He's a good man with cattle. I'd like to have him. Do you know if he was laid off?"

Longmont laughed. "He was laid off all right. But I don't think he'll be making any trail drives with you."

"Why not? Me'n Billy's always got along. And I know that Smoke will match whatever he was getting' over at the Double Tree," Pearlie said.

"Yeah, well, Billy is in jail, and he's likely to be there until spring."

"Why is that?"

"Seems Billy got upset with a drummer from Denver. He didn't like the way the drummer was actin' around Chris Candy."

"What do you mean the way he was actin' around Chris Candy? Chris Candy's a whore," Pearlie said. "Billy can't get upset with ever' man who has anything to do with her. That's her job."

"Well, it ain't her job to get her eye blackened, and that's what the drummer did."

"Oh," Pearlie said.

"So Billy blackened both the drummer's eyes, and he broke the drummer's nose. If Sheriff Carson hadn't pulled him off when he did, why, like as not Billy would've broken both the drummer's hands as well."

"How long is he in jail for?" Cal asked.

"Well, the judge gave him thirty days or thirty dollars. Since Billy didn't have thirty dollars, he's servin' the thirty days."

"Do you think Sheriff Carson would turn him over to us if we paid his fine?" Cal asked.

Longmont nodded.

"I reckon he would," he said. "Especially if he knew

that Billy was going to be out of town and out of his hair for a while."

"Then Smoke will pay his fine."

"Hold on now, Pearlie," Cal said. "Hadn't we better take that up with Smoke first?"

"Didn't he say he would trust us to get good men?" Pearlie replied.

"Yes, but . . ."

"But nothin'. Billy's one of the best cowboys around. Everyone knows that. He's well worth paying off his fine to have him with us."

"All right, if you think so," Cal said, though the "all right" was somewhat reluctant.

"If Smoke don't like it, I'll take all the responsibility," Pearlie said. "And I'll pay the fine myself."

Cal shook his head. "No need for that," he said. I'll back you on it with Smoke, and I'll pay half the fine."

"Good," Pearlie said. He took another drink of his beer. "Now we only need two."

"You don't need to go nowhere else," Billy said when Pearlie and Cal came down to the jail to hire him. Billy pointed to the two men in the cell next to him. "These here is the Butrum boys, LeRoy and Hank. Hire them and you'll have everyone you need."

"I can't just hire anybody," Pearlie said. "They need to have some skills."

"I've punched cows with these boys for most of the past year," Billy said. "They're good hands, both of 'em."

"Why are they in jail?" Pearlie asked.

"Well, because they . . ." Billy began, then stopped. "Truth to tell, I don't know why they're in jail. They was already here when Sheriff Carson brung me in. Hey, LeRoy," he called.

Both Butrums were asleep, or appeared to be, as they were lying on their bunks with their hats pulled down over their eyes.

"LeRoy," Billy called again.

"What do you want?" LeRoy answered from under his hat.

"What for are you and Hank in jail?"

"For stealin' back what was our'n," LeRoy answered. He had still not removed his hat.

"What do you mean, stealing back what was yours?"

LeRoy finally removed his hat and sat up on his bunk. "Do you know that low-assed pipsqueak named Josiah Pogue?"

"Yes, he owns the leather-goods shop," Pearlie said. "I don't know him well, but I know who he is."

"He done some work for me, then he tried to charge too much. When I couldn't pay it, he took my saddle," LeRoy said.

"Well, that's not stealin', that's legal," Pearlie said.

"Yeah, well, what he done was put a fender on. When I couldn't pay for the fender, I took it off and give it back to him, but that wasn't good enough. He wanted my whole saddle. So me'n Hank took the saddle anyway."

"Which is when the deputy showed up, and that's how we wound up in here," Hank said, finishing the story.

"If me'n Cal can get this cleared up, would you two boys agree to work for Sugarloaf?"

Hank nodded. "Yeah, we'll come work for Sugarloaf, won't we, LeRoy?"

"Sure. It's better than bein' in here."

* * *

A little bell rang as the door to Pogue's leather-goods store was opened.

"I'll be right with you," a reed-thin voice called from the back of the store.

A moment later a small, bald-headed man appeared. He was wearing an apron, and it was apparent he had been doing some leatherwork in the shop behind the store. Examples of his work were on display about the store, and Cal had to admit that the man was an artisan.

"Yes, sir, can I help you gentlemen?" Pogue asked. Then, recognizing them, he smiled. "You two men work for Mr. Smoke Jensen, don't you?"

"Yes," Pearlie said.

"He's a fine man. Are you perhaps looking for something for him?"

Cal was looking at a belt, holding it up to examine the intricate scrolling in the leather.

"That is a fine belt, if I do say so myself," Pogue said.

"Yes, sir, it is pretty all right," Cal agreed.

"I can make you a very good price for it."

"Uh, no, sir, we ain't here to buy nothin'," Pearlie said.

The smile left Pogue's face.

"Then why are you here?" he asked.

"We want to talk to you about the Butrum brothers."

"Oh, them," Pogue said. "They are brutish men, the two of them. I hope the sheriff sends them to prison. They need to learn that they can't just come in here and take what doesn't belong to them."

"But the saddle did belong to them, didn't it? It was LeRoy's saddle, I believe."

"In a manner of speaking, it was his saddle," Pogue agreed. "But I had a legitimate lien against it. And until that lien is satisfied, the saddle belongs to me."

"Would it square things with you if the lien was paid off?" Pearlie asked.

"As far as not makin' a claim on the saddle, yes, it would," Pogue said. "But I would still like to see them punished."

"Why?"

"Why? Because they need to know that they can't just run roughshod over decent citizens. Besides, I'm a little frightened of them," Pogue added.

"Suppose you were paid off the ten dollars, and the Butrums left town so there would be no possibility of them causing you any more trouble. Would that satisfy you?"

Pogue studied Pearlie for a moment. "Why are you so interested in what happens to the Butrums?"

"Because Smoke is going to drive a herd of cows north, and we want to hire the Butrum boys to help us. But we can't as long as they are in jail."

"How far north?"

"All the way to Wyoming."

Pogue whistled quietly. "That's a long way to drive cattle."

"Yes. And it should certainly be far enough to keep the boys out of your hair," Pearlie said.

"What hair?" Cal asked, laughing out loud.

For a moment, the expression on Pogue's face was one of irritation over the allusion to his lack of hair. Then, he began to laugh, and he rubbed his hand across his bald head.

"Yes, what hair indeed?" he replied. "All right, boys. If you see to it that I get my ten dollars, I'll inform Sheriff Carson that I don't intend to press charges."

"Thank you," Pearlie said. He pulled out his billfold, then extracted ten dollars and gave it to Pogue.

"Thanks," Pogue said, taking the money. He took a pencil and piece of paper from behind the shelf, then wrote out:

I, Josiah Pogue, having been duly satisfied as to the debt owed me by the Butrum brothers, do hereby free them of any further financial obligations toward me, and relinquish any claim to the saddle belonging to LeRoy Butrum. I also withdraw the charges I filed against them.

"Are you sure you want to do this? I mean, have you really thought about what you are doing?" Sheriff Carson asked a few minutes later as he released Billy, Hank, and LeRoy to Pearlie and Cal.

"I'm sure," Pearlie answered. "I know Billy to be a good hand, and if he vouches for the other two, that's good enough for me."

Sheriff Carson chuckled. "I'm not talkin' about that," he said. "I know all three of those boys and they probably will make you good hands. I'm talkin' about this foolishness of trying to drive a herd that far north at this time of year."

"You know Smoke as well as anyone, Sheriff," Cal said. "If he says he can do it, I believe he can do it."

"Well, I'll give you this," Sheriff Carson said. "If any man alive can take a herd of—how many cows did you say it was?"

"Three thousand head," Cal answered.

Sheriff Carson gave a low whistle. "Three thousand head," he repeated. "Well, like I was about to say, if any man alive can take a herd of three thousand head all the way to Wyoming this late in the season, Smoke Jensen is that man. But I certainly don't envy any of you."

"Hold it," LeRoy said. "What are you talking about? What do you mean taking three thousand head of cattle to Wyoming? I thought you said we was comin' to work at Sugarloaf."

"That's right," Pearlie said. "And the work you're goin' to be doin' is takin' a herd to Wyoming."

"When?"

"Now," Pearlie said.

"Now! Are you crazy? It's damn near winter."

"Yes, that's why we need to get started right away," Pearlie said.

LeRoy shook his head. "Huh-uh," he said. "You didn't say nothin' about drivin' no herd north when you hired us. All you said was that you was lookin' for some more hands."

"If you don't want to go, I'm sure we can arrange for you to stay here in jail," Pearlie said. "I can always get someone else."

"Yeah? Well, you just . . ." LeRoy began, but Hank interrupted him in mid-sentence.

"No!" he said. "You don't need anyone else. Don't pay my brother no never-mind. Me'n LeRoy will do it."

The wagon was about half-loaded by the time Pearlie, Cal, Billy, Hank, and LeRoy arrived. Mike, Billy, and the Butrums already knew each other, but Andy and Dooley had to introduce themselves. Pearlie noticed that both former soldiers were now wearing new jeans and plaid shirts.

"Yeah," Andy said. "Don't they look nice? Miz Sally

bought 'em for us. First time I've had 'nything other'n an army uniform on in four years."

"Come on, boys," Pearlie said, picking up a bundle. "Let's get the wagon loaded so we can get back to the ranch in time for supper."

Chapter Eight

The Cheyenne village of Red Eagle

The village was typical of all the villages of the Plains Indians. The tepees were erected in a series of concentric circles with the openings facing east. They were pitched alongside a fast-flowing stream, which provided not only water for drinking, cooking, and washing, but also fresh fish. Although there were no addresses as such, everyone knew where everyone else lived by their position within the circles.

Fall had already come and the bright yellow aspen trees stood out from the dark green conifers interspersed with a spattering of red and brown from the willow, oak, and maple that climbed the nearby mountainsides. Smoke curled from the tops of the lodges as the women prepared meals while the men watched over the herd of horses, or worked at cleaning their rifles or making bows and arrows. Children played beside the water.

The chief of the village was a man named Red Eagle. Red Eagle was once the great warrior chief of a proud people, but now he was a chief in name only. In compliance with a treaty signed with the soldiers, Red Eagle had moved his people onto a reservation.

The reservation guaranteed peace with the soldiers, but it stripped his people of all identity and pride. Now, they were totally dependent upon the white man for their very survival. They were not allowed to hunt buffalo, for to do so would require them to leave their designated area. But there were few buffalo anyway, the herds having been greatly diminished by the white men who had hunted to supply meat for the work crews that were building the railroads, or worse, the buffers who took only the hides and left the prairie strewn with rotting meat and bleaching bones.

Red Eagle's people were dispirited. Without the buffalo, there was little to eat. They had been promised a ration of beef by the agency, but the promised beef had not materialized. Even if it had, it was a poor substitute for the buffalo. Red Eagle did not care much for beef, and he knew that his people felt as he did. But if it was a choice of beef or starvation, they would take beef.

Not everyone agreed with Red Eagle. There were some who wanted to leave the reservation, to be free to hunt what buffalo remained. But Red Eagle had no wish to see his village subjected to the kind of murderous attack he and his wife had lived through at White Antelope's village at Sand Creek, so he counseled his people to stay on the reservation.

Sand Creek proved, however, that even obedience to the white man's law would not always protect you. There, Colonel John M. Chivington and his Colorado militia had murdered men, women, and children, even as the terrified Indians were gathering around a tepee flying the American flag.

White Antelope, the head of the Sand Creek village, was Red Eagle's very good friend. An old man of seventy-one, White Antelope was convinced that the soldiers were attacking because they didn't understand that his people were a peaceful band. In order to prove that his village was friendly, he raised the American flag over his tepee. Then, in order to reinforce his declaration of peace, he started walking toward Colonel Chivington carrying a white flag.

Despite White Antelope's efforts to show the soldiers that neither he nor his people represented a danger to the soldiers, he was shot down. Red Eagle had screamed out in anger and grief at seeing his friend murdered.

That had been many years ago, but sometimes Red Eagle still believed he could hear the old chief singing the Cheyenne death song as he lay dying.

"There is not a thing that lives forever
Except the earth and the mountains."

Red Eagle realized then that if he stayed, he would be killed, despite the protection of the American flag and the flag of surrender. He grabbed his wife by the hand and they darted down a ravine, miraculously escaping Chivington's band.

Now, Red Eagle was the leader of his own village, and he was determined not to let his people be slaughtered as had been the villagers under White Antelope's protection. If the soldiers demanded that Red Eagle keep his people on the reservation, then that is exactly what he would do. And if Walking Bear and the band of young firebrands who followed him wanted to make trouble off the reservation, then they would have to deal with the soldiers themselves, because he would not make council on their behalf.

As the shadows of evening pushed away the last vestiges of color in the west, Red Eagle came out into the village circle to sit near the fire. The village circle acted as a community center for the village. It was an area of dry grass, smooth logs, and gentle rises making it a very good sitting place. Every night that weather permitted, men, women, and children from the village would gather around the fire's light and talk of the events of the day.

The village circle was a place where problems were discussed, group decisions made, and young men and young women could court under the watchful eyes of the village. It was also a place of entertainment, sometimes consisting of dancing, but often a place where stories were told.

One of the reasons Red Eagle was a leader of the village was because he was an old man who had lived through many winters, and had experienced a lot of adventures. That made him a particularly good storyteller when he was in the mood, and tonight he was in just such a mood. Besides, he thought, a good story would lift his people's spirits so that they would not think of the hunger that was gnawing at their bellies.

"Listen," Red Eagle said, "and I will tell you a story."

Those who were around him, the men of the council, the warriors, and those who would be warriors, drew closer to hear his words. The women and children grew quiet, not only because it was forbidden to make noise while stories were being told around the campfires, but also because they knew it would be a good story and it filled them with excitement to hear it.

As the fire burned, it cast an orange light upon Red Eagle, making his skin glow and his eyes gleam. A small gas pocket in one of the burning logs popped, and it sent a shower of sparks climbing into the sky, red stars among the blue. Red Eagle held his hand up and crooked his finger as he began to talk.

"Once there was a time before the people, before Kiowa,

before Arapaho, before Commanche, before Lakota, even before Cheyenne."

"What time was this, Grandfather?" one of the children asked. Red Eagle was not the young questioner's biological grandfather, but he was the spiritual grandfather of them all, and so the child's innocent question reflected that.

"This was the time before time," Red Eagle replied. "This was in the time of the beginning, before the winter-count, before there was dry land. Then, there was only water and the Great Spirit, who floated on the water. With him were only things that could swim, like the fish and the swan, the goose, and the duck.

"The Great Spirit wanted to have people, but to do that, had to make land to walk upon. So he asked someone to dive to the bottom. 'Let me try,' a little duck said.

"The swan laughed at the little duck. 'You are much too small. I am a mighty swan, the most noble of all creatures. I will dive to the bottom and find earth.'

"So the swan dove down through the water to try and find the earth. But when he came up, his bill was empty.

"'The water is much too deep,' the swan said. 'I could not find the bottom.'

"'Let me try and find the bottom,' the little duck said.

"But the goose laughed at the duck. 'You are much too little and too weak to find the bottom. I am a goose. I am big and strong. I will find the bottom.'

"So the goose took a deep breath and dove very deep, but he couldn't reach the bottom either. He came up, gasping for breath, and he said, 'Great Spirit, I think you are playing tricks with us. I think there is no bottom.'

"'Please, let me try,' the little duck said again.

"Both the swan and the goose laughed. 'Foolish little

duck,' they said. 'If we could not find the bottom, what makes you think you can?'"

"'I believe I can do it,' the little duck said again.

"'You may try,' the Great Spirit said.

"The little duck took a deep breath and plunged down through the water. He was underwater for a long time, and everyone thought that the little duck had drowned and they were very sad. 'You should not have let him try,' they said to the Great Spirit, but the Great Spirit told them to have patience.

"Then, when it seemed that all was lost, the little duck came back up with a bit of mud in its bill.

"'How could he do that when we could not?' the swan asked. 'He is small and we are big.'

"'He is small, but his heart is big and his soul is good. That gives him very strong medicine, and that is why he succeeded where you failed,' the Great Spirit said.

"Then, taking the mud from the bill of the little duck, the Great Spirit worked it in his hands until it was dry, and with it, he made little piles of land on the water surface. That land grew and grew until it made solid land everywhere." Red Eagle held his arm out and took in all the land around him. "And that is what we see today."

"And then did our people come to live on the land?" one of the children asked.

"Yes," Red Eagle said. "Two young men and two young women who were looking for food walked for eight days and eight nights without eating, or drinking, or sleeping. They saw a high peak and decided to go to it to die, for it would be a marker to show their burying place. But when they got there, they saw a yellow-haired woman who showed them the buffalo. The men hunted the buffalo and got food to eat, and the women bore many sons. The sons took many wives and bore more children. I am the child of one of those children, just as you are the children of my children. And thus we are all Cheyenne."

Once Red Eagle finished his story, others began to tell stories as well. If the story was to be a tale of bravery in battle, the one who spoke would walk over to the lodge pole and strike it with his coup stick. Then everyone would know that he was going to tell a story of an enemy killed in battle. In such stories the enemy warriors were always brave and skilled, because that made the warrior's own exploits all the greater.

Not all stories were of enemies killed in battle. Some of the stories were of hunting exploits, and some told of things that had happened in the time of their father's father's father that had been handed down through the generations to be preserved as part of their history.

One of those who spoke little, but of whom many tales were told, was Walking Bear. A few days earlier, Walking Bear had led a war party against a small establishment that consisted of a military stockade, stagecoach station, and telegraph office. The stockade was manned by about fifty soldiers, and when Walking Bear tried a frontal attack against the soldiers, he was driven back by cannon fire and by the long-range fire of the soldier's rifles. As the soldiers were protected by the heavy timbers of the stockade, Walking Bear was unable to dislodge them, even though he had superior numbers.

Walking Bear tried a few ploys. He sent ten warriors down toward the soldiers to act as decoys, but they were unable to draw the soldiers out. The next morning he sent twenty, and this time the soldiers came out as far as the bridge, but would come no farther.

Some suggested the warriors should slip down at night and set fire to the stockade, but Walking Bear insisted that only cowards fight in such a way. They finally decided that they would try another frontal assault the next day, massing all their numbers. Before they could launch their attack, though, they were surprised to see an entire platoon of cavalrymen ride out of the fort, cross the bridge, then head westward at a trot. The soldiers had come out of the fort to provide an escort for an approaching wagon train.

Elated at their good fortune, Walking Bear mounted all his warriors and they swarmed down on the wagons and the escorting soldiers.

The soldiers reached the wagons, then, in a classic formation, circled the wagons and dug in. The soldiers fought bravely, and Walking Bear's own brother was killed in the first few minutes of fighting. Angered and grieving, Walking Bear led the Cheyenne into ever-decreasing circles around the wagons, lashing their ponies to make them go faster and faster. Walking Bear was wearing his medicine bonnet and carrying his sacred shield, so he knew that no bullets would strike him.

As the circle tightened closer to the wagons, the soldiers continued their firing until, finally, all the soldiers were out of ammunition. When the soldiers stopped firing, the Cheyenne charged straight for the wagons and killed all the soldiers. They fell upon the wagons in eager anticipation, but were very disappointed by what they found. Though they had hoped for weapons and ammunition, there was nothing in the wagons but bedding and mess chests.

When Walking Bear returned, he told the others in the council that the white men had been taught a lesson and would now obey the treaty they had signed.

"No," Red Eagle said. "I fear that all you have done is anger the white man so that we will get no beef."

"You want beef?" Walking Bear retorted, angry that

Red Eagle did not respect his story of bravery in battle. "I will get beef for you. I will get all the beef you can eat."

"How will you do such a thing?" Red Eagle asked.

"Are you an old man that you have forgotten the way of our people? I will get beef the way Cheyenne have always gotten food. I will find it, and I will bring it back. I will not wait for the white man to give it to us, as if we are children, pawing and mewing to suckle at the teat."

Walking Bear's words were angry and disrespectful of an old man who had, long ago, earned the respect of all his people. As a result, many who heard the words gasped.

Red Eagle stood up, and pulled his robe about him. He pointed. "Go," he said. "Leave our village before you bring evil to us."

"And if I say I do not wish to go, what can you do?" Walking Bear asked. He laughed, a disrespectful, guttural laugh. "You can do nothing, old man," he taunted. "You are old and weak, and you have no medicine."

Red Eagle said nothing, but he raised his hand into the air, then made a circular motion with his fingers. Then, there was the whirring sound of wind through feathers. A large eagle suddenly appeared swooping down out of the darkness. He made a pass at Walking Bear's head, legs extended, claws bared. The eagle raked his claws across Walking Bear's face, leaving three, parallel, bleeding gashes on his cheek. Then, with a graceful but powerful beat of his wings, the eagle soared back up to disappear in the darkness.

Those who watched the incident gasped and called out in shock and fear, but no one was more shocked or more frightened by what had just happened than Walking Bear himself.

Walking Bear put his hand to his cheek, ran the fingers

across the cuts, then held them out to look at the blood, shining darkly in the firelight.

"How . . . ?" Walking Bear started to ask, but he never finished his question.

"Leave," Red Eagle said again, this time speaking very quietly, but with great authority.

"I will go," Walking Bear replied. "I am not going because you have ordered me to, but because I can no longer live with men who fear to walk the path of a warrior. Who will come with me?" he asked loudly.

About two dozen young men stood up, standing silently in the night, their eyes shining red from the light of the fire.

Red Eagle looked at all of the young men, then nodded.

"Do you see that the bravest of our people have joined me?" Walking Bear asked.

"Go," Red Eagle said. "Take your women and your children with you. You are no longer a part of this village."

"Eeeyahhhh!!!!" Walking Bear shouted, and those who had stood to go returned the shout.

As Walking Bear and those who followed him left the village, their departure was greeted with silence, partly in stunned disbelief over what they were witnessing and partly in grief at losing members of their village.

Red Eagle spoke to the village. "I will say for the last time the name of Walking Bear. I tell you now to speak the names of those who left us. Then, after this day, do not say their names again, for they are no more."

The villagers shouted the names of the warriors, and of the women and children of the warriors who left with them; then they began singing the lament of the dead for, as far as they were concerned, those who left the village that day were dead.

* * *

As Walking Bear and his warriors and their families moved away from Red Eagle's village, he could hear the sounds of the death songs. He could also hear the sound of weeping from the women and children of his band as they mourned those who were left behind.

"Warriors!" he called. "Be of stout heart! We ride the path of the brave! Eeeyaaah!!!!"

The other warriors with him joined in the yell, as much to buck up their own spirits as to shut out the mournful sounds from the village.

Chapter Nine

Puxico, Wyoming Territory

"Oyez, oyez, oyez, this here court is about to convene, the Honorable Judge Spenser Clark presidin'," the bailiff shouted.

"Ha, this ain't no court! This here's a saloon," someone shouted. His shout was met with laughter from others who were present.

"Crawford, one more outburst like that, and you'll spend thirty days in the jail," the bailiff said, pointing to the offending customer/spectator. "This here saloon is a court whenever His Honor decides to make it a court, and that's what he's done. Now, everybody stand up'n make sure you ain't wearin' no hat or nothin' like that while the judge comes in. And McCall, you better not let me catch you servin' no liquor durin' the trial."

"I know the rules, George. I ain't served nary a drop since the judge ordered the saloon closed," McCall replied.

The Honorable Spenser Clark came out of the back room of the saloon and took a seat at his "bench," which was the best table in the saloon. The table sat upon a raised platform that had been built just for this purpose.

The saloon was used as a court because it was the

largest building in town. An ancillary reason for holding court in the saloon was because it was always crowded, thus making it easy for the judge to empanel a jury by rounding up twelve sober men, good and true. If it was sometimes difficult to find twelve sober men, then the judge could stretch the definition of sobriety enough to meet the needs of the court. The "good and true," however, had to be taken upon faith.

Quince Pardeen was being charged with the murder of Sheriff John Logan. There was no question that he had killed Sheriff Logan, because he had done so on the main street of the town in front of no fewer than thirty witnesses.

There was some question, however, as to whether or not it could actually be considered murder. That was because it was clear that Sheriff Logan drew his pistol first. Prosecution contended that the sheriff did so in the line of duty while attempting to arrest a man for whom there were wanted posters in obvious circulation.

The city of Puxico had only two lawyers, David Varner and Bailey Gilmore, neither of whom was a prosecuting attorney. Because of that, Judge Clark brought the two men into his hotel room prior to the trial.

"I don't suppose Pardeen has hired either of you to represent him, has he?" he asked.

"It is my understanding he is going to ask that a lawyer be appointed," Varner replied.

Judge Clark sighed. "Do either of you volunteer for defense?"

Varner and Gilmore looked at each other, but neither spoke.

"Very well, we'll flip a coin," the judge said, pulling a nickel from his pocket.

Varner called heads, it came up heads, and he asked to prosecute. That made Gilmore Pardeen's defense attorney.

Gilmore was conscientious enough to believe in providing the best defense possible, regardless of the heinousness of the crime, and he sat out to do just that. He made a very strong argument that Pardeen saw only the draw, and perceiving that his life was in danger, reacted as anyone would.

"Pardeen might be a wanted man," Gilmore said in his closing argument. "But even wanted men do not surrender their right to self-preservation.

"I lament the fact that Sheriff Logan was killed, and for that, his dear widow has our sincerest sympathy." Gilmore glanced over at Mrs. Logan, who, still wearing widows weeds, lifted her black veil to dab at her eyes with a silk handkerchief.

"Indeed," Gilmore continued, "the entire town of Puxico has our sympathy, for Sheriff Logan was known far and wide as a good and decent man."

"What the hell are you doin', lawyer?" Pardeen yelled angrily from the defense table. "Whose side are you on anyhow?"

"Mr. Pardeen, one more outburst like that and I'll have you bound and gagged," Judge Clark warned. "You may continue with your argument, Counselor."

The defense attorney nodded, then brought his closing argument to its conclusion. "Gentlemen of the jury, any way you look at this fracas, no matter how good and decent a man Logan was, if you are fair and honest in your deliberation, you will agree that Mr. Pardeen acted in self-defense."

Varner waited until Gilmore had taken his seat before he rose to address the jury. Before he said a word he made a sarcastic show of applauding, clapping his hands together so quietly that they could not be heard.

"I applaud the esteemed counselor for the defense," he said. "He is a good man who believes that anyone—even a person as evil and as obviously guilty as Quince Pardeen—deserves a good defense. He chose, of course, the only option open to him. He chose to make his plea, one of self-defense. But despite my esteemed colleague's most sincere attempt, the truth is"—Varner paused and looked directly at Pardeen—"Mr. Gilmore's noble effort was an exercise in futility. Quince Pardeen is a cold-blooded murderer. Many a good man has fallen before his gun—none finer than our own sheriff. By his lifetime of evil, Pardeen has forfeited forever any claim to self-defense."

After Varner sat down, Judge Clark instructed the jury and they withdrew to a room at the back of the saloon to make their decision. After only five minutes of deliberation, the jury sent word that they had reached a verdict.

After retaking his seat at the "bench," Judge Clark put on his glasses, slipping the end pieces over one ear at a time. Then he blew his nose and cleared his throat.

"Are counsel and defendant present?" He pronounced the word as "defend-ant."

"Counsel and defendant are both present at the table," Gilmore replied.

"Is the prosecutor present?"

"Hell, Judge, you can see him right in front of your face," one of the spectators shouted. "Get this over so we can get back to our drinkin'."

There was some nervous laughter, terminated by the rap of the judge's gavel. "Mr. Matthews, that little outburst just cost you twenty dollars," Clark said.

"Wait a minute, I ain't the only one who—" Matthews began, but he was interrupted by the judge.

"Now it's twenty-five dollars. Do you want to open your mouth again?"

This time Matthews's reply was a silent shaking of his head.

"I thought you might come to your senses," Judge Clark said. "Now, would the bailiff please summon the jury?"

The bailiff, who was leaning against the bar with his arms folded across his chest, spit a quid of tobacco into the brass spittoon, then walked over to a door, opened it, and called inside.

"The judge has called for the jury," he said.

At the bailiff's call, the twelve men shuffled from the room where they had conducted their deliberations, and out onto the main floor of the saloon, to the chairs that had been set out for them in two lines of six. They took their seats, then waited for further instructions from the judge.

"Mr. Foreman of the Jury, have you reached a verdict?" the judge asked.

"We have, Judge."

"Your Honor," the bailiff said.

"Say what?"

"When addressing His Honor the judge, you will say Your Honor," the bailiff directed.

"Oh, yeah, I'm sorry, I forgot about that. We have reached a verdict, Your Honor."

"Please publish the verdict."

"Do what?"

Judge Clark sighed. "Tell the court what the jury has found."

"Oh. Well, sir, Your Honor, we have found this guilty son of bitch guilty," the foreman said.

"You goddamn well better have!" someone shouted from the court.

The judge banged his gavel on the table.

"Order!" he called. "I will have order in my court." He looked over at the foreman. "So say you all?" he asked.

"So say we all," the foreman replied.

The judge took off his glasses and began polishing them.

"Bailiff, escort the defendant to the bench, please," the judge said.

Pardeen was handcuffed, and he had shackles on his ankles. He shuffled up to stand in front of the judge.

Pardeen was not a very large man. In a normal world, any belligerency on the part of a man as small as Pardeen would have been regarded as unimportant, or at least manageable. But this was not an ordinary world because Pardeen's small stature was offset by the fact that he possessed extraordinary skill with a handgun. But even more important than his skill with a pistol was the diabolical disregard of human life that would allow him to use that skill. It was said of Pardeen that he could kill a human being with no more thought than stepping on a bug.

Pardeen's hair was dark and his eyes were brown. One of his eyes was what people called "lazy," and it had a tendency to give the illusion that he was looking at two things at once.

"Quince Pardeen, it is said that you have killed fifteen men, and that you may be one of the deadliest gunmen in the West. I could not try you for all those killings—I could only try you for killing Sheriff Logan, and that I have done. You have been tried by a jury of your peers and you have been found guilty of the crime of murder," he said. "Before this court passes sentence, have you anything to say?"

"Nah, I ain't got nothin' to say," Pardeen said.

"Then draw near for sentencing," the judge said solemly. "It is the sentence of this court that you be taken from this place and put in jail long enough to witness one more night pass from this mortal coil. At dawn's light on the morrow, you are to be taken from jail and transported to a place where you will be hanged."

"Your Honor, we can't hang 'im in the mornin'. We ain't built no gallows yet," the deputy who was now acting sheriff said.

Judge Clark held up his hand to silence the deputy, indicating that he had already taken that into consideration. "This court authorizes the use of a tree, a lamppost, a hay-loading stanchion, or any other device, fixture, apparatus, contrivance, agent, or means as may be sufficient to suspend Mr. Pardeen's carcass above the ground, bringing about the effect of breaking his neck, collapsing his windpipe and, in any and all ways, squeezing the last breath of life from his worthless, vile, and miserable body."

The gallery broke into loud applause and cheers and shouts.

"Hey, Pardeen, how does it feel? You'll be in hell this time tomorrow!" someone shouted.

"Hell is too good for you!" another said.

Judge Clark banged his gavel a few times, then realizing the futility of it, looked at the deputy.

"Get his sorry carcass out of here," he said.

Acting Sheriff Lewis Baker had been napping at his desk when something awakened him. Opening his eyes, he looked around the inside of the sheriff's office. The room was dimly lit by a low-burning kerosene lantern. A breath of wind moved softly through the open window, causing the wanted posters to flutter on the bulletin board.

A pot of coffee sat on a small, wood-burning stove filling the room with its rich armoa. The Regulator clock on the wall swept its pendulum back and forth in a measured "tick-tock," the hands on the face pointing to ten minutes after two. The acting sheriff rubbed his eyes, then stood up and stretched. Stepping over to the stove, he used his hat as a heat pad and grabbed the metal handle to pour himself a cup of coffee. Taking a sip of his coffee, he glanced over toward the jail cell. He was surprised to see that Pardeen wasn't asleep, but was sitting up on his bunk.

Baker chuckled. "What's the matter, Pardeen?" he asked. He took another slurping drink of his coffee. "Can't sleep?"

"No," Pardeen growled.

"Well, I don't know as I blame you none," the acting sheriff said. "I mean, you're goin' to die in about four more hours, so you may as well stay awake and enjoy what little time you got left on this earth." He took another swallow of his coffee.

"Ahhh," he said. "Coffee is one of the sweetest pleasures of life, don't you think? But then, life itself is sweet, ain't it?" He laughed again, then turned away from the cell.

He gasped in surprise when he saw someone standing between himself and his desk. He had not heard the man come in.

"Who the hell are you?" Baker asked gruffly. "And what the hell are you doing in here? You aren't supposed to be in here."

"My name is Corbett. I've come to visit Mr. Pardeen."

"There ain't no visitors authorized right now," Baker said.

"I've got some sad news for him."

"Sad news?"

"Yeah, his brother was killed."

Unexpectedly, Baker chuckled. "Is that a fact? His brother was killed, was he? Well, now, I wouldn't want to keep our prisoner from getting any sad news," he said. He made a motion toward the cell. "You just go ahead and tell Pardeen about his brother. The son of a bitch is going to be dead in four more hours. I'd like to do everything in my power to make his last hours as unpleasant as I can." Baker laughed again.

Corbett nodded, then walked over to the cell. "Pardeen, I hate to be the one to tell you this, but your brother Emerson got hisself kilt last week."

"Who killed him?"

"A fella by the name of Smoke Jensen. You ever hear of him?"

"Yeah, I've heard of him. How'd it happen?"

"Damn'dest thing you ever saw. Emerson had his gun drawed already, and he was comin' back on the hammer when Smoke Jensen drawed his gun and shot him."

"You seen this, did you?" Pardeen asked.

"Yeah, I seen it."

"He must be pretty fast."

"He is fast. He's faster'n anyone I ever seen."

"Yeah, well, I don't care how fast he is. I'm goin' to kill him."

Acting Sheriff Baker laughed so hard that he sprayed coffee. "You're going to kill him? And how are you going to do that? Come sunrise, you're goin' to be hangin' by your neck." He put his fist by his neck, then make a rasping sound with his voice and tilted his head in a pantomime of hanging.

"Give me your gun," Pardeen said quietly.

Nodding, Corbett drew his pistol and passed it through the bars to Pardeen.

"Sheriff, you want to step over here for a moment?" Pardeen called.

"What do you want?" the acting sheriff asked. Then, shocked at seeing a pistol in Pardeen's hand, he threw up his arms. "No!" he shouted in fear.

Without so much as another word, Pardeen shot the deputy.

"When you get to hell, tell my brother hello for me," Pardeen said.

"Where are the keys?" Corbett asked.

"They're over there, hanging on a hook behind the desk," Pardeen said, pointing.

Corbett stepped quickly over to the hook, took down the keys, then returned to unlock the cell door. "I've got a couple of horses in the alley," he said.

"I appreciate you doin' this for me."

"Well, your brother was my friend. I'd like to see the son of a bitch who killed him pay for it. And I figure you're the one who can make him do it."

The two men stepped out into the alley, but instead of going toward the two horses that were tied off in back, Pardeen turned and started walking up the dark alley.

"Hey, the horses is over here," Corbett called.

"I got somewhere else I'm goin' to first," Pardeen said with an impatient grunt.

"Where you got to go that's so important we can't ride outta here while we have the chance?" Corbett asked.

"The hotel."

"Why we goin' to the hotel?"

"You'll see when I get there," Pardeen replied. "That is, if you're a'comin' with me."

"Yeah," Corbett answered. "Yeah, I'm comin' with you."

The two men moved silently through the dark shadows of the alley until they reached the hotel. Slipping in through the front door, they could hear the snores of the night clerk who was on duty. Crossing the darkened lobby, Pardeen turned the registration book around so he could read the entries.

"What are you lookin' for?" Corbett whispered.

"Ain't lookin'. I found it," Pardeen replied, also in a whisper. He reached over behind the sleeping clerk and took a key down from a board filled with keys. Recrossing the lobby, Pardeen started up the stairs with Corbett, still unsure as to what they were doing, climbing the stairs behind him.

Reaching the second floor, the two men stopped for just a moment. A couple of candles that were set in wall sconces lit the hallway in a flickering orange light. The snoring of the various residents could be heard through the closed doors.

"He's down this way," Pardeen hissed.

"Who is?"

"The judge."

"We're lookin' for a judge? Why?"

"He's the son of a bitch that sentenced me to hang," Pardeen said. "I want to send a message to all the other judges so that if I ever get in this position again, they'll think twice before trying to hang me."

They walked quietly down the carpeted hallway until they found the door Pardeen was looking for. Slowly, he unlocked the door, then pushed it open.

The judge was snoring peacefully.

Pardeen pulled his gun and pointed it toward the judge. Then, having second thoughts, he put the gun away.

"You got a knife?" he asked.

"Yeah, I got a knife," Corbett answered.

"Let me borrow it."

Corbett pulled his knife from its sheath and handed it

to Pardeen. Pardeen raised the knife over the judge, paused for a moment, then pulled it back down.

"What is it? What's wrong?" Corbett hissed.

"I want the son of a bitch to wake up long enough to know what's happening to him, and to see who is doing it."

Corbett nodded.

Pardeen reached down to cover the judge's mouth with his hand.

"Wake up, you son of a bitch," he said.

The judge snorted in mid-snore, then opened his eyes. For just a moment there was confusion in his eyes, but when he recognized Pardeen, the confusion turned to fear, then terror. He tried to speak, but couldn't because Pardeen's hand was clamped down over his mouth.

"Ha! Bet you never thought you'd see me again, did you?"

The judge tried to speak again, but it came out as a squeak.

"Oh, I guess you're wonderin' how I got here, huh? Well, I tell you, Judge. I just killed the deputy and broke jail, and now I've come to kill you. What was it you said in court? Something about finding a contrivance or means to suspend me from the ground long enough to break my neck?"

Pardeen laughed a guttural laugh that was without humor.

"Well, this here knife is all the contrivance I need, Judge."

Pardeen pulled his hand away from the judge's mouth. The judge tried to sit up, but before he could, Pardeen brought his knife across the judge's neck. The judge put his hands up to his throat, then, with a gurgling sound, fell back down onto the pillow. He flopped once or twice like a fish out of water, then lay still in a growing pool of blood.

"Is he dead?" Corbett asked.

"Yeah, he's dead."

Corbett went over to the window and tried to raise it.

"What are you doin'?"

"Killin' a judge like we done, maybe we ought to go out this way before somebody comes after us," Corbett said.

Pardeen laughed. "Who's goin' to come after us, Corbett? I killed the sheriff last week, the deputy and the judge tonight. They ain't nobody left to come after us."

Corbett thought for a moment, then laughed out loud. "Yeah," he said. "Yeah, there ain't nobody left to come after us."

Chapter Ten

Sugarloaf Ranch

Smoke was surprised when he saw several head of cattle being pushed onto Sugarloaf. Riding out to see what was going on, he found a small, wiry young man, whistling and shouting as he drove the herd. He was riding one horse, and leading another.

When the young man saw Smoke, he rode toward him, touching the brim of his hat as he reached him. The hat was oversized, with a particularly high crown, almost as if the boy was trying to use it to make up for his small stature.

"You Smoke Jensen?" he asked.

"I am."

The boy smiled and stuck out his hand. "Mr. Jensen, I heard you was plannin' on makin' a big cattle drive up north."

"That's right."

"Well, these here is your cows that was way down on the south range. I reckon you would'a got around to 'em in time, but I thought I'd save you the trouble. The name's Sanders. Jules Sanders. I come to join you on your drive, if you'll have me."

"Jules, don't get the wrong idea here, but how old are you?" Smoke asked.

"Tell me how old you want me to be and I'll accommodate you," Jules said.

Smoke chuckled. "That's not what I asked," he said. "I'll be honest with you, you don't look a day over fifteen."

Jules didn't answer. "Where you want me to put these cows?"

"You say you drove them up from the south range?" Smoke asked.

"Yes."

"That's twelve miles from here. You brought—how many are there?"

"Sixty-three head," Jules said.

"You brought sixty-three head up from the south range all by yourself?"

"Yes."

Smoke stroked his chin. "That's a pretty good drive for someone to make all by themselves, no matter how old they might be. You knew we'd be coming down there to get them, didn't you?"

"Yes, sir," Jules said. "I knew you'd be comin' for 'em."

"Then why didn't you just leave them there for us?"

"I wanted to impress you," Jules said.

"Well, I must confess, you did do that."

"Mr. Jensen, I need the job," Jules said.

"Jules, this is going to be one difficult drive. It's late in the year and we've got a long way to go. We'll be gone for some time. How would your mom and dad feel about that?"

"They're the reason I need to do it," Jules said. "My ma is bringin' in washin' and sech, all the while she's doin' for my dad. My dad is laid up with what the doc calls the cancer. I got to do somethin' to help out, Mr. Jensen."

Smoke was quiet for a moment, then he nodded. "All right, Jules. I reckon if you can bring this many head this far all by yourself, then you're man enough to do the job."

A big smile spread across Jules's face, and he stuck out his hand. "Thanks, Mr. Jensen," he said. "I can't tell you what this means to me."

Smoke shook Jules's hand. "One thing, though, Jules."

"Yes, sir, anything."

"We're sort of one big family here. I'm Smoke to all the men."

"Yes, sir, Mister—uh, Smoke," Jules said. He looked back at the cattle he had brought up. "Uh, what do I do with these critters?"

"Take 'em out to the north range, join them with the others you see there, then go on down to the house and see Sally."

"Sally?"

"My wife," Smoke said. "She's taking care of the business end of this. She'll make sure you're on the payroll. Uh, by the way, could you use a little advance to send back to your folks?"

Jules shook his head. "No, sir," he said. "I appreciate the offer, I purely do. But I don't want nothin' till I've earned it."

Smoke smiled, and nodded. "You're a good man, Jules," he said. "I don't care how old you are, you're a good man."

"Thanks."

"When's the last time you ate?"

"I had me some jerky back this mornin'," Jules said.

"Well, I know you don't want any money before you've earned it, but you wouldn't mind eatin' with us, would you?"

The broad smile returned. "No, sir, I wouldn't mind that," he said. "I wouldn't mind that none at all."

"When you get back to the house, tell Sally there'll be one more for supper."

"Yes, sir!" Jules said. He turned to the cattle he had brought up. "Get along, cows. They's grass for you and vittles for me."

Smoke watched Jules ride off, driving the cattle before him. He didn't really need another man, but there was something about this young man that reminded him of Matt, and there was no way he was going to turn him down.

Pearlie came riding up shortly after Jules rode off.

"Who was that?" Pearlie asked.

"Our new man."

"I thought we had everyone we needed."

"There's always room for one more," Smoke said.

Pearlie smiled. "Uh-huh," he said. "And if you particular like a person, why, I reckon you'd make room for him even if there weren't none."

"I made room for you once, didn't I?" Smoke asked.

Pearlie nodded. "Yes, sir, you done that all right," Pearlie said. They were referring to the fact that Pearlie, who had once been hired as a gunman to run Smoke off his ranch, had wound up joining the same man he was supposed to kill.

As a means of allowing everyone to get better acquainted with each other, Sally invited all the cowboys to have supper in the big house that night. She fixed roast beef, mashed potatoes with brown gravy, lima beans, and hot rolls.

"Do you folks eat like this all the time?" Jules asked.

"We sure do," Pearlie said.

"Ha!" Cal laughed. "Pearlie wishes we did."

"I figure that during the trail drive," said Sally, "there are bound to be times when you boys are going to get pretty frustrated by pushing a bunch of cows. So, if they start giving you too much trouble, maybe you can take some solace in having eaten their cousin tonight."

The others laughed.

"Say, Smoke, the county fair starts tomorrow," Cal said. "You reckon we could all go in for a bit? I mean, especially as we are going to be on the trail drive for so long."

"I don't see why not," Smoke said.

"You know what we ought to do? We ought to play a baseball game," Jules said.

"What?" Billy asked.

"We ought to play a baseball game," Jules said again. "We've got enough for a baseball team. There's Pearlie, Cal, Andy, Dooley, Hank, LeRoy, Billy, Mike, and me. That's nine people."

"What about Smoke?" Billy asked.

"Smoke can be our manager."

"What's a manager?"

"A manager is someone who doesn't play, but sort of bosses the ones that do."

"Ha! That's Smoke all right," Cal said. "The bossin' part, I mean."

"Well, tell me just who we are goin' to play with this baseball team?" Pearlie asked.

"The St. Louis Unions."

"The what?"

"The St. Louis Unions," Jules repeated. "They are a professional baseball team and they go around playing local teams. If you beat them, they'll give you two hundred dollars."

"Two hundred dollars? That's a lot of money," LeRoy said.

"Yeah, that would be twenty dollars apiece," Dooley added.

"You can forget that," Pearlie said.

"What do you mean, we can forget it?" Jules asked. "It would be good to leave twenty dollars with my mom before we started on this trail drive."

"You can forget it, because we ain't likely to win."

"Well, come on, don't give up before we even try," Jules said.

"Didn't you say this St. Louis Unions was a bunch of professional baseball players?"

"Yes."

"Then that means that they play baseball all the time. I prob'ly ain't played more'n two or three times in my entire life."

"Me'n Dooley have played a lot," Andy said. "We used to have baseball games out at the fort."

"Yeah, and Andy's real good at it," Dooley said.

"I've played a lot too," Jules said. "Come on, we can at least try."

"Jules, you're young so I don't hold it against you none that you ain't really got no sense," Pearlie said. "But this whole idea of playing a baseball game against a bunch of people who make a living playing baseball is a . . ."

"Great idea," Sally said, finishing Pearlie's sentence.

"What?" several of the others replied at the same time.

"I think Jules has a great idea," Sally said. "I think you should play a baseball game against these people."

"Sally, I tend to agree with Pearlie," Smoke said. "Why humiliate ourselves before our neighbors against a bunch of professionals?"

"We're going to be working together for the next several weeks, right?" Sally asked.

"Yes."

"Then what better way to learn to work together than to play a baseball game now? I think it will create a sense of cooperation and belonging."

"Even if we lose?" Cal asked.

"Yes, even if you lose," Sally said. "Win or lose, if you all play together, you are going to come out ahead. Go on, Smoke, sign them up to play a game."

Smoke chuckled and shook his head. "All right," he said, "I'll challenge the—what are they called?"

"The St. Louis Unions," Jules said.

"I'll challenge the St. Louis Unions. But if we are humiliated, it's on your shoulders."

"I can take it," Sally said.

As Smoke, Sally, and the contingent from Sugarloaf rode into town, they passed under a banner that was stretched across the street, tied up on one side at Andersons's Apothecary and on the other at Miller's Meat Market. In big red letters the sign read:

WELCOME TO COUNTY FAIR

A series of exploding firecrackers made Billy's horse rear up, but Billy got it under control very quickly. The young boys who had set off the firecrackers laughed as they ran up the street.

Several vendors had set up booths in the street and were selling such things as taffy, roasted peanuts, fudge, and slices of pie. The city band, resplendent in their red and black uniforms, was seated on a temporary stage, playing a rousing march.

"Look, over there," Jules said, pointing to an open field. There, several men wearing identical straw hats, white shirts, and matching trousers were throwing a ball back and forth.

"Why are they all dressed alike?" Cal asked.

"They are in their uniforms," Jules answered.

"Uniforms? You mean like the suits the soldiers wear?"

"Sort of like that," Jules said. "They all wear the same uniform so you can tell who is on your side."

"Well, now, that don't make no sense a'tall," LeRoy said. "I mean, all you got to do is look at who the person is."

"It's probably for a little intimidation as well," Sally suggested.

"What does that mean?" Cal asked.

"It's just a way of giving them an edge," Sally explained.

"I see. Well, it ain't workin', whatever it's supposed to be doin'," Cal said.

"Shall we go over there and challenge them?" Smoke asked.

"Yeah," Pearlie said. "Let's do it."

"Really? You were one of the ones who thought it was such a crazy idea," Jules said.

"Yeah, but that was before I saw what a bunch of sissies these guys are. I think we won't have any trouble with them."

Smoke cut his horse over toward the field where the uniformed baseball players were throwing the ball around. Half-a-dozen kids were sitting on the top of a split-rail fence, watching the players.

"Who's in charge here?" Smoke called when he rode up.

At Smoke's call, one of the players threw a ball to

another, put his glove in his back pocket, expectorated a wad of chewing tobacco, wiped his mouth with the back of his hand, then came over to talk to Smoke.

"I'm in charge here," he said. "What do you need?"

"Is it true that you will give two hundred dollars to any team that can beat you?" Smoke asked.

"Well, to a degree, that is true," the player said.

"What isn't true?"

"We don't just give the money away. You have to enter the contest. And enterin' the contest is goin' to cost you money."

"How much?"

"Fifty dollars."

"Fifty dollars?" Jules groaned. "Why does it cost fifty dollars?"

"Where do you think we get the money to pay those who beat us?" the player asked.

"Does anyone ever actually beat you?" Smoke asked.

"Not very often," the ballplayer admitted.

"When can we play?" Smoke asked.

"As soon as we get the fifty dollars."

"Smoke, I'm sorry," Jules said. "I didn't have no idea it was going to cost money to play."

"That's all right," Smoke said, taking out the money and giving it to the ballplayer. "Here's your money, mister," he said. "Let's play."

"Yes."

Chapter Eleven

Big Rock

Word spread quickly around town that there would be a baseball match between the professional players who called themselves the St. Louis Unions and an aggregate of players from in and around Big Rock. As a result, nearly all the town gathered to watch the game.

Baseball was not unknown in Big Rock. There had been games contested between men from Big Rock and teams from nearby towns. But this was the first time that a touring professional team had ever come to town, so interest was high.

"Do you think our boys have a chance of winning?" someone asked.

"Not a snowball's chance in hell," another answered. "But that won't keep me from cheering them on."

"No, me neither. I'd like to see those St. Louis boys get their comeuppance."

The Unions, dressed in their white uniforms, were on the field giving a display of their skills by batting the ball, scooping it up from the ground, and throwing it sharply from base to base. After several minutes of such activity, the manager of the St. Louis Unions walked across the field to speak with Smoke.

"The game will commence in thirty minutes, and we will play by the Cartwright Rules," he said. He handed Smoke a booklet. "If you don't know the rules, they are in this book. Three strikes and you are out. Three outs and the other team comes to bat. When each team has made three outs, that will be an inning. We will play nine innings, unless the game is tied. Then we will continue to play until the tie is broken."

"We know the rules, mister," Pearlie said.

"Pearlie, Mr. Thayer is just extending a courtesy," Smoke said.

"I think he's trying to—to intimidate us," Pearlie said, recalling Sally's word. "But it ain't goin' to work, mister. It ain't goin' to work."

"I will tell my players to go easy on you," Thayer said as he turned to walk away."

"Oh, I'd love for us to give his team a good beating," Pearlie said.

"I wonder where Miss Sally is," Cal said. "I thought she would be here to watch us play."

"Maybe she don't want to see us lose," Mike said.

"Lose? We haven't played the first pitch yet and you are already talking about losing. Now, that's a fine way to look at it, don't you think?" Jules asked.

"Well, come on, Jules, look at them people. They got them fancy clothes they're a'wearin'. They got them fancy gloves."

"They've provided us with gloves," Jules said.

"Yeah, but they're nothin' like them fancy gloves they all got."

"Here comes Sally now," Smoke said. "I wonder what she's carrying."

Sally was carrying a bundle and as she approached them, she smiled broadly, then put the bundle down on a bench.

"What have you got there?" Smoke asked.

"Open it," Sally said. "The St. Louis Unions aren't the only ones with uniforms."

"You bought us uniforms?" Jules asked excitedly.

"I bought all of you matching red shirts," Sally said. "That, with your blue denim trousers, will make a uniform."

"Oh, yeah!" Jules said as he held up one of the shirts. "And these here is a lot better-lookin' than them white pajama-lookin' things those folks is wearin'."

Within minutes, every one of Smoke's men was smartly outfitted with the new red shirt and the result was dramatic. They took on the same aura as the uniformed St. Louis Unions.

Sheriff Carson agreed to be the umpire, and he walked out onto the ball field, leaned over to brush off the home plate, then stood up to bellow out as loud as he could:

"Play ball!"

They had played eight and a half innings of baseball and though the St. Louis Unions were leading, the score, at four to one, was much closer than anyone had thought possible. As it turned out, Jules was a very good baseball player, and Mike, Andy, and Leroy were also quite skilled. The others were good enough to keep the game from getting embarrassingly out of hand.

Now, in the last half of the ninth inning, with none out, Billy was walked, giving them a man on base. Cal singled, but Billy was held at third. Hank popped up and the ball was caught by the Unions' second baseman. LeRoy struck out, and that brought Jules to the plate.

"Come on, Jules, a home run would tie the game!" Pearlie shouted.

Jules nodded, then struck his bat against the plate a couple of times before looking at the pitcher.

"Boy," the catcher said from behind him. "I've been watching you. You're a pretty good ballplayer. What are you doing with this bunch of yokels? Why don't you leave them and come with us?"

"You really think I'm good enough to play with you fellas?" Jules asked.

"I sure do."

The pitcher fired the first ball to the plate. Jules swung, but missed.

"That didn't look all that good," Jules said to the catcher.

"Ah, don't worry about it. Tommy is a very good pitcher. You've hit him three times today, and not even the best batter can hit him every time. That's why if you strike out, nobody would ever suspect you did it on purpose."

"What do you mean, on purpose?" Jules asked.

"Well, we divide up the gate from every game. If anyone beats us and we have to pay two hundred dollars, it comes out of our pocket. Your pocket, if you join us. So, why don't you just strike out now and end this game? It'll be better for all of us if you do."

Jules swung and missed at the second pitch.

"Attaboy," the catcher said. "Miss this pitch and you'll be one of us."

Jules turned to look at the catcher.

"Mister, if I strike out, it ain't a'goin' to be on purpose," Jules said. "And I wouldn't want to play with people like you anyway."

The catcher chuckled. "Have it your way, kid," he said. Then he called to the pitcher. "Quit playin' around with him, Tommy. Throw it past him!"

"No batter, no batter, no batter," the shortstop called.

"Throw it by him, Tommy. Let's collect our money and go have a few beers," the first baseman called.

The left fielder started whistling.

Jules scraped at the ground with his feet and watched as the pitcher wound up, then threw. Jules swung the bat, and had the satisfying feeling of making contact with the ball on the sweet spot of the bat. The ball flew high over the left fielder's head. Jules tossed the bat aside and started for first base.

Billy came home and Cal rounded second, headed for third, rounded third, and streaked home. Jules was right behind Billy, rounding second as Billy started home. Jules saw the left fielder run for the ball, then pick it up just before Jules reached third. Jules rounded third and started for home as the crowd cheered for him.

Then, to Jules's surprise, the left fielder made a tremendous throw, and Jules saw the ball fly into the catcher's mitt just before he reached home plate. Jules slid into home plate, but the catcher was waiting for him and he put the tag on him before he reached the plate.

"You're out!" the umpire called.

The cheers turned to groans.

"You should've took me up on my offer, boy," the catcher said. "You wound up being out anyway, and now you got nothing to show for it."

"Yeah, I've got something to show for it," Jules said and he stood up and wiped the dust from the seat of his pants. "I've got my honor."

* * *

The high, skirling sound of a fiddle could be heard from one end of the street to the other as the dancers dipped and whirled to the caller's patter:

"A right and left around the ring
While the roosters crow and the birdies sing.
All join hands and circle wide,
Spread right out like an old cow hide.
All jump up and never come down,
Swing your pretty girl round and round."

Even though Smoke's baseball team had lost to the professionals of St. Louis, they had played so well that they were being heralded as heroes by the citizens of Big Rock. As a result, none of the boys had any difficulty in finding young girls who were willing to dance with them. In fact, several of the girls came up to the boys, hinting that they were thirsty, or suggesting that their dance card was empty for the next dance.

The only ones who were not having a good time at the dance were the ballplayers of the St. Louis Unions. When they saw that the girls were more interested in the young men of Smoke's baseball team, they began to get angry and they started taunting Smoke's men.

"Perhaps we should have lost the game. Then the girls would have taken pity on us, as they have these poor rubes," one of the players suggested.

"I think we should have played the girls," another player said. "They would have given us a better game."

One insult led into another, until finally one of the Unions reached out and tripped Jules as he was dancing. When Jules fell, all the Unions laughed loudly.

"What's the matter, boy? Are you so clumsy that you can't even keep your feet?" one of the players called out.

"You tripped me!" Jules shouted, jumping up and confronting the one who had done it.

The St. Louis player pushed Jules back, and another St. Louis player tripped him again.

"My word, they are as clumsy on the dance floor as they are on the baseball diamond."

This time when Jules jumped up, he came up swinging, connecting with a right jab to the chin of the one who was tormenting him. The player went down, but another player attacked Jules.

Within seconds, the rest of Smoke's men joined in the action and the entire dance came to a halt as the young men from both camps traded blows. The fight continued in a grand scale with tables and chairs turning over, punch bowls being spilled, and men and women shouting, some in alarm and some in encouragement.

The fight lasted for several minutes until, eventually, Smoke, Sheriff Carson, and two of his deputies managed to break it up. As the fight finally came to an end, it became obvious that Smoke's men had gotten much the better of the St. Louis Unions, all of whom were now nursing black eyes and bloody noses.

As the cowboys rode back out to Sugarloaf that night, they were laughing and singing.

"Well, they may have beaten us at baseball, but we sure gave 'em a licking where it counts," Cal said.

"We sure did," LeRoy said.

"You won on the baseball diamond as well," Smoke said.

"No, we lost, four to three," Jules said.

"Uh-huh," Smoke said. "Only their manager bet me

two hundred dollars that they would win by at least five runs."

"They only beat us by one run," Jules said.

"That's right," Smoke said. He reached into his pocket and pulled out a wad of bills. "And that's why we won two hundred dollars. You fellas can divide it up exactly as you would have had we won the game."

"Then I can leave my mom twenty dollars before we leave," Jules said excitedly.

"Forty dollars," Pearlie said. "You can have my share."

"Sixty," Cal offered.

"I'd give you my money too, Jules, only I ain't had no work in near two months now," Billy said.

"Me neither," LeRoy echoed.

"I thank you, but Ma don't need no more money than this," Jules said. "This'll keep her till we get back." He looked at Pearlie and Cal. "Thanks to you two," he added.

"Ah," Pearlie said. "It wasn't nothin'."

"You didn't really make a bet with that baseball team, did you?" Sally asked that night as she lay in bed beside Smoke.

"What makes you think I didn't?"

"Because I was with you all day, remember? You couldn't have made such a bet without me knowing about it."

"Well, suppose I didn't."

Sally laughed. "Nothing, except you are a wonderfully generous man, Kirby Jensen."

"So are Pearlie and Cal. They gave their money to Jules."

"I know. You have been a wonderful influence on them."

"Ha!" Smoke said. "We all know who has been the real

influence on them. No tellin' where those two would be now if it weren't for you."

Sally snuggled up against Smoke. "Let's face it," she said. "You and I make a wonderful team. That's why I know we are going to get there first."

Smoke lay quietly for just a second. Then he raised himself up on one elbow and looked down at Sally.

"What did you say?"

"I said we make a wonderful team."

"Yeah, I heard that part. I mean, what did you say after that? Something about getting there first?"

"Yes. I said that's why I know we are going to get there first."

"Get where first?"

"To Sorento."

"What does getting there first have to do with it? First before who?"

"First before anyone else," Sally said.

"Sally, darlin', you aren't making sense. Did you or did you not tell me that Mr. Abernathy will buy our cattle at thirty-five dollars a head?"

"Yes," Sally answered.

"Then what does getting there first have to do with it?"

"Well, actually what he said was, he will buy the first three thousand head of cattle delivered to him," Sally said. "I just assumed it would be us."

Smoke let out a sigh, then fell back on his pillow. "You just assumed?"

"Yes. Darling, I know we will get there first," Sally said.

"We damn well better get there first," Smoke said. "Otherwise, we'll be worse off than we are now. I'd hate to be somewhere on the trail, facing a winter like the one we faced before."

"It's a simple thing," Sally said.

"A simple thing?"

"Yes. Our cows are here, we want them in Sorento. All we have to do is take them there."

"Right, that's all we have to do."

Sally rolled into Smoke and kissed him, not a longtime married kiss, but a deep, lover's kiss.

"Oh," Smoke said when she pulled her lips from him. "That was quite a kiss."

"No matter what happens, Smoke, I know you will get us there. I have all the confidence in the world in you," Sally said.

"With trust like that, how can I let you down?" Smoke asked.

Chapter Twelve

The first pink fingers of dawn touched the sagebrush, and the light was soft and the air was cool. This was Smoke's favorite time of day and as he stood by the fire, drinking coffee, he watched his cowboys moving the herd together for the start of the drive.

Behind him he heard the sound of pots and pans being moved around, and he smelled the aroma of frying bacon and baking biscuits. He also caught a whiff of the sweet smell of Sally's patented bear claws. Turning, he saw Sally working at the chuck wagon.

Damn, he thought, he was one lucky man to have found someone like Sally. Sally was Smoke's second wife. After his first wife, Nicole, and their baby were killed, Smoke went on the blood trail, tracking down and killing the men who had so destroyed his life.

After that, Smoke didn't think he would ever be able to love again. But he met a beautiful and spirited young schoolteacher who changed his mind. This was not to say that he had forgotten Nicole; she would always have a place in his heart and Sally understood that. In fact, Sally was so confident in her own position that, though she had never met Nicole, she thought of Smoke's dead wife as a sister to her.

Smoke was so deep in concentration that, for a moment, he didn't realize Sally was staring at him with a bemused expression on her face.

"Good morning," Smoke said.

Sally chuckled. "Good morning," she replied. "If you want to call the boys in, breakfast is about ready."

Sally had gotten up even before sunrise to cook a full breakfast meal for eleven people. After breakfast, she would pack up the chuck wagon and leave, going out ahead of the herd. The men would lunch in the saddle with strips of jerky and cold biscuits. They wouldn't see Sally again until supper.

It was not only Sally's job to get into position in time to fix supper, it was also her job to find a place where the herd could bed down for the night. This was a very responsible job, but Smoke had absolutely no qualms about her ability to perform the tasks assigned.

Smoke walked over to the chuck wagon to see the breakfast she had prepared. She had scrambled eggs, fried potatoes, sausage, stewed apples, and biscuits and gravy.

Smoke whistled in amazement as he eyed the spread.

"Good Lord, Sally, I hope you don't feed them this big a breakfast every morning," he said. "My Lord, they'll get so fat they can't even ride."

Sally laughed.

"This is the first day," she said. "It's just my way of getting things started on the right foot."

"Yeah, well, I hope you don't spoil them into thinking that they are going to eat like this for every meal. I mean, you aren't going to feed them like this, are you?"

"Maybe not quite this well," Sally replied. "But don't forget, a well-fed cowboy is a happy cowboy."

"You didn't pack your china and silver, did you?" Smoke asked sarcastically.

"Oh, that's a good idea," Sally teased. "Maybe I will do that."

"Right," Smoke replied sarcastically.

Sally laughed. "Call the boys in, Smoke," she said. "I need to get going if I'm going to get ahead of the drive."

The drive had been out for four days and nights so far, and there had been no real problems except fatigue. Smoke was pleased with the job Pearlie and Cal had done in picking hands for the drive. Billy Cantrell and the Butrum brothers had proven to be great hands. Mike Kennedy had as well. Only the two former soldiers, Andy and Dooley, were inexperienced, but not even that was causing much of a problem. They were good workers and eager to learn from the more experienced of the outfit.

It was early in the morning of the fifth day, and the last morning star made a bright pinpoint of light over the purple mountains that lay in a ragged line far to the north and west. The coals from the campfire of the night before were still glowing, and Smoke watched as Pearlie threw chunks of wood onto them, then stirred the fire into crackling flames, which danced merrily against the bottom of the suspended coffeepot.

A rustle of wind through feathers caused Smoke to look up just in time to see a golden eagle diving on its prey. The eagle swooped back into the air carrying a tiny field mouse, which kicked fearfully in the eagle's claws. A rabbit bounded quickly into its hole, frightened by the sudden appearance of the eagle.

"Want some coffee, Smoke?" Pearlie called.

"Yes, thanks," Smoke answered.

Pearlie used his hat as a heat pad against the blue-iron handle and poured a cup, then brought it over to Smoke.

"Who's watching the herd?" Smoke asked.

"Billy and Mike ate their breakfast early and have gone out to relieve Cal and Andy."

"Cal and Andy were riding nighthawk?"

"Yes."

"Hmm, I didn't think Cal would have the nerve to be alone with Andy after that joke he pulled on him," Smoke said.

Smoke's comment referred to an incident on their first day out. Cal had told Andy that the feces from some cows were edible, and to prove his point, he went over to pick up a handful of cow manure and eat it.

While all the other cowboys laughed, Andy fought hard to keep from gagging. Then, feeling sorry for him, Pearlie explained that what Cal had eaten was actually a piece of Sally's gingerbread.

"Well, sir, Andy took it pretty good and I think Cal is sort of ashamed of himself for the joke, so they've been gettin' along just real good since then," Pearlie said.

"Speak of the devils, here they come," Smoke said, nodding toward two riders who were coming into the camp then.

Both men dismounted, then went over and poured themselves cups of coffee. Andy walked over to a log and sat down with some of the others to wait for breakfast, while Cal came up to Smoke and Pearlie. Cal's coffee was black and steaming and he had to blow on it before he could suck it through his lips.

"Cows quiet through the night?" Smoke asked.

"Bedded down like they had blankets and pillows," Cal responded.

"That's good."

"You know what I'm beginnin' to think?" Cal asked. "I'm beginnin' to think we might just pull this off. I mean, look, we've been out for four full days now, and there ain't been no trouble of any kind."

Pearlie chuckled. "We've only been out for four days. Hell, we're barely off Sugarloaf, and you're already talkin' about how easy it's goin' to be."

"No," Cal responded quickly. "I'm not sayin' it's goin' to be easy. I'm just sayin' I believe we can do it."

Pearlie snorted. "I didn't know you ever doubted it."

Cal looked back toward the chuck wagon. "I tell you what, this coffee was good, but I'm gettin' a little hungry. I wouldn't mind havin' a biscuit or two."

"I seen Sally put some in the Dutch oven just a little while ago," Pearlie said. "I expect breakfast will be ready in a minute or two." He looked over at a couple of lumps on the ground. The lumps were actually bedrolls and right now, both were occupied by the men who had been on nighthawk from midnight until four. "I guess I'd better wake up Billy and Hank."

"No, let me do it," Cal said. "They seemed to take particular pleasure in waking me up this mornin' at four when it was time for me to take the watch. I am going to enjoy returning the favor."

"Be my guest," Pearlie invited.

Cal crept over very quietly until he was positioned exactly between the two sleeping men. He stood there for a moment, listening to their soft snoring as he smiled in anticipation of the moment. Then he yelled, at the top of his voice.

"All right you two, let's go! Get 'em up an' head 'em out! We can't wait around here till Christmas!"

Billy and Hank awoke with a start, Billy letting out a little shout of surprise as he did so.

"What is it? What's happening?" Billy asked.

Cal laughed.

Hank groaned. "Damn you, Cal, what do you mean a'wakin' me up like that. I was talkin' to the purtiest little lady you ever did see, in my dream. And iffen I had seen you in my dream doin' somethin' like what you just done, why, I would'a shot you down and that's a fact."

Cal laughed. "You'll dream her up again, I'm sure," he said. "'Cause, truth to tell, dreams are about the only place you'll ever be talkin' to a pretty girl anyway."

"Oh, yeah? Well, what about after that baseball game? I danced with lots of pretty girls."

"They wasn't dancin' with you," Cal said. "They was dancin' with a baseball player. Anyhow, what are we standin' here gabbin' for when Miz Sally has gone to all the trouble of cookin' up a good breakfast. I figured you'd want to eat the biscuits while they're still hot."

"I tell you what I would like to do with those biscuits while they're still hot," Billy grumbled. "And it ain't got nothin' to do with eatin' 'em."

Cal laughed. "Come on, boys, we're burnin' sunlight," he said more softly.

After breakfast, all the cowboys saddled their mounts, then rode out to get the herd moving again. Nearby, three thousand head of cattle, fully awake on this, a new day, milled around nervously. The animals, used to the freedom of the open range, were now forced together in one large, controlled herd. That made them acutely aware of different sights, sounds, smells, and sensations, and they were growing increasingly anxious over the change in what had been their normal routine. So far there had been no trouble, but Smoke knew that the least little thing could spook them: a wolf, a lightning flash, or a loud noise.

He listened with an analytical ear to the crying and

bawling of cattle. He was also aware of the shouts and whistles of the wranglers as they started the herd moving.

Although Sally's job was to cook, sometimes in the morning she would saddle her own horse and help the others get the cattle moving. Smoke watched her dash forward to intercept three or four steers who had moved away from the herd. She stopped the stragglers and pushed them back into the herd. Smoke couldn't help but marvel at how well his wife could ride. It was almost as if she and the horse were sharing the same musculature and nerve endings.

Once the herd was actually under way, though, Sally returned to the chuck wagon. The vehicle was being drawn by a particularly fine-looking team of mules. Smoke had hitched up the team for her, and he was standing alongside the wagon as Sally approached.

"Maybe you should break those three steers up," Sally suggested, pointing toward the animals she had just pushed back into the herd. "I swear, this is the third day in a row I've had to deal with them. I believe if they were separated, we wouldn't have a problem."

"Or maybe we would have a problem three times as large," Smoke suggested. "How do you know each one of the cows wouldn't just recruit new cows to help them out? Then you'd have three eruptions instead of just one."

Sally nodded. "You may be right," she said. "I guess I can push them back in tomorrow, or every day as far as that goes, just as long as we're on the trail."

"That's my girl," Smoke said with a broad smile.

Sally walked up to the side of the chuck wagon and tied a knot in a hanging piece of rawhide cord. Each knot represented a day, while a double knot indicated a Sunday. As they knew what day they left, the strip of rawhide would serve as an effective calendar.

"How is the chuck wagon working out for you?" Smoke asked. "Is there anything we need to change?"

"Nothing needs to be changed," Sally said. "I have to hand it to you, Smoke. When you built this wagon, you did a great job."

"All I did was put it together," Smoke said. "You're the one that had it all laid out." Smoke ran his hand lightly across the chuck box, which was a shelf of honeycombs and cubbyholes.

"Well, I guess I'd better get going," Sally said. Kissing him, she climbed up onto the wagon seat and, with a slap of the reins against the backs of the team, the wagon moved forward.

Smoke watched Sally move out at a rather brisk rate, going much faster than the herd. It was her job each day not only to find a spot that would be suitable to bed down the herd for the night, but also to have the camp established and the supper cooked. By the time the weary cowboys arrived with the herd, they would be ready to eat, then turn in, leaving Sally to clean up and roll out the bread dough for the next day.

Smoke watched Sally drive her wagon by the herd. Then he swung into the saddle and turned his attention to the task at hand, moving the herd another twenty miles.

Chapter Thirteen

The cowboys knew something was different one morning a few days later when Sally did not go ahead of them, but stayed with the herd as it started out. Then, at mid-morning, Smoke called a halt and gathered all the cowboys around him.

"Boys, just over that rise there is the little town of Braggadocio." He pointed to the east. "Sally says we're going to need a few more supplies, so I'm going to send some of you into town to pick them up."

"I'll go," LeRoy said quickly.

"Yeah, me too," Andy said.

"Heck, I want to go as well," Mike said.

"May I go?" Jules asked.

Smoke held up his hands. "You can't all go," he said. "I've got to keep some of you back to watch over the herd."

"I'll stay back," Pearlie offered.

Smoke shook his head. "No, I want you to go in with the others. Cal, you stay back."

"All right," Cal said.

"What about sending half of us in now, then we switch so the other half can go into town tomorrow?" Andy suggested.

Smoke shook his head. "I wish I could let you do that,"

he said. "But the truth is we can't take the time to spend two days here. So what I want is for those of you who do go into town to buy the groceries on Sally's list, then get back out here."

"Wait," LeRoy said. "You mean we can't even go into the saloon for a beer?"

Smoke chuckled. "I'm not that hard of a slave driver," he said. "You can spend a little time in the saloon, as long as you remember that I want you back here by nightfall."

"I'll keep an eye on them, Smoke," Pearlie said.

Sally chuckled. "You are going to keep an eye on them? Isn't that a little like setting the fox to watch the hen-house?"

"Oh, now, Miz Sally," Pearlie said. "Do you really think that?" He was obviously hurt by her insinuation.

Sally laughed out loud and reached out to touch him. "I was teasing you, Pearlie," she said. "I know you aren't going to get into any trouble."

Pearlie smiled as well. "I didn't think you meant nothin' by that," he said.

"All right, who is going and who is staying?" Smoke asked.

"You already told me I was stayin'," Cal said.

"Cal, if you want, I'll stay and you can go," Jules volunteered.

Cal chuckled. "Nah, you go ahead. I don't mind stayin'."

"I'll stay," Billy offered.

"I'll stay," Dooley said.

Finally, it was agreed that Cal, Hank, Dooley, and Billy would stay with the herd. Pearlie, Andy, LeRoy, Mike, and Jules would go into town.

Sally presented Pearlie with the shopping list and some money. "This is what I want," she said.

"I'll get ever'thing you got on that list, Miz Sally," Pearlie promised. "You can count on it."

"I know I can," Sally said.

"What are you boys waitin' around here for?" Smoke asked. "We're in the middle of fall and it's getting dark earlier every day. If you're going to be back by nightfall, you had better get going."

"Yahoo!" LeRoy shouted. "Come on, boys, let's go! I aim to spend me some of that baseball money."

"Jules?" Billy called.

Jules looked back toward Billy.

"Would you see if you can find me some horehound candy? I'm just real partial to that."

Jules smiled and nodded. "Sure thing, Billy, I'll bring you some back," he promised.

"Thanks," Billy said with a big smile.

After they bought the supplies, they walked out of the store and Pearlie tied the bag of groceries to his saddle horn.

"Let's find us a saloon," LeRoy suggested.

"I don't know, I think we should get on back," Pearlie said.

"Pearlie, come on, Smoke said we could stay in town for a while. I plan on havin' a couple of drinks, and maybe eatin' in a place where I can sit in a chair at a table. What do you say?"

Pearlie stroked his chin as he considered it, but didn't say anything.

"Look, you're our boss," LeRoy said. "So if you say we

got to go back, why, we'll all go back. I'm just tellin' you that Smoke did say we could stay for a while."

Pearlie sighed, then nodded. "All right," he said. "You can stay. But just remember what Smoke said about staying out of trouble. Oh, and be sure and get back before nightfall tonight."

"We will," LeRoy promised.

"Mike?" Pearlie said.

"I'll look after 'em," Mike promised.

Pearlie nodded again, then mounted his horse. "Before nightfall," he said again, and the others nodded at him.

The cowboys watched Pearlie ride off before they started looking for the saloon. Then, finding it, they tied up to the hitching rail out front, pushed through the batwing doors, and strode up to the bar, catching the bartender's eye.

"Jules, I don't want to embarrass you or anything in here, so, what'll it be? Beer or sarsaparilla?" Mike asked.

Jules thought for a moment. He had tried beer before, and he didn't particularly like the taste, whereas he did like the taste of sarsaparilla. On the other hand, he was now a working cowboy, doing the same job as the other cowboys. He decided he should drink as the others as well.

"I'll have a beer," he said.

"Good man," Mike replied.

After ordering beers for each of them, LeRoy asked the bartender where they might find a whorehouse.

"Ain't nothin' exactly like that in Braggadocio," the bartender replied. He pointed toward the stairs. "But we got a top floor here with private rooms and beds, and half-a-dozen whores that look as good as any you're goin' to find in some big city somewhere."

As the bartender was talking, he saw Jules take a sip of

his beer, then make a face at its bitterness. The bartender looked at LeRoy as he pointed to Jules.

"Ain't this here boy kinda young to be runnin' with you fellas? Most especial if you are talkin' about whores and such."

Jules's eyes narrowed. "Mister, you got somethin' to say about me, you say it to me. Don't be talkin' around me."

"All right, I'm tellin' you, I think you are still a little too wet behind the ears to be in here."

Jules took another swallow of his beer, this time making certain not to react to the beer's bitter taste. "You know, I heard there was lots of young fellas no older'n me killin' and dyin' in the late war. If it was to come down to that again, do you think I would be old enough to go to war?"

"Well, I reckon you might be," the bartender admitted.

"So that means I'm old enough to die?" Jules asked.

"I suppose so."

"That makes me old enough."

The bartender had a puzzled look on his face. "How does that make you old enough?"

"Well, now, a fella doesn't get any older than dead, does he?" Jules asked.

Suddenly, the bartender laughed. "I reckon you got a point there, boy," he said. "Yes, sir, I reckon you got a point."

"Whereat is a good place to eat?" LeRoy asked.

"Jenny's Place, just next door," the bartender replied.

"Well, sir, me an' my friends is goin' over to this here Jenny's Place to get us somethin' to eat," LeRoy said. "Then we're goin' to come back for some serious drinking and to make a run on them whores. Don't you let them get away."

"Oh, don't worry none about that. They'll be here."

The cowboys left the saloon, then turned into Jenny's Place, which was next door. Their orders came quickly, but while Mike, Andy, and LeRoy wolfed down their meals, Jules merely picked at his food.

"You plannin' on eatin' the rest of them taters?" LeRoy asked Jules. When Jules shook his head, LeRoy took Jules's plate and shoveled the uneaten potatoes off onto his own.

LeRoy spent the rest of the meal instructing Jules on the proper techniques of whoring. "You're prob'ly thinkin' you should get yourself a real young whore, ain't you? Maybe someone about your own age?"

"I don't know," Jules replied in a mumble.

"Come on, boy, pay attention," LeRoy said. "I'm tryin' to learn you somethin' about whorin' here."

"LeRoy, leave the boy alone," Mike said.

"I ain't doin' nothin' wrong," LeRoy replied. "I'm just tryin' to learn the boy a few things. You got no trouble with that, do you, boy?"

"No," Jules said. "It's just that . . ."

"It's just what?"

"If Pearlie was still here, I don't think we'd be doin' this."

"Doin' what?"

"Talkin' about goin' with whores and such," Jules said.

"Yeah, well, Pearlie ain't here," LeRoy said. "And he didn't say don't go with no whores now, did he?"

"No."

"So that takes care of that. Now, how 'bout what I asked you a while ago? If you was to have your choice betwixt a young whore and a old whore, which one would you choose?"

"I'd choose the young whore, I reckon."

"Why?"

"Well, 'cause I'm young," Jules said.

"Uh-huh, and that's just where you'd be makin' a big mistake," LeRoy insisted.

"Why would that be a mistake?" Jules asked.

"Because if she's that young, she won't be a'knowin' a whole lot more about it than you, for all that she is a whore," LeRoy explained. "What you need is to find yourself the oldest one in the place. See, that way, there ain' no kind of way she ain' never been rode, an' no kind of man she ain't never throwed. Besides which, the older the whores get, the younger they like their men. An old whore would be a real good one for breakin' you in."

Mike laughed. "LeRoy, will you leave the boy alone? You're as full of shit as a Christmas goose, you know that? Don't go listening to him, Jules. He's just tryin' to make sure he gets the youngest and prettiest one for himself. By the way, you goin' to eat the rest of your steak?"

Without answering, Jules forked the rest of his steak off his plate and onto Mike's.

"That's where you're wrong," LeRoy said to Mike. "I for sure don't want the prettiest one. The prettiest ones think their good looks is all they need. The ugly ones, now, will do whatever you want 'cause they want to stay on your good side. Unless you get one that's ugly, but don't know that she's ugly." LeRoy laughed. "Them's the worst kind, 'cause they figure they're pretty enough for looks to get them by, and they don't try none at all. An ugly woman that thinks she's pretty and don't try . . . well, you sure don't want that kind of whore if you can help it."

Mike laughed. "I keep tellin' LeRoy he ought to write a book. I mean, as much as he knows about whorin' 'n all."

"That's a fact all right," LeRoy said. "I could write me a good book."

"If you could write," Mike said, and all around the table laughed.

"Boy, you're lookin' a little peekid," LeRoy said to Jules. "You feelin' all right?"

"Sure, I feel fine," Jules said.

Though he wouldn't tell the others, he had butterflies in his stomach just from thinking about being with a woman.

When they returned to the saloon after their meal, they found a table and sat there having a few drinks while they were waiting.

As they waited, Jules studied the women who were at the moment working the men for drinks. One seemed to have a softer smile and a gentler disposition than the others. Somehow she seemed less threatening to him.

"If we do this, that's the one I want," he said to the others, pointing to one of the women. It was the first comment he had made in several minutes.

"What do you mean 'if' we do this? Of course we are going to do this," LeRoy said. LeRoy turned to look. "Which one is it you're a'lookin' at?"

When Jules pointed her out, LeRoy shook his head. "No," he said. "That ain't the one you want. Give me a few minutes, I'll find the right one for you."

"I don't want you to find one for me," Jules insisted. "That's the one I want."

"Boy, you didn't listen to nothin' I said, did you?" LeRoy said.

"That's the one I want," Jules insisted.

Finally, LeRoy shook his head. "All right, but don't say I didn't warn you none."

Even as they were talking, one of the women came over to the table where the four men were sitting. Putting a hand on her hip and thrusting her hip out provocatively, she leaned over the table. "The bartender says you fellas want some company tonight."

"Company, yeah," LeRoy said.

The woman straightened up. "First, we must get the unpleasant business of money out of the way. Our company will cost you gentlemen a dollar each, or two dollars apiece for the whole night."

"We can't stay all night," LeRoy said. "Fact is, we can't stay very long a'tall so we was wonderin', I mean, seein' as we can't none of us stay very long, we was wonderin' if maybe you'd give us a cheaper price."

"My, my, ain't you boys cheap? Sorry, boys, but we can't give it to you no cheaper'n a dollar. But if you are willin' to pay for it, why, we can sure show you a good time." The woman smiled. "My name's Tillie."

"Tillie, I'm layin' me a claim on you right now," LeRoy said. "And the young'un here"—LeRoy pointed to Jules—"wants that one over there." He pointed to the girl Jules had chosen.

"Have you ever been with a woman before, honey?" Tillie asked Jules.

Jules felt his cheeks burning in embarrassment. "No, ma'am," he answered, barely mumbling the words.

"Then you've made a wise choice," Tillie said. "Doney is just real good with young boys who're doing it for the first time. It's almost as if she has a calling for it."

Tillie signaled the other three whores, and they came over to the table to stand beside her. She made the introductions, ending with Doney.

"Doney, this little sweetheart is one of your specials, if you get my meaning," Tillie said.

"She means he ain't never done it before," LeRoy added, and Jules felt his cheeks flush again.

"Is that right?" Doney asked.

"Yes, ma'am," Jules replied in a quiet voice.

Doney reached out to take Jules's hand in hers.

"Don't you be worryin' none about it, honey," Doney said to Jules. "We're goin' to have us a fine time, you'll see."

"Well, shall we all go upstairs?" Tillie invited.

"I reckon so, unless you're wantin' to do it right down here on the table," LeRoy said. "And I'm that ready I'm about to bust."

"Well, we certainly don't want to see him bust, do we?" Tillie said, laughing. "Come on, ladies, I do believe these gentlemen are badly in need of our services."

As they all climbed the stairs, Jules was certain that everyone in the saloon was watching them. But as they reached the first landing, he happened to glance into the mirror hanging behind the bar, and it didn't appear that anyone in the saloon was paying the slightest bit of attention to him and his friends. He was surprised by that, but it did make him feel a bit less embarrassed.

Once he and Doney were in her room, Doney shut the door behind them, then lit a single candle. She turned and smiled at Jules as she began stripping off her clothes. Jules watched, spellbound, as the smooth skin of Doney's shoulders was exposed. Then she turned so that he saw only her back as she removed the rest of her clothes. Calling on all the tricks of her professional experience, she used a shadow here, a soft light there, and a movement to hold her body just so. As if by magic, she seemed to lose so many years in age and gain so much in mystery that she became as sensual a creature as anyone who had ever appeared in Jules's fantasies. Finally, raising the corner of the sheet, she managed to slip into bed using the shadows in such a way that he wasn't sure whether he had seen anything or not.

She looked at Jules and laughed.

"What is it?" he asked. "What's wrong?"

"Are you just going to stand there like that?"

"Like what?"

"Like that?" Doney said. She pointed. "Honey, you still have your clothes on. Do you plan to keep your clothes on?"

"Oh," Jules said.

Jules just stood there.

"Well?"

"Well what?"

Doney sighed. "Honey, are you going to undress or not?"

"Oh," Jules said again. "Uh—Doney, would you mind if we . . .?"

Jules paused in mid-sentence.

"If we what?"

"If we—uh—didn't really do anything? I mean, you can keep the money. It's just that—well—I don't think my ma would approve."

Doney smiled and patted the bed. "Sit here beside me, honey," she said.

Jules sat down.

"Unless I miss my guess, your friends are waiting just outside the door."

"Waiting outside the door? Why would they be waiting outside the door?" Jules asked.

"To see if you really do anything," Doney said. "If they don't hear anything going on in here, they are going to tease you unmercifully."

"Oh."

Doney's smile broadened. "I tell you what. Let's give 'em a show."

"What do you mean?"

"Start bouncing up and down on the bed," Doney said.

Now, as he understood what Doney was suggesting, a broad smile spread across Jules's face.

Outside the door, LeRoy, Andy, Mike, and the three women with them were straining to hear what was going on inside.

"How come there ain't nothin' happenin'?" LeRoy asked.

"Give 'em time, honey," Tillie said. "The kid is green. Doney will have to work on him for a while."

Suddenly, from the other side of the door, they heard the bed squeaking. LeRoy grinned broadly.

"There they go!" he said. "Hot damn, they are at it now."

The squeaking of the bed became more pronounced; then the squeaking was joined by squeals and groans.

"Oh, honey, oh, honey!" Doney was saying. "Oh, honey, yes, you are wonderful! You are magnificent!"

"Damn!" Mike said. "What's that boy doin' that's so great?"

"Honey, that's not a boy," Tillie said. "Sounds to me like he's all man."

* * *

Inside the room, Jules and Doney continued to bounce on the bed. Then, as she held up her hand as a signal, Doney's squeal reached a climax.

"Yes, yes, yes, yes!" she shouted. With a cutting motion of her hand, she signaled for them to stop.

"Okay, honey," she whispered. "Wait a minute, then go on out. I promise you, you won't be teased."

"Thanks," Jules said.

"You're a sweet boy," Doney said. "Come back and see me in a couple of years."

The sun was setting as the four young cowboys returned to the encampment.

"Well," Smoke said. "All back in one piece, I see."

"Yes, sir, Smoke. You said get back a'fore sundown and that's just what we done," LeRoy said.

"Did you have a good time?"

"We had a fine time," LeRoy said. "But I don't reckon none of us had as fine a time as Jules here."

"Oh?"

"Yes, sir," LeRoy said. "He had him a fine time. Just ask him. Maybe he'll tell you about it. He won't say nothin' at all to us."

"Well, I'm glad you boys had a chance to enjoy yourselves. That means that by tomorrow, you'll all be bright-eyed, bushy-tailed, and ready to go."

"Yes, sir, we will at that," LeRoy said. "Come on, boys, let's get the horses into the remuda."

"Sally held some supper for you," Smoke called to them.

When the other cowboys left, Jules hung back for a moment.

"Uh, Smoke?" he said.

"Yes?"

"Uh, truth to tell, I didn't do nothin'. Me'n Doney just made 'em think I did. But, don't tell 'em, all right?"

Smoke smiled, then reached out to squeeze Jules's shoulder.

"Don't worry," he said. "Your secret is safe with me."

Chapter Fourteen

One morning, less than a week after their stop at Braggadocio, Smoke noticed that Billy Cantrell seemed a little detached. While the others laughed and joked over breakfast, visiting for the last few minutes before getting the herd under way, Billy was walking around the encampment, pulling stems of grass and sucking on the roots, snapping twigs and smelling them, and scooping up handfuls of dirt to examine them very closely.

Smoke had already done those same things, and he knew exactly what Billy was looking for. He walked over to talk to the young cowboy. Billy looked up at him, but before he could say anything, Smoke spoke up. "I know," he said.

"Do you?"

"Billy, I was sucking on grass roots before you were born. I know exactly what you are doing."

"What's the name of that river you say we'll be crossing next?"

"The Eagle River."

"How far do you make it from here?"

"I'd say another forty miles," Smoke said.

"They're going to be dry miles," Billy said.

"Yeah, I know," Smoke said. "From the looks of the sign, there hasn't been a rain here in quite a spell, which means that any narrow streams or watering holes between here and the Eagle will, more than likely, be dried up."

"Forty miles. That means what? Two more days without water?" Billy asked.

Smoke nodded grimly. "I'm afraid so," he said.

"You prob'ly know this country better'n I do, Smoke. You know of any year-round streams or creeks between here and Eagle River?"

"There aren't any."

"Damn," Billy said. "That means the herd is going to get awfully thirsty."

"Yeah, which means they will spook easily," Smoke said. "You boys will just have to be very careful when you are driving them. Don't make any sudden movements or noises. The least little thing, a sneeze or taking off your hat too fast, could spook them into a stampede."

"We'll have to tell the others," Billy said.

"Billy, have you ever seen a stampede?" Smoke asked.

"No, I haven't. Have you?"

"Yeah, but not one with this many cows. If this herd goes, I can promise you, we will have our hands full."

"You got any suggestions on the best way to handle 'em if they start?" Billy asked.

"Yeah, my suggestion would be to get the hell out of their way," Smoke replied.

Billy chuckled. "Most likely, that ain't somethin' we'll have to tell 'em. I reckon if anyone sees a whole herd of cows comin' down on 'em at a gallop, they'll just natural get out of the way."

Smoke laughed as well. "You may have a point there," he said. "Next thing after you get out of the way, is just to follow them, and when they run down a little so that you can turn them, try and head them back in the right direction. But the best thing to do is keep them from stampeding in the first place."

Over the next two days, they pushed the cows through the dry area as gingerly as if the animals were made of glass. They made no sudden moves, whether mounted or not, and when they spoke to each other, they spoke in whispers. Finally, when Cal rode ahead and returned to tell them that they were now only ten miles away from water, it looked as if they would make it through with no real trouble.

Smoke signaled to the others that they would camp by water that night, and the others responded with grateful waves as they continued to work around the perimeters, keeping the cows moving forward steadily and confidently. Despite what had to be a terrible thirst, the herd was well under control.

That all changed when Dooley Thomas's horse was spooked by a rattler. The horse whinnied loudly, then reared up on its back legs. The cows nearest the snake-spooked horse started running, and that spread through the rest of the herd. Then, like a wild prairie fire before a wind, it took only seconds for the entire herd to be out of control.

"Stampede! Stampede!" Billy shouted from the front, and his cry was carried in relay until everyone knew about it.

"Stampede!"

There was obvious fright in the voices that shouted the warning, but there was grim determination as well, for every man knew what was at stake, and moved quickly to do what he could to stop the stampede.

Smoke was riding on the left flank and, fortunately for him, when the stampede started, the herd veered away from him, toward the right, a living tidal wave of thundering hoofbeats, a million aggregate pounds of muscle and bone, horn and hair, red eyes, dry tongues, and running noses. Although the herd consisted of three thousand individual animals, they were moving as one entity, huge and ferocious. Their pounding hooves churned up a huge cloud of dust to hang in the air, leaving the air so thick that within moments Smoke could see nothing. It was as if he were caught in the thickest fog one could imagine, but this fog was brown, and it burned the eyes and clogged the nostrils and stung his face with its fury. And it was filled with thousands of pounding hooves and clacking, slashing horns.

Leaning forward in his saddle, Smoke urged his horse to its top speed, allowing him to overtake the herd. Then he rode on their right in a desperate attempt to turn them back into the proper direction. He, like the others, was shouting and whistling and waving his hat at the herd, trying to get them to respond.

Then, to Smoke's horror, he saw Dooley fall from his horse. The stampeding cows adjusted their direction toward the helpless rider, almost as if they were intentionally trying to do him harm. Dooley regained his feet, but without a horse, all he could do was try to outrun them on foot. It quickly became clear that he was going to lose the race. Smoke watched the young ex-soldier go down.

Smoke raced to Dooley, but even before he dismounted, he knew the young man was dead. The entire herd had passed over him, their slashing and pounding hooves leaving his body lying in the dirt behind them, battered and torn.

Looking up toward the herd, Smoke saw that the cattle had slowed their run to a brisk trot, and as they did, the rest of the wranglers were able to turn them back in the direction they were supposed to be going. The stampede had at last come to an end, brought under control by the courage and will of the young men who had been pushing the herd.

With the herd once more under control, Andy and Pearlie came riding back to where Smoke was standing.

"Dooley! Dooley!" Andy shouted anxiously as he rode up. He leaped from his saddle and knelt on the ground beside his friend. "Dooley," he repeated, then shook his head as tears began streaming down his cheeks.

Smoke reached down to put his hand on Andy's shoulder.

"I'm sorry," Smoke said.

"Me'n Dooley was together from the time we come into the army at Jefferson Barracks back in St. Louis," Andy explained. "We mucked stalls together, walked guard together, put up with sergeants that was the scum of the earth, and fought the Indians in a dozen or more campaigns, all with nary a scratch between us. And now this."

Cal came back then, leading Dooley's horse.

"Get him on the horse," Smoke said. "We'll bury him tonight."

Cal nodded, then got down and reached for Dooley.

"I'll put 'im up," Andy said. "He was my friend."

"He was a friend to us all," Cal said.

Andy nodded, then stepped back to allow Cal to help him. They put Dooley belly-down across his saddle.

* * *

Within another hour, the herd caught the scent of water as they approached the Eagle River. They began running again, not stampeding, but moving toward the water at a gait that brought them quickly to the water's edge.

The lead cows moved out into the river and for a moment, Smoke was afraid that the cows coming up from behind would push the front ranks into deep water where they would drown. Fortunately, the herd had approached the river where a huge sandbar formed a natural ford, and the cattle were able to spread out enough that all could drink their fill. Although they had only come twenty miles today, it had been an unusually rapid twenty miles, so rapid in fact that they had overtaken, then outpaced the chuck wagon. Smoke called a halt to the drive, declaring that they would spend the next twenty-four hours right there.

Ordinarily, arriving at water after such a long, dry spell would be cause for a celebration. But though everyone was thankful for the water, no one felt like celebrating.

As Cal came riding toward the chuck wagon, Sally recognized him by the way he sat his horse, even before she could make out his features. She smiled at him.

"I saw the herd go by," she said. "I expect they've all drunk their fill by now."

"Yes'm, I reckon so," Cal said. Something in the tone of his voice alerted Sally.

"Cal, what is it? What's wrong?" Sally asked. She felt a quick stab of fear go through her.

"We had an accident," Cal said.

"Oh, my God, no!" Sally gasped. "It's not Smoke?"

"No, no, Miz Sally!" Cal shouted quickly, holding up

his hand. "It ain't Smoke, he's fine. I didn't mean to scare you like that. It was Dooley."

"Dooley," Sally said with a sigh, thankful that it wasn't Smoke.

"Yes'm. It was Dooley—and—the thing is, he got hisself kilt."

"Oh!" Sally said, feeling guilty now over her sense of relief in learning that it had been Dooley and not Smoke.

"Smoke sent me out to tell you, and to ride into camp with you."

"Thanks," Sally said. "I appreciate the company."

After supper that night, they buried Dooley on top of a small hill that overlooked the Eagle River. Andy asked if he could say a few words.

"Of course you can," Smoke replied.

Andy stood over the mound of fresh dirt, holding his hat in his hands as he spoke.

"Me'n Dooley was friends," Andy said. "Now, ever'-body has friends, but if you ain't never been in the army, then you don't know how important army friends is.

"You see, most of us in the army is a long ways from home, so Dooley was more'n a friend; he was my brother. Like the song says, we rode forty miles a day on beans and hay. Mosquitoes was worse than Indians, boredom was worse than fear, loneliness was worse than brutal sergeants. But we managed to come through it all, because we was friends."

Andy paused for a moment and looked at the bowed heads around him. "You was all good friends to the two of us, and I reckon I'll get through this all right because of friends like you. I thank you for letting me speak these words."

One by one the others came by to shake Andy's hand, and say a word or two of comfort to him. Sally embraced him, then all went to spread their bedrolls. Smoke let everyone sleep through the night, secure in the knowledge that the herd was not likely to wander away from water.

Over the next two days it turned cold, and by nightfall of the thirteenth day out, it was so cold that a constant fog of vapor hung over the herd and issued from the noses and mouths of horses and men alike. The campfire that night was as welcome for its heat as it was for the fact that it cooked their supper meal and furnished the light.

Smoke and Sally slept in the chuck wagon. The others spread out a canvas from the side of the wagon and, building the fire up for maximum warmth, spread their rolls out under the canvas.

During the night, unnoticed by Smoke, Sally, or the sleeping cowboys, huge, white flakes began drifting down from the sky. The snowfall was heavy, continuous, and silent.

Smoke and his cowboys slept peacefully, warm in their bedrolls, completely unaware of the silent snowfall. While they were sleeping, the world around them was changing. There was no grass, no dirt, no rocks. Even the trees and shrubbery had become unidentifiable lumps. The entire world had become one all-encompassing pall of white.

Because she had to prepare breakfast, Sally was always the first to awaken. When she opened the back flap of the wagon and looked outside, she was greeted by such a white, featureless landscape that, for a moment, she thought she might still be asleep. Then, with a gasp, she realized what she was seeing.

"No!" she said aloud.

"What is it, Sal?" Smoke's question was mumbled from the warmth of his blankets.

"Smoke, look at this."

There was a such a sense of dread and foreboding in Sally's voice that Smoke roused himself from the blankets, then crawled to the back of the wagon to look outside.

"Oh, damn," Smoke said.

"What will we do, Smoke?"

"We keep going," Smoke said.

"How? We have three thousand head of cattle, and snow that is at least two feet deep. How are we going to move?" Sally asked.

"I haven't figured that part out yet," Smoke said. "But we are going to move. We've got no choice. It's either move, or stay here and lose the entire herd."

After Smoke was dressed, he jumped down from the chuck wagon, then crawled up under the canvas to talk to the others. They were all awake and squatting on their heels, looking out at the snow.

"Mornin', boys," Smoke said.

"Damn, Smoke, I thought the whole reason for takin' the herd up to Wyoming was so we wouldn't have to go through this," Pearlie said.

"Yeah, it was. But you know what they say. Man proposes, God disposes," Smoke replied. "I reckon this is just His way of testing us."

"Some test," Pearlie said.

"What are we goin' to do?" Andy asked.

"We're goin' on," Smoke said.

"What do you mean we're goin' on?" LeRoy asked. He pointed to the snow-covered terrain. "In case you ain't noticed, there's more'n two feet of snow out there."

Smoke stared at him. "I'm goin' on," Smoke said. "You can go on with me, or you can turn around and go back."

"Then I'm goin' back," LeRoy said.

"Go back to what?" Hank asked. "We don't have anything to go back to."

"I don't care whether we have anything to go back to or not," LeRoy said. "Anything is better'n this."

Hank shook his head. "You can go back if you want to, LeRoy, but I'm stayin'."

"Come on, Hank, stayin' to do what?" LeRoy asked. "You know damn well we can't drive cows through two feet of snow. Not if we got behind each and every one of them and pushed."

Hank pointed to Smoke. "This man got us out of jail and I gave my word that I would go to Wyoming with him," Hank said. "And I aim to keep that word. As long as he is willin' to keep goin', then I'm staying with him."

"Hank?" LeRoy said, questioning, without actually forming a question.

"I'll see you when I get back."

"If you get back," LeRoy said. He sighed, then looked over at Billy. "Billy, you got more sense than this, don't you?"

"Tell all the painted ladies back in Big Rock I said hello, will you?" Billy asked.

"And tell my mom I'm doin' fine," Jules added.

LeRoy looked over at Andy. "What about you?" he asked.

"Dooley died tryin' to get these cows up to Wyoming," Andy answered. "Seems to me like iffen I'd stop now, well, I'd sort of be lettin' him down. No, sir, I reckon I'll be stayin' with Mr. Jensen and the others."

"LeRoy, if you're goin', get all your good-byes said and be goin'," Smoke said. "We've got work today."

"Damnit! Damnit, damnit, damnit!" LeRoy said, hitting his hand into his fist. "I ain't goin'."

"What do you mean you ain't goin'?" Pearlie asked. "Why not?"

" 'Cause I reckon when you get right down to it, I'm as crazy as all the rest of you," LeRoy said, laughing as he spoke.

The others laughed as well.

"I figured you were too good a man to just pull up and leave a job undone," Smoke said. "I'm glad to have you with us."

"But what I want to know now is, how the hell are we going to do this?" LeRoy asked. "How are we going to get out of here?"

"We're goin' to ride out," Smoke said.

"That's easy enough to say. A horse will break trail in snow. A cow won't."

Smoke smiled broadly and held up a finger. "Then we'll break a trail for them," he said.

Chapter Fifteen

All that day the silence of the white-covered scene was broken by the sound of sawing and the shouts of men as they went about their labors, cutting limbs from the trees, then tying them into place. By nightfall they were ready, but because it was too dark to proceed, they made plans to get under way the next morning.

Exhausted and cold, the men built a big fire, then huddled under the tarp to take advantage of what warmth the fire put out. Pearlie was the one who noticed it first.

"I'll be damn!" he said, smiling broadly. "I'll be damn!"

"What is it?" Mike asked.

"Can't you smell it?"

Several of the men sniffed the air. "I can't smell nothin' but cold," Andy said.

"That's 'cause you ain't never smelt Miz Sally's apple pie before. Nor ate none of it either."

Cal nodded. "He's right!" he said. "I smell it too."

Soon, the rich aroma of cinnamon and apple permeated the entire area and everyone could smell it.

Supper was biscuits and a satisfying stew, but everybody's thoughts were of the apple pies Sally had made.

After supper, she brought them out, three of them, which she carved into very generous portions for everyone.

"I thought that, after a day like today, a big piece of apple pie and a hot cup of coffee might lift everyone's spirits," she said.

"Yes, ma'am," Jules said as he took a huge bite of his pie. "You thought right."

The men's spirits were lifted and as they ate their pie and drank their coffee, they exchanged stories. Sally and the men laughed at a story Andy told about how he and Dooley had put one over on the same sergeant Mike had gotten into a fight with.

"Say, Jules, where'd you learn to play baseball like that?" LeRoy asked. "You were purt' near as good as them boys in them white pajamas."

The others laughed at LeRoy's reference to the uniforms of the St. Louis Unions.

"Pretty near as good? He was a lot better'n any of 'em," Cal said.

"Yeah," Andy said. "Where did you learn to play like that?"

"I don't know," Jules said. "Seems like from the first time I ever saw the game, I could play. I think it would be great to play ball and get paid for it like them boys was."

"But you have too much honor," Smoke said.

"Honor? What do you mean he has too much honor?" Pearlie asked. "I mean, yeah, I think he's got honor and all, but what does that have to do with playing baseball?"

"It don't have nothin' to do with it really," Jules said self-consciously,

"That's not what Sheriff Carson says," Smoke said.

"Tell them, Smoke," Sally said. Smoke had obviously shared the story with Sally.

"Sheriff Carson? What does he have to do with it?" Billy asked.

"He was umpire, remember?" Smoke said.

"Yeah, I remember."

"Sheriff Carson said that our man Jules here was offered the chance to play for the Unions, and to get paid for playing. But they wanted him to strike out his last time at bat."

"Strike out? What? They tried to talk him into striking out?" Billy asked.

"They told him if he would strike out that he could play for them. And he would make a lot of money, more money than he can make being a cowboy."

"Why, those dirty bastards," Hank said. Then, quickly, he looked over toward Sally. "Beggin' your pardon, ma'am, for the cussin'," he said.

"That's quite all right," Sally said. "Anyone who would try and get someone to cheat is a bastard," she said. The others laughed.

"Why didn't you do it?" Mike asked Jules

"Mike, you aren't serious," Billy said.

"Well, I mean, think about it," Mike said. "This was just one game that didn't really mean nothin'. He could'a made a lot of money."

"It wouldn't of been right," Jules said. "And I don't think you would've done it either."

Mike thought for a minute, then smiled. "Well, I reckon not," he said. "Of course, the question never come up because I ain't a good enough baseball player. But if it had come up, I reckon I would'a done the same thing as you done. Though I might of stopped to think about it a little."

The others laughed at Mike's admission.

"Say, Smoke, why don't you tell us about Matt?" Pearlie asked.

"Who?" Andy asked.

"Smoke rode all the way to Denver just to see a fella get some kind of award from the governor," Pearlie explained. "A fella by the name of Matt Jensen."

"Matt Jensen?" Andy said. "I've heard of him. They say he's fast as lightnin' with a gun. Say, you've got the same name. Is he your kin?"

"He's not blood kin," Smoke said. "But I raised him from the time he was twelve. That's how he came to take my name."

"Tell us about when you found him," Pearlie said. Pearlie looked over at Andy, Mike, Billy, and the Butrum brothers. "This is a good story," he said. "You'll like it."

"Well, it started in weather just about like this," Smoke said. "I got caught up in a snowstorm and I needed to be on the other side of the mountain range before the snow closed the pass. So, although every ounce of me wanted to hole up somewhere long enough to ride the storm out, I pushed on through, fighting the cold, stinging snow in my face until I reached the top of the pass. I made it through, then started looking for a place to spend the night when I saw the boy."

"That's when you seen him? In the middle of a snowstorm?" Mike asked.

"Yes. I almost missed him. There was a big drift of snow so that only the boy's head and shoulders were sticking out. He was under an overhanging ledge, and his head was back and his eyes were closed, so I didn't know if he was sleeping or if he was dead.

"The boy's face and lips were blue, and there were ice crystals in his eyebrows and hair. The only protection he had against the cold was a blanket that he had wrapped around him, and that blanket was frozen stiff."

"Damn, what did you do?" Andy asked.

"I put my fingers on his neck. It was cold, but I could feel a pulse. But I knew that if I didn't get him back to my cabin soon, he would die. So I cut some limbs and built a travois. Then, stuffing moss in between a couple of blankets, I made an insulated bedroll, and tying the boy onto the bedroll, started down the other side of the mountain.

"The snow continued to fall and walking was hard. I knew it was going to be hard enough for the horse to move, even without pulling a travois, so I walked in front of the horse, holding onto his bridle.

"It was so cold that the air hurt my lungs as I sucked it down. And I didn't have any snowshoes so, often, I would sink nearly waist-deep into the drifts.

"Because of the clear air, the unbroken whiteness, and the way distance was contorted, it seemed like I was getting nowhere. I remember once, I had been working really hard for two hours, and yet when I looked back over my shoulder, it was almost as if I had just left—I could still see the rock overhang where I found the boy, and if it had not been for the fact that I knew exactly where I was, and how far I had to go, I would've been pretty disheartened. But I knew that I would be to the cabin before nightfall.

"I trudged on through the snow for at least another three hours until, finally, the little cabin came into view.

"I have to admit that the cabin I lived in then wasn't much to look at. But considering the alternative at the time, it looked better than the finest mansion you could imagine.

"I picked the boy up from the travois and carried him inside, then deposited him on the bed. Then, after I took care of the horse, I came back in and fixed supper."

"Did you make him apple pie?" Pearlie asked.

"I'm afraid not," he said. "That was a little beyond my capability."

"What did you make him?" Billy asked.

"Beaver stew."

"Beaver stew? Hmm," Billy said. "I don't know as I've ever et any beaver stew."

Smoke laughed. "That's what the boy said."

"That he'd never et beaver stew before?"

"That's it," Smoke said. "He didn't ask who I was, or where he was, or what was going to happen to him. All he said was that he didn't think he had ever eaten beaver stew before. I figured then that if he couldn't be shaken by nearly freezing to death, then winding up in a total stranger's house eating something he had never eaten before, then he had to be a boy with gumption."

"From what I've heard of the fella, he's proved you right," Andy said.

"Yes," Smoke said. "Matt has made me very proud over the years."

Smoke stretched and yawned. "I don't know about you boys," he said. "But I worked hard today, and I figure I'll be working just as hard tomorrow, so I plan to get some sleep."

"Smoke, do we need nighthawks tonight?" Pearlie asked.

"I wouldn't think so," Smoke replied. "Where would the cattle go? No, you can let everyone sleep in tonight."

"Ha," Mike said. "That almost makes the snow worth it."

By daybreak the next day, Smoke and the others were in position. As part of the outfit, every man had two horses in the remuda so as to always have one that was fresh. But on this morning every one of them was using both horses paired as a team, for a total of ten teams. They had tied a log crossways behind each team. All nine teams were abreast, and in front of them was the chuck wagon, its wheels lashed to poles that were running parallel with the wagon. The poles had the effect of creating runners, so that the chuck wagon was converted to a sleigh. In addition to the team of mules that normally pulled the wagon, the two horses that would have belonged to Dooley had been put in harness with the mules.

"Smoke, maybe you ain't thought of it," Andy said. "But if all of us is up here, there ain't nobody ridin' to keep the herd goin' straight."

Billy laughed.

"What is it? What did I say that was so funny?" Andy asked.

"You ain't got to worry none about them cows goin' nowhere," Billy said. "They're goin' to follow the road we'll be makin' for 'em."

"Billy's right," Smoke said. "We'll be cutting a trail for them and they'll follow along behind like some old yellow dog."

Andy nodded, then smiled. "Yeah," he said. "Yeah, I can see that. Damn, that's smart. How'd you come up with that idea?"

"You don't have to worry none about how Smoke comes up with ideas," Cal said. "He's 'bout the smartest person I know. 'Cept maybe Miz Sally."

In good-natured fun, Smoke threw a snowball at Cal, and Sally, who was close enough to hear the conversation, laughed out loud.

"Sally, don't you be paying any attention to him now," Smoke teased. "He's just buttering you up for more pie."

Sally laughed. "Well, when's the last time *you* made him a pie?"

Smoke laughed as well. "I guess you have a point there," he said.

Smoke looked out at all the men. All were standing on the ground behind their teams, holding the reins as if they were plowing a field.

"Is everyone ready?"

"We're ready at this end, Smoke," Pearlie called back.

"All ready on this end," Cal said.

"Then, let's move 'em out."

Smoke was an active participant for, like the others, he had a team hitched to one of the logs and he urged his horses forward.

To Smoke's relief, the horses appeared to be able to pull the logs without too much effort. From time to time a rather large mound of snow would pile up in front of a log and whoever was driving that team would have to clear the snow away before they could proceed.

They had gone no more than twenty-five yards when Smoke turned to look behind them. His plan was working. Not only was there a wide swath through the snow behind him—the cattle were following along.

They plowed their way through the snow for the rest of that day and halfway through the next, until they came to an area where the snow was so sparse that vegetation was showing through. By then the cows, hungry after two days of not being able to graze, began to feed.

That night the cowboys celebrated with some of Sally's bear claws.

"So, LeRoy," Billy said. "What do you think about drivin' cattle through snow now?"

"Ah," LeRoy said with a dismissive wave of his hand. "I knowed all along that we could do it."

Chapter Sixteen

Salcedo

It was nine o'clock on a Tuesday morning and Trent Williams was in the barbershop getting his weekly shave.

"Have you seen Jason Adams yet?" Cook asked as he applied the razor to Williams's face.

"No, not yet," Williams said. "But I expect to be seeing him today."

"Yes, sir, I expect you will," Cook said. "Jason is one happy man."

"Well, I'm glad he is taking it so well," Williams said. "When I first offered him the deal, he seemed a little hesitant. But as I explained to him, it is the only way he can save his ranch."

"Hesitant? Why would he be hesitant?" Cook asked.

"Well, let's face it. In order to keep from having his ranch go into foreclosure, he is going to have to give up his entire herd. That's quite a sacrifice to make, but at least it will save his ranch."

"Oh, he isn't going to have to give up his ranch," Cook said. He made another stroke across Williams's face. "He isn't going to have to give up anything. He's coming in to pay off the loan."

"What?" Williams shouted, sitting up so fast that Cook cut his face. "Damn it, man, you have cut me!"

"I'm sorry, sir!" Cook said, chagrined at his mistake. He began wiping off the lather to examine the cut. "You rose up so quickly that . . ."

"Here, give me that!" Williams shouted, grabbing the towel. He wiped off his face and examined the cut. It was very small and was barely bleeding.

"Fortunately, it doesn't look very bad," Cook said, reaching up to touch it.

"Just leave it alone," Williams said irritably. Williams treated his own cut for a moment; then, when it was obvious that it wasn't going to bleed anymore, he looked over at Cook.

"What do you mean Adams is going to pay off the loan? How the hell is he going to pay off his loan?"

"Well, after old Mr. Devaney died, Jason said it seemed like the right thing for him to do."

"Devaney? Abner Devaney?"

"Yes, sir, that's the one."

"What does Devaney dying have to do with whether or not Adams pays off his note?"

"Well, sir, as I'm sure you know, Mr. Devaney was Millie Adams's father. When he died, he left all his money to her."

"All his money?" Williams shook his head. "What are you talking about? That old fool didn't have any money."

Cook chuckled. "Oh, yes, sir, he did. Turns out he had quite a bit of money. I'm surprised you didn't know that."

"But how could he have money? He didn't have as much as one dime in the bank."

"No, sir, he didn't, but that don't mean he didn't have no money. He said he didn't believe in banks. He always kept his money in a jar, buried out back of his place."

"How much money was it?"

"According to Jason, it was a little over three thousand dollars. I don't know how much he owes, but he says that's enough to pay off his note."

"Yes," Williams said in a low, growling type voice. "Yes, that is quite enough."

Cook smiled broadly. "Well, there you go then. I know you told me that you bought the note. You must be happy, knowing that you aren't going to be stuck with the note."

"Yes, very happy," Williams replied, though the expression on his face indicated that he was anything but happy. Where would he get his cows now?

With Walking Bear

Walking Bear stood on the rock and looked far down into the valley at the two wagons moving slowly along the road that paralleled Wind River. Four soldiers rode in front of the wagons and four soldiers rode behind. One who had stripes on his sleeves rode alongside. Walking Bear knew that a soldier who had stripes on his sleeves was a soldier chief, and that could only mean one thing. Something very valuable was being carried by the wagons.

Looking behind him, Walking Bear saw twenty mounted warriors awaiting his orders. He felt a swelling of pride because so many had left the camp of Red Eagle to follow him. Red Eagle was an old man whose time had passed. Walking Bear was young and strong and unafraid of the white man. Soon, all in Red Eagle's camp would follow him, and perhaps other camps as well. He would lead not twenty, but many times twenty, a mighty nation of warriors, and they would drive the white man away from the ancient land of the Cheyenne once and for all.

He came back down from the rock.

"What did you see, Walking Bear?" one of the warriors asked.

"Two wagons," Walking Bear reported. "They are heavy with things the white man values."

"Are there soldiers?"

"Yes, soldiers in front and in the back. A soldier chief rides alongside."

"Perhaps we should let the wagons pass," one of the others suggested.

"If you are a woman, too frightened to do battle, you may stay," Walking Bear said. He beat his fist against his chest. "I will attack the soldiers and take what is in the wagons. Brave hearts will go with me, cowards will stay behind."

The Indian who suggested that they should let the wagons pass was shamed by Walking Bear's words and, to redeem himself, he rode to the front, then turned to face the other warriors. He held his rifle over his head.

"I, Little Hawk, will ride by the side of Walking Bear when we attack the soldiers!" he shouted.

The others let out a shout of defiance and held their rifles aloft as well.

Walking Bear nodded in appreciation, then turned and started riding behind the ridgeline, approaching the wagons and soldiers in a way that kept the warriors out of sight.

When he reached the end of the valley, he led them up to the top of the ridgeline. As he had planned, the wagons were now beyond so that, as the warriors came down the hill, they would be approaching the wagons from the rear.

Lifting his rifle to his shoulder, Walking Bear aimed at the soldier riding at the end. He fired, and the soldier tumbled from the saddle.

"Eeeeeyaahhh!" Walking Bear yelled, and the shout was picked up by the other warriors.

"Indians!" one of the soldiers called, his voice cracking with fear.

The wagon drivers urged their teams into a gallop, but the wagons were too heavily laden and Walking Bear and his warriors overtook them easily. Walking Bear divided his men into two columns, sending one to one side of the wagons and the other to the other side. Recognizing the leader of the soldiers by the stripes on his sleeves, Walking Bear shot him.

With their leader down, the remaining soldiers seemed unsure of what to do. Half of them slowed their horses and attempted to give battle, but the others galloped away, abandoning their fellow soldiers and the wagons.

Little Hawk, perhaps in a attempt to make up for his earlier hesitancy, rode up close enough to leap from his horse into one of the wagons. He killed the driver with his war club, then, even as he was holding up his hands, whooping in victory, was shot. He tumbled from the wagon and was run over by the wheels.

The second wagon driver was killed. Then the two remaining soldiers, realizing that they were now alone, tried to flee, but they were both run down and killed.

The Indians overtook the lumbering wagons and brought them to a halt.

Walking Bear beamed with pride over the tremendous success of his adventure. Behind him in the road lay seven dead soldiers, including the soldier leader and the two drivers. Only four of the soldiers had gotten away, and they had not even attempted to give battle. As for the losses Walking Bear suffered, Little Hawk was the only warrior killed.

"Get the food from the wagons," Walking Bear said.

"We will take it to the village of Red Eagle. Let us see him tell the people they cannot take food from us."

Several of his warriors leaped up onto the wagons and rolled back the tarpaulin cover. Both wagons were filled with boxes and the Indians proceeded to break into the boxes.

"Iron!" one of the Indians said in exasperation when he saw that the box contained nothing but large pieces of blued iron. "Why would they put iron in boxes?"

"No food, Walking Bear," one of the others said in disgust. "You said there would be food, but there is no food."

Walking Bear stared at the boxes, nearly all of which had been opened now. There was white man's writing on the outside of the boxes, but he was unable to read it.

STOVE, HEATING
DISASSEMBLED

"Aaaarggghh!" Walking Bear shouted in anger and frustration as he watched his triumph slip away from him.

Sorento, Wyoming Territory

A train sat on the tracks at the depot, its relief valve venting steam. A small white sign nailed to the railroad depot identified the town as Sorento, Wyoming Territory. The town was small, with a posted population of two hundred fifteen, but it was busy beyond its size because it was a railhead to which surrounding ranchers brought their cattle.

The air of the town was perfumed with the strong odor of the several hundred cows that were now waiting in feeder lots awaiting shipment.

Trent Williams dismounted in front of a small building

that had a sign out front identifying it as the Indian agency. A small bell was attached to the door, and it rang as he opened it to step inside. The inside of the building was bare of any type of decoration, and consisted only of a waist-high counter that separated the entrance from the rest of the building.

Shortly after Williams stepped inside, a large man with muttonchops and chin whiskers came into the room. He was wearing a three-piece suit with a vest that was stretched by his girth.

"Yes, can I help you?" he asked.

"I'm looking for Mr. Abernathey. Colin Abernathy."

"I'm afraid Mr. Abernathy isn't here. His office is in Laramie. My name is Cephus Malone. May I help you?"

"I don't understand. Isn't Abernathy the purchasing agent for cattle to be used to supply the Indians?"

"Yes, he is, but he is in Washington right now and won't be back until the fifth of next month," the man answered. "In the meantime, I am authorized to accept delivery of the cattle, and to give you a receipt which will be redeemed by Mr. Abernathy for the appropriate amount. I'm Cephus Malone. Do you have cattle?"

"Yes," Williams said.

Malone smiled. "Ahh, then you must be Mr. Kirby Jensen. Well, Mr. Jensen, I must confess that you got here much sooner than I thought you would. You have three thousand head for me, I believe?"

Williams didn't know anything about Kirby Jensen or his cattle, but for the time being he thought it might be a good idea to go along with Malone's belief that he was Jensen.

"Yes, three thousand head."

"Good, good. As soon as I make an inventory of the

cattle, I can issue a government draft for the funds. Where are the cattle? Just outside of town?"

"Uh, no, the herd isn't here yet."

"Well, I can understand," Malone said. "It's a long way up here from Big Rock, Colorado. But the sooner you can get them here, the better."

"Yes, well, I just wanted to check and see if you still wanted to purchase the cattle."

"Mind you, in order to secure the purchase you must be the first one to deliver the cattle," Malone said. "And I must warn you, you are not the only one in the picture. A man named Trent Williams has also contacted us for possible delivery."

"Yes, I understand," Williams replied. "I'll rejoin the herd and bring them up as fast as I can."

As Williams left Malone's office, his mind was racing with possibilities. If he could deliver over three thousand head, that would be over one hundred thousand dollars. All he had to do was get control of the three thousand head of cattle that a man named Kirby Jensen was bringing up from Colorado.

The way Williams saw it, there were two problems to contend with.

Problem number one was to find the herd.

Well, that shouldn't be too difficult. After all, given the mountains, passes, and rivers, how many ways up from Big Rock, Colorado, were there?

Problem number two would be to take the herd once he found it.

That shouldn't be too difficult either. With three thousand head, he could afford to hire a band of men to do the job for him and still have more money than he would have had had he been able to take Jason Adams's herd.

He could afford such a band of men, and he knew just where to find them.

Before going to bed that night, Trent Williams sent a telegram back to Salcedo. The recipient of the telegram was a man name Will Staley. Staley was the former sheriff, but had been defeated in the last election because of accusations that he had been in cahoots with a cattle rustler.

Staley denied the accusations, but was defeated anyway. Now he operated a private cattle protective agency going after rustlers. Although he was no longer a sheriff, and no longer had territorial authority to make arrests, he compensated for that by declaring himself a bounty hunter, and indeed, he did collect bounty on those who were wanted. But his primary income came from the cattlemen who hired him. There were those who said that Staley didn't always let the law get in the way of getting the job done, especially if there was enough money involved.

Williams was sure that he could offer Staley enough money to get the job done. But he could pay only if Staley succeeded in getting a herd for him. And the herd Malone had mentioned, the one belonging to a man named Kirby Jensen, would be that herd.

Chapter Seventeen

It had been five days since they came through the snow and were again on dry ground. In fact, as far as Andy was concerned, it was too dry. The reason for that was that he was riding drag and eating the dust kicked up by the herd.

It was because he was riding drag that he was the first to see the Indians. He wasn't sure he actually saw them because it was only a slight movement, a shadow within a shadow that caught his eye. He dismounted and pretended to be working on his saddle while actually looking behind him.

There! He saw it again, and this time there was no question. Three Indians, riding in line, moved through a cut in the ridge. They were bending low over their horses, obviously trying to remain unseen.

Andy remounted, then rode, not at a gallop but at a quick pace, until he caught up with Smoke.

"Smoke, there's some Indians on our tail," he said.

"How many?"

"I don't know," Andy said. "But they are trying their damn'dest to stay out of sight, so I know that they are up to no good."

Smoke stroked his chin and looked out over the herd.

"Andy, do you think you can get to the other side of the herd without letting the Indians know that you are on to them?"

"Yeah," Andy said. "I think so."

"All right, you get over there, tell Billy, Mike, and the Butrum boys that, at my signal, I want them to get the herd moving as fast as we can. The river's not more than a mile ahead and Sally is already set up there. If we can get the herd across, we'll make our stand there."

"Right," Andy said as he started around the herd.

"Pearlie!" Smoke called.

Pearlie turned his horse and rode back to see what Smoke wanted.

"Andy has spotted some Indians behind us. We're going to try and get the herd across the river, then turn to face them. Send Cal on up to be with Sally. Have them pick out some defensive positions for us, then help the others drive the herd."

"Smoke, isn't there a chance of spookin' the cows into a stampede if we try and hurry them now?"

"I don't think so. They're tired and they're headed toward water. I don't think they'll scatter. And I know this area. Once they get on the other side, there's no way they can go except the way we want them to go. Hell, I hope they do run, it'll keep 'em out of the line of fire. Now, get goin'."

"Right," Pearlie replied.

Smoke watched Pearlie ride back up to deliver his message to Cal. He saw Cal ride off at a rapid clip, and not until Cal was at least half a mile away did he raise his pistol and fire.

"Let's go!" he shouted. "Move 'em out! Move 'em out!"

The cattle started forward at a gallop with the cowboys

on both sides urging them on with whoops and shouts and waving their hats.

"Here, cows, run!" Smoke heard Billy calling. "Run, cows, run!"

Smoke rode to the rear of the herd, pulled his rifle, then looked back. The Indians, realizing then that they had been seen, gave up all pretense of trying to keep out of sight. They started after the cattle.

Smoke sighted on one of the Indians and squeezed the trigger. The Indian grabbed his chest, then fell from his galloping pony. That caused the other Indians to pull up for a moment. It was a moment only, but that gave Smoke the chance to turn and catch up with the herd.

By now the leading animals of the herd were crossing the river, their hooves churning up water ahead of the onrushing cattle behind them.

"Pearlie, you and Andy grab your rifles," Smoke said. He pointed to the neck of a small island that faced the western bank of the river, the direction from which they had just come.

"See if the two of you can squirm down through the tall grass. Take a position as near to the point as you can get, and do as much damage as you can when the Indians start across the water."

"Right!" Pearlie called back. "Andy, let's go!"

"The rest of you," Smoke ordered. "Find yourselves a good spot and get ready."

As the men got on their knees and began looking around for a rock or hill or tree log to provide them with cover and concealment, Smoke walked back to the chuck wagon, where he saw Sally making herself a firing position from behind one of the wheels.

"Sally, you're on your own," Smoke said. "When the shooting starts, I'm going to be moving around."

"You do what you have to do, Smoke," Sally replied. "I've got a good position here. I'll be all right and, I suspect, I might even get off a shot or two."

Despite the seriousness of the situation, Smoke laughed. "You might get off a shot or two, huh?" he said. He knew that, next to him, Sally was probably the best shot there. And he knew that nobody had more courage. "Just make sure you know who you are shooting."

"Any more snide remarks like that, Smoke Jensen, and you'll be my target," Sally quipped.

Smoke kissed her, and they held the kiss a moment longer than they normally would have.

"You be careful with all your moving around," Sally said as Smoke took his leave of her.

Smoke hurried back to see how the others were positioned, and where they were deployed.

"All right, now remember, Pearlie and Andy will shoot first!" Smoke said. "So don't be spooked into shooting when you hear them. I want you to hold your fire until the last possible moment. Then make your shots count!"

"Smoke, here they are! I can hear 'em coming!" Jules said nervously. His announcement wasn't necessary, however, for by then everyone could hear them. Above the drumming of the hoofbeats came the cries of the warriors themselves, yipping and barking and screaming at the top of their lungs.

The Indians crested the bluff just before the river; then, without a pause, they rushed down the hill toward the water, their horses sounding like thunder.

"Remember, hold your fire until the last possible

moment," Smoke shouted to the others. "In fact, hold your fire until I give you the word!"

The Indians stopped just at the water's edge, then holding their rifles over their heads, began shouting guttural challenges to the men who were dug in on the island.

"Hu ihpeya wicayapo!"

"Huka!"

"Huka hey!"

"They're working up their courage," Smoke said. "Check your rifles, make sure you have a shell in the chamber."

The men opened the breaches and checked the chambers, then closed them and prepared for the attack.

The Indians rushed into the water, riding hard across the fifty-yard-wide shallows, whooping, hollering, and gesturing with rifles and lances. Then two of warriors pulled ahead of the others, and when they were halfway across the water, Smoke heard two distinct shots from the point of the island. The two warriors in front went down.

The remaining Indians crossed the river, then started up the sandy point.

"Fire!" Smoke shouted.

Smoke, Sally, Billy, Mike, Hank, LeRoy, and Jules fired as one. Four of the Indians went down, not because a couple of them had missed, but because a couple of them had fired at the same target. The devastating volley was effective, for the warriors who survived swerved to the right and left, riding by, rather than over, the cowboys' positions.

The Indians regrouped on the east bank of the river.

"Turn around!" Smoke yelled. "They'll be coming from behind us this time!"

The cowboys had just barely managed to switch positions when the Indians turned and rode back in a second charge. They were met with another volley, this one as crushing as the first had been. Again, a significant number of the Indians in the middle of the charge went down.

The Cheyenne pulled back to the west bank of the river to regroup, watched anxiously by the men on the island. By now the river was strewn with dead Indians. There were at least eight or ten of them, lying facedown in the shallow water as the current parted around them.

"Anyone hit?" Smoke called.

"Yeah, I been hit," LeRoy called back, his voice strained.

"How bad is it?" Smoke asked.

"I—I reckon it's killed me," LeRoy said, his voice growing weaker.

"LeRoy!" Hank called, moving quickly to his brother's side.

"Hang on, LeRoy," Smoke said. "We're going to get out of here. We'll be having drinks in a saloon in a few days, telling tall tales about this fight."

"You fellas have a drink to me," LeRoy said.

"LeRoy! LeRoy!" Hank called anxiously.

"How is he?" Smoke called.

"He's dead," Hank said in a tone that reflected both his shock and his sorrow. "I can't believe this. My brother is dead."

"I'm sorry, Hank. He was a good man." Smoke looked at all who had gathered around him. "You are all good men," he said.

"Smoke, what about Pearlie and Andy?" Cal asked. "You think they are all right?"

"Good question. I'd better go get them."

"Why don't you just call 'em in?" Billy asked.

"No, I can't do that. If the Indians hear us, that will make Pearlie and Andy easy targets. I'll go get them. Cal, you're in charge while I'm gone."

"Right," Cal replied.

Smoke worked his way down through the tall grass until he reached the point. Looking up, he saw both Pearlie and Andy behind tall clumps of grass, just on the other side of an open sandbar.

"Pearlie, you and Andy all right?" Smoke called to them, just loudly enough to be heard.

"Yeah, we're fine," Pearlie replied.

"Come on back with the rest of us now," Smoke said. "We've lost whatever advantage we had by having you out here."

"All right," Pearlie said. "Andy, you go first, I'll cover you."

Nodding, Andy bent over at the waist and darted across the open bar of sand until he reached the tall grass.

"All right, Pearlie, it's your turn," Andy called back.

Duplicating Andy, Pearlie darted across the sandbar, then dived into the grass alongside Smoke and Andy.

"Anyone hit back there?" Pearlie asked.

"Yeah. LeRoy was killed," Smoke said grimly.

"Damn."

"Come on, let's get back."

The three men wriggled through the grass on their bellies until the reached a slight depression that allowed them to stand up. Once up, they were able to move quickly until they were back with the others.

"You think they're going to come back?" Mike asked.

Smoke shook his head. "I don't know," he said. "I wish I could see them well enough to know what is going on."

"I have a pair of army binoculars," Andy offered. "Would that help?"

"It might," Smoke said. "Let me see them."

Andy hurried back to where the horses were tied. He

fished the binoculars from his saddlebag, then took them back and handed them to Smoke.

"These are good-looking glasses," Smoke said.

"Yeah," Andy replied. He smiled. "I took them from Sergeant Caviness."

"Good," Mike said. "I hope the son of a bitch had to pay the army for them."

The others laughed.

Smoke raised the binoculars to look across the water. He saw one Indian who was obviously in charge, riding back and forth in front of the others, holding a rifle over his head and shouting.

"Somebody seems to be stirring them up," Smoke said.

"May I take a look?" Andy asked.

"Sure, they're your glasses," Smoke said, handing the binoculars to the former soldier.

Andy lifted the binoculars to study the Indians. "I'll be damned," he said.

"What is it?"

"It's Walking Bear," Andy said.

"Who?"

"Walking Bear," Andy said, lowering his glasses.

"You know him, Andy?" Billy asked.

Andy shook his head. "Can't say as I know him exactly," he replied. "But he's been givin' the army some trouble for a long time now. He was part of Red Eagle's camp, but when Red Eagle went to reservation, Walking Bear took a lot of warriors with him and left. The army's been after him ever since then, but he's been like a ghost. No one's been able to find him."

"Looks like we just did," Smoke said.

"Yes, sir, it does at that," Andy said.

"How bad is this Walking Bear fella?" Mike asked.

"Pretty bad. Just before I got out of the army, Walking

Bear attacked a platoon of soldiers that was escortin' a supply wagon. He kilt ever' soldier in that platoon."

"Are you sure this is Walking Bear?" Smoke asked.

Andy nodded. "Oh, yeah, I'm sure," he said.

"Sally," Smoke called. "Come here for a moment, would you?"

Sally walked over to where Smoke and Andy were standing. Smoke took the binoculars from Andy and handed them to Sally.

"Take a look at the Indian in front," Smoke said. "The one riding back and forth, yelling at the others. Do you see him?"

Sally held the binoculars to her eyes for a moment.

"I see him," she said.

"Next time they come after us, shoot him. Take your time, get a good shot. But you need to kill him."

"All right," Sally answered. She handed the glasses back to Andy.

"Whoa, hold it," Hank said. "You're giving that job to her?"

"Yes."

"But she's a woman."

Pearlie and Cal laughed.

"What is it?" Hank asked.

"She may be a woman but when it comes to shootin'," said Pearlie, "'bout the only one here better'n she is with a rifle would be Smoke his ownself. And I'm not all that sure he's better."

"Smoke," Andy said, lowering the binoculars. "Looks like ole' Walkin' Bear's got 'em worked up into comin' again."

"All right, everyone, get ready! They're coming back!" Smoke warned.

Looking around, he saw that Sally had repositioned

herself. No longer behind the wagon wheel, she was now behind a fallen tree, resting the barrel of her rifle on the log. She thumbed back the hammer, then sighted down the barrel.

With Walking Bear in the lead, the Cheyenne started another attack.

The Indians came again, their horses leaping over the bodies of the warriors and horses who had fallen before. Sally waited for a good shot, but Walking Bear was bending low over his horse in such a way as to keep behind his horse. It was difficult for Sally to get a good sight picture, and the first time she fired, she missed.

Quickly, she jacked another shell into the chamber and waited for another opportunity.

For some unknown reason, Walking Bear sat upright for just a second, and that gave Sally the opening she was looking for. She squeezed the trigger and her bullet hit Walking Bear right in the middle of his chest. She saw the look of surprise on his face; then she saw him drop his rifle and clasp his hand over his wound. He weaved back and forth for just a second before tumbling from the saddle.

When the others saw their leader go down, they stopped and milled about for a moment, uncertain as to what they should do. One or two started forward, but it wasn't a concerted charge and, like Walking Bear before them, they were shot down.

By now well over half their party lay dead on both banks of the river, in the water, and on the sandy beaches of the island. They had started the fight with the numerical advantage, but realized now that they were outnumbered.

One of the Indians turned and started riding away. Almost instantly, the others followed.

"Run! Run, you cowards!" Andy shouted, shooting at them as they fled.

The other cowboys began shooting as well, making certain to give the Indians a good send-off. Then, they began laughing and congratulating each other on the good fight.

"If you want to know who gets the most congratulatin', it should be Miz Sally," Andy said. "When she took ole Walkin' Bear down, she took the fight right out of 'em."

"Let's hear it for Miz Sally!" Billy shouted.

"Hurrah! Hurrah!" the others called.

With all the laughing and self-congratulations, the men forgot all about Hank, until Sally spoke up. She saw him over by his brother's body, hanging his head in sorrow.

"Hank," she said. "We want you to know how sorry we are about LeRoy. He was a good man."

"Thank you, ma'am," Hank said.

Chapter Eighteen

A range in Wyoming

A small herd of no more than one hundred cows moved through the darkness, watched over by three riders. A calf called for its mother and, in the distance, a coyote sent up its long, lonesome wail. The moon was a thin sliver of silver, but the night was alive with stars . . . from the very bright, shining lights all the way down to those stars that weren't visible as individual bodies at all, but whose glow added to the luminous powder that dusted the distant sky.

"Damn, Bobby, but it's cold," one of the riders said, the vapor of his breath glowing in the moonlight.

"Yeah, well, I tell you, if it wasn't this cold, we prob'ly wouldn't of been able to steal these critters. They'd of been someone watchin' 'em," Bobby said.

"Pat's right, though. Stealin' cows on a cold night like this is damn near as hard as punchin' 'em," a third rider said.

"Well, now, let me ask you this, Deekus. Would you rather be ridin' out here in the cold tonight, pushin' cows we'll be gettin' five, maybe ten dollars a head for? Or would you rather be punchin' cows for someone at twenty dollars a month and found?" Bobby asked.

"Hell, you put it like that, I can take bein' cold for a while," Deekus said.

"Hey, Deekus, what are you goin' to do with your money?" Pat asked.

"I'm goin' to a whorehouse and get me a woman," Deekus said. "What about you?"

"I don't know, get some new duds, I reckon."

"Duds? You goin' to waste your money on clothes when you could get you a woman?"

"Why, dress me up in some new duds and I can get me a woman without payin' for it," Pat said.

"Whoo, boy," Deekus said, laughing. "Did you hear that, Bobby? We got us a lover boy here."

Bobby laughed.

"Yeah, well, you just watch," Pat said. "You spend all your money on a woman and it's over with. You make yourself look good so's a woman wants you, why, you can get you a woman anytime you want, and you still got your new duds."

Bobby laughed again. "Seems like ole Pat has got it all figured out," he said.

The calf's call for his mother came again, this time with more insistence. The mother's answer had a degree of anxiousness to it.

"Damn," Bobby said. "I told you we should'a left the heifer and her calf alone. Now I got to go get 'em back together."

"Hell, why bother? It'll find its own way back."

"I don't think so. And if it starts settin' up too much of a racket, well, the three of us won't be able to handle the rest of the cows," Bobby said, slapping his legs against the side of his horse and riding off, disappearing in the darkness.

"Bobby's as bad as an ole mama cow himself," Deekus said, "watchin' out for 'em like that."

"Yeah, but he's prob'ly right. In this cold, we don't need the cows givin' us any trouble."

Suddenly, from the darkness came the sound of a gunshot.

"What was that?" Pat asked.

"Sounded like a gunshot," Deekus answered.

"Bobby must'a seen a snake or something."

"At night?" Deekus asked.

"A wolf maybe?"

The two boys waited for a moment longer, but heard nothing else.

"He ought to be back by now, shouldn't he?" Pat asked.

They were quiet for a moment longer. Then Deekus called out. "Bobby? Bobby, you out there?"

"Bobby?" Pat shouted, adding his own call.

"I don't like this," Deekus said.

"What do you think is going on?"

"I don't know, but I think we better check."

Pulling their guns, Deekus and Pat rode into the night in search of their friend.

A moment later, gunshots erupted in the night, the muzzle flashes lighting up the herd.

"Jesus! What's happening? Who is it? They're all around us!" Pat shouted in terror, firing his gun wildly in the dark.

"Throw down your guns!" a voice called from the dark. "Do it now, or we'll kill your friend, then we'll kill you!"

"Pat, Deekus, do what they say!" Bobby called from the darkness. "They're all around you!"

Neither Deekus nor Pat reacted, and there was another shot from the dark.

"Oww!" Deekus called out as a bullet hit him in the shoulder. He dropped his gun.

Seeing Deekus hit, Pat threw down his gun as well. He put his hands in the air.

"We quit! We quit!" he called.

The two young men sat quietly as they watched over a dozen riders materialize from the dark.

"Who are you?" Pat asked.

One rider rode in front of the others. He was a powerfully built man with hat pulled low over a bald head and brow-less eyes.

"The name is Staley, boys. Will Staley," the rider said. "You should'a known better than to steal them cows in my country."

"Staley? What are you doin' here? You ain't the sheriff no more," Pat said.

"Nope, I ain't," Staley said.

"Then that means you got no jurisdiction over us."

Staley chuckled. "No, all that means is that the judge and jury got no jurisdiction over me."

"The judge and jury got no jurisdiction over you? What are you talkin' about?" Pat asked.

"I'm talkin' about hangin' you boys as cow thieves," Staley said. "When I was sheriff, I had to have a judge give me the word to do it. Now, I don't need nobody's word."

"What?" Deekus asked, suddenly understanding what Staley had in mind. "No, what are you doing?"

"Get 'em over there under that tree," Staley said.

"Wait, you can't do this! You got no right!" Pat said, but even as he was calling out in terror, Staley's men were coming toward him.

Within minutes, Deekus, Pat, and Bobby were sitting on their horses, their hands bound behind them. Three ropes were tossed over an outstretched tree limb; then the nooses were looped around the necks of the young cattle rustlers.

"You boys got 'ny last words?" Staley asked.

"You got no right to do this, Staley," Deekus said. "You ain't no lawman."

"You had no right to steal them cows," Staley replied.

"Stealin' a few cows ain't the same as murder and you know it. What you're doin' here is no more'n murder."

"That your say?"

"That's my say," Deekus said.

"What about you other two boys? You got 'nything to say before you go to meet your Maker?"

Bobby and Pat gritted their teeth to keep from crying out in terror. They looked at Staley and his riders through eyes that reflected their panic, but they said nothing.

"All right, you boys don't want to say nothin', I'll go along with that," Staley said.

Staley looked at the three men who were behind the horses of the rustlers. He nodded, and all three struck the rustlers' horses. The three horses leaped ahead, and the ropes that hung down from the tree pulled the rustlers from their saddles. The limb creaked and bent, but not before jerking the men up short. Pat and Bobby died quickly, but Deekus didn't. He hung there for several minutes, lifting his legs up as if by so doing he could ease the pressure on his neck. He made guttural, gurgling sounds and his eyes were opened wide in terror. One of the men pulled his pistol and pointed it Deekus.

"No!" Staley called out. "Let 'im die natural."

It took almost another full minute for Deekus to die. Finally, he quit twitching and hung there as quietly and as still as the other two.

"Put the signs on 'em," Staley said. "We'll leave 'em here as a warnin' to other cow thieves."

One of Staley's men rode up to the three dead rustlers, then pinned a sign onto each one of them.

COW RUSTLERS

CAUGHT AND HUNG BY

THE CATTLEMEN'S PROTECTIVE

ASSOCIATION

"That's, good," Staley said. "Now we'll take the fifty cows back to Dawkins and collect our pay."

"Fifty cows? You mean we ain't goin' to take 'em all back? They's about a hunnert cows here," one of Staley's deputies said.

"No, you are mistaken. I only see fifty cows here," Staley said pointedly.

The deputy realized then what Staley was saying. "Oh," he replied, nodding in agreement. "Yeah, now that I re-count them, fifty is all I get as well."

Trent Williams was standing at the front window of the bank, looking out onto Salcedo's main street when he saw Staley and his men riding back into town. They made a rather imposing sight, ten men, all wearing long trench coats and wide-brimmed hats pulled low over their eyes. Stopping in front of a building that bore a sign reading CATTLEMEN'S PROTECTIVE ASSOCIATION, Staley dismounted, then gave the reins of his horse to one of the others. All the rest of the men rode on down to the livery, but Staley, after raking the bottoms of his boots in the edge of the board porch, went into his office.

Williams turned away from the window and saw Gilbert, his chief teller, dealing with a customer. The customer, a woman, received a deposit slip, then turned toward the door. She smiled and nodded her head at Williams.

"Mr. Williams," she said.

"Mrs. Rittenhouse," Williams replied.

Williams waited until Mrs. Rittenhouse left the bank. Then he called out to his teller.

"Mr. Gilbert?"

"Yes, Mr. Williams?" Gilbert replied.

"I'm going to be out of the bank for a short while. You handle anything that comes up."

"Yes, Mr. Williams."

Williams returned to his office, got his hat, then left the bank.

When Williams stepped into the building belonging to the Cattlemen's Protective Association a few minutes later, he saw that Staley had the door of the little stove open and was throwing wood into the flames. Though the fire was going, it had not yet built up enough heat to push back the cold, and Staley was still wearing his coat.

"Sheriff Staley?" Williams said.

"I'm no longer the sheriff," Staley said.

"I'm sorry. You were sheriff for so long that it seems natural to call you that."

"What do you want, Williams?"

"I, uh . . ." Williams cleared his throat. "Did you get my telegram, Sheri—uh, Mr. Staley?"

Staley turned toward him. "Yeah, I got your telegram," he said.

"Then you know that I have a proposition for you."

"I believe what you said was that you had a *profitable* proposition for me," Staley said, emphasizing the word "profitable."

"Yes. Indeed, it could be very profitable," Williams replied.

"How profitable?"

"Five thousand dollars profitable," Williams said.

"Seventy-five hundred," Staley replied.

"Seventy-five hundred?" Williams gasped. "What makes you think it should be seventy-five hundred dollars? You don't even know what the proposition is. Five thousand dollars is a lot of money, Mr. Staley."

"Yes, it is a lot of money," Staley agreed. "And it doesn't matter what the proposition is. If you are willing to pay me five thousand to do whatever it is you want done, that means you are making a lot more money than you are going to be paying me. I want seven thousand five hundred dollars from you or we don't do business."

Williams stroked his chin for a moment as he contemplated the demand. Finally, he nodded.

"All right, seventy-five hundred dollars," he said. He pointed to Staley. "But I can only pay the money after the job is done."

"What is the job?"

"There is a herd of cattle coming up from Colorado," Williams said. "I need that herd."

"I see," Staley said. "You say you want the herd but . . ."

"I didn't say I *want* the herd, I said I *need* the herd," Williams replied. "Everything depends on it. Especially your"—he paused as if saying the amount of money was distasteful to him—"seventy-five hundred dollars."

"Uh-huh," Staley replied. The stove was beginning to put out a little warmth now and he took his coat off to hang on a hook on the wall. He was wearing a pistol belt and the holster was hanging low on the right side. The pistol was kicked out so that as his hand hung naturally, it was no more than an inch or so from the butt. Staley turned toward Williams.

"You aren't talking about buying this herd, are you?"

Williams shook his head in the negative.

"So what you are asking me to do is steal the herd?"

Williams let out a nervous sigh before he answered. "Yes."

"You do know, don't you, that I own the Cattlemen's Protective Association?" Staley said. "Stealing cows is not my business. My business is running down the outlaws who *do* steal cows, and dealing with them. In fact, we just came back from running down the outlaws who stole cows from Eric Dawkins."

"You found them?" Williams asked.

Staley nodded. "Found 'em and hung 'em. They're danglin' from a tree near Cobb's Crossing right now as a warnin' to anyone else who thinks they can get away with stealin' cows."

"I see," Williams said nervously. He put his finger to his shirt collar and pulled it away from his neck.

"And now you are asking me to steal cows?"

"I, uh, I'm sorry," Williams said. "I was led to believe that I could do business with you if the price was right."

Suddenly, and inexplicably, the frown on Staley's face was replaced by a smile.

"We can do business if the price is right," he said.

"Seventy-five hundred dollars?"

"Ten thousand."

Williams was silent for a long moment. Then, finally, he nodded.

"Ten thousand," he agreed.

"Write out a letter, hiring me to recover your stolen herd," Staley said.

"What? No, you don't understand. The herd isn't stolen, it's . . ."

"No, *you* don't understand," Staley told him. "If I'm goin' after those cows, I'm not going to be left hanging out to dry. You're going to write a letter hiring the Cattlemen's Protective Association to recover your stolen herd."

"Wait a minute," Williams said. "If anything goes wrong, that would automatically transfer all the guilt to me."

Williams smiled. "Yeah, it will, won't it?" he said.

"All right, all right. You're a difficult man to work with, Mr. Staley, but I don't see as I have any choice. I'll do as you say."

"Good. That means that if you do everything I tell you to do, we'll get along just real good. Now, where do I find these cows?"

Chapter Nineteen

Mike was riding nighthawk when he heard the sound of hooves, not a restless shuffling of cows repositioning themselves in the night, but a steady clack of hooves on rock. Since the herd was at a halt, he looked around to discover the source of the sound. Then, in the moonlight, he saw a long dark line, ragged with heads and horns, moving away from the main herd.

At first, he wasn't sure of exactly what was going on; then, all at once, he realized what was happening. These cattle weren't merely wandering away; they were being taken away.

"Billy!" he shouted to the man who was riding nighthawk with him. "Look out! We got rustlers! Call the others!"

Billy was closer to the main camp than Mike, and he shouted back toward the chuck wagon where the others were sleeping.

"Smoke! Pearlie! Cal! Turn out! We got rustlers!"

Billy's shout not only awakened Smoke and the others, it also alerted the thieves to the fact that they had been spotted. Instantly thereafter, one of them fired a shot at the sound of Billy's voice. Billy saw the muzzle flash, then heard the bullet whiz by, amazingly close for a wild shot in the dark.

Billy shot back, and the crack of the guns right over the head of the stolen cows started them running. By now, rapid and sustained gunfire was coming from the camp itself as Smoke and the others rolled out of their blankets and began shooting. Sally was standing in the wagon, firing a rifle, adding her own effort to the fight.

Billy put his pistol away and raised his rifle. He aimed toward the dust and the swirling melee of cattle, waiting for one of the robbers to present a target. One horse appeared, but its saddle was empty. Then another horse appeared, this time with a rider who was shooting wildly.

Billy fired and the robber's horse broke stride, then fell, carrying his rider down with him, right in front of the running cattle. Downed horse and rider disappeared under the hooves of the maddened beasts.

So far, only the cattle that had been stolen were running. The main herd, though made restless by the flashes and explosions in the night, milled around, but resisted running.

Cal appeared alongside Billy then, having mounted more quickly than any of the others.

"Are the others coming?" Billy asked.

"Yes, they're right behind me," Cal replied. He pointed toward the running cattle. "Come on, let's get our cows back!"

By now Smoke, Pearlie, and Andy had joined them, and they spurred their horses into a gallop toward the fleeing cows. Within minutes they were riding alongside the running, lumbering animals.

"We've got to get to the front!" Smoke called.

Billy nodded, but didn't answer.

The cows were running as fast as they could run, which

was about three quarters of the speed of the horses. But what the cattle lacked in speed, they made up for with their momentum. With lowered heads, wild eyes, and flopping tongues, the cattle ran as if there were no tomorrow.

Finally, Smoke reached the head of the column, rode to the front, and was able to turn them. Once the cows were turned, they lost their forward momentum, slowed their running to a trot, and finally to a walk. When that happened, the riders were able to turn them and start them back.

"What happened to the rustlers?" Pearlie asked.

"One of 'em went down," Billy said. "The others must've run away."

Suddenly they heard shots from back at the camp.

"What's that?" Mike asked. "What's going on?"

"Damn!" Smoke said. "These cows were just a diversion! They're after the entire herd!"

Sally, Jules, and Hank were firing as fast as they could operate the levers of their rifles.

"Lord!" Hank said. "There's got to be at least twenty of them. Where did they all . . . uhnnn!"

Grabbing his chest, Hank went down.

"Hank!" Jules shouted. He knelt beside his friend and put his hand on Hank's face. "Hank!"

Hank made no response.

"Miz Sally, Hank's been hit!" Jules called.

"Get up here, Jules," Sally called back to him. "Get up here in the wagon!"

"But Hank! I can't leave him!" Jules shouted.

Looking down toward the young cowboy, Sally could

tell by the way Hank was spread-eagled on the ground that he was dead.

"Never mind Hank, it's too late for him," Sally said. Even as she was calling out to him, she was sighting down the barrel of her rifle. She pulled the trigger, the rifle kicked back against her shoulder, and she saw the outlaw in her sights go down.

With one final look at Hank to confirm that he really was dead, Jules dashed across the open area toward the wagon.

Sally saw one of the rustlers taking aim at Jules, and quickly jacking a shell into the chamber, she snapped a shot toward him. She missed, but she did keep him from shooting at Jules.

Jules scrambled up over the side and down into the wagon.

"Are you all right?" Sally called.

"Yes, ma'am, I ain't been hit none," Jules responded.

A bullet slammed into one of the bow frames of the wagon, then whistled off into the night, a darkened missile of death.

"Get up here and start shooting," Sally ordered.

"Yes, ma'am!"

For the next thirty seconds, Sally and Jules exchanged shots with the rustlers.

"Where'd all these folks come from?" Jules asked. "I thought Smoke was chasin' 'em down."

"That's what they wanted to happen," Sally replied. "They wanted to pull away all the men so they could waltz right in and take the cattle."

Sally punctuated her remarks with another shot from her rifle.

"Really?" Jules said, laughing. "Well, they sure made

a mistake thinkin' that if all the men was gone they could just waltz in here."

Sally laughed as well. "You may be young, Jules Sanders, but if you can laugh at a time like this, you are a man in my book."

"Why, thank you, Miz Sally," Jules said as he fired at the rustlers.

"Staley, we've lost three men already," one of Staley's riders said.

"All right, Cord, break off the fight," Staley said. "Start moving the cows out."

"With them shootin' at us?"

"They're in a wagon," Staley said. "You think they're goin' to be able to run us down in a wagon?"

Cord laughed. "No."

"Then do like I said and start movin' out them cows before the others come back."

"Where did they go?" Jules asked, lowering his rifle and staring through the gun smoke out into the darkness. "I don't see any of them."

"I don't either," Sally said.

"Hoo boy, we must'a run 'em off!" Jules said excitedly.

Sally shook her head. "I don't think so," she said. "I think they have something else . . . the cows!" she suddenly said.

"What?"

"They're going after the herd!"

"What'll we do?"

Before Sally could answer, they heard the report of several gunshots from the darkness.

Sally smiled. "We don't have to do anything," she said. "Smoke's back!"

From their position in the chuck wagon, they couldn't actually see what was going on, but they could see the muzzle flashes in the night, and they could hear the reports of the guns being fired.

"I wish I was out there," Jules said. "I feel like I ain't doin' my part."

"Don't be silly," Sally said. "If you hadn't been here to hold them down for a while, they would already have the herd and be gone."

Jules smiled. "Yeah, that's right, ain't it? We held them down here until Smoke could get back."

The sound of the hoofbeats of the galloping horses spread its thunder over the valley. As Smoke led his men back to the herd, he saw the cattle rustlers moving into position to steal the herd. Pearlie saw it too.

"They're takin' the cows!" Pearlie shouted.

"Like hell they are," Smoke replied, firing the first shot.

The rustlers, surprised by the fact that someone was in front of them, returned fire. Bullets whistled back and forth in the dark; then, one of Smoke's men cried out.

"I'm hit!"

Looking around, Smoke saw that it was Andy. Andy weaved back and forth in the saddle, then grabbed hold of the saddle horn to keep from falling.

"Mike, see to him!" Smoke called.

"Hold on, Andy, I'm comin'!" Mike called, riding toward the stricken cowboy.

Even as Mike was moving toward Andy, Smoke shot at another one of the rustlers, a stocky, powerfully built man.

As the man tumbled from his saddle he lost his hat, and Smoke could see that he was bald.

"Damn, they got Staley!" Cord called.

"We're outnumbered now," one of the other outlaws said. "I'm gettin' out of here!"

"I'm leavin' too," another said.

Cord watched the two men leave, then saw that only he and one other man remained.

"Let's go!" Cord shouted.

"What about Staley?"

"To hell with him!"

"Should we go after 'em, Smoke?" Pearlie called.

"No," Smoke said. "We need to get the herd back together. And we need to see to Andy. Anyone else hit?"

A quick appraisal of their situation showed that only Andy had been shot. Smoke hurried over to the young cowboy, who was now lying on the ground beside his horse. Mike was squatting down beside him.

"How bad is it?" Smoke asked.

"He's hurt bad," Mike replied. "We need to get him in to a doctor."

"Hrmmph," Andy said in a disapproving growl. "We both know there ain't nothin' a doctor could do for me, even if you could get me there in time. Which you can't."

"We'll get you back to the wagon," Smoke said. "Sally is about as good on patching up gunshot wounds as any doctor. Lord knows, she's patched me up a few times."

"I ain't goin' to make it, Smoke," Andy said. "There's no sense in you tryin' to fool me none."

Smoke sighed, then nodded. "I won't lie to you, Andy. You're hit hard."

Andy chuckled.

"What the hell you findin' to laugh about, Andy?" Billy asked.

"I owed Dooley ten dollars," Andy said. "I figured when he died I wouldn't have to pay it. Don't you know now that the first thing ole' Dooley is goin' to do when he sees me is hold out his hand for that money."

Despite the seriousness of Andy's wound, both Billy and Mike laughed. Smoke laughed as well.

"Boys, I'll tell you somethin' maybe you didn't know," Andy said. "This here dyin' ain't hurtin' me none a'tall."

Andy gasped a few more breaths, then stopped breathing.

"All right, boys, get him up on his horse. Mike, you take him back to the wagon. Pearlie, Cal, Billy, let's take care of the cows."

It was nearly dawn by the time all the cows that had been run off were back with the herd.

"What are we goin' to do now, Smoke?" Pearlie asked. "Them cows is near dead they're so tired. We goin' to have to give 'em a little break."

"We'll stay here twenty-four hours," Smoke said. "We could use a rest too. And it'll give us time to get Andy buried."

"And Hank," Jules said, coming up to join them.

"Hank too?"

Jules nodded. "Yes, sir, me 'n Mike got 'em both lyin' under canvas back at the wagon. Oh, and Miz Sally say's she's near 'bout got breakfast ready."

"Good, I've done worked up an appetite," Pearlie said.

"Miz Sally was a regular hellion, shootin' the bad guys with one hand and cookin' breakfast with the other."

"What?" Billy asked, shocked by the revelation. "You mean to tell me Miz Sally was fixin' breakfast and shootin' the bad guys all at the same time?"

"Well, maybe not for real," Jules agreed. "But she almost was. You should see her when she's got her dander up, Smoke," Jules said.

Smoke chuckled. "I have seen her, Jules," he said. "Believe me, I have seen her."

Chapter Twenty

The corpses of Hank and Andy were dressed in their best shirts as they lay side by side on the canvas that had been spread out alongside the two graves that had been dug for them. The cowboys had put on their best shirts as well for the impromptu funeral that Smoke was about to conduct.

"Are the others taken care of?" Smoke asked Pearlie. He was referring to the outlaws who had lost their lives in the failed attempt at cattle rustling.

"They're took care of," Pearlie said. "We found a draw that was big enough to hold them. The sides of the draw was real soft and it was easy enough to just drop the bodies into the hole and push all the dirt in. They're buried, all six of 'em."

"Did you recognize any of them?"

"No," Pearlie answered. "We pretty near figured out which one is the leader, though. Was the leader, I mean, seein' as he's as dead as the others."

"Are you talking about the stocky bald-headed one?" Smoke asked.

"Yeah," Pearlie answered. "How'd you know that?"

"After he went down, the fight seemed to go out of all the others," Smoke said.

"Yeah, that's pretty much the way I noticed it too."

"Smoke, are you goin' to say a few words for Hank and Andy?" Sally asked.

Smoke nodded and the men took off their hats, then stood, holding their hats in front of them.

Smoke cleared his throat.

"Lord, I don't have to tell you that I'm not much for prayin'," he said. "But I figure that when I'm prayin' for someone else, you'll more than likely listen, even to someone like me.

"I don't know much about what kind of life these two boys lived before they joined us on this drive. But on this drive they were good men. They rode night-hawk without complaining, their partners could always count on them to be wherever they were supposed to be on time, and they died with courage and honor.

"Lord, all the preachers tell us that you have a special place for men like these two we're sendin' you today. I want you to welcome them there. Go easy on them, Lord. They've been through blizzards, drought, Indian raids, and rustlers. I know you've got some good men with you up there, Lord. Well, sir, here are two more.

"Amen."

"Amen," the others said.

The men put their hats back on. Then Cal cleared his throat and looked at Mike and Billy.

"Better get your old shirts back on," he said. "We need to get these boys in the ground."

"All right," Billy said.

"Jules, you come with me, we need to get us a good count of how many cows we got left," Pearlie said.

"Yes, sir," Jules replied, starting toward his horse.

Smoke watched Jules and Pearlie ride away. Then he turned his attention to the bodies of Hank and Andy. Sally sewed the canvas covers closed around the two bodies; then, gently, Billy, Mike, and Cal, using ropes, lowered Hank and Andy into their graves. Smoke watched until the graves were closed, leaving two fresh mounds of dirt.

Sally scattered a few pieces of brightly colored glass over the two mounds.

"I broke this glass a few days ago," Sally said. "I intended to throw it away, I don't know why I kept it, but now I'm glad I did. It's not as nice as putting flowers on their graves, but it does add a little color."

"It's nice," Smoke said without elaboration.

With the funeral over, the others began drifting away. Sally had something that needed her attention and, for some time, Smoke was alone. He walked over to stand over the two graves. Finally, he saw Pearlie and Jules returning to the camp. Swinging down from his horse, Pearlie gave the reins of his horse to Jules, then walked over to give the report to Smoke.

"We got a good count, Smoke," Pearlie said. "We've still got a little over twenty-nine hundred. That means that on this whole drive, we've lost less than a hundred cows."

"And four good men," Smoke added, looking at the side-by-side graves where Hank and Andy lay buried. He was referring also to Dooley and LeRoy, who were buried on the trail behind them.

"Yeah," Pearlie agreed. "They were four good men, all right."

"I'd trade every cow in the herd for them," Smoke said.

"Things like this happen, Smoke," Pearlie said. "You know this better'n anyone."

"Yeah, I know," Smoke said as he stroked his jaw. "Things like this happen."

Smoke walked over to the fire and poured himself a cup of coffee. He had just taken a swallow when Sally came up to him with her own cup. Seeing her, Smoke reached for the pot and poured her a cup as well.

"Are you all right?" Sally asked.

"I wish you hadn't come," Smoke said, making no reference to Sally's comment.

"Why?"

Smoke sighed. "A lot has happened."

"Smoke, I'm not made of sugar and spice and everything nice," she said, quoting the old nursery rhyme.

Smoke chuckled. "Well, I'll second the 'you aren't very nice' part," he said.

"What? Why, Smoke Jensen!" Sally gasped. "Are you saying I'm not nice?"

"No, I'm just saying that, sometimes, you can be a little difficult."

Sally made as if to throw her coffee on him. "Why, if I weren't nice, I'd throw this scalding cup on you right now," she said, laughing.

"Nah, that's not what's stopping you," Smoke said, laughing with her. "You just don't want to waste the coffee, that's all."

"You found me out," Sally teased, laughing some more. "You didn't answer me," she added.

"What was the question?"

"I asked if you were all right."

"Yeah," Smoke replied. "Yeah, I'm all right."

"It was good to see the two of you laughing a moment ago," Cal said, coming up to them then.

"Why do you say that?" Smoke asked.

"No reason in particular," Cal said. "It's just that some of the boys was beginnin' to think that you was so upset over losin' Hank and LeRoy, and Andy and Dooley, that you wouldn't be able to keep goin'."

"Do the others want to turn back?" Smoke asked.

Cal shook his head. "No, sir, not a one of us wants to turn back," he said. "We started out on this here journey, and we aim to see to it that you get your cows through."

"Four good men lost their lives to get the cows this far," Smoke said.

"Yes, but think about it, Smoke. If we don't' go on, then those boys died for nothin'. Besides, it's farther to go back now than it is to go on ahead. Looks to me like we got no choice."

Smoke nodded. "That's true," he said. He sighed. "We've got no choice. Tell the boys to get a good day's rest. We're going on ahead tomorrow."

Cal smiled broadly. "Yes, sir!" he said. "I'll tell 'em just that."

Sally looked up at Smoke after Cal left. "What was that all about?" she asked.

"What was what all about?"

"You weren't about to turn back."

"No, I wasn't," Smoke said. "But this way, the men think they have talked me into it. And sometimes it's good to let a man think he is controlling his own destiny, even if he isn't."

Trent Williams looked up from his desk when Gilbert stepped into his office.

"Mr. Williams there is a—gentleman—here to see you," the teller said. The way he set the word "gentleman" apart from the rest of the sentence indicated that he believed the man was anything but a gentleman.

"Who is it?" Williams asked.

"I don't know, sir," Gilbert replied. "He didn't give his name, but he said that it had to do with some—cow—business. He said you would understand."

"Cow business?" Williams thought for a moment, then realized what it must be. "Very well, show him in."

Williams leaned back in his chair waiting, expecting to see Will Staley come through the door.

It wasn't Staley.

"Who are you?" Williams asked.

"The name is Cord. Trace Cord," the man said.

"What can I do for you, Mr. Cord? My teller said it had something to do with the cow business."

"Yes," Cord said.

"What sort of cow business?"

"The kind of business you hired Will Staley for."

"Oh," Williams said. He drummed his fingers on the desk for a moment or two. "I see. So tell me, Mr. Cord, why didn't Mr. Staley come to discuss this?"

"He didn't come 'cause he's dead."

"Dead?" Williams asked, sitting back in his chair, surprised by the statement.

"Yeah, him and five others."

"What happened?"

"We ran into a hornets' nest, that's what happened."

"Am I to understand that you did not get the herd?"

"You ain't been listenin' to nothin' I've said, have you?" Cord asked. "No, we didn't get the herd. We're damn lucky they didn't kill all of us."

"I see," Williams said. "What am I to do now?"

"I don't care what you do now. All I care about is gettin' the money."

"What money would that be?"

"The money Staley was supposed to pay us."

Williams's smile was without mirth. "Why, Mr. Cord,

you don't really think I'm going to pay you for failure, do you?"

"There wasn't nothin' said about failure. Only thing Staley said was that he would pay us to go with him. Besides, you set us up, you son of a bitch. You didn't tell us we was goin' to run into an army."

"When I pay to have something done, how it is done is none of my business," Williams said.

"Yeah, well, that's just it. I went with him, and now I want my pay."

"And if I refuse?"

"I'll go to the sheriff and tell him what you had planned," Cord said.

Williams stroked his chin. "You wouldn't do that. You would be incriminating yourself."

"Hell, I don't care nothin' about that. I've been in prison before, wouldn't bother me none to go back in. But a highfalutin fella like yourself? You'd have a real hard time in prison."

"How much did Staley say he would pay you?"

"Two hun . . . uh, five hundred dollars," Cord said.

"Five hundred dollars is a lot of money."

"Yeah. But that's what he said he would pay us."

"Us?"

"I'll be splitting the money with the others."

"I see," Williams said. He nodded. "All right, I suppose what's right is right. I'll give you the money."

"I thought you might see it my way," Cord said with a self-satisfied smile.

Williams opened the middle drawer of his desk, reached his hand in, wrapped his fingers around the butt of a Colt .44, then pulled the gun out.

"What?" Cord asked, surprised by the sudden appearance of the gun. "What are you doing?"

"I'll not be blackmailed," Williams said, pulling the trigger.

The sound of the gunshot was exceptionally loud. The bullet caught Cord in the heart, and though he lived long enough to slap his hand over the wound in his chest, he was dead by the time his body hit the floor.

"Mr. Gilbert! Mr. Gilbert, come in here quickly!" Williams shouted.

Gilbert, the teller who had come in earlier, now came running into the room carrying a poker over his head. Williams was standing over Cord's body, holding a smoking pistol in his hand.

"Mr. Williams, what happened, sir?" Gilbert asked.

"I don't know," Williams answered, his face registering shock. "This man came in here and threatened to hold up the bank. I tried to talk him out of it, but he was quite obdurate. Then, it all happened so quickly. One minute I was arguing with him and the next minute"—Williams held up the pistol—"I was holding a smoking pistol and he was lying on the floor."

"Yes, well, don't worry, Mr. Williams," Gilbert said. "You did the right thing. A bank robber like that should be shot."

Chapter Twenty-one

The sheriff's inquiry had been fast and nonthreatening. Gilbert testified that Cord had come into the bank and presented himself in a belligerent manner, demanding to see Trent Williams. Gilbert further testified that he was worried about Mr. Williams, and therefore kept a close eye on the door to the bank office. Then, he heard Williams call out, heard a shot, and when he entered the office he saw Cord lying on the floor and Williams standing over him, holding a smoking gun.

Trent Williams did not dissent from Gilbert's account. He explained that Cord had come into the office, demanding that Williams empty the safe and give him all the money.

"Did he have a gun?" Williams was asked.

"Yes."

"Was the gun in his holster, or was he holding it in his hand?"

"I don't know," Williams said.

"Come on, Sheriff, what are you askin' Mr. Williams all these questions for?" Gilbert asked. "We've already told you what happened."

The sheriff nodded. "All right, Mr. Williams, you're free to go. There will be no charges."

"Thank you," Williams said.

Williams told himself that shooting Cord had been necessary, but he was unnerved. He wasn't unnerved because he had had to shoot Cord. He was unnerved because Staley had failed to get the herd for him. Now what was he going to do?

At this very moment the answer to Williams's dilemma was just down the street from the bank, playing a game of solitaire in the saloon. The man was dressed all in black, including his hat, though the starkness was offset by the glitter of the silver and turquoise hatband. This was Quince Pardeen, and though he would have preferred a game of poker, nobody would play with him because everyone was afraid of him. Pardeen's reputation preceeded him now, even in the smallest towns.

Pardeen counted out three cards, but couldn't find a play. The second card of the three was a black seven. There would have been a play had the black seven come up on top, but unfortunately, it was one card down and therefore useless to him. Pardeen glared at it for a moment, then, with a shrug, played it anyway.

The batwing doors swung open and a cowboy came in and walked over to the bar. He ordered a whiskey, then looked around and saw Pardeen sitting at the table, calmly playing cards.

"Ain't you the one they call Pardeen?" the cowboy asked.

Pardeen didn't answer.

"Yeah, that's who you are, all right," the cowboy said. "You're Quince Pardeen."

Though the cowboy wasn't telling the people in the saloon anything they didn't already know, everyone remained silent. The cowboy's tone of voice was challenging, and everyone knew that Pardeen was not a man to be challenged.

"My name is Carl Logan," the cowboy said. "My brother's name was John Logan. I reckon you've heard that name."

Pardeen made no response.

"John was a sheriff, an honest man whose only job was to protect the people of his town. But you shot him down in cold blood," the cowboy continued.

"Mister, do you know who you are talkin' to?" another man asked.

The cowboy looked at the questioner. "Yeah," he replied, "I know who I'm talkin' to. And I know who you are too, Corbett. You're the little piece of dung that hangs on Pardeen's ass all the time. They's some that says you're the one that helped Pardeen break out of jail where he was waitin' to be hung for killin' my brother."

Finally, Pardeen looked up from his cards. The expression on his face was one of boredom, as if he shouldn't have to deal with people like this belligerent cowboy.

"You talkin' to me, friend?"

"Mister, I'm not your friend."

Pardeen smiled coldly. "Oh, that's too bad," he said. "You see, I generally give my friends some leeway when they make a mistake. But seein' as you aren't my friend, then I don't see much need in cuttin' you any slack a'tall."

"I ain't askin' for any slack from you, you low-assed son of a bitch," the cowboy said.

The others in the saloon gasped at the audacity of Logan's words.

"I'm tryin' to get you riled enough to fight," Logan said. He doubled his fists. "Because I aim to beat you to a pulp."

Pardeen looked up from the cards again. This time the nonchalance was gone. Instead, his eyes were narrowed menacingly.

"If you got somethin' stickin' in your craw, cowboy, I think maybe you'd better just spit it out," Pardeen said coldly.

"I done spit it out," Logan said. "I told you, I aim to beat you to a pulp; then I'm goin' to personally turn you over to the sheriff so you can get hung proper."

Pardeen looked surprised. "A fistfight?" he asked. "Did I hear you right? You are challenging me to a fistfight?"

"Yeah," Logan said. He looked over at Corbett. "I know there's two of you and one of me. But I'd say that makes the odds about even. Come on, I think I'm goin' to enjoy this." He made his hands into fists, then held them out in front of his face, moving his right hand in tiny circles. "Come on," he said. "I'm goin' to put the lights out for both of you."

Pardeen smiled, a low, evil smile. "Huh-uh," he said. "If me'n you are goin' to fight, mister, it's goin' to be permanent."

"You mean a gunfight? No, I ain't goin' to get into no gunfight with the likes of you," Logan said. "Besides, like I said, there's two of you. I figure with the two of you, it might just about make a fistfight come out even."

"You can keep me out of this one, mister," Corbett said. "This is just between the two of you." Corbett stood up and walked away, leaving the floor to the two players. Pardeen, in the meantime, stood up and stepped away from the table. He let his arm hang down alongside his pistol and he looked at the cowboy through cold, ruthless eyes.

"Well, what about it, Mr. Logan?" Pardeen said. "You're the one that asked me to dance."

Logan shook his head. "No, I told you, this ain't the kind of fight I'm talkin' about."

"I'll let you draw first," Pardeen offered.

"I told you, I ain't drawin' on you," Logan said. He doubled up his fists again. "But if you'd like to come over here and take your beatin' like a man, I'd be glad to oblige you."

"I said draw," Pardeen repeated in a cold, flat voice.

The others in the saloon began, quietly but deliberately, to get out of the way of any flying lead.

Logan shook his head slowly. "I told you, I ain't goin' to draw on you," he said. He smiled. "You might'a noticed that I'm not wearin' a gun."

"I'll give you time to get yourself heeled," Pardeen offered.

"I told you, I ain't goin' to get into no gunfight with you."

"Somebody give Mr. Logan a gun," Pardeen said coldly. He pulled his lips into a sinister smile. "He seems to have come to this fight unprepared."

"I don't want a gun," Peabody said.

When no one offered Logan their gun, Pardeen pointed to a cowboy who was standing at the far end of the bar. "I see that you are wearing a gun. Give it to him."

"He don't want a gun," the man said. "I ain't goin' to do that. If I give him a gun, you'll kill him."

"That's right."

"Well, I don't want no part of it."

"You got no choice, friend. You'll either give him your gun or you had better be ready to use it yourself," Pardeen said. He turned three quarters of the way toward the armed cowboy. "Which will it be?"

The cowboy paused for just a moment longer, then sighed in defeat. "All right, all right. If you put it that way, I reckon I'll do whatever you want." He took his gun out of the holster and laid it on the bar. "Sorry, Logan," he said. He gave the gun a shove and it slid halfway down the bar, knocking two glasses aside, then stopping just beside Logan's hand. It rocked back and forth for a moment, making a little sound that, in the now-silent bar, seemed amost deafening.

"Pick it up," Pardeen said to Logan.

Logan looked at the pistol, but made no effort to pick it up. A line of perspiration beads broke out on his upper lip.

"No, I ain't goin' to do it."

Pardeen drew his pistol and fired. There was a flash of light and a roar of exploding gunpowder. A billowing cloud of acrid, blue smoke rolled from the end of Pardeen's pistol, then began rising to the ceiling.

For a moment the entire saloon thought Pardeen had killed Logan, but that impression dissolved when they saw that Logan was still standing. He wasn't unscathed, though, for he was holding his hand to the side of his head with blood spilling through his fingers. Pardeen had shot off a piece of Logan's earlobe.

"Pick up the gun," Pardeen ordered.

"No."

There was a second shot and Peabody's right earlobe, like his left, turned into a ragged, bloody piece of flesh.

"Mister, you better do somethin'," Corbett said. "Else ole Quince here is goin' to carve you up like a Christmas turkey."

Logan stood there holding his hands over his ears as he stared at Pardeen. Both hands were red with blood.

"Pick it up!"

"No!"

"Are you left-handed or right-handed?" Pardeen asked.

"What?"

"Left or right."

"Why do you ask that?"

"I figure you are probably right-handed," Pardeen said. "Am I right?"

"Whether I'm right-handed or left-handed ain't none of your business," Logan said.

"You better hope I'm right," Pardeen said. He pulled his gun and shot a third time. This time his bullet took one of the fingers off Logan's left hand.

Logan cried out in pain, then grabbed his hand. "You're crazy!" he said.

"Pick up the gun," Pardeen said calmly.

Logan stared at Pardeen through eyes that were wide with fear. Then the fear was replaced by blind rage. Logan reached for the pistol.

"I'll send you to hell, you son of a bitch!" Logan yelled.

Pardeen played with Logan the way a cat will play with a mouse. He waited until Logan had the gun in hand before he drew again. This time his bullet caught Logan in the forehead. Logan fell back against the bar, then slid down, dead before he reached the floor.

The sound of the gunshot brought two or three outsiders into the saloon, including the sheriff. He saw Logan sitting down against the bar, his eyes open and sightless, his hand clenched tightly around the unfired pistol.

"Oh, hell," the sheriff said quietly. He looked over at Pardeen. "Did you do this?"

"Yeah, I done it," Pardeen said. "But it was self-defense. Look at the gun in his hand. He was goin' to shoot me."

"Pardeen forced him into it, Sheriff," the bartender said. "Logan didn't want to fight but Pardeen egged him on."

"Pardeen didn't have any choice, Sheriff," a voice from the back of the saloon said. "He had to force a showdown now."

The sheriff looked toward the sound of the voice and saw Trent Williams.

"Mr. Williams, you are taking up for Pardeen?" the sheriff asked, surprised by the statement.

"Believe me, it's not something I want to do," Williams said. "But when Mr. Logan spoke to me earlier today, he let it be known that he intended to kill Quince Pardeen. I believe if Pardeen had not forced a showdown here, Logan would have shot him in the back."

"Yeah," Corbett said. "That's what I think too."

"What have you got to say about this, Pardeen?" the sheriff asked.

"You heard what the man said, Sheriff," Pardeen replied. "I didn't have no choice. If I hadn't killed him, he would'a killed me."

The sheriff shook his head. "I don't know if I believe you or not," he said.

Pardeen smiled. "Oh, yeah, you believe me all right," he said easily. "You believe me because you are afraid to go against me. Otherwise, you would have arrested me the moment I came into town."

"No, I—I couldn't arrest you," the sheriff said. "I've

heard what you did back in Puxico, but I've received no paper on you and I've got no authority."

"Well, Sheriff, if you do get some paper on me and you want to come arrest me, you know where you can find me," Pardeen taunted.

"You just—you just watch your step around here," the sheriff said, trying hard to keep his voice from breaking in fear. Turning, he walked out of the saloon, leaving Logan's body dead on the floor behind him.

Pardeen chuckled as the sheriff left; then, turning, he saw Trent Williams staring at him. He walked over to talk to him.

"Logan didn't really tell you he was going to kill me, did he?" Pardeen asked.

"No."

"Then why did you say that?"

Williams looked around the saloon to see if anyone was close enough to overhear their conversation. As everyone seemed to want to give Pardeen a very wide berth, there was nobody close by.

"I spoke up for you because I want to hire your services," Williams said.

"I'm not interested," Pardeen replied.

Pardeen's dismissive comment surprised Williams. "You're not interested? Why not? You haven't even heard what I want you to do."

"I know what you want me to do. You want me to kill someone. The answer is no. Kill him yourself," Pardeen said.

"You haven't heard my offer."

"It would have to be a very good offer to get me to change my mind," Pardeen said.

"Is ten thousand dollars good enough?" Williams asked.

“What?” Pardeen replied with a gasp. “Did you say ten thousand dollars?”

“Yes.”

A smile spread across Pardeen’s face, and this time the smile was genuine.

“I’ll do it.”

“You haven’t asked who it is I want you to kill.”

“I don’t care who it is. For ten thousand dollars I’d kill my own grandma.”

Chapter Twenty-two

Sorento, Wyoming Territory

The town was cold and dark when Williams, Pardeen, and Corbett arrived at around one in the morning. Tying their horses off behind the saloon, the three men moved up the alley toward the office of the Indian agency.

They were startled by the screech of a cat that jumped down from a fence, then ran across the alley in front of them.

The yap of a dog caused them to stop, then move into the shadows. The dog continued to bark.

"Cody, hush up!" an irritated voice shouted.

The dog continued to bark.

"I said shut up!" the voice shouted again.

The dog barked one more time, but this time its bark was interrupted by a yelp of pain.

"Damnit, when I tell you to shut up, I mean shut up," the voice said angrily.

A baby began crying.

The three men waited a moment longer; then when everything had calmed down, they resumed their cautious movement down the alley.

"He lives in a small shack behind the agency," Williams said.

"What about the other man?" Pardeen asked. "The one who is the actual agent?"

"Don't worry about him. He lives in Laramie."

"I still don't know how killin' this man is going to get us any money."

"It's simple," Williams said. "Kirby Jensen—"

"Smoke Jensen," Pardeen said, interrupting.

"All right, Smoke Jensen," Williams continued. "He's bringing in three thousand head of cattle. He will turn the cattle over to Malone in return for a receipt, which he can then redeem for cash from Abernathy. Only, he isn't going to turn the cattle over to Malone, he's going to turn them over to me."

"Because?" Pardeen asked.

"Because he is going to think that I am Cephus Malone."

Reaching the little building behind the Indian agency, Williams tried the front door.

"I'll be damned," he whispered. "It isn't locked."

"Yeah, a lot of people don't lock their doors in these little towns," Pardeen replied, also in a whisper. "They figure they know everyone in town, so they figure they're safe."

Williams started in, then stopped and stepped back out onto the porch.

"What is it? What's wrong?"

"Don't make any noise, and tell me when it's done," Williams said.

Pardeen chuckled, then disappeared into the darkened interior of the little house. Williams and Corbett waited outside.

"Who's there? What is it?" a voice said from inside. "What are you doing in here?"

That was as far as the voice got until it turned into a muffled squealing sound.

A moment later, Pardeen came back outside. "It's done," he said.

"Are you sure he's dead?" Williams asked.

"Oh, yeah, he's dead," Pardeen said. "I cut his throat from ear to ear."

"Lock the door," Williams said. "By the time anyone discovers him it will be too late."

Smoke's riders didn't see the town until they reached the top of a long, sloping ridgeline. Jules was riding point, so he was the first to see Sorento, which was no more than a small group of buildings clustered around a railroad depot.

"Yahoo!" Jules shouted, taking off his hat and waving it over his head. Turning his horse, he galloped back to the others.

"We're here!" he shouted happily. "It's just over the hill! We're here, we're here, we're here!"

It had been twenty-eight days since Smoke and his outfit had left Sugarloaf. Twenty-eight days of drought, stampede, blizzard, and attacks from Indians and cattle rustlers. They had come through, though not without its cost. Four good men lay dead on the trail behind them.

Because they would be spending this night in town, Sally had not gone ahead of them this morning as she normally did. On this, the last day of the drive, she kept the wagon alongside the herd.

Smoke stopped them when they reached the crest of the hill. They sat there for a moment, looking down at the little town below them.

"It sure don't look like much," Pearlie said. "Comin'

all this way only to see a town that ain't even as big as Big Rock seems sort of . . ." He struggled for a word. "Sort of . . ."

"Anticlimactic," Sally suggested.

"Yeah, that," Pearlie said, though he had no idea what the word meant.

"Well, we didn't come here to visit the town," Smoke said. "We came here to sell our cattle. And if we can do that, then it doesn't matter what size the town is."

"You got that right," Cal said. "But the question now is, did we make it in time? Are we the first ones here?"

"We're the first ones here," Sally said.

"How do you know?"

"Look at the feeder lots," Sally said. "There aren't more than a couple of dozen cattle down there."

"Could be they already been delivered to the Indians," Billy said.

"No," Sally said. "If there had been that many cattle in the pens, we would still be able to smell it. We're the first."

"So, what do we do now, Smoke?" Billy asked.

"We'll keep the herd here while I go into town and contact Mr. Malone," Smoke answered. "Then, soon as I make the arrangements, I'll pay you boys off, then make arrangements for you and the horses to go back by train."

"Whooee," Jules said. "Think about that, boys. We'll be goin' home on the train. I ain't never been on no train before. I wonder what that'll be like."

"Why, shoot, it won't be like nothin'," Cal said. "You just sit there on the train and ride along with it, that's all."

"Sally, you want to come into town with me?" Smoke asked.

"Not yet," Sally said. "Since we won't be taking the wagon back, I'll need to spend some time packing the things that we will be shipping back home. But I tell you what, find us a hotel room while you are in town, would you? I wouldn't mind spending this night in a real bed."

"Yeah, I could go along with that myself," Smoke said. He swung into his saddle and looked back at the others. "I can't tell you how proud I am of you," he said. "Not many men could do what you just did, driving three thousand head of cattle five hundred miles in the wintertime."

"The reason not many men could do it is because there ain't that many dumb enough to try," Billy replied, and the others laughed.

"I'll be back in a couple of hours," Smoke said as he turned toward the town.

A small bell was suspended from the door so that it jingled as Smoke stepped into the Indian agency office.

"I'll be with you in just a moment," someone called from the back.

"No hurry," Smoke answered. "It's taken me a month to get here. I can wait a few more minutes, I reckon."

The man laughed as he came out front. "May I help you?"

"My name is Smoke Jensen," Smoke said. "Are you are Cephus Malone?"

"I am indeed, sir. Cephus Malone at your service."

"Then you are the man I'm looking for. I'm here to sell my cattle. That is, assuming I am the first."

"You are the first."

"Then, I take it that you are still interested in buying." Smoke chuckled. "Otherwise, I've had a hell of a long drive for nothing."

"Oh, yes, I am quite willing to buy your herd. As soon as you put your cows in the holding pens, I will issue you a receipt for payment. Then, all you have to do is send the receipt to Washington and they'll send you a bank draft for the amount."

"I have to send the receipt to Washington for payment? I thought all I had to do was present the receipt to Mr. Abernathy."

"No, no, Abernathy need not get involved. I'm the only one you will have to deal with. That is, except for the Indian Bureau in Washington."

"Yes, in Washington," Smoke repeated. It was obvious by the tone of his voice that he was not too thrilled with the idea of having to wait for payment.

"I can see that it is making you a little nervous to have to wait for your money. But if you can't depend on the United States government, who can you depend on?"

"I guess you're right," Smoke said. "All right, I'll go bring in the herd. I have them just outside town."

"Good, good. Believe me, Mr. Jensen, there are going to be a lot of happy Indians when these cattle are delivered."

"I hope so," Smoke said. "A happy Indian is a peaceful Indian."

The man chuckled. "That's true, Mr. Jensen," he said. "Yes, sir, truer words were never spoken. I like that. I may use that the next time I talk to the bureaucrats in Washington. A happy Indian is a peaceful Indian."

"You will want the cattle delivered to the holding pens, I suppose?"

"Yes."

"All right," Smoke said as he started toward the door.

"Wait, Mr. Jensen, don't you want the receipt?"

Smoke stopped. "Don't you want to count them first?"

"Oh, yes. Yes, indeed. I guess I was getting a little ahead

of myself, wasn't I? Please, by all means, bring the cattle in. I'll count them, then I'll issue the receipt."

Smoke nodded, then left.

Pardeen came out of the back room then. "So that was the great Smoke Jensen," he said.

"That is how he identified himself," Williams, who had been posing as Cephus Malone, said. "I have no way of knowing for sure, since I've never met the man. But I have no reason to doubt that he is who he says he is, especially as he has delivered the herd."

"Not yet he ain't delivered it," Pardeen said.

"Oh, he's delivered it all right," Williams insisted. "He just hasn't put them in the feeder pens for us."

"Yeah, well, you'd better keep an eye on that one," Pardeen said. "He's as slick as they come."

"No," Williams replied. "It isn't my job to keep an eye on him. That's your job."

"Oh, you don't worry about that," Pardeen said. "I have something special in mind for him just as soon as all this is over."

The town of Sorento existed for the sole purpose of providing a railhead to ship out cattle for the neighboring ranches. Because of that, the facilities at the depot were equal to those of cities much bigger.

Included in the facilities were two very large feeder lots, and Smoke used both of them. While Cal, Billy, Mike, and Jules pushed the cows into the two large pens, Pearlie and Smoke sat on the top rail of the pens, counting them. Smoke had one pen and Pearlie the other. They counted the cows by the simple method of making a knot in a string of rawhide for every fifty cows that passed through the gate.

This controlled counting method allowed them to arrive at a much more accurate number than the hasty count that had been taken in the field after the attempted rustling.

"I make if thirteen hundred and forty-two, Pearlie said.

"I've got fourteen hundred and eleven," Smoke said.

"That's twenty-seven hundred and fifty three," Pearlie said. He shook his head. "I didn't think we had lost that many."

"Pearlie, when you consider everything that we went through, I'm very pleasantly surprise we didn't lose more," Smoke said.

"Yeah, I guess you are right," Pearlie said. He smiled. "But I reckon it's enough to make the drive worth it, don't you think?"

"Oh, yes, it's more than worth it," Smoke agreed. "Especially considering that we might have as bad a winter as we did before."

"Here comes our man," Smoke said when he saw Trent Williams, the man he thought was Cephus Malone, coming toward him. Williams was carrying two pieces of paper.

"Well, you got them all counted, I see," Williams said.

"Twenty-seven hundred and fifty-three," Smoke said.

"Two thousand, seven hundred, and fifty-three," Williams repeated. "All right, all I need you to do is sign this bill of sale over to me, and I'll give you your receipt."

Smoke nodded, then signed the bill of sale.

Williams handed him a receipt. "Send this in to Washington, friend, and you'll be a rich man," he said. "And may I say that it was a pleasure doing business with you?"

"Thank you," Smoke replied. "Now, I want to treat my cowboys to the best dinner in town. Where do you recommend I take them?"

"Oh, well, I wouldn't presume to recommend one place

over another," Williams said. "But knowing cowboys, I imagine anyplace that would let them in would be a welcome change to men who are used to nothing but whorehouses and saloons."

Smoke glared at Williams. "I don't think of my cowboys in that way, mister," he said. "I consider them to be good men. In fact, I would go so far as to say that I consider them to be among the finest men I have ever met."

Williams cleared his throat. "Well—uh—certainly I meant no disrespect to either you or your men," he said.

Sally came up to Smoke as Williams was walking away.

"What's wrong?" she asked.

"Nothing's wrong," Smoke replied. He held up the receipt. "We have the receipt, but I'll tell you the truth, Sally, if it weren't for the money, that's a fella I'd just as soon avoid."

Sally smiled. "Well, after this, we can avoid him," she said.

As it turned out, the hotel had a banquet room and Smoke rented it for the evening. He ordered a dinner to be prepared for his men, and all showed up, freshly scrubbed and wearing their best clothes.

As the wine was poured, Smoke lifted his glass to propose a toast.

"Sally, men," he said. "I would like to drink a toast to ones who didn't make it here with us but who, by their effort and their sacrifice, enabled us to make it. Here's to Dooley, Andy, Hank, and LeRoy."

"Hear, hear," Pearlie said, and all of them drank.

"And I'd like to propose a toast to the man who led us," Billy said.

"And to the woman who led him," Cal added, eliciting laughter as he held his glass toward Sally.

Again they drank a toast. Then waiters began bringing in the food.

"Oh, that looks good," Billy said as a plate was put before him.

"I heard that you men just brought a herd of cattle up," the headwaiter said. "I suppose after eating bad food on the trail, anything would look good to you."

Jules started to say something, but Billy held up his hand to stop him.

"Mister, I said this food looks good. I didn't say nothin' about how we ate on the trail 'cause the truth is, there ain't nothin' this here café can serve that will come close to bein' as good."

"Trail food?" the headwaiter asked incredulously. "I hardly think so."

"Mister, Miz Sally cooked all our food on the trail," Mike said. "And if you make another remark about how it wasn't no good, why I reckon I'll just have to box your ears for you."

"Mike!" Sally said.

"Miz Sally, I'm just takin' up for you is all," Mike said.

Despite herself, Sally couldn't help but laugh at her young "protector."

"Well, I thank you very much. But boxing this gentleman's ears is no way to do it."

"Madam," the headwaiter said. "Believe me, I meant no disrespect."

"And no disrespect was taken," Sally replied graciously.

"Say, Smoke, what time does the train leave tomorrow?" Billy asked.

"Around nine o'clock, I think," Smoke said. "I'll find

out for sure right after breakfast tomorrow when I get the tickets."

"There ain't no reason we can't go out and have us a good time tonight, is there?" Billy asked.

"No reason at all," Smoke said. "You are all on your own time now."

"Good," Billy said. "It's been a long time on the trail. I aim to wash some of that trail dust away."

Chapter Twenty-three

Billy was standing in the Cattleman's Saloon when he looked up at the clock and saw that it was nearly midnight.

"Whoa," he said to the soiled dove who was keeping him company. "I'd better get back to the hotel and go to bed. I'm catching a train out of here tomorrow."

"Honey, you don't have to go all the way to the hotel just to get in bed," the girl said.

Billy laughed. "I have to give you credit, Lucy, you are all business," he said. "But Mr. Jensen has gone to all the trouble to rent hotel rooms for us. It ain't that often I get to stay in a hotel, and I aim to take advantage of it."

"You will buy me one more drink, though, won't you?" Lucy asked.

"Damn right I will," Billy said. "In fact, I'll have one with you."

Billy tapped his finger on the empty glass and when the bartender came to refill it, indicated that Lucy's glass should be refilled as well.

"Not from that bottle, Jake," Lucy said.

"I know your special bottle," Jake replied, putting the whiskey bottle away and getting another bottle from under the bar.

"Ha. That's tea, ain't it?" Billy said.

"Well, I . . ."

"I don't care if it's tea," Billy said. "Hell, you couldn't stay here and drink ever' night without becomin' a drunk."

"I'm glad you understand," Lucy said. She took a swallow of her tea, then smiled at him. "Go on, you were tellin' me about the cattle drive you were on."

"Yes, ma'am, I was, wasn't I? Well, it was quite a trip up here, I tell you."

"Oh, I think it would have been very frightening to have to face so many Indians," the girl said.

"Well, I don't mind tellin' you that some of the boys was afraid," Billy said. He took a swallow of his whiskey, then ran the back of his hand across his mouth. "But I wasn't none afraid, no, sir. And I helped Smoke buck up some of the others."

"Smoke?"

"Smoke Jensen is his name. He was our trail boss," Billy said. "Well, he was more'n that 'cause he actually owned the cows."

"That's a funny name," the girl said.

"It may be a funny name," Billy said. "But he's about the best man I've ever known. Faster with a gun than greased lightnin', but you'd never know it just to know him 'cause he's a fella that don't get riled any too easy." Billy waved his finger back and forth. "But you have to pity the fella that ever does get him riled."

"I've heard of Smoke Jensen before," a man standing just down the bar said. The man was dressed all in black, including his hat, though the starkness was offset by the glitter of the silver and turquoise hatband. He continued to stare into his glass as he spoke.

"You've heard of him, have you, mister?" Billy said.

"Well, then you can verify what I'm saying about the type man he is."

"I'll tell you what I know about him," the man in black said. "I know him to be a lying, back-shooting coward."

Upon hearing that unexpected description of Smoke, Billy slammed the glass down hard on the bar, then turned to face the man who had spoken.

"What did you say, mister?"

The man at the bar turned to face Billy. "You heard what I said. I said that Smoke Jensen is a yellow-bellied, lying coward."

"Mister, maybe you don't know this, but Smoke Jensen is a friend of mine," Billy said. "And I'll be askin' you to take that back."

"And if I don't?"

"If you don't, you'll be answerin' to me," Billy said.

"Are you challengin' me to a gunfight, boy?"

Billy had not intended for the altercation to go this far. He had thought that a few harsh words, if necessary even a few punches, would be called for. He had no idea that it was being pushed to a gunfight.

"Well, no, not that," Billy said, thinking quickly. "I was thinkin' more along the lines of wipin' up this here saloon floor with your hide. I mean, you spoke some harsh and even rude words, but I'm not ready to get into a gunfight over it."

"Mister, it's too late for you to back out now," the man said. "You're the one who invited me to this ball. Now either dance with me, or admit that you are a yellow-bellied, lying coward just like your friend Smoke Jensen."

Those were killing words and everyone in the saloon, including Lucy, moved out of the way to give the two men room.

"Pardeen, the boy's been drinkin'," the bartender said. "Ease up on him."

"You stay out of this, barkeep," Pardeen said.

Billy's face went white. "Pardeen?" Billy said. "Did he call you Pardeen?"

"Yeah, he called me Pardeen 'cause that's my name," Pardeen said. "You got a problem with my name, boy?"

"No, it's not that—it's just that . . ." Billy took a deep breath. "Well, maybe we got off on the wrong foot." Billy tried to force a smile. "Why don't we just both forget about some of the things we've said and go back to drinkin' in peace?"

"Too late for that, boy. You should'a thought of that before you called me out."

"I didn't exactly call you out," Billy said. "I just said that you would have to—answer to me," he finished, barely saying the last three words.

"I'm going to count to three," Pardeen said. "When I get to three, I'm going to kill you. So I expect you had better draw your gun."

"No—I . . ."

"One."

"Look, I don't want to do this!"

"Two."

Suddenly, Billy made a desperate grab for his pistol. He had the gun out and was coming up with it before Pardeen even started his draw. For just a second, Billy actually thought that he might have a chance, and he felt a surge of hope.

That hope was dashed, even as it was forming in his mind, when he felt a sudden crushing blow to his chest. Pardeen had drawn and fired so quickly that by the time Billy realized Pardeen had the gun in his hand, he had already been shot.

The impact of the bullet knocked Billy back against the bar. He dropped his pistol and slapped his hand over the wound in his chest. Then, turning his hand out, he watched in horror as the palm of his hand filled to overflowing with his blood.

Billy looked around the saloon, into the faces of those who had just witnessed this. He saw horror and sadness in Lucy's face. He held his hand out toward her, tried to take a step, then collapsed.

The knocking was loud and insistent and even as Smoke was waking up, he was drawing his pistol from the holster that hung over the bedstead. He motioned for Sally to get out of bed and get into the corner.

"Yeah, who is it?" he called. Immediately after he called out, he moved to one side so as not to be where his voice had been.

"Mr. Jensen, my name is Joe Titus. I'm the deputy sheriff. I need to talk to you."

"What about?" Smoke called. Once more he moved after he had called out.

"Do you have a man working for you by the name of Billy Cantrell?"

Smiling, Smoke sighed and lowered his gun. He opened the door. The deputy was an older man, tall and weathered, with gunmetal-gray hair.

"What kind of trouble has Billy got himself into?" he asked. "A barroom fight?"

"No, sir," the deputy answered. "I'm sorry to have to tell you this, Mr. Jensen, but Billy Cantrell is dead."

"What? Are you serious?"

"Yes, sir. He got into a gunfight with a man by the name of Quince Pardeen. Pardeen killed him."

Smoke lowered his head and pinched the bridge of his nose.

"Did you say Quince Pardeen?"

"Yes, sir. Do you know him?"

"I've never met him, but I know who he is," Smoke said.

"Well, sir, then you know he's what they call a gunfighter. Too bad your man, Cantrell, didn't know that. If he had known that, he might not have started the fight."

"Wait a minute? Are you telling me that Billy started the fight with Pardeen?"

"Yes, sir, that's what ever'body in the saloon said. They was near all of 'em witnesses, and they all said that Cantrell called Pardeen out."

"Billy might have challenged him to a fistfight," Smoke said. "He had a habit of doing that. But he would have never challenged anyone to a gunfight, let alone someone like Pardeen."

"Yes, sir, that don't seem to make no sense to me neither," the deputy said. "But like I said, ever'one who witnessed the fight says that's exactly what happened."

"Where is Billy now?"

"He's down to the Welch Mortuary," the deputy said. "You can see him first thing in the morning if you'd like."

Smoke nodded. "Yes," he said. "I'd like to, thank you."

"It's me Pardeen is after," Smoke said to Sally after the deputy left. "He killed Billy to get to me."

"You don't know that," Sally said.

Smoke nodded. "Yeah, Sally, the sad truth is, I do know it."

* * *

The next morning, Smoke, Sally, Pearlie, Cal, Mike, and Jules were waiting outside the mortuary when Welch turned the sign from CLOSED to OPEN.

"Yes, sir, what can I do for you?" Welch asked as he opened the door.

"You have our friend's body here," Smoke said. "We would like to see him."

"Well, sir, I haven't prepared the body for viewing yet," Welch said.

"I don't care whether he is prepared for viewing yet or not. I want to see him," Smoke said with more insistence."

"Very good, sir," Welch replied. "As long as you know that the remains are in a distressed state."

"Where is he?"

"He is right in here, sir."

Smoke and the others followed Welch into the back room of the building where they saw not one, but two bodies.

"Was someone else killed last night?" Smoke asked. "I thought Billy was the only one killed in the shoot-out."

"Oh, no, that is Mr. Malone," Welch said, pointing to the other body. "The poor fellow was found murdered in his bed yesterday morning."

"Malone?"

"Yes, Cephus Malone. Did you know him?"

Smoke walked over to look at the body. He turned toward Welch.

"Are you saying *this* is Cephus Malone?"

"Yes."

"The Indian agent Cephus Malone?"

"Yes, do you know him?"

"And he was killed yesterday morning?"

"Apparently night before last," Welch said. "As I said, he was discovered yesterday morning. Someone broke into his house and cut his throat. The sheriff thinks it was robbery." Welch shook his head. "It is frightening to think that we would have such a person in our small town."

"Smoke, that's not—" Sally began, but Smoke interrupted her.

"—the man we gave our cattle to," he said, concluding her sentence.

At that very moment, the man Smoke did give his cattle to was standing down at the feeder lot, addressing the ten men Pardeen had rounded up for him.

"One hundred dollars," Williams was saying. "One hundred dollars to every man who helps me drive these cattle to the Indian agency in Laramie."

"Mister, am I hearing you right?" one of the men said. "All we have to do is drive these here cows no more'n ten miles, and you're givin' us one hundred dollars?"

"That's right."

The men started talking excitedly among themselves; then one of them asked the question that was on all their minds.

"What's the catch?"

"No catch."

"You say there is no catch, but when Pardeen hired us, he asked if we were willing to use our guns. Now he wouldn't ask that if he didn't think there was a chance we'd have to use them."

"It's not a catch exactly. It's more like a complication," Williams said.

"All right, what is the complication?"

"There may be some who don't want us to do this,"

Williams said. "They may try and stop us. I don't intend to be stopped."

"If any of you have a problem with that, walk away now," Pardeen said. "Because when the shooting starts, I'll kill anyone who tries to run away."

"You say some people may try to stop us. How many people are you talking about?"

"One less than they started out with," Pardeen said. "I killed one of them last night."

"That was the fella in the saloon?" one of the men asked.

"Yeah."

"I seen that happen. I was wonderin' why you was bracing him so. Now I guess I know."

"So, you still ain't told us how many there are," one of the others said.

"There's only six of 'em," Pardeen said. "And that's countin' both Jensen and his wife."

"Jensen?" someone said. "That wouldn't be a fella they call Smoke Jensen, would it?"

Pardeen stared at the questioner for a moment before he answered.

"You don't be worryin' about that," he said. "I'll take care of Mr. Smoke Jensen. And his wife," he added.

"So what you are sayin' is, while you're takin' care of Jensen, we're to take care of the rest?"

"Yes. That would be nine of you, and four of them."

"For one hundred dollars?"

"Yes."

"Hell, sounds like easy money to me."

"Me too," one of the others said.

"Count me in."

"What if the sheriff and his deputy get involved?" one of the men asked.

"Are you talking about Dawson and Titus?" one of the others asked. "Ha! If they think there's likely to be shooting, they'll both be hidin' under a bed somewhere. You don't have to worry about them."

"McHenry," Pardeen said. "How about wandering back up into town to see what you can find out?"

"All right," McHenry said.

Leaving the undertaker's establishment, Smoke, Sally, Pearlie, Cal, Mike, and Jules walked down to the sheriff's office to find out what they could about the murder of Billy Cantrell, and to report the theft of their herd. Sheriff Dawson met them outside on the boardwalk.

"What can I do for you?" Dawson asked.

"Well, to start with, you can arrest the man who killed Billy Cantrell," Smoke said. "Then you can serve a warrant on the man who killed Cephus Malone and stole my cattle."

"Hold on there," Dawson said. "What do you mean the man who killed Cephus Malone? How do you know who killed Cephus Malone?"

"I know because yesterday I sold my cattle to a man who claimed to be Cephus Malone. Obviously, he wasn't Malone since Malone was already dead."

"His name is Trent Williams," Sheriff Dawson said.

"What? You already know about this?"

"You are talking about the man whose cattle are in the feeder lot right now?"

"Yes," Smoke said. "Only they aren't his cows, they are my cows."

"Well, seems to me like that is a civil dispute. I don't get involved in civil disputes."

"You call murder a civil dispute?" Smoke asked incredulously.

"Murder? Well, now, that's a serious accusation," Dawson said. "You have no proof of that, though I admit it does look suspicious."

"Suspicious?" Smoke replied. "Sheriff, how much evidence do you need? I have a receipt, signed by a man who claims to be Cephus Malone. Only it turns out that he isn't Cephus Malone. That can only mean that he murdered Cephus Malone in order to get control of my cattle. I also think it is suspicious that Quince Pardeen, the man who murdered Billy Cantrell, has been seen down at the feeder lot this morning."

Sheriff Dawson shook his head. "Titus and I both talked to the eyewitnesses; they all said that your man drew first."

"Are you serious? Billy was forced into it," Smoke said. "I talked to those same witnesses, Sheriff, and they said that Pardeen told Billy he was going to kill him at the count of three—then he began counting."

"That was just a bluff. If your man had not drawn his pistol and then Pardeen killed him, it would have been murder."

"And Billy would have still been dead," Smoke said.

"Yes, well, the fact is, your man did draw first," the sheriff said. "And as long as all the witnesses swear to what they saw, no charges can be made."

"What about the fact that Pardeen and whoever he is with are about to steal my cattle?"

Dawson ran his hand through his hair, clearly agitated by the way the discussion was going.

The sheriff pointed toward the cow pens. "Maybe you

don't know it, mister, but there are ten men down there, in addition to Pardeen. I've only got one deputy."

"So you have looked into it," Smoke said. "You do know that Williams is down there with my cattle."

"Yeah, I've looked into it," Dawson replied. "Like I said, it is suspicious. But I have no proof that anything illegal has happened."

"And you aren't going to get proof unless you go down there and ask a few questions," Smoke said.

Dawson shook his head. "Maybe you don't know this, but the men down there aren't just cowboys. They are a bad lot, all of them. More than half of them have been in jail at one time or another for robbery, assault, you name it."

"They aren't regular cowboys?"

"No."

"Then that is more evidence, isn't it? Sheriff, they are stealing my herd right before your eyes."

"Well, what do you want me to do about it? I told you, there's just me and Titus."

"Deputize us," Smoke said, taking in the others with a sweep of his hand. "We'll take care of the situation ourselves."

"I don't know that I can do that."

"Of course you can do it," Smoke said. "In fact, I am already a deputy back in Big Rock. All you have to do is grant me a professional courtesy as a visiting lawman. It's done all the time."

"All right, all right," Sheriff Dawson said. "You're deputized. Do what you feel must be done. But don't count on any help from either me or my deputy."

"At this point, Sheriff, you and your deputy would just get in our way," Smoke said.

Chapter Twenty-four

Jarred McHenry came back to the feeder lot to report to Williams and Pardeen on what he had just learned.

"The sheriff has deputized Smoke Jensen and the others," he said.

"Well, now, this is getting interesting," Pardeen said. They were holding the conversation just outside the fence of the feeder lot, and the air was redolent with the pungent smell of manure. Nearby was a stable where a half-dozen buckboards and wagons were parked and waiting to be rented. Someone from the stable was working on the wheel of one of the wagons, totally unaware of the impending showdown.

"We about to have us a shoot-out, ain't we?" one of the men asked, his voice betraying his nervousness over the prospect.

"I sure as hell hope so," Pardeen said.

"What do you mean, you hope so?"

"The stage has been set for me'n Smoke Jensen to have us a meeting for a long time now," Pardeen said. "And this is as good a time and place as any."

"Well, I don't mind telling you boys, this isn't what I

wanted," Williams said. He sighed. "But I'm afraid the fat is in the fire now."

Suddenly, and inexplicably, Jarred laughed.

"What it is? What are you laughin' at?" one of the others asked.

"Devil's food cake," Jarred said.

"What?"

"Devil's food cake," Jarred repeated. "You think it really is devil's food? What I'm askin' is, come supper time in hell tonight, you think they'll serve devil's food cake?"

One of the others shook his head. "Jarred, you are dumber than a cow turd."

They were quiet for a moment. Then Jarred growled, "We goin' to stand around 'n talk all day? Or are we goin' to get this thing done?"

"You're anxious, are you?" Pardeen asked.

"Some," Jarred admitted. "If we're goin' to do this, let's get it done." He started toward town and some of the others began to follow.

"Wait," Williams called. The others turned to look at him. "Didn't you say they were coming to us?"

"Yeah, that's what it sounded like," Jarred said.

"Then let's make them come to us. That way, we'll have the advantage. And when it's over, there won't be no question about it bein' murder or anything."

"Yeah, good idea," Pardeen said. "Hey, you," he called to the man who was working on the wagon wheel.

The man looked over toward Pardeen. "You talkin' to me?"

"Yeah, you," Pardeen repeated. "Come here."

Responding to the call, the man got up and walked over toward them, wiping his hands with a rag he carried in his back pocket.

"What's your name?" Pardeen asked.

"The name is Cooksie. I own this place." He pointed to the livery. "You need to board your horse, or rent a horse or a wagon?"

"Nah," Pardeen said. As he was talking, he took out his pistol and began checking the loads in the cylinder. Seeing this, the others did the same thing. "We need you to do something for us."

The expression on Cooksie's face reflected some anxiousness over seeing everyone suddenly check their pistols.

"What's going on here? What are you men about to do?"

"We're about to conduct a prayer meetin'," Pardeen said, and the others laughed.

"Yeah, a prayer meetin'," Jarred repeated with a low laugh.

"What?" Cooksie asked.

"Never you mind what we're about to do," Pardeen said. "You just go on down to the sheriff's office and tell them new deputies he just swore in that we're down here waitin' for 'em."

"You're about to get into a gunfight here, aren't you?" Cooksie asked.

"That's right."

Cooksie shook his head. "You boys don't really want to do this," he said, his voice high-pitched and nervous.

"Yeah," Pardeen said, looking pointedly at him. "We do. Now, you go down there and get them like we said. Then you stay the hell out of the way."

Smoke and the others were still standing in front of the sheriff's office, discussing the best way to deal with the situation at hand, when Cooksie came up to them.

"Is the sheriff and his new deputies in the office?" the stable owner asked.

"We're his new deputies," Smoke replied.

"You ain't wearin' no stars."

"We don't need any stars," Smoke said. "But if you doubt we are deputies, you can check with the sheriff. He is just inside."

"No, that's all right. Now that I think about it, I reckon you're the ones they was talkin' about anyway. They said new deputies."

"Who said it?"

"Well, the only ones I know are Jarred McHenry, Abner Coleman, Whizzer Magee, Lou Smith, the Parker brothers, and maybe three or four more with 'em."

"What about them?" Smoke asked.

"Well, sir, I don't rightly know what this is all about, but they said to tell you that they are down at the feeder lot waitin' for you."

"Are they now?" Smoke asked.

"Yes, sir. And that fella Pardeen? He's with them too."

Pearlie grinned broadly. "Pardeen too? Well, what do you know, Smoke?" he said. "We must've been livin' right. Christmas is comin' early this year."

"Pardeen belongs to me," Smoke said.

"Dead is dead," Mike said. "The son of a bitch killed Billy, so I don't care who kills him, as long as he's dead." Then, realizing that Sally had overheard him swear, Mike apologized.

"Sorry 'bout usin' them words like that, Miz Sally."

"No need to apologize, Mike," Sally replied. "Pardeen is a son of a bitch."

Jules laughed. Then he and the others checked their

guns and the loads, then replaced the weapons loosely in their holsters.

"A shoot-out!" Cooksie shouted then, running down the street. "Stay off the streets, ever'body, there's going to be a shoot-out!"

Cooksie's shouts were picked up by others, but what he intended to be a warning had just the opposite effect. People began pouring out into the street from all the stores and houses. What they saw was five men and a woman walking resolutely toward this rendevous with destiny. What they didn't see was one ounce of emotion in any of the faces of the six.

When they looked back toward the eleven the six would be facing, though, they saw faces that reflected the gamut of emotion, from resignation to fear to excitement. On Quince Pardeen's face was an expression of detachment.

Sheriff Dawson suddenly appeared, stepping out into the street. He held his hand up to stop Smoke and the others.

"Stop right there," he called. "I don't intend to have a bloodbath in my town."

"You want to go down there and arrest them, Sheriff?" Smoke asked.

Dawson looked at Smoke and the others for a moment. Then, shaking his head, he stepped back out of the street. "No," he said. "You folks are on your own now. I wash my hands of it."

Sally chuckled. "Why not?" she asked. "It worked for Pontius Pilate."

As Smoke, Sally, Pearlie, Cal, Mike, and Jules approached, Williams, Pardeen, and the others stepped out of the livery barn and stood facing them. The two groups stood no more than ten feet apart. Williams, Pardeen,

McHenry, and the others were now boxed in, for the feeder lot was behind them, the livery barn on one side, and a house on the other. Smoke, Sally, Pearlie, Cal, Mike, and Jules were standing out in the open close to the street.

There was a moment of silence as the two parties confronted each other.

"Williams, this doesn't have to happen. You and your men lay your guns on the ground, then walk away and leave my cattle here, and this will all be over," Smoke said.

"Oh, it has to happen," Pardeen said. "Yes, sir, it has to happen." Pardeen allowed a snide smile to spread across his face.

"Pardeen, you aren't a part of this offer. I was talking to Williams," Smoke said. "You killed Billy, so I'm going to kill you, no matter what Williams does."

The smile left Pardeen's face. Then he made the first move, reaching for and pulling his .45 so fast that to some of the bystanders, it appeared as if he had been holding the gun all along.

"No!" Williams suddenly shouted. He took a couple of hesitant steps backward. "No, wait! We'll be killed!" Williams turned and ran through the open door of the barn behind them. "No, don't shoot us, don't shoot us!" he begged.

"Williams, you lily-livered coward!" Jarred McHenry shouted.

Although Pardeen had drawn first, the first shot came from Smoke's gun. He fired and the recoil kicked his hand up. Pardeen called out in pain, then grabbed his stomach as blood spilled between his fingers. But even as Pardeen went down, Magee shot at Smoke but missed. Sally shot Magee, hitting him in the chest. Smith fired at Mike as Pearlie fired at Coleman, hitting him between the eyes.

After that, guns began to roar in rapid succession. Both

Parkers went down, then three other gunmen, leaving only Smith and McHenry. Smoke killed Smith, while a bullet from Cal's pistol tore through McHenry's right hand. Another hit him in the chest.

McHenry staggered back against a window of the vacant house, then slid slowly to the ground. He switched his pistol to his left hand. Sitting there on the ground with his legs crossed, and resting his pistol on his shattered arm, he shot with his left hand. His bullet hit Sally in the arm, spinning her around. Smoke shot McHenry again, this time in the forehead, knocking him back against the house.

"Sally, are you all right?" Smoke shouted.

"Yes," Sally answered. "It's not much more than a nick."

Suddenly, out of the corner of her eye, Sally saw Williams reappear in the door of the barn, holding a rifle. Williams fired, and Mike went down. Smoke, Pearlie, and Cal all fired at the same time and their bullets slammed into Williams's chest. He stumbled out into the street and lurched over toward the people who had crowded around to watch. Unable to shoot for fear of hitting someone in the crowd, Smoke held his fire.

Williams grabbed onto the post that supported the roof over the boot repair shop. He coughed once and blood bubbled from his lips; then he fell back, dead in the dirt.

Of all those involved in the fight, not one of the gunmen with Williams was left alive. Smoke, Pearlie, Cal, and Jules were unscathed. Sally had a bullet in her arm, and Mike was dead.

"Mike!" Sally shouted. "Oh, Smoke, they got Mike."

Smoke went over to look down at the young man, then shook his head sadly.

The fight had been witnessed by scores of people, and

now Smoke could see them moving closer to look at the bodies of the slain. None of the townspeople said anything. Their looks weren't of pity, or compassion, or even hate. Most were of morbid curiosity, as if they were experiencing a sensual pleasure from being so close to death while themselves avoiding it.

"Did you ever seen anythin' like this?" someone asked.

"Never," another answered.

"It was over in a hurry, wasn't it?" someone asked.

"Thirty-seven seconds," another said, holding a watch in his hand. "I timed it."

One of them came over to look down at Mike.

"Get away from him," Smoke said.

"I don't mean nothin' by it, mister. I'm just goin' to look."

"I said get away!" Smoke shouted, pulling his pistol and pointing it at the curious townsman. The citizen backed away quickly, holding his hands up.

Two days later, Smoke, Sally, Pearlie, Cal, and Jules were standing on the platform at the depot, waiting for the train that would take them back home. Sally had been treated by a doctor and her arm was in a sling. The bodies of Mike and Billy were in coffins, and would be put on the baggage car of the same train. The cattle were gone, and Smoke had a certified bank draft for $97,250.00, the amount he and Colin Abernathy agreed upon after Abernathy came personally to take delivery of the cattle. They heard the sound of the train in the distance.

"Here it comes," Jules said excitedly.

"Are you anxious to get home?" Sally asked.

"Yes, ma'am," Jules said. "I'll be glad to give this money

to Ma and Pa. Plus," he added with a broad grin, "this here will be the first time I ever rode on a train."

The smile left his lips. "It's the first time either Billy or Mike ever rode on a train too. They was really lookin' forward to it."

Sheriff Dawson came up to them then. "I thought you might like to know that an inquest was held, and it was found that the shootin' and killin' was all justified," he said.

Smoke just nodded, but said nothing.

Dawson smiled. "And you'll be goin' home with almost one hundred thousand dollars. I reckon this is one trip you'll be real glad you made."

"Oh, yeah, I'm just all broke out with joy," Smoke replied.

"You don't sound all that happy."

"Mike, Billy, Hank, Andy, LeRoy, and Dooley," Smoke said.

"I don't understand."

"No," Smoke said. "You wouldn't."

The train pulled into the station then, chugging, clanging, spewing steam and dripping glowing embers onto the track bed.

"Come on, Sally," Smoke said. "Let's go home."

J. A. Johnstone on William W. Johnstone
"When the Truth Becomes Legend"

William W. Johnstone was born in southern Missouri, the youngest of four children. He was raised with strong moral and family values by his minister father, and tutored by his schoolteacher mother. Despite this, he quit school at age fifteen.

"I have the highest respect for education," he says, "but such is the folly of youth, and wanting to see the world beyond the four walls and the blackboard." True to this vow, Bill attempted to enlist in the French Foreign Legion ("I saw Gary Cooper in *Beau Geste* when I was a kid and I thought the French Foreign Legion would be fun") but was rejected, thankfully, for being underage. Instead, he joined a traveling carnival and did all kinds of odd jobs. It was listening to the veteran carny folk, some of whom had been on the circuit since the late 1800s, telling amazing tales about their experiences which planted the storytelling seed in Bill's imagination.

"They were honest people, despite the bad reputation traveling carny shows had back then," Bill remembers. "Of course, there were exceptions. There was one guy named Picky, who got that name because he was a master pickpocket. He could steal a man's socks right off his feet without him knowing. Believe me, Picky got us chased out of more than a few towns."

After a few months of this grueling existence, Bill returned home and finished high school. Next came stints as a deputy sheriff in the Tallulah, LA. Sheriff's Department, followed by a hitch in the U.S. Army. Then he began a career in radio broadcasting at KTLD in Tallulah, Louisiana, that would last sixteen years. It was here that he fine-tuned his storytelling skills. He turned to writing in 1970, but it wouldn't be until 1979 until his first novel, *The Devil's Kiss*, was published. Thus began the full-time writing career of William W. Johnstone. He wrote horror (*The Uninvited*), thrillers (*The Last of the Dog Team*), even a romance novel or two. Then, in February 1983, *Out of the Ashes* was published. Searching for his missing family in the aftermath of a post-apocalyptic America, rebel mercenary and patriot Ben Raines is united with the civilians of the Resistance forces and moves to the forefront of a revolution for the nation's future.

Out of the Ashes was a smash. The series would continue for the next twenty years, winning Bill three generations of fans all over the world. The series was often imitated but never duplicated. "We all tried to copy *The Ashes* series," said one publishing executive, "but Bill's uncanny ability, both then and now, to predict in which direction the political winds were blowing, brought a dead-on timeliness to the table no one else could capture." *The Ashes* series would end its run with more than thirty-four books and twenty million copies in print, making it one of the most successful men's action series in American book publishing. (*The Ashes* series also, Bill notes with a touch of pride, got him on the FBI's Watch List for its less than flattering portrayal of spineless politicians and the growing power of big government over our lives, among other things. "In that respect," says collaborator J. A. Johnstone, "Bill was years ahead of his time.")

Always steps ahead of the political curve, Bill's recent thrillers, written with J. A. Johnstone, include *Vengeance Is Mine, Invasion USA, Border War, Jackknife, Remember the Alamo, Home Invasion, Phoenix Rising, The Blood of Patriots, The Bleeding Edge,* and the upcoming *Suicide Mission.*

It is with the Western, though, that Bill found his greatest success and propelled him onto both the *USA Today* and *New York Times* bestseller lists.

Bill's western series, co-authored by J. A. Johnstone, include *The Mountain Man, Matt Jensen the Last Mountain Man, Preacher, The Family Jensen, Luke Jensen Bounty Hunter, Eagles, MacCallister* (an *Eagles* spin-off), *Sidewinders, The Brothers O'Brien, Sixkiller, Blood Bond, The Last Gunfighter,* and the upcoming new series *Flintlock* and *The Trail West* is the hardcover western *Butch Cassidy, The Lost Years.*

"The Western," Bill says, "is one of the few true art forms that is one hundred percent American. I liken the Western as America's version of England's Arthurian legends, like the Knights of the Round Table or Robin Hood and his Merry Men. Starting with the 1902 publication of *The Virginian* by Owen Wister, and followed by the greats like Zane Grey, Max Brand, Ernest Haycox, and of course Louis L'Amour, the Western has helped to shape the cultural landscape of America.

"I'm no goggle-eyed college academic, so when my fans ask me why the Western is as popular now as it was a century ago, I don't offer a 200-page thesis. Instead, I can only offer this: The Western is honest. In this great country, which is suffering under the yoke of political correctness, the Western harks back to an era when justice was sure and swift. Steal a man's horse, rustle his cattle, rob a bank, a stagecoach, or a train, you were hunted down and fitted with a hangman's noose. One size fit all.

"Sure, we westerners are prone to a little embellishment and exaggeration and, I admit it, occasionally play a little fast and loose with the facts. But we do so for a very good reason—to enhance the enjoyment of readers.

"It was Owen Wister, in *The Virginian*, who first coined the phrase '*When you call me that, smile.*' Legend has it that Wister actually heard those words spoken by a deputy sheriff in Medicine Bow, Wyoming, when another poker player called him a son-of-a-bitch.

"Did it really happen, or is it one of those myths that have passed down from one generation to the next? I honestly don't know. But there's a line in one of my favorite Westerns of all time, *The Man Who Shot Liberty Valance*, where the newspaper editor tells the young reporter, 'When the truth becomes legend, print the legend.'

"These are the words I live by."